Alexander Fullerton has bee
interpreter, shipping agen
Through nearly all those perio
he has lived solely on his wri
several bestsellers to his credit.

WITHDRAWN

Also by Alexander Fullerton:

SURFACE!	STORE
BURY THE PAST	THE ESCAPISTS
OLD MOKE	OTHER MEN'S WIVES
NO MAN'S MISTRESS	PIPER'S LEAVE
A WREN CALLED SMITH	REGENESIS
THE WHITE MEN SANG	THE APHRODITE CARGO
THE YELLOW FORD	JOHNSON'S BIRD
SOLDIER FROM THE SEA	BLOODY SUNSET
THE WAITING GAME	LOOK TO THE WOLVES
THE THUNDER AND THE FLAME	LOVE FOR AN ENEMY
LIONHEART	NOT THINKING OF DEATH
CHIEF EXECUTIVE	BAND OF BROTHERS
THE PUBLISHER	RETURN TO THE FIELD

The Everard series of naval novels

THE BLOODING OF THE GUNS
SIXTY MINUTES FOR ST GEORGE
PATROL TO THE GOLDEN HORN
STORM FORCE TO NARVIK
LAST LIFT FROM CRETE
ALL THE DROWNING SEAS
A SHARE OF HONOUR
THE TORCH BEARERS
THE GATECRASHERS

The SBS Trilogy

SPECIAL DELIVERANCE
SPECIAL DYNAMIC
SPECIAL DECEPTION

INTO
THE FIRE

Alexander Fullerton

WARNER BOOKS

A *Warner* Book

First published in Great Britain in 1995 by Little, Brown and Company
This edition published in 1997 by Warner Books

Copyright © Alexander Fullerton 1995

The moral right of the author has been asserted.

*All characters in this publication are fictitious and
any resemblance to real persons, living or dead,
is purely coincidental.*

All rights reserved.
No part of this publication may be reproduced,
stored in a retrieval system, or transmitted, in any
form or by any means, without the prior
permission in writing of the publisher, nor be
otherwise circulated in any form of binding or
cover other than that in which it is published and
without a similar condition including this
condition being imposed on the subsequent purchaser.

A CIP catalogue record for this book is
available from the British Library.

ISBN 0 7515 1807 7

Typeset by Solidus (Bristol) Limited
Printed and bound in Great Britain by
Mackays of Chatham plc, Chatham, Kent

Warner Books
A Division of
Little, Brown and Company (UK)
Brettenham House
Lancaster Place
London WC2E 7EN

To Priscilla – again – with love

604097
MORAY COUNCIL
Department of Technical
& Leisure Services

1

As the train slowed for some halt, she was remembering her farewell interview with Maurice Buckmaster in his flat in Portman Square, earlier in the day; how in her mind when he'd set the ball rolling with a cheerful 'Ready for the off, are you, Rosie?' had been the thought that it was only when they gave you the cyanide pill you could *really* say you were 'off'.

She hadn't got it yet. Marilyn Stuart – blonde, smartly uniformed as a 2nd Officer in the W.R.N.S. – would be handing it over to her later on. Together with a few other items, and after searching for and confiscating any give-aways such as an English railway ticket or ten-bob note, English cigarettes or book of matches – items which, if you had the bad luck to be searched and they came to light, could be enough to get you shot or hanged. After, as likely as not, some period of incarceration and torture. Images of which sprang all too readily to mind at the thought of the little pill which had to be reposing now in that locked briefcase ... She'd also have some French pocket money for her – as well as a package containing a very much larger sum – and identity papers and a ration card in the name of Jeanne-Marie Lefèvre; and French cigarettes and matches, probably also a few extra props of the kind Marilyn specialized in producing at such times: a love letter for instance, or a scrap of one, some crumpled tram or Metro tickets. She'd already checked that Rosie's clothes bore only French labels and laundry marks.

Last time – her first mission, last September – September '42, that was, two days after her twenty-fourth birthday – she'd left from Tempsford in a Whitley of the R.A.F.'s Special Duties squadron and landed by parachute near Cahors, en route to join the network in Toulouse. At Tempsford there was an S.O.E. hut in which all such final checks were made, and she could remember all too clearly how she'd felt standing there with the suicide pill in its little postage-stamp sized packet in the palm of her hand, asking herself in a suddenly overwhelming conviction of personal inadequacy as well as sickening fright, *Am I strong enough for this? Fit for it? Am I, Johnny?*

But would *he* have been? Johnny – who'd been her husband and was dead – and had cheated on her – whose image in her thoughts of him was no longer of his dark good looks and strong, muscled body, only of a Spitfire burning, falling, trailing smoke, exploding into the blue heave of the Channel – how about *his* powers of self-control? Or might there be no connection between inner moral strength and the kind attributed to heroes?

Exeter, this was. She'd pulled back the edge of the window blind to peep out, just as a whistle blew and the train gasped and thumped into motion. While they'd been stopped the catch on the compartment's door had been tried several times, but it was locked, she and Marilyn isolated in their own secret, tight-nerved world. Avoiding strangers' questions, however innocent or well-meaning, or eyes that might be less innocent, sharp enough to retain a visual memory; and of course to allow for exchanges of conversation, last-minute queries or reminders, reassurances either way. All of which according to the rules should have been in French, at this stage – getting her back into the habit of it. The train was rolling again now, anyway, accelerating back into its former pounding rhythm and in a long haul round to the left. Turning south, she realized, visualizing the coastline where it curved down towards Torquay: and recalling again those moments of panic at Tempsford, thankful that having been subjected to her baptism of fire, seven months of it – hectic months at that, culminating in the *réseau* – network – being penetrated by Gestapo agents so that it had had to be closed down – she'd got out through Spain and Portugal three months ago, but out of Toulouse initially only by the skin of her back teeth. Having weathered that, she had fewer self-doubts than she'd had that night at Tempsford.

Still scared stiff, of course. As was natural, and – as she *now* knew – didn't have to be hidden from Marilyn; hadn't, for that matter, had to be denied in Buckmaster's flat this morning. Anyone who was not scared at such a time would have to be so bone-headed that she'd be useless. You did your best not to advertise it, that was all. Not to shake, or visibly sweat.

It was Colonel Buckmaster's custom to invite agents to what was known as the 'briefing flat' for a final chat before their departure for the field. 'Buck' had had the command of 'F' Section of S.O.E. – Special Operations Executive – since the autumn of '41. A tall man, spare, slightly stoop-shouldered, with a humorous look about him and a great deal of charm. After Eton he'd lived and worked in France for a number of years – first as a tutor, then as a reporter on the newspaper *Le Matin*, finally as assistant manager of the Ford Motor Company, with its headquarters in Paris. Prior to transferring to S.O.E. he'd been serving as Intelligence Officer of the 50th Division.

In Portman Square this morning – it was an easy stroll from 'F' Section's headquarters at 62–64 Baker Street – he'd had Rosie's file on his knee, but had opened it only after his butler – Park, who pre-war had been a bank messenger in Paris – had brought coffee and biscuits, and withdrawn. Marilyn Stuart had been with them too: from here they'd be going straight to Paddington.

'I see we're calling you "Angel", this time. Whereas actually you're Jeanne-Marie Lefèvre. War widow. Visiting your former mother-in-law near Brest – leaving the child with her. Yes, that's good ... Golly, what a lot of money. Million and a quarter – strewth ... Of course, the quarter-million's for – what's her name—'

'Jacqueline Clermont, alias "La Minette".' She added, 'It's a bulky package, all those francs. I'm hoping it'll cram in with the transceiver.'

He'd stared at her for a moment, then nodded. 'Because if they found one or other they might as well find both. *Would*, no doubt. But—' reaching to touch wood, he shook his head. 'Please God ...' He glanced at Marilyn: 'She's taking the new Mark III, did you say?'

A Mark III transmitter/receiver was the latest to become available, and until now it had only been available to field agents of S.I.S. Its provision to Rosie for this mission was obviously not unconnected with the fact that she'd be doing some work for them, as well as her own job.

The essential difference being that S.I.S. were intelligence gatherers, and S.O.E. agents were not. This trip, she would be.

'Now. This private brief of yours, Rosie. Colonel – what's his name ...' Flipping a page over, nodding. 'Colonel Walther. The Clermont woman being his mistress, we're told.'

'Yes.'

'But whether that means she hasn't placed her final bet – do we have a view on that?'

'I'll have to form one on the spot. The impression meanwhile – down the road – is that she's a good-time girl with a sharp commercial instinct. Likes men, too.'

'Including Germans, evidently.' He'd sighed. 'I can't say I like it much.'

'No. Well ...'

'What I was leading to, though – you're expected to keep the whole thing to yourself, I gather. Not letting even César in on it.'

César was to be her boss, organizer of the new *réseau* that was to be built up now in Rouen. If all had gone as planned he'd be setting up shop in Rouen at about this time, taking under his wing – initially – a courier-radio operator code-named Romeo, sole survivor of the previously blown *réseau*.

Buckmaster suggested, 'If you did find you needed help, César would be your man. Especially since at this stage Romeo's a doubtful quantity. Nothing conclusive about it, but – well, you've got to face this, Rosie – if he's a traitor, your cover'll be blown the minute you contact him.'

'Yes.'

She'd talked this out with the other people. And knew that Buckmaster needed to have her in there anyway because Romeo had been told to stay off the air – for obvious reasons – and until she arrived with her own transmitter there'd be no line of communication at all, to or from César. You had to take *some* risks.

'César, thank God, is gilt-edged. A rock of a man. And as experienced as anyone we've got. Give him my personal regards, will you, when you see him?' She'd nodded. Buckmaster added, 'I'm stressing his reliability because you may well find you need his help – with your private brief, I mean. *They* want you to play it solo—' he'd jerked his head, pointing it vaguely in the direction of St James', and referring to S.I.S. – 'and understandably, quite properly, I suppose – but they know as well as you and I do, Rosie, that that whole area is a minefield now. Our doubts of Romeo, and those other arrests – and the para-drop leak ... Incidentally, why have S.I.S. asked us to do this job for them, do you imagine?'

'Because a search for rocket-launching sites rather over-laps with our prospecting for arms-dropping ones. There's also the usefulness of our links with Maquis and local French *réseaux*. It does seem to be up our street, or so I'd have *thought*.'

'That end of it – yes, I agree. But the top end – the apex, if one could so call it – Colonel Walther and his little – er

– hairdresser . . .' He shook his head. 'Rosie, I'm telling you, and I'm going to tell *them*, that these are my personal orders to you. One, unless "La Minette" is prepared to cooperate, and you're certain she can be used *safely* – don't push it. Back off, look for answers in the deep field. Coincide rather better with your normal S.O.E. activities anyway, wouldn't it? Two, don't tell Romeo a damn thing – don't let him guess you have any sideline. And three, if you find yourself in trouble you'd be well advised to take César into your confidence. All the more so because it *is* a matter of such huge importance – as well as urgency. Effectively, in fact, I'll be offering them César as a backup – to be brought in only on your say-so, of course. All right?'

The train had stopped again; there was shunting in progress. Marilyn said, 'Newton Abbot. Our part gets detached here for the Paignton and Kingswear line.'

'Not far, then.'

'No.' A smile. 'Not far.'

Rosie thought, *Like going back to school. Mummy saying 'Be a brave girl, now . . .'*

Thinking again then about this morning's talk with Maurice Buckmaster, and the fact that some of his observations might have seemed contradictory. On the one hand 'It's vital and urgent', and on the other, 'If the going's hard, lay off.' What he'd really been saying, she guessed, was that he'd had to agree to S.O.E. taking on this job – against his own judgement, therefore as likely as not under pressure from some higher level – and that he fully understood how important the task was, but was deeply concerned that Rosie might find herself out of her depth.

He tried to take care of his own, that was the thing. He liked to get his agents back: and all three of them this morning had been well aware that he sometimes did not.

Which took one's mind back to the cyanide pill: and to the final stages of S.O.E. agents' training, techniques of resistance to interrogation and torture. The basic aim, as taught on the course, was to hold out for forty-eight hours, the period regarded as minimal but adequate for other members of the *réseau* to go to ground.

Could be the longest forty-eight hours of one's life, she imagined. Especially as one knew that once they decided you'd be of no further use to them – either that you weren't going to talk or that you had no more to tell them – their standard practice was to send you to the concentration camp at Ravensbruck. Or Dachau, or in some cases Buchenvald, but more usually to the women's camp at Ravensbruck. The French called it *L'Enfer des Femmes*.

The train was rolling again, on the branch line now. End of the line, where they'd disembark, would be Kingswear, the terminus for Dartmouth, on this side of the Dart estuary. There'd be a boat of some kind to meet them and take them out to an old paddle-steamer, the *Westward Ho!*, which was moored there as a depot-ship for the 15th Motor Gunboat Flotilla.

She met Marilyn's thoughtful gaze, and smiled. 'Please God it'll be calm tonight.'

'Not a good sailor?'

'Lousy!'

Marilyn held up a hand with two fingers crossed: slender fingers with nails lacquered blush-pink. Totally unlike Rosie's, which were not only unpainted but rather short: not exactly stubby, but – well, it was the physical difference between the two of them in more general terms as well, Marilyn being taller, slimmer – and blonde, almost ash-blonde, in contrast to Rosie's middling brown, naturally wavy locks ...

A rough crossing was the very last thing she wanted, tonight: even when it was calm, the sea was anything but her natural habitat, and a motor gunboat did sound like a very small craft in which to cross to Brittany.

It would be a fast trip, she'd been told. A dash of something over a hundred miles, in this moonless period. They only made the crossing when there was no moon.

She glanced up at Marilyn. '*Quoi?*'

Marilyn repeated – in French – 'Your name?'

She swallowed: and *became* the French war widow . . .

'Jeanne-Marie Lefèvre.'

'Date of birth?'

'September the tenth, 1918.'

'Maiden name?'

'Chrestien.'

'Husband's name?'

'Henri. Lieutenant Henri Lefèvre. He was killed in 1940.'

'Why are you on this train?'

'I've left my daughter with her grandmother – on the farm. Near St Saveur. I'm going to Paris about a job – I need money, for the child and—'

She'd let her desperation show for a moment, but Marilyn cut in again: 'What sort of job?'

'Selling perfume. From the *parfumeries* at Grasse – well, a merchant in Paris who's a sort of cousin—'

'Your child's name and age?'

'Juliette. She's three and a half. I hope to God the old woman will be kind to her. But to hold down any job that pays enough for us to *live*—'

'No need to scream at me. We have to know who's who, that's all. Heil Hitler!'

'Heil sodding Hitler . . .'

Relaxing. For about two minutes she'd had no doubt at all that she was Jeanne-Marie Lefèvre, a war widow. Well, she *was* – a war widow – and might easily have had a child; had no difficulty at all in imagining how she'd feel about it if she had.

The train's rhythm was slowing again.

'Kingswear coming up, Rosie.'

Breaking out of thoughts: not idle ones, but projections to Rouen where she'd be making contact with César and with the one who was under suspicion – Romeo. He was a Mauritian, Colonel B. had told her. There were several

Mauritians working for S.O.E.; it was one partial solution to the problem of finding enough suitable recruits who were completely at home in the language. The rendezvous with César would be at a certain café where he'd be sitting with two cups on his table, both spoons in one saucer. After they'd met and agreed whatever arrangements were necessary, it would be up to him to arrange her introduction to Romeo; but she did have a way of getting in touch with Romeo directly – for better or for worse – if for instance César had been arrested before she got there. The number she had to call initially wasn't his – Romeo's – but an intermediary's, so if anything disastrous had happened it would serve as a cut-out.

Touch wood. There was a lot to remember. You needed a good memory almost as much as you needed fluency in French.

She lifted her suitcase down from the rack. Marilyn's only burden was a briefcase with the money, radio and other items in it. The suitcase was as scuffed and battered as you'd expect a penniless young French widow to be lugging around with her – as often as not on a bicycle, even over quite long distances.

Sea air: there was a light breeze from the southwest. Not enough of it to make the sea rough, she hoped. Quite a few other people – mostly naval, but a handful of civilians too – were getting out; a railway official shouted 'Ferry leaves in five minutes! Ferry for Dartmouth town, five minutes!

'We won't need *that* . . .'

'Second Officer Stuart?'

A stocky lad – nineteen or twenty, no more – with the single wavy stripe of an R.N.V.R. sub-lieutenant on each sleeve: saluting her, smiling. Marilyn in her Wren hat managing to look officer-like as well as ultra-feminine. The sub-lieutenant was smiling at Rosie, though: 'I'm Nick Ball, of M.G.B. 600. You must be our passenger. I've a boat here – motorboat—'

'I'm coming too.' Marilyn looked steely, as if she was

expecting argument. 'I take it I can be landed again before the train leaves?'

'Of course. All fixed. This way ... Oh, sorry, let me—'

'How kind.'

He took the scruffy case from her and went ahead of them through the ticket inspector's barrier, waited while Rosie gave up her railway warrant and Marilyn showed hers. 'I'm going back on this train. How long have I got?'

'Oh—' checking the time on a pocket-watch: 'Forty-five minutes, miss. Thereabouts ...'

They followed the young officer out of the station and down to a jetty near the slipway. The ferry was just berthing, its wires scattering water like rain as they quivered taut, and a motorboat nearby – Ball led them to it – had three sailors in it who watched their approach. A leading seaman at the helm, a stoker at the engine and another sailor at the bow with a line looped through one of the iron rings. Ball passed the suitcase down, and the three of them embarked. Another, larger boat was filling up with naval people further along the jetty.

'Let's go, cox'n.' Ball told them, pointing, 'That's where we're going. Called *Westward Ho!* Used to plug up and down full of trippers, now she's what you might call our mother-ship. This boat's hers; ours is just a little dinghy. The kind one rows – you know, with oars?'

Rosie glanced at him sharply. 'Will it be calm enough?'

'Oh, we manage somehow. Irrespective.' Grinning, as the motorboat chugged out into the estuary: the depot-ship wasn't more than a hundred yards away. Further out, other ships lay at anchor, their hulls and superstructures mirrored in the still water of the estuary. Destroyers, she guessed. She asked him – insisting on a straight answer – '*Will* it be a smooth crossing?'

'Millpond. Absolutely. Mind you – well, *you'll* be all right. By about dawn, though, we're told it's going to blow up to something like force nine. So we'll have a wet trip home.' He pointed again: 'You can see our boat's bows, poking out there. See?'

On *Westward Ho!*'s other side: a low, grey-painted prow. It did look as if it might be fast – what she'd heard referred to as 'racy lines', no doubt ... Out of sight again now, though, as the motorboat curved in towards a gangway near the paddle-steamer's stern. Marilyn had asked Ball, 'How many gunboats in your flotilla?' and he'd told her, 'Three. But the other two are currently elsewhere.' The boat's engine cut out. Swinging in; the engine revving again, going astern – and stopped. A boathook held them alongside at the bow, and the coxswain had grabbed at a rope back at this end where the wooden gangway slanted up. Ball murmured, 'After you, ladies ...'

It had been Marilyn who'd seen her off last time, too – at Tempsford, seen her right into the aircraft. She'd been her Conducting Officer, as they called it, during the months of training, March to August of last year. An unlikely mother-hen, with her slim figure, impeccable grooming, rarely a hair out of place: but she'd done it all too, could match the instructors in all those esoteric arts. At Wanborough Manor through the selection course and initial training, then at Arisaig in Inverness-shire for night operations, bridge-blowing and fieldcraft, living off the land; the instructors were commandos, poachers and ex-convicts. Safe-breaking was one of the subjects; industrial sabotage another, and of course parachuting. That was at Ringway, near Manchester. To Beaulieu then, where 'school' was a stately home and the trainees were billeted in various cottages and lodges while they studied codes, microphotography, forgery, techniques in the use of safe letter boxes, and as much as was known of enemy counter-intelligence. Finally, 'Experience of Interrogation'.

The radio stuff had been a walkover for her, because she'd already been a trained operator – or 'pianist', as it was called in the Resistance. She'd been working for quite a long time at S.O.E.'s message-receiving centre at Sevenoaks, before the crisis point when Johnny had been killed and she'd wheedled her way into training as an agent – thanks to

Maurice Buckmaster – and she'd only needed to familiarize herself with the Mark II sets which were then in use. That way, she'd saved months.

They were on the deck of *Westward Ho!* by this time, looking down at M.G.B. 600. Not making all that much of it – except that it was long and low, with guns of differing shapes and sizes under grey canvas covers here and there: in fact one was uncovered, two sailors in overalls working on it, bits and pieces lying around. The gunboat wasn't *quite* as small as she'd expected – having seen photographs of M.T.B.s – but it was still no cruise-liner. A hundred feet long, she guessed; or a bit more. Not *much* more ...

Nick Ball reappeared beside them. 'I've put your case in the cabin. Show you down, when you're ready. C.O.'ll meet you on board later, he's in the Ops Room at the moment. Would you like to get your business done right away?'

A cabin was being lent to them in this steamer, and the 'business' would be Marilyn's – transferring the money, packing it and other things in with the radio, and finding homes in Rosie's pockets for odds and ends of French origin: other agents brought them back, and Marilyn squirrelled them away. She asked the sub-lieutenant, 'Can we hear the start of the news at six, please? The preliminaries?'

Those ostensibly meaningless messages in French, she meant. The BBC put them out every evening. Ball nodded. 'There'll be a speaker in the cabin. I'll make sure the main set's tuned in.'

It wasn't far short of six now; sailing time had been given as 1900. There was a lot of movement out there: boats going to and from ships and the shore – and a warship of some kind nosing in, by the look of it preparing to drop anchor. Immediately below them, too, on the gunboat: a derrick had been swung out and a wire sling was being lowered with a heavy-looking crate in it: sailors were standing ready to receive it. Ball told her, 'We'll be *man*-handling that ashore, later on.' She checked the time on her wristwatch – an old, cheap one, and Swiss-made, therefore OK ... But this all seemed so damned *routine*, she thought. Didn't they even *suspect* there were times when one's heart felt as though it might shake itself loose?

Probably not. No reason they should, she supposed. They'd have their own problems, wouldn't they. Like getting you to the right place at the right time, under the Germans' noses.

Ball had raised his hand in greeting to an officer who'd appeared on the M.G.B.'s deck, emerging from a hatchway – an R.N.V.R. lieutenant, bearded, heading for the gangway into this depot-ship with a rolled chart under his arm. He'd paused, staring up at them.

At Rosie: with his eyes slitted against the brightness of the sky behind them, the lowering sun. The curve of a smile – then incredulity ... Marilyn heard Rosie's intake of breath, her mutter of 'Oh, my God!'

Why'd he grow a beard, for God's sake?

Marilyn's quiet voice, at her shoulder: 'Friend of yours?'

Ball said, 'Ben Quarry. Our hot-shot navigator. Aussie. Hell of a nice chap.' He caught on, then: 'Hey, d'you know each other?'

2

For a moment or two she'd been dazed. *Not* wanting a reunion with him here or now; but aware that it was inevitable, that she was going to have to do it – get it over, pass it off ... Meanwhile he'd disappeared – up into this ship, presumably, might appear here with them at any moment. She was showing interest meanwhile in the activity on the gunboat's deck; they were getting that crate out of the sling, and other boxes were being carried on board. Marilyn came to her aid then: 'We'd better go down, Rosie. If we're going to catch this broadcast. Not essential, but—'

'You've the train to catch, too.'

He still hadn't appeared, and she remembered as they moved away that the sub-lieutenant had said something about a conference in the Ops Room – and that Ben had been carrying a chart. Late for the meeting, she guessed. Ball seemed relieved that they'd decided to go below: no doubt he'd have more important things to do, just before sailing time, than entertaining passengers.

Marilyn asked her when they were alone – the cabin door shut, her briefcase and Rosie's suitcase open on a bunk – '*Old* friend of yours, Rosie?'

'Oh. Not really.' She was emptying her pockets and bag: English money, cigarettes and so forth. She wouldn't be taking the bag, only a purse. 'Year and a half ago, roughly. We met in Baker Street, as it happens.'

A year and a half ago, and a *day* and a half after Johnny

had been shot down. They'd given her a few days off from her job at the W/T centre and she'd come up to Baker Street to volunteer for the field-agents' training course. She'd made an appointment first by telephone – without any trouble once she'd mentioned that she was fluent in French – but the middle-aged Army captain who'd interviewed her – one of Buckmaster's administrative assistants, a dug-out with '14–'18 medal ribbons on his tunic – had been determinedly discouraging. His reason – implied, not actually stated – had been that she was in a state of shock and grief, therefore in no mental state to take a decision of such magnitude. Potentially, he'd implied, her motive might even be suicidal. Give it a few months, he'd urged gently, carry on meanwhile with the excellent and valuable work you're doing for us down there, Mrs Ewing. Then if you still feel you want to do it, let's hear from you again. She'd assured him that she had no death-wish whatsoever, would have volunteered much sooner except that her husband had been against it and she'd felt he needed her – to come home to, as it were. (Although she hadn't been the *only* woman he'd 'come home to', on occasion.) On top of having an absolutely normal inclination to remain alive as long as possible, she'd pointed out, she spoke French as naturally as she spoke English, and was already a trained radio operator. He'd agreed that this made her eminently well qualified, but repeated, 'Give it six months', and added that officially they weren't yet recruiting women agents. It was coming: Colonel Buckmaster had been pressing for it but as yet hadn't received formal authority from above.

And that had seemed to be that. Depressed, frustrated, angry – on top of Johnny's death, although the reality of that hadn't hit her as hard as it was going to within the next few days – she'd blundered down the stairs, stalked angrily through the narrow, gloomy hallway: the door had opened just as she'd been putting her hand out to it, and the man on his way in – naval uniform, a lieutenant – had been Ben Quarry.

She told Marilyn, 'Almost knocked me down. I was in a bit of a state, you can imagine.'

'And?'

'Oh, you could say I let him pick me up. We went on a pub crawl and I poured all my woes into his ear. What I needed, I suppose. He was in some Staff job ... Oh, yes – in St James', some naval department of S.I.S.?'

'N.I.D.(C), you mean. Its chief is known as D.D.O.D.(I). I *think* that stands for Deputy Director Operations Division brackets Irregular.'

'You're just showing off, now.'

'They run *this* lot, Rosie. This flotilla. So – less of a coincidence than you might have thought. Let's get on with this, shall we?'

'I'm going to have one last decent cigarette.'

Caporals, thereafter. Marilyn wouldn't leave her the English packet in case she forgot and took it with her.

'Want one?'

A shake of her blonde head. 'Look here, now ...'

She and Ben Quarry had got drunk together that night, had woken together in a single bed in the Charing Cross Hotel.

'Here. Identity documents. Driving licence. Your late husband got it for you. No test, then. Clothes coupons – not many left, I'm afraid. And ration cards – yours, and the child's.'

'But I'd have left that one with the old woman!'

'Right, you should have. So you can be in a panic – if they inspect your papers in the train, for instance. You can be absolutely mortified – burst into tears, if you like. First chance you have you'll be posting it back to St Saveur, meanwhile you're frantic, the kid might be starving, for all you know.'

'Well, I must say—'

'Hush ...' Lifting a finger: and cocking an ear to the BBC, the start of apparently senseless French-language messages. One about dark clouds heralding rain, and a second to the effect that Paul's boots had been repaired and awaited collection. Third: *Au bord de la rivière poussent des saules.*

'That was it.' Marilyn looked relieved. 'Show's on the road.'

The leader of a *réseau* in northwest Brittany would have been waiting for it too. He wouldn't much care whether willows grew on the river bank or didn't, but he'd be relieved to know that there'd been no snags and the gunboat was coming as arranged. The message would have gone out first at midday, and this repetition of it was the clincher.

'Hey, just a minute . . .'

The Allied troops who'd landed in Sicily yesterday, Bruce Belfridge was saying, had been consolidating their beach-heads, while advance units of parachute and glider troops had captured an inland airfield.

'Watch this space.' Marilyn switched off the speaker. 'But look here, now . . .'

On the day she'd met Ben Quarry, Rosie was remembering, Singapore had been surrendered to the Japanese. Great events and very small ones, she thought: the import of them depended on where one was standing at the time. As an Australian, Ben had been particularly shocked by that news from the East, but his own private *good* news had still called for celebration: just as now those Sicilian beaches were pretty well obscured by her own image of a small, dark Breton cove. Marilyn meanwhile was producing more of her bits and pieces: 'Bus tickets. Only a few weeks old, and they came from Landerneau – the station you'll probably be using. Perhaps you took ma-in-law into town for shopping. But look – this is really quite important. A note to you from "Louis" saying he hopes he may have good news by the time you get back to Paris – "if you could bear to live and work in the sticks", he says. Meaning Rouen, the job you're hoping for.'

'Did he write this himself?'

'He did indeed. A very dependable old queen, is Louis. Well connected, too. Oh, here's your map. And now, money . . .' Some coins and crumpled, rather dirty notes, to go in the purse. 'And look at *this* – snapshot of your little darling.'

'Crikey...'

'Fairly repulsive, I agree. But you think it's the bee's knees, obviously. Rosie, here's the *big* money now.'

The wrapped package of banknotes, which she'd actually counted – more or less – before she'd signed for it, would serve as padding to hold the Mark III radio transceiver in place. The set was impressively compact – ten inches by seven by five, with a spool on which seventy feet of aerial was wound – and it wouldn't have done it any good to be rattling around. Its battery was the heaviest single item. The quartz crystals were – as always – carried separately, in their own little bag inside a sponge bag with her toothbrush and other such items. Including French toothpaste, of course.

'Cypher key.'

'Pretty.' Silk – like the map – overprinted with a jumble of letters. Far less bulky than the one-time pads she'd had last time. Easy to dispose of, too; you could burn each strip of silk after the transmission, and it would leave practically no ash. 'That's about it, then.' Folding some rather tatty items of clothing back into the case ... 'Oh, except—'

'Last but not least.'

The suicide pill.

'Be sure to bring the beastly little thing back with you, eh?'

'New kind of package?'

'Rice paper. Don't have to unwrap it, you see. Just pop it in as it is, and—'

'*Don't* they make it easy for us!'

They both laughed. Knowing it wasn't in the least funny: only that for some reason you needed to make it seem so. To seem unreal – despite full awareness of the reality, and certain names and faces that sprang to mind. The odds *were* against you, logically they had to be; and one statistic – sufficiently unattractive to be taken with a pinch of salt – was that the average working life of an S.O.E. pianist at this stage in the battle was six weeks. Rosie felt she really *could* discount it, anyway: the main factor in recent German successes had been the increased efficiency of their radio-direction-finding equipment, and she'd been given special directives this time as to where and when she should or should not transmit. Never from the same place twice – not even from the same district, if she could help it, and preferably from rural areas.

Which was why you needed a battery, of course. But also, not to transmit at all if it wasn't absolutely necessary – and/ or on César's orders – and with a limit on the duration of any one transmission. On no account any 'skeds', such as agents had worked to and in some cases still did. 'Skeds' being schedules, regular transmissions at set times, which would obviously have made things easier for the bastards.

The little rice-paper packet went into a tiny slot inside her French-made bra. Left side, not far from the armpit. Her own idea and needlework. She was buttoning her blouse now. And that was about the lot. Jersey. Coat ... All right, so it was a heavy coat for midsummer, but summer wasn't going to last for ever, and meanwhile she'd either wear it open or carry it over her arm: it had a suitably nondescript look, she thought.

It would be cold tonight, anyway. In the early hours, in that little rowing boat.

Marilyn locked her briefcase. 'Don't *think* we've forgotten anything. You're clear on the details for the drops, are you?'

'As clear as I'll ever be.'

She'd memorized it all: the locations, names of Resistance leaders, dates and times of the drops and the phrases which would be broadcast to confirm them. All locked in her head. Not many months ago an agent had been arrested in the south with a briefcase full of written notes including the names of other agents, who'd then also been arrested. Chances were that they were dead.

'You don't want a pistol, do you?' Tapping the briefcase. 'I've a .32 Beretta here, if you did.'

She shook her head. 'Thanks all the same.'

Because the risk of it being found in some routine search outweighed any likelihood of her ever using it. Marilyn agreed, 'Dare say you're wise. But that's about all there is, Rosie dear. Get some rest if you can, on the way over?'

'I expect I will.'

'And remember, no distractions.'

'What?'

'You looked as if you'd seen a ghost, up there.'

'Oh. That.' She shook her head. 'Surprise, that's all. One hardly expects—'

'You've got to start being Jeanne-Marie Lefèvre now – you know?'

'Oddly enough, I do.' She nodded. 'And thanks – for everything, Marilyn. Heaven knows where any of us would be without you.'

They hugged each other. 'God bless you, Rosie.'

She saw Marilyn off to catch her train back to London, waving goodbye to her from the top of the paddle-steamer's gangway, and she'd still been there when Sub-Lieutenant Ball brought his C.O. along to meet her. M.G.B. 600's captain was an R.N.V.R. lieutenant by name of Hughes: pink-faced, fair-haired, solid, she guessed in his early thirties. He told her that in 'real' life he was a solicitor in Ross-on-Wye. He didn't chat for long, though, only long enough to offer her the use of his cabin. 'More closet than cabin, really – but you'll want to get some shut-eye, won't you? Weather looks like holding for a while, you shouldn't find it too uncomfortable.'

Even that brief meeting had been more than she'd have expected. She'd been told that the gunboat's officers and crew were discouraged from socializing with their passengers – for security reasons, also because agents usually preferred to be left to themselves. As in fact was the case with the two other passengers, Frenchmen, who came off from shore in the motorboat after it had landed Marilyn and

went straight on board the gunboat. They'd either be
B.C.R.A., she guessed – de Gaulle's lot, *Bureau Central de
Renseignements et d'Action* – or independents of some kind.
There were several groups or factions, not all of them the
best of friends – especially French Gaullists and non-
Gaullists. In fact S.O.E. and B.C.R.A. had very little to do
with each other here in England, at administrative levels,
largely because de Gaulle resented the existence of S.O.E.
and their potential control of a secret army which he felt
should more appropriately be under *his* wing; but agents in
the field still helped each other when the need arose.
Anyway, these two would presumably be landing with her in
Ball's dinghy in pitch darkness on some rocky beach: they
could hardly ignore each others' existence, and she asked
Ball when he came back to her who they were. All he knew
was that the name of the little one had been listed as
Mitterrand and then changed to Morland. Neither would be
his real name, she guessed.

Glancing round: still no sign of Ben. 'Should I go on
board too?'

The gunboat's engines were started at that moment. A
deep, resonant growl from the other side of the old steamer.
Ball told her – having to raise his voice, over the volume of
sound – 'Warming through.' That boyish grin: 'Don't worry,
you won't be left behind. That's only two engines' worth,
incidentally, we run on four once we get outside. But – yes
– actually I came to suggest it. I'll take you down. Oh, and
the pilot said he'll show you over the boat, if you like, before
we shove off.'

'Pilot?'

'Navigator. Ben Quarry – chap you saw – you knew each
other vaguely some time ago, he said.'

Vaguely . . . As in a glass darkly, she thought. A whole *lot*
of glasses. Whatever had been in them. Micky Finns in that
nightclub, she'd thought ever since. Some gut-rot hooch:
there was a lot of it about. She was remembering, though, as
she followed the boy down, the moment when she'd first set

eyes on Ben. Coming down the stairs in Baker Street – angry, thoroughly depressed – down into the hall and through it to the street door, thinking *God's sake, I need a drink* … Except, though – shaking her head: the tears she'd been holding at bay – since a flood of them the night before – well, strong drink such as she felt the need of might not help at all. If the reaction up there had been *Yes, Mrs Ewing, you're an answer to our prayers* – well, that would have been the right medicine. Instead of which – that stupid man's 'Daddy knows best' attitude … And the problem which then faced her: what the hell *could* she do? The idea of life continuing just as it had before Johnny's death appalled her.

Try S.I.S.?

Yes. First thing, tomorrow. She had actually thought of them before. But having a connection already with S.O.E. … Well – Foreign Office, a call to them might point her in the right—

The front door had crashed open, inwards, and this naval lieutenant had come barging in, colliding with her. She was only on her feet because they were grasping each other's arms.

'Hell – *sorry*—'

'Probably my fault – partly—'

'Definitely was not.' Still hanging on to her. Tallish, and enough of him that she couldn't easily have got past. 'You know damn well it wasn't.'

'You're Australian.'

'Got it in one. Work here, do you?'

'No. I do not.' She'd pulled free. 'As it happens.'

'Meaning, if it's any of my damn business?'

'No – not at all. But if you'd let me by, please—'

'You have a – kind of strained look. If it's from being crashed into by strange Australians—'

'It's not.' She made herself smile, relax a little. 'It's just that I've had a very bad day – including an interview just concluded, with an idiot.'

'Might a drink help?'

'It might.' She nodded. 'Might well. Thanks for the inspiration.'

'What I meant was,' – he'd put a hand on her arm again – 'well, all I have to do here is get a signature for *this*' – a long brown envelope which he'd pulled out of his greatcoat pocket: red seals on it, something secret obviously – 'have your idiot make his mark for it, maybe. Then – fact is I've something terrific to celebrate.'

'Loss of Singapore?'

'Now don't spoil it. I really do have something to celebrate – forget bloody Singapore. And drinking alone's no fun, is it? Look – one for my good news, another to drown your sorrows. You can tell me about 'em – I'm deaf in one ear, I'll lend you the other. What d'you say?'

He looked almost imploring: he really did want her company. And it was certainly a better prospect than that stinking train, cold sober, then about twelve hours' solitary in the digs in Sevenoaks where until a day ago there'd always been the hope that Johnny would come breezing in. Sevenoaks being where she worked, and close enough to Biggin Hill where he'd been stationed. He'd got himself to and fro in an MG midget, a 1936 TC in which he'd claimed he only touched the ground at corners. She'd have to do something about that little car, she realized, ring the adjutant or someone.

She'd nodded. 'All right.'

'*Good* on you, that's *marvellous*!' He'd virtually shouted the last word. 'Look, I'll be two minutes, maximum. Don't go and vanish now, uh?'

Alone, she began to wonder if it mightn't be more sensible if she did just that. Whether either a drink or two or a sympathetic hearing mightn't bring on the tears: the two together might just about guarantee it. It struck her again what a different world this would have been around her if that man upstairs had said 'Yes' – or even 'In a month or two, when we *will* be recruiting women agents' ...

'That was *half* a minute – OK?'

He'd called it down to her, and she'd turned, looking up at him as he came bounding down the stairs. Brown, curly-looking hair – pushing his naval cap more or less straight on it. Not good-looking as Johnny had been – Johnny had known it, too – but not *bad* looking, either. Blue eyes, light-brown hair, and this sort of wild enthusiasm. Raising a forefinger in warning: '*I*'ll open the door this time . . .'

He hadn't changed much, either. Except for the beard. On the gunboat's deck, cluttered with weaponry and other gear – holding both her hands in his: 'Rosie, how absolutely *marvellous*!'

Familiar word, familiar tone of voice: even to the shouting, which of course was necessary, over the engines' noise. But he looked slightly less wild than he had in her mental image of him.

'*What* a surprise, Ben.' Searching for something to say that wouldn't reflect the past, or any lingering emotional involvement. 'You were going off on a course in navigation – and here you are, a full-blown navigator!'

'Be odder if I'd wound up as a full-blown pastry-cook.'

'Oh, you *haven't* changed.'

'Give you a quick tour of this vessel, shall I? Upper deck first – before they get busy. Haven't long, see.' He looked across at Ball: 'Sub, will you dump that in the skipper's cabin?'

The suitcase. Ball nodded. 'I was going to.' He disappeared with it. Ben asked her, 'How've you been, Rosie?'

'All right. Fine.'

'And you got what *you* wanted.' There was a reek of petrol suddenly: then it cleared, just as suddenly. 'Despite that bloke turning you down. Crikey, you were spitting mad, weren't you?'

Shaking his head, gazing down at her. 'Doesn't it *scare* you mad, now you've got it?'

What she'd wondered earlier – whether any of them even guessed . . . No comment, though. She pointed: 'What's this?'

'Well, OK. The guided tour.' He reached up, grasping one of the lower rails that ran around some kind of gun-mounting. 'What we call the bandstand. That's a twin Oerlikon up there, twenty millimetre. And further aft here, six-pounder Hotchkiss. For'ard there's a two-pounder and twin point-fives. And Vickers in the bridge. We're a D-class motor gunboat, incidentally. Length one-twenty feet, crew of thirty plus four officers, displaces about a hundred and twenty tons. I did try to get in touch, Rosie. Slightly disadvantaged by not knowing your surname, or for that matter where to start – except the R.A.F. at Biggin Hill. I tried there, nobody knew of anyone called Rosie. Didn't at S.O.E.'s 'F' Section either – which was a long shot, obviously, seeing as they'd turned you down.'

'I asked you *not* to try.'

He nodded: glancing round, then turning back to her. 'That's why I – desisted.'

'This tiny little boat is the one I'll be landed in, I gather.'

It was on this starboard side, about midway along between the 'bandstand' and the six-pounder. A sailor was tightening lashings over its canvas cover. Ben nodded. 'Ten-foot SN dinghy, special design for the job. Nick Ball's job. Two oarsmen, and he steers from the back end with a scull, compass between his knees.'

'Sounds – primitive . . .'

'Not easy. Best way of doing it, though. And he knows his stuff, don't worry . . . Christ, Rosie, I wish you weren't doing this. Here we get to see each other again at last, and—'

'What's that?'

He sighed, moving aft with her. 'Depth charge. One the other side too. Mostly for use against E-boats. Not that we go looking for them, it's all softly, softly, this racket . . . And that – before you ask, and not that you actually give a damn – that's chemical smoke apparatus. When we need to lay a screen . . . Better be quick now, I'll just point out the main features. Oh, Petty Officers' mess down there.' He led the way back towards the bow. 'Engine-room hatch. As you can

hear ... There you have the mast – carries our W/T aerials
and also radar – a 291 ... Quick shufti in the bridge now?
Up here. *Very* quick, skipper'll be down in two shakes. Oh,
hi, Don.' Introducing yet another R.N.V.R. lieutenant as they
came off the ladderway into the rest of the bridge. 'Don
Shepherd, our first lieutenant.'

She smiled at him and nodded, and he saluted her. A
Johnny type, she thought – smoothly handsome. *Too* smooth
– as Johnny had been. He'd turned to Ben: 'Shoving off any
minute, you know.'

'Right.' Ben pointed. 'The wheel. And this is Petty
Officer Ambrose, who handles it, steers us hither and yon.'

'How do, miss.' A voice called from a voicepipe, and he
stooped to it. Ben pointed again: 'Down there – where we'll
go now, out of these blokes' way – is my plot. Chart-room's
another word for it.' He went ahead down steps into a
cramped, low-roofed space with a chart-table on this port
side – a chart spread on it, which was how she knew what
it was – a rack of books, manuals – some dials and switches
and so forth. Windows gave a view forward and to the sides.
A voice called, 'C.O.'s coming aboard, sir!'

'Down here now, Rosie.' Another ladderway, this one
near-vertical. 'Galley flat, we call this. Wardroom's here to
port; French passengers'll be dossing in there. That's the
galley, next to it. And this side, starboard – officers' heads
– lavatory, with a washbasin, the one you can use – then this
is the W/T office, and last but by no means least, skipper's
cabin. Door at the end there leads into the for'ard mess,
some of the ship's company's living space. Are you a good
sailor, by the way?'

'Rotten.'

'Looks like it's going to be smooth enough, anyway. Here
you are, C.O.'s cabin – all yours. But Rosie—'

The noise had doubled, suddenly. He paused, touched his
good ear. He was deaf in the other, she remembered him
telling her that evening in London, from having been blown
up in a motor torpedo boat in the winter of 1941. Telling her

now, 'That's the two centre engines warming up. We leave harbour on just the outers, go on to four then and work up to cruising speed. Twenty-three knots, this trip. Rosie – you'll need something to eat before you turn in, won't you?'

'Since you mention it . . .'

'So come up to the plot, when you feel like it, after we've sailed. I get the pleasure of your company, you get some nosh. Sandwiches – all right?' She was in the cabin, and he was stooping in the small doorway, on the point of shutting it. There was a lot of noise and movement overhead by this time. 'Rosie – tell me your surname?'

'Can't. Not allowed to. Sorry.' Then, seeing his expression, '*Honestly*, Ben. *Officially* I can't.' Officially, in fact, she didn't have one at this stage; only her code-name, and the French pseudonym, which wouldn't have been any use to him. Eighteen months ago she hadn't let him know it, because – well, partly because it was Johnny's name, not hers. Her thinking had been confused and contradictory even before she'd got drunk, but essentially she'd wanted to be herself, not Johnny's widow. She'd told him – told Ben Quarry, in the taxi after they'd left Baker Street – that her name was Rosie, and that she'd been born Rosalie de Bosque.

Alone in the cabin, she kicked off her shoes and got up on the bunk. Remembering that taxi-ride: that she'd still been asking herself what the hell she was doing, but telling him 'My father was French. A lawyer – actually in Monte Carlo. He died when I was twelve. Until then we hardly spoke anything *but* French, but we came home then – Mama being English, family here, and so forth.'

'Where, exactly?'

She hadn't answered this. Hadn't told him anything about her wireless-operator's job in Sevenoaks, either. So – she realized now, without any really clear recollection of her reasons at the time – she'd obviously not wanted him to be able to track her down.

Because she'd had some intention right from the outset to behave the way she had?

She was sure she hadn't. Not even a thought of it.

She'd told him about Johnny at some point: she'd thought she had, knew it now because otherwise he wouldn't have tried to find her via Biggin Hill. On a more practical level, though, she might have not wanted to be traceable because at that stage she couldn't have been sure she'd want to see him again.

He'd told her – in the New Yorker, in Park Lane, to which they'd taken the taxi from Baker Street – 'I speak a few words of French, myself. *Very* few, mind you.'

'Australian schoolboy French?'

'Uh-huh. Australian-messing-around-in-Paris French. I was there a couple of years, but most of my chums weren't French speakers, and I'm no linguist. Middle '37 to September '39. Trying to be an artist, would you believe it?'

'No reason I shouldn't.'

'Want ice in that?'

'Please.' In her gimlet. Swirling it then to get some of the ice to melt and weaken it. 'You haven't yet told me what the good news is that we're celebrating.'

He touched her glass with his. 'My imminent return to seagoing. *That*'s what.'

'Good thing, is it?'

He'd swallowed some whisky. 'Nothing short of bloody marvellous. Even miraculous.' He put the glass down half-empty. 'Is this going to bore you, Rosie?'

She'd laughed. 'Bit late to worry about *that*.'

'I'll give it to you in a nutshell. I was at sea – Coastal Forces, small, fast craft called M.T.B.s. Motor torpedo boats. Wearing one stripe, not two; I joined as an O.D. – Ordinary Seaman, that stands for, don't ask me how – then got commissioned, for some reason, and shortly after – well, blown up, sort of. Winter of '41, this was, night action off the Dutch coast. We got a real pasting – Hun destroyers – but we got the boat back – that's to say the others did – with me in it, not all that conscious. Which is why I don't have a functional eardrum now on this side, and I was thereafter no bloody use to Coastal Forces. See, in M.T.B.s. and M.G.B.s. – gunboats, no torpedoes – we'd often enough stop engines off that coast or on the convoy route and lie quiet in the dark, listening for E-boats. Hear 'em for bloody miles, when you're out there. But lacking one eardrum . . .' He'd paused, and engaged the barman's attention: 'Same again, please.' Glancing back at Rosie: 'OK?'

'Second and last – as agreed.'

'But I haven't told you my story yet. And there's still yours to come . . . Where'd I got to – well, the naval hospital at Haslar, is where I was. And this lieutenant-commander – something to do with Coastal Forces, I forget what. Must have included officers' appointments, anyway. This was after they'd stitched me together, I was about ready to come out. Spring of last year. This bloke sort of ticked off various items – M.T.B.s., talks some French – must've shot that line when I got commissioned, so it'd have been on my record – ditto pre-war residence in Gay Paree, and yachting – before I'd left Brisbane I'd sailed quite a lot. Anyway, the geezer winds up with "So happens, Quarry, there's a staff job in London needs filling, connected with all those things, including Coastal Forces. And as you're now unfit for sea duty . . .'

He'd raised his new glass. 'Here's to you, Rosalie.'

'And to your seagoing. But how come?'

'I was fed up to here with the desk job. When all your chums are at sea – you know . . . In St James' is where I've been working, a department of Naval Intelligence run by an R.N. four-striper, name of Slocum. Some character, I tell you – it's thanks to him I'm getting back to sea. He's swung it on the grounds that in Coastal Forces – well, motor gunboats – a navigator doesn't need sharp ears, not like a skipper and a first lieutenant do. Navigator's stuck below with his charts. And I've done *some* navigating. So they're giving me this crash course down at Bursledon – in Hampshire, eh? – and as long as I pass out of it well enough – which believe me I bloody *will*—'

'I'm sure you will.'

'Bet your life, Rosie. And life then begins again.'

'Congratulations.'

'Thanks. Must say, Rosie, you're a peach. Let's have a drink. I want to hear what these troubles are you said needed drowning. Barman—'

'Why did you leave Australia in the first place?'

'Glutton for punishment, aren't you? Yeah – same, please ... Rosie, this *will* bore you. When you've heard enough, shut me up. Answering the question, though – my dad wanted me in his business, which is timber. He had a Master's ticket in the Merchant Navy – British – settled out there after he'd met and married my Aussie mother. He was going to build boats – her brother was in that business – but he sort of branched off. Cheers, Rosie ... Fact, it was the boat interest got me sailing – from about knee-high onwards. That, and painting, I'd wanted to paint since I don't remember when. So, '37, when I left College, he said OK, son, give it a go if you have to, take a year off *then* join the business. I wanted to see England and Europe too, and – you know, Paris being where all the painters go, that's where I went. Worked my passage cutting up cabbages and stuff in the *Strathmore*'s kitchens – P. and O. Line – lovely ships, those *Straths*. And there I was – Paris, London, all over. Mostly Paris. Full of bastard Boches now – doesn't it make your flesh creep?'

'Yes, it does.' She'd sipped at her gin. 'Ever sell any paintings?'

'One. Just *one* damn canvas, ever. I took some to London, they wouldn't look at 'em. The one I sold was on the Dover–Calais boat – to a Yank. He was pie-eyed, really stewed ... So – what you're wondering – I got jobs now and then. Kitchen work mostly, and a delivery van one time. Family kept writing come on home, and I kept saying yes, on my way next month. Always telling myself *This'll be break-through month* – you know?'

'There must have been a girl.'

'Painting, is what there was.'

'*And* a girl.'

'You're really gifted, Rosie. Put a shawl over your head and sling some beads on, crystal ball on the table: *I see a girl...*'

'Where is she now?'

'Oh.' A shrug. 'Have it your way. I don't know. She only slummed for a while, went back to greener pastures.'

'Poor you.'

'Poor me, hell. Barman!'

'Oh, now look—'

The boat was moving. On her back in this little box of a cabin she'd become aware of a change in the engines' note and rhythm, and felt some kind of motion. Changing again now: getting clear of the old paddle-steamer's side, she guessed – trying to visualize it, interpret the variations in sound and vibration. Conscious also that this was the moment of severance of contact, that from here on she'd be on her own. No further refreshing of memory, for instance: code-names, addresses, telephone numbers . . .

Buckmaster hadn't mentioned the drops, in his résumé this morning, and she was glad he hadn't. The intention was that she'd tell no-one at all, except the Resistance people who'd receive them. If Buckmaster had remembered it you could bet he'd have said something like 'You'll keep César informed, of course': and she'd have had to. It was S.O.E.'s own business, no-one else's. A different thing entirely from the S.I.S. operation. But as he *hadn't* issued any such instruction, she could stick to what had been agreed. Even allowing for César being – as Buckmaster had said – 'gilt-edged': suppose for instance he decided – wrongly – that it was all right to bring the suspect Romeo into it?

Romeo was the stiffest fence she'd be facing, at the start. He might be perfectly OK but if he *had* been turned by the Germans – as Baker Street suspected – they'd have her on toast. Unless César had sorted him out before she got there, and decided to stay clear of him. But on the S.I.S. job, 'La Minette' was potentially no less dangerous, and there was no way to stay clear of *her* – no matter what Maurice Buckmaster thought ... She'd been the protégée of an independent agent known as 'La Chatte', who'd been playing both ends against the middle to no small effect. A year ago, this had been. 'La Minette' – meaning kitten – had only been doing odd jobs for her – entertaining men for or with her had been her primary function up to the time of La Chatte's arrest. La Chatte had then saved her own neck by agreeing to work for the Germans, and at the same time she'd got rid of her part-time employee, presumably because she couldn't trust her to toe the new line. Otherwise, why sack her – when she (La Chatte) was still in business? 'La Minette' might therefore be fundamentally anti-German, and clever enough not to have let the Germans know it. Whether or not S.I.S. had other reasons for believing this, one didn't know, but it was the basis on which they'd decided she might be useable: her value being solely that she was – allegedly – Colonel Walther's mistress.

"La Chatte" was out of it. She'd sold the Germans the idea of her working for them right in the heart of S.O.E., in London, the Gestapo had connived at her 'escape' from their custody and an S.O.E. agent whom she then contacted had allowed her to believe he'd swallowed her story whole. He'd taken her to England with him on board a gunboat of this 15th Flotilla, and she was now in Holloway women's prison. But she'd made her mark, all right. German use of her radio, probably with her as the pianist, had convinced S.I.S. and Naval Intelligence that the warships *Scharnhorst*, *Gneisenau* and *Prinz Eugen* had no intentions of leaving Brest; and in the middle of February of last year – a few days before Johnny's death and Rosie's first visit to Baker Street – they'd broken out and escaped up-Channel to German ports.

The engines were fairly deafening now. All four, Rosie guessed. And the gunboat's angle in the water was changing, its bow lifting as it gathered speed.

3

'César' stared back at his interrogator. About his own
age – middle thirties. Civilian clothes. He'd introduced himself as an officer of the S.D. – *Sicherheitsdienst*,
intelligence branch of the S.S. – which made sense in a way
because although this – the Hotel Terminus – was the Lyon
Gestapo headquarters, not S.D., its presiding genius was a
fairly notorious thug by name of Klaus Barbie, who was
himself an S.S. lieutenant.

Ernst Hauffe, this one's name was.

'An absolute fool, Rossier. *Think* about it!'

About the offer he'd made him: he'd be a fool to turn it
down, was the assertion. They knew a great deal about him
already, Hauffe had pointed out, there were only a few
details to fill in. The conversation was all in French, of
course.

'If we have to get it out of you the hard way – well, we
will. But I really would recommend the alternative. Easier
for us, and *much* easier for you. You have my word on it as
a German officer: in return for your full cooperation, either
you'll walk free if you agree to be on our payroll, or you'll
go to an ordinary prison here in France – for the duration of
the war, of course, but at least you'd be alive to join in the
celebrations of our victory. It's for you to choose, Rossier.'

'Since when did a German officer keep his word?'

The other one – behind him, behind the heavy timber
chair on to which they'd forced him with his wrists chained

behind his back – stooped and grasped his arms just below the elbows. Hauffe checked him with a gesture: the hands loosened as if reluctantly.

Standard gambits, Michel thought. Preliminaries, like lovers' foreplay.

Not that the analogy was a very good one.

That was one of the things they did to you, though. Hands cuffed behind the back, then the arms forced up. Try it even halfway, you'd begin to know what pain was. On occasion they'd hung prisoners up that way, but it was self-defeating since the victim invariably fainted.

'Your wife's in Ireland, it seems.' Touching her letter: several sheets of blue paper covered with Andrea's rounded writing. They hadn't let him read it. Hauffe added, 'We have our own people in Dublin, you know. Do I have to point out that it may not be only you who suffers?'

Again, par for the course. Bribery, then threats to one's nearest and dearest.

'Shall I read this to you?'

'No, thank you.'

'She was Irish-born, one gathers – from these references to various family connections. Also to some man who seems to have – shall we say, engaged her affections. Well, well . . .' He turned that page over, read a line or two more, and shrugged. 'Leave 'em too long, it's bound to happen, isn't it? And typically, she can't even see it coming – so blind to it she's even telling *you* about him.' He'd sat back, moving the letter aside. 'When you finally persuade yourself to start talking, you mustn't forget to tell me how that letter got to Lyon without a stamp on it. My *guess* is that it might have come via London. So who brought it here, and by what route? Eh? Well, never mind, you'll tell me later. Here's an idea, though – what about sending her a recent portrait of yourself?'

Some silly game. He stared at Hauffe, expressionless, ignoring it. Knowing that he'd lied about Andrea, who if she was contemplating or indulging in some kind of an *affaire* wouldn't be either so stupid or so cruel as to drop hints to him about it. She wasn't Irish-born either: the Irish relations were all his – and distant, from way back. The family name had been Mullins, but when Grandfather had settled in Bordeaux and married into the wine trade he'd added a 'de' and an 'o' and dropped one 'l' to make the name de Moulins. That was César's real name, Michel de Moulins: while the name on his papers was Michel Rossier. Also among his papers was a certificate to the effect that he'd been honourably discharged from the French army – cavalry – in 1938, following injury when a horse had fallen on him. This accounted for his limp, although in fact it was the result of a parachuting accident in England in 1940.

Hauffe had picked up his telephone and asked someone – in German – where the photographer had got to. Hanging up, he explained, 'Before we ruin your good looks, Rossier. It does seem to be inevitable.'

He'd arrived from Marseille late yesterday afternoon, and called the *planque* – safe house – in the Rue Bonnel from a telephone in the Café de la Gare. A male voice had answered, and in reply to the question was Jacques Deschamps at home the answer had been 'Deschamps?' – and then after a second's hesitation, 'Oh, *him*. He's out, at this instant. But he'll be back in half an hour. Why don't you come along? Can I say what time you'll be here?' It had been enough to tell Michel that the Pension d'Alsace was a safe house no longer, in fact was obviously staked out: he'd never heard of anyone called Jacques Deschamps.

It was a major setback. There was to have been a mail drop at the pension, and he'd been hoping to have a letter – or two, or three – from Andrea. Brought by hand and addressed to him as Michel Rossier: 'Mick, ma cher', or 'Mick, mon amour' . . . No danger in it: He'd had letters from her before, elsewhere, and she was meticulous in mentioning nothing but family and other entirely personal matters. Touch wood, there'd have been no other communications – nothing from Baker Street.

Arrangements for contacting Romeo and/or Angel – which was what he'd stopped off in Lyon for – were to be passed to him verbally by a silk merchant on the Quai Perrache.

He'd visit him in the morning, he'd decided. If they'd shut up shop for the night before he got there he'd have gone a long way for nothing; he knew nowhere to stay the night in that immediate area, and there was the curfew to think about. So he'd walked – too long a hike for his gammy leg – to the Grand Nouvel Hotel, which he'd used once before, and had an early meal – again, because of the curfew – at a Greek restaurant close by.

He'd woken at about two in the morning, and sweated for a couple of hours, thinking about the pension stake-out and the possible ramifications, the mail drop and how much they might have learnt from it. That 'come along' invitation proved it was a stake-out, but whether they'd have been waiting for him personally was guesswork. If there'd been a letter or letters from Andrea, they might well have been. But there'd have been nothing to tell them that Michel Rossier's ultimate destination was Rouen. Not even if they'd caught others in the *planque* who'd talked. The silk merchant – code-named 'Fabien' – was the one and only contact to be made here, the pension only a place to stay and to pick up any mail.

He'd make the approach to Fabien's establishment very carefully, all the same.

Go to the famous Monique's first?

Park the luggage, and ask for a bed there for the night. It was a brothel, in the Old Town, *Vieux Lyon*. He'd never been there, but he'd been told she always had room for people like himself. And two nights in this hotel would be one too many. Suspicions were easily aroused – in night porters, cleaning women, any of them. Plenty of potential informers around, interested in both ingratiating and enriching themselves.

Monique's, therefore, *then* the silk emporium. It was going to entail a lot of legwork, but using taxis was as risky as putting up at small hotels.

Long telephone calls too. Some lines were tapped.

He'd slept, eventually. Woken, bathed in tepid water, breakfasted on rolls and chemical-tasting jam, and on an impulse – because his knee still ached from over-use the day before – taken a taxi to the Old Town. It was such a hell of a long haul: across the town and over both rivers, the Rhône and the Saône: wouldn't be exactly a short step after that, either, down to the Quai Perrache. And then back *again* . . . He'd been thinking about it – that there was a time factor as well – when a *gazo* taxi had come bumbling out of the Gare La Part Dieu, and that had clinched it.

'Vieux Lyon. Rue Saint Jean.'

The driver had a face like a rat, teeth like a rat's too when he smiled, which he did when Michel paid him off just short of a corner and then waited, immobile – partly so as not to demonstrate his limp – until he'd got going again and was out of sight. Guessing, maybe: although this was hardly a time of day for brothels. He'd have brought solitary men here before, though, he might well have made that assumption. Good thing if he had – the Germans would hardly pay for *that* sort of information.

It certainly wasn't the right time of day for Monique or her girls. He'd located the house, finally, some way up a near-vertical flight of stairs that led up from the *place* at the top of the road, and having hauled himself up there, step by step, had more than enough time to get his breath back before his ring was answered. It was Monique herself who came down. Fiftyish, built like a prize-fighter, swathed in a purple *robe de chambre* and highly suspicious at first, then alarmed – for which you could hardly blame her, when the penalty for helping a British agent was death – but less so, although still cautious, once he was inside with the door securely bolted.

'Have you been here before, monsieur?'

'No, but friends of mine have. You don't let your Boche customers up to the top floor, they told me.'

'I don't know what you're talking about!'

'Madame—'

'How can I be certain *you're* not a Boche – trying to set me up, hunh?'

After he'd satisfied her that he wasn't, she'd shown him to an attic room, where he'd left his suitcase. It would be safe, she assured him, he could take the key of the room with him if he liked. He *did* like – not that it made much difference, there'd be other keys – and told her he'd be back some time later – please God. She'd repeated that plea soundlessly with her eyes shut, then taken him down and let him out. And having now established his temporary base, he'd been thinking about the silk merchant: in essence, the simple truth was that however carefully he made the approach, since he'd eventually have to walk in and ask for 'Fabien' – well, if they'd got there ahead of him, he'd have had it.

Chances about evens, maybe. Obviously they'd have made a few arrests in the Pension d'Alsace: and having only limited faith in his fellow beings he could only hope and pray that none of them had ever heard of 'Fabien'. Limping southward, down the Quai Fulchiron – the shortest route, he'd decided, would be to stay this side of the river down as far as the Kitchener bridge – he made himself stroll, not hurry, and not limp more noticeably than he could help. It was the start of a beautiful day: mist on the river rising and dissipating as the early sun burnt through.

He was still thinking about Fabien's place: that 'care' in the approach could only amount to keeping his eyes open for Germans who might be hanging around or waiting in parked vehicles.

Which you could bet they wouldn't be. They were a lot of things but they weren't fools.

He'd paused on the bridge, leaning on the parapet with his weight off that leg, gazing down at the sun's sparkle on the water and also back the way he'd come – looking for any face or figure he might have noticed earlier and might still be with him. Two girls in summer dresses passed close, arm in arm; the dark one smiled at him – the kind of small, private smile that was infinitely more interesting than mere bonhomie. She'd probably thought he'd been giving *her* the eye. But he did have an alternative, he'd realized: to play this *really* cautiously, he could stay away from Fabien, make contact with some other *réseau* – through Monique perhaps, it was known she had Resistance links – and get a message sent to Baker Street informing them of the debacle in the Rue Bonnel and asking for the Rouen rendezvous arrangements to be wirelessed to him.

Incidentally, the sooner London heard about the Pension d'Alsace, the better.

But it would mean delay. Several days at least to make that contact – which might in any case be extremely difficult, since no-one in this business could afford to take anyone else on trust – and then a long wait for the exchange of signals. And he was already late: Romeo had been told to expect him a week or more ago. On top of all that, he had no sound reason to suspect there was any connection between the Pension d'Alsace and this silk man: so he'd have caused a lot of disruption and delay quite unnecessarily.

He walked on – across the bridge and the glittering river and straight on, along the Cours de Verdun with the railway line and the Gare Perrache off to his right. Then left, along the west bank of the Rhône, looking for Jules Martin et Cie.

And by Jesus, there it was!

Stone-faced, with intervals of patterned brickwork, wide entrance doors shut and chained, with the company name painted across them and a notice with an arrow pointing to a small door at the side: *Renseignements*.

For 'Jules', read 'Fabien'?

He walked on past, on the river side of the road. A man out for a stroll, enjoying the scenery and the sun's warmth. The nearest vehicle was a farm cart with a seedy-looking horse between its shafts, and forty metres beyond that a brown van with its doors open and two boys unloading what looked like cases of wine. A woman on a bicycle. A string of barges in mid-river, in tow of a steam tug.

Having passed under the railway bridge, he was crossing the road when a *Wehrmacht* truck which had come over the river by the Pont Galliéni swung left with screeching tyres, forcing him to hurry, to get out of its way. Reaching the kerb, he looked back over his shoulder and saw helmeted soldiers inside, facing each other from the side benches like identical stuffed dummies, each with a rifle vertical between its knees.

Still accelerating. Nothing to do with anything that mattered here. Only that the sight of them still set one's teeth on edge. As if the swine took it for granted they had some right to *be* here.

Get this over, now. Limping on past Jules Martin's vehicle-entrance doors, coming to the small one ... Pushing it open, he found himself in a shop-cum-storeroom – a counter facing him, bolts of silk in racks which looked as if they might have been there a hundred years. Mahogany, all that timber: the counter too, on which there was a brass bell, which he rang.

'Oui, monsieur?'

A small, grey-haired woman had appeared from a doorway in the wall behind the counter. Like a mouse popping out of its hole. She'd left that door open but it was along to the right so that he had no view into the nether regions.

'Perhaps I'm mistaken ...' – he'd cleared his throat – 'Could be I've come to the wrong place. I'm looking for – someone by name of Fabien, is there?'

A male voice called, 'Show the gentleman in, Françoise!'

She'd raised a flap in the counter. He'd have to pass through that gap and then along behind the counter. 'Monsieur ...'

At close range, a second or two later, he saw that she was shaking all over and that her little eyes were popping like those of a petrified rabbit. He'd limped through the opening in the counter by that time – then glancing her way again had seen her state of fright and realized immediately that this *was* a trap and that he was in it.

Well – not *quite* . . .

'I'm interested in buying silk, you understand.' Edging out, getting ready to bolt, talking only for the ear of the man inside. Aware that he'd have stood only a slim chance even if he'd not been lame. Beginning to retreat anyway, to get as far as possible before that one knew he was on his way: covering it with 'I was told that Monsieur Fabien – that's to say, if one was to buy in sufficient quantity—'

'Any quantity you like! Please, come in!'

Then the street door had opened: the woman's rounded eyes also jerked that way. His own sharp intake of breath coincided with a kind of mew from her: there was an S.S. trooper – inside now – with a Luger in his fist. The stuff nightmares were made of: and a momentary, desperate hope that this *was* nightmare, that he'd wake in a moment in his bed in the hotel. Then again it was the woman's reaction that caused him to turn: the one from inside had come out and was covering him with yet another Luger. He had it in both hands, with his elbows planted on the counter.

'Your hands behind your back, please. César, is it? I regret, the person you know as "Fabien" is – detained elsewhere.' There was a clink of metal, then the cold steel of the cuffs as the soldier clamped them on him. Also consciousness of disaster, and – even at that moment – of his personal responsibility for it. The man at the counter had straightened from his marksman's pose: 'My name is Hauffe. Ernst Hauffe. What might yours be – other than "César"?'

They'd pushed him into a pitch-dark cell and left him there all day with nothing to eat or drink, and now after questioning him for about an hour – it was past midnight, he'd heard a clock strike some time ago – they were taking photographs of him with a magnesium flash.

Front, face-on – left profile – right profile. God alone

knew what for ... Well – to be able to prove to some other prisoner that they'd got him?

'Let's have one from behind too. While we're at it.' Hauffe switched back into French: 'I dare say you're wondering why we're doing this.'

'Well.' He shrugged. 'It's painless.'

'Well, indeed.' The narrow, dark head nodded. 'And you must have expected that we'd be hurting you by this time.' He said quietly in German, 'The film's to go immediately by despatch rider to Avenue Foch. Mark it for the attention of Sturmbannfuhrer Kieffer. It's urgent, don't waste any time.'

The other one moved up close behind him again. Avenue Foch meant head office, the S.D. headquarters in Paris, Avenue Foch 82/86. The beginnings of understanding, suddenly. Except that he'd have thought they'd send *him*, the object itself, not just pictures. Just as a preliminary, perhaps: faster, by despatch rider, they could start working on it in Paris while Hauffe got on with his interrogation here.

This *had* to be the answer. He felt actually sick, as the logic of it hardened in his imagination: together with awareness of his own impotence – compounding carelessness, the lives he'd put at stake by taking a chance instead of playing safe, going the long way round.

Might have known. Really, should *have known* ...

Hauffe picked up his telephone. 'Get me Avenue Foch, Sturmbannfuhrer Kieffer.' He nodded. 'If he's not, ask for his private number – or wherever he can be found.'

He'd hung up. 'Speaking of hurting you, Rossier ... There's one question – well two, two in one, really – which might avert the need for it completely – if you'd give me a straight and truthful answer. Are you interested?'

'Your French is excellent.'

'Thank you. The question's this. There's a young woman, code-name "Angel", and a male you're calling "Romeo". I want to know what they look like.'

'I bet you do.'

Fabien must have been talking his head off. But actually,

Michel thought, while this sod obviously wouldn't mind having a description of Angel and Romeo – which as it happened he wouldn't have been able to supply, having never set eyes on either of them – what the bastard really wanted to know was whether either of *them* knew what he – César – looked like.

'Well?'

'I'm trying to remember.'

Needing a moment or two to think it out. The possibility that he might not be quite so impotent after all. If he could convince them that Romeo and Angel would know César when they saw him – more to the point, would know at a glance that an impostor was *not* César – it might stop this thing in its tracks.

Hauffe was hardly likely to believe that he'd abruptly give in – not to the extent of betraying his fellow agents ...

'Are you going to tell me?'

'You know damn well I'm not. So you may as well get on with it.'

'Is it because you know the woman personally, that you won't describe her?'

He'd been right: here was the *real* question, and he jumped on it. 'Even if I *didn't* know her—'

'If you did not, the question of describing her wouldn't arise in any case, would it?' A slight shrug ... 'What about the man – "Romeo"?'

'I'm not answering *any* questions.'

'You just tried to tell me something, though – didn't you?'

Canny bastard. But it made no difference, he realized. If they saw even a faint chance of pulling it off, what would they stand to lose by trying?

He shut his eyes. Knowing the savagery would start soon. *God, give me strength ...*

4

She'd been more dozing than sleeping, and the bang on the cabin door had her awake at once. It was Ball, the sub-lieutenant, telling her 'Be there in half an hour. If you like – when you're ready – you could move up to the plot.'

'Right. Thank you.'

It felt like only about half an hour since he'd banged on the door like that and told her 'Skipper's compliments, we're about to test the guns. Makes a bit of a racket, might alarm you if you weren't expecting it.' But actually that had been not long after they'd sailed; and after the gunboat had sounded and felt as if it had been blowing up – its numerous guns all blasting off simultaneously – she'd gone up to join Ben in the plot as he'd suggested. Ball added now, 'Only thing is – word of warning – pilot's going to be concentrating like mad. Tricky approach, this one.'

She smiled. 'Won't speak unless I'm spoken to.'

'Leave your suitcase in here, for the time being?'

There was a lot more movement on the boat than there had been: an irregular plunging motion and thudding impacts of the sea as the bow smashed through it. No feeling of seasickness though – as yet. She slid down from the bunk, and put her shoes on: thinking how much easier it would have been to go in by Lysander, or even by parachute as she'd done last time. You landed, and there you were; either the reception party had a bicycle for you, or there was transport – a farm lorry, milk cart or some such, to some safe house or a railway station. A lot simpler than rowing-boats, beaches and cliffs, God knew what else, all in pitch darkness.

A wash, and a pee. The last of either for some time, probably ... There was another knock, though. 'Like tea, miss?'

'Oh, *would* I!'

The sailor looked about sixteen. 'Bacon sandwich here an' all. I put one sugar in the tea.'

'As good as the Ritz.'

'Ah. Well.' He seemed embarrassed. 'Best of luck, miss.'

Sipping the hot tea, she wondered whether that warning about Ben concentrating on his work had come from young Ball or from Ben himself. She'd spent some time up there, after the gun-testing, and he'd had thick, mustardy ham sandwiches brought up from the galley. The last of the light had been going, the sun dipping behind a distant streak of land; it was Lizard Point, he'd told her, about sixty miles away. And behind, on the quarter, Start Point ... 'Prawle Point there – entrance to Salcombe.' Her last sight of England for how long, she'd wondered: England at its most beautiful, at that, with the light dying in a golden glow over the littoral behind the darkening coast.

He'd shown her on a chart where they were going: a remote crack in the Breton coast called L'Abervrac'h. In fact it was going to be worse than that: L'Abervrac'h was an indenture in the mainland, but she was to be put ashore on some small island from which there'd be a second boat-trip to an even smaller one, followed by what looked like quite a long slog – on foot – over a sandpit which only at low tide connected it to the mainland. She'd asked him 'Couldn't you have made it *really* difficult?'

'Not easy even from my angle. Navigationally. Have to more or less feel our way along this channel – see? Rocks right, left and centre. And to add to the joys of spring,' – he'd touched the coastline with the tip of a pencil – 'here, here and here – Boche lookout positions.'

'You're having me on, Ben.'

'You might well think so. But that's one advantage – they wouldn't believe anyone in his right mind would come near the place, would they?'

It was a point . . . 'You've been there before, anyway.'

'Lots of times. Coming from Falmouth more often than Dartmouth – shorter trip. Doesn't make much odds to this hooker, though, we have the range and some to spare. It's the furthest west of our pinpoints, this one – as well as the trickiest approach. But it's not just a matter of picking some beach and saying "OK, here's a good one"; there's a heck of a lot more to it. Takes months to set one up. There's got to be a local *réseau* who can handle it – people and material in and out, routes to and fro – on shore, I mean. And lines of communication beyond that – I suppose you'd know that end of it – routes right across France, for escapees, British and Yank shot-down flyers, escaped P.O.W.s sometimes. Mail, too – secret stuff from all over Europe.' He'd paused, then added, 'And last but certainly not least, people like you. To whom, let me say this while I have the chance, Rosie – I take off my hat. I really do. I wish you weren't doing it, but – in my book, you're the bravest of the brave.'

'Whatever induced you to grow a beard?'

'Laziness, mostly. Saves shaving. Disapprove, do you?'

'No. Well –' she'd shrugged – 'hardly my business, is it?'

'I'd like it to be. Really, *love* it to be.'

'All right. Shave it off, then.'

He nodded. 'Back alongside, first thing I'll do.'

'I wasn't being serious, Ben. What's this?'

'Message carrier, between me here and the W/T office. Lanyard here through the pipe – signal's stuffed into this little bucket, gets pulled up or down . . . Tell me how I can get in touch with you – at some later stage?'

'Ben – I can't see there'd be much point. In any case I may be away a *very* long time.'

'Not for ever, though.'

'Well – I hope not. But—'

'What's the other thing?'

She'd shaken her head.

'Listen. Please. What happened that night – I want you to know I'd no such thing in mind, no intention at *all*—'

'I do know that. But it still happened.'

'Well, you say that, but—'

'I'd like *you* to know that if I hadn't been blind drunk—'

'The hooch they sold us. That joint where we danced. My fault, I'd persuaded you to come along, should've looked after you. Bloody *should*'ve. If you'd ever trust me again, Rosie, I *swear*—'

'It's nothing to do with trust. Sorry, but – simply *no*. Quite apart from the fact that whenever I have any time off I go home – which is nowhere near London ... I'm sorry, Ben.'

'Still don't want to tell me where "home" is, either ...'

She shook her head again. 'Can't we just leave it?'

'Well.' Shrugging. 'Have to, if you insist ... D'you reckon your family wouldn't like me, is that it? Bloody colonial, wouldn't fit in?'

'Nothing even remotely of that kind. Even to think it could be you must have a totally wrong impression of me.'

'OK. So – new question – how did you get into this, after that bloke turned you down?'

'I was contacted at work.'

'What work was that?'

'At Sevenoaks, the S.O.E. wireless reception centre. I was what you might call a dotter and dasher.'

'I'm sure you never told me that.'

'Dare say I didn't.'

'Didn't tell me a damn thing. We made a joke of it, remember – sang a song?

> *Ask no questions*
> *You'll be told no lies ...*

Remember we sang that all over London?'

In the Gay Nineties, they'd first put it to music. After she'd refused repeatedly to tell him her surname or where she lived, and he'd gone on arguing about it, she'd trotted out that old rejoinder and he'd made a jingle out of it. Those two lines and then on a basso note a sort of chorus of *No lies. No lies. No lies ...*

In the street – quite a number of streets, probably – blundering through the fog – a real pea-souper, that night – they'd sung it in duet. Shivering, clinging together, they'd still been warbling it when they'd made a complete circuit and were back at the same policeman of whom half an hour earlier they'd asked the way. It was how they'd ended up in the hotel, where the night porter had taken pity on them although there'd been only one single room available: he'd told them doubtfully, 'Does have its own bathroom', and Ben had slurred 'S'all right then – I'll sleep in the bath.'

The hell he had.

He'd told her, when the gunboat had left Start Point well astern and was steering south 22 degrees west at about 24 knots, 'Stayed with me ever since, that song. Over and over, day in, day out.' There'd been a call from the bridge then, which he'd answered, something about a log-reading and the speed-made-good: then he'd turned back to her ... 'Rosie – something else I have to say. Hope it won't annoy you. That evening – night – well, early morning anyway – OK, so I'm totally to blame for how it ended, I apologize and I'd give my soul for a chance to prove to you I'm not the heel you think I am – but up to that point, that night out with you – you know, I never had such a bloody marvellous evening in my life?'

Now – this second visit, when she'd been warned not to make a nuisance of herself, she propped herself in a corner on the starboard side, as far removed from him as she could get. And Ben, stooped over the chart and checking frequently on various instruments, didn't even glance at her. Leaning to the voicepipe, suddenly, after peering closely at the thing that whirred all the time: 'Bridge? La Libenter, skipper. Go to silent running?'

There was a gruff answer of some kind, then a considerable reduction in the engine noise. He'd mentioned, when he'd been showing her the Brittany-coast chart, that before they entered that narrow, rock-strewn channel they'd slow right down, and that the engines had what he'd called Dumbflows on them – silencers.

Not one, or two, but *three* German lookout posts, she remembered. You'd need silencers, all right. Invisibility too ... She checked the time – five past eleven, Central European Time. She'd put her watch back by two hours last night, after checking that their ETA at the island, 0130 G.M.T., would be 2330 C.E.T., the time she'd be using from here on.

She'd met the Frenchmen down there, a few minutes earlier. One of them had tried the door of the officers' heads when she'd been in there, and she'd called 'Won't be a minute!' – in English, then realized it might be one of those two. So when she came out she'd looked into the wardroom, which was across the flat from the cabin she'd been using, introduced herself and shook hands with them – rather liking the look of the small one, whose name Ball had mentioned earlier – despite his manner being only coldly polite, perhaps indicative of a high degree of professional aloofness.

And why not? Her own attitude should have been the same. Remembering Marilyn's caution, *no distractions* ... She had, in fact, made some effort to put Ben Quarry out of mind when she'd come back down here, concentrating her thoughts instead – in French – on César and Romeo, La Minette, Louis, wondering whether it might be wiser to accept Buckmaster's advice and tell César about the sideline S.I.S. job. She'd decided that there was plenty of time to make up her mind.

Ben called up the voicepipe, 'Come three degrees to starboard.' Attention was back on the chart then. Like a different man, she thought. Intent, absorbed in *his* own expertise. The gunboat was lifting on a swell and rolling hard, a ton or more of sea crashing against this forepart as she started down again. Rosie wondered how it would be possible to hold a course with anything like that degree of accuracy – three degrees this way or that – when the ship was being flung around as she was. She was feeling the effect now: telling herself that it was all in the mind, ignore it . . . She focused on Ben's bearded face, part-lit by the lamp over the chart and the glow from the instruments, including the machine that whirred and which seemed to be churning out some kind of graph to which he referred every few seconds. That and the compass and some other gadget had most of his attention. They didn't switch on their radar anywhere near the coast, he'd told her, because German equipment might detect it. Didn't need it anyway, having this, that and the other – topographical features – fairly accurately in mind, being able to recognize all the more prominent rocks by their shape and height above the water. He worked out the height-above-water from tide tables, he'd told her, before each trip.

She was glad *she* didn't have to. Here and now, with an increasingly queasy feeling from the gunboat's motion – there seemed to be more of it since they'd slowed down – all she wanted was to get it over, get to the damned island. Terra firma, even when occupied by Germans, had a lot going for it.

A quick glance . . . 'Rosie – sorry. Soon as we're anchored, though—'

There was a call from the bridge, then: some buoy in sight to starboard. He shouted back, 'La Petite Fourche. Spot on. Come round to –' hesitating for a second – 'make it south four west. When the buoy's abeam, revs for six knots.'

'Abeam be buggered, south four west we'll hit the bloody thing!'

'Make it south six west, then.'

Muttering to himself as he thought about it . . . Face at the pipe again, then: 'Skipper – when that buoy's abeam, come back two degrees to port.'

'Coming up close now. Wind's getting up too.'

She thought ironically, in a wave of nausea – *That*'s good news . . .

Creeping in . . .

The voice from the bridge had called down, 'Guenioc's in sight fine to port. Come up if you want.'

He turned to her: in that instant, visibly relaxed. 'That's it – my bit of it, for the time being. How're you, Rosie?'

'Seasick.'

'Fresh air'll fix that. Rosie – in the longer term – I'll be praying for you. And I'll find you again somehow, you can take that as fact.'

'I'll fetch my suitcase.'

'I know where to start looking now, you see.'

'I'll just get it.'

She started down the ladder. The gunboat's engines were only muttering to themselves now, and she thought – touch wood – that there might be less movement than there had been. Unless it was only wishful thinking . . .

Probably had been. That was the heaviest roll so far. Turning, she guessed. Up to now there'd been more pitch than roll. The taller of the two Frenchmen, holding on to the open wardroom door and looking green, asked her, 'Are we arrived, madame?'

'Just about.' Her own language, her *first* language; she loved it. Ducking into the cabin for her case: the Frenchman reached for it as she came out again, murmuring '*Permettez*', but she hung on to it and started up the ladder. 'Thank you, but I can manage.' She'd be lugging the damn thing across France during the next few days, might as well get used to it. Besides it contained a million and a quarter francs, as well as the Mark III. Ben took it from her anyway, as she arrived at the top, telling her 'I'll pass it down to you when you're in the dinghy.'

'It has some frightfully precious things in it.'

'I'm sure. But look here, now. Mae West, this is called. You won't be doing any swimming, but if you had to it would help to hold you up.' He showed her how to put it on and blow it up if/when she had to. The engines meanwhile, which hadn't even been mumbling, started up again: but the hum of sound and vibration lasted only a few seconds. Ben told her, 'Anchored. That was a touch astern to dig it in.' The gunboat was still rolling, but the sea's impacts were on the port side now. Obviously they'd turned ... The taller Frenchman slipped and staggered as he came off the ladder, and Rosie put out a hand to steady him: he still looked green around the gills. Ben passed Mae Wests to both of them, and they put them on without assistance. Neither of them had any luggage.

'Pilot –' the voicepipe – 'passengers on deck, please.'

'Aye aye, sir.' He turned back to them. 'We'll go through the bridge into the afterpart, and wait until the boat's in the water and there's a ladder over. Wooden steps, chain sides, you go down it backwards. Main thing is we need to be as quiet as possible. Would you translate that, Rosie?'

On her way through the bridge then, following Ben into cool night air that tasted of salt with a slight flavouring of high-octane petrol, the voice which had conducted most of the voicepipe exchanges murmured 'Good luck. Not just *saying* it either – believe me.' The C.O. – solicitor from Ross-on-Wye: she thanked him for having lent her his cabin. She could see the rolling as well as feel it now, the surge of white water lifting threateningly and then sucking down as the gunboat rolled back. It was white all round the island too: she wondered how on earth anyone could land without at least *half* drowning. Following Ben down the ladder from the back end of the bridge she was hearing a voice that came in snatches from up there behind them: someone using a radio telephone. Making contact with the reception party, she guessed, and Ben confirmed it. He'd mentioned before that they also had something he'd called an S-phone, which was a walky-talky too but more directional, for communication between the gunboat and the dinghy.

They were launching the dinghy on the starboard side,

dark shapes of sailors getting the lashings off and then carrying it over. It would be lifted over the guardrail and lowered on ropes, he'd told her. No davits, which would have been noisier.

Ball – a shape detaching itself from the boat-launching group – came to them, checking that his three passengers were ready and that she had her suitcase. Then he was summoned to the bridge, and on his return told Ben, 'Complications.' Adding to Rosie, 'None that'll affect you, though. Listen – when you come down the ladder, chaps already in the boat'll give you a hand in. And it really won't be nearly as bad as you imagine. That dinghy's specially designed for the job.'

'And I'll help from the ship's side, then pass this case down.' Ball had left them. Ben added, 'He'll put you nearest the stern, these two in the sharp end behind the oarsmen.'

'How far is it to the island?'

'Cable's length – couple of hundred yards. But you'll land on sand that's exposed now because the tide's off it. Same as where you'll be crossing later on.'

'What about the cargo?'

'It'll go on the second trip. Nick'll have a couple of extra men on board to lug it up on to the rocks. But you'll be well on your way over to Tariec by then. Slightly larger boat, incidentally, they use.'

She was glad of the tweed coat, collar turned up, and her back to the wind and occasional bursts of spray. She asked him, 'So does the French boat make a second trip too?'

'Uh-huh. Time being, the stuff stays on Guenioc. We bury it, more or less, and they'll shift it piecemeal over the next few days.'

'With Germans watching?'

'Crossing the sands, our friends are seaweed gatherers. They're terrific blokes, believe me.'

The *réseau* leader's code-name was Vidor, she remembered.

Ball came back to them. 'All set?'

*

They'd told her it would be less bad than she'd thought, when she'd been on board the gunboat, with its heavy rolling and the long swells smashing themselves into foam along the coast and over the rocks making her wonder how a small dinghy could possibly survive in it. Then during the crossing, waves higher than her head and their tops curling white, there were moments when she'd thought it was *worse* than she'd expected. With Ben's words an echo in her memory, *I'll find you again somehow, you can take that as fact*: she'd thought even at the time that he'd been begging a few questions. She was still in abject fear as the two oarsmen drove the little craft headlong into the boil of surf surrounding the island, Nick Ball yelling at them more or less incomprehensibly and using his sweep oar to keep the stern to the rollers and ride them in. Then they were suddenly in very shallow water, the boat's keel scraping on sand, and one of two men – knee-deep in surf, one each side of the boat – invited her to get on his back, then carried her up on to dry sand. Behind her the dinghy was being dragged up too.

'You're Angel?'

'Yes. Vidor?'

'No, I'm the other one. Léon. Wait here, a small moment?'

She was damp, but not soaked as she'd been sure she would be. Climbing down the ladder into the bobbing dinghy she'd accepted it as inevitable and told herself *There's bound to be some place where I can dry out . . .*

All the same – next time, a Lysander. Damn well insist on it.

If there *was* a next time.

'Didn't get too wet?'

Nick Ball: she'd heard him scrunching towards her up the beach, and he was beside her now. She told him, 'Thanks to you and Léon, no, I didn't. What about the other two?'

'They're all right. Talking to Vidor. He'll be with us shortly. Come on up to the island, eh?'

'Isn't this it?'

'Nope. This is sand. Island's all rock.' A tall figure was already looming up beside them: others following him would be the French passengers and Léon. Ball told her, 'This is Vidor.'

'I'm Angel. Heard a lot about you, Vidor.'

'Don't believe it, it's all lies.' There was a pleasant timbre to his voice. 'One minute, Angel, I'll be with you.'

He had to show Ball where the crate was to be cached, higher up the slope of rock. Guns and ammunition, plastic explosive, grenades – whatever the Resistance had asked for. She could hear those two talking – in English, Vidor's a variety of pidgin, and Ball's slow, carefully enunciated. Asking now, 'What's happened to the airmen?'

She called, 'Like me to interpret?'

'Oh, yes – *please* ...' Behind her, Léon was in conversation with the others. Ball explained to her. 'There were supposed to be five or six airmen to embark. We'd have done it easily in the two trips, d'you see? But there aren't any. He told us so over the walky-talky – and I *think* he's saying they'll be here tomorrow. But *we* won't – not unless—'

'Hold on ...'

She began the translation, but Vidor had caught most of it, interrupting her to explain that the airmen had been lodged in safe houses in Brest while awaiting this moonless period, but there'd been a sudden and unprecented clampdown of German security – reasons for it as yet unknown – with checkpoints on all roads and unusually thorough searching of all trains coming out of Brest northward and eastward. So the escapers were being brought by roundabout country routes, but should be lodged under cover locally by tomorrow night – instead of last night, as they would have been. He finished, 'We have two more nights with no moon. Will the ship return perhaps not tomorrow but the night after? Otherwise it's three weeks more to hide them – and the Boche already stirred up, eh?'

Ball was sure they'd come back. 'Us or one of the others.

London'll have to confirm it, tell him. Need a broadcast, I suppose.'

'Yes. I have, here.' Vidor had made a note of a message he'd send when he had the fliers ready to ship out, and for the BBC to broadcast twice on the chosen day. He gave it to Ball, a folded sheet of paper, and told Rosie, 'Another thing different he should know is it's not five men now, it's twelve. For sure – perhaps more, but twelve as we know it now.'

She translated this. Ball agreed, again, 'We'll have to come back, obviously ... I'd better get cracking now, though.' He said goodbye to Rosie and the Frenchmen first, and collected their Mae Wests. Vidor didn't want to hang around; they had a few hundred yards to row – from the island's eastern end, where he and Léon had beached their boat – and then that expanse of sand to cross before it was covered by the rising tide.

The gunboat was tugging at her anchor, outer engines rumbling, all guns manned and an O.D. still standing by the anchor's grass line with an axe, as he had for the two and a half hours they'd been lying here, in case of emergency and the need to cut and run. In fact she'd be leaving in good order now, Ball having completed his second trip, and the dinghy inboard, being lashed down. There was a chain cable for the anchor, and a windlass, but anchoring would then have been noisy enough to be heard at the lookout posts – two of them less than 1200 yards away – whereas using the grass line, lowering and raising the hook by hand, wasn't audible even in the gunboat's bridge. When you'd anchored you weighted the line at water level, so that if it was cut on deck it would sink: otherwise the grass line might have wound itself round a propeller as the boat moved ahead.

Shepherd, the first lieutenant, murmured 'Shorten in', and two hands – Leading Seaman Mollison, second coxswain, and Ordinary Seaman Walbrook, the axe-man – began hauling the line in hand over hand, coordinating their movements with the rise and fall of the boat's stem.

The weather was much as it had been when they'd arrived. Ben Quarry, in the bridge with his C.O., had expected worse, going by the forecast. With luck, this return crossing mightn't be too bad.

Shepherd had come aft along the starboard side, past the six-pounder and the twin point-fives: his voice floated out of the darkness down there, 'Anchor's up and down, sir.'

'Weigh.'

Ben was in the bridge because at this stage the C.O. didn't need to be given courses to steer. The blackness of Guenioc was visible through binoculars, and once the anchor was out of the ground P.O. Ambrose would steer her around it and then slightly west of north: by which time she *would* need navigating, up the narrow channel between the rocks to the La Petite Fourche buoy and from there more or less due north – with allowance for the prevailing tidal stream – passing over the western end of the Libenter bank. The echo-sounder would tell him when she was crossing it, as it had done during the approach.

'Anchor's aweigh, sir!'

'Slow ahead both outers. Eight hundred revs. Port twenty.'

Hughes was increasing his distance from the island – or rather, from its surrounding shallows – before starting round it. The shallow fringe extended as much as six hundred yards, in places. Those two engines were in silent running, of course – Dumbflow silencers and underwater exhausts, systems which could only be used at low speeds, as now. Ben had his binoculars trained astern, over the port quarter, for Tariec: but it wasn't visible. Only about half a mile away, but it was even lower than Guenioc. Rosie, he guessed, would be on the mainland by this time. Still with a long hike ahead of her.

He swung his glasses back to Guenioc.

'Could come round now, sir. North thirty west'd do it. I'll go down.'

'Bring her round, Cox'n.'

'Aye aye, sir.' P.O. Ambrose's stocky figure ducked slightly, bending at the knees as he swung the wheel around. Engines' rumble a deep growl in the night, roll and pitch increasing as she turned her bow into the wind and out of it again: the weather was on her port side then, and he was easing the helm to steady her on north thirty west.

In his plot, Ben set the echo-sounder running. He knew they were in about five fathoms here but also that there was a smallish shallow patch of just less than two which would be under her in a few minutes' time. At any rate he hoped it would be, so he'd have an absolutely accurate point of departure, on which all subsequent reckonings would be based. The sounder was his primary navigational aid, at this stage. It wouldn't have been safe to use radar, with the risk of detection by enemy direction-finding stations, and the QH – R.A.F. equipment originally, used in conjunction with specially gridded charts – was more use out in the open sea than in this clutter of rocks and islands where you had to work to a degree of accuracy of a few yards, rather than say half a mile.

Extraordinary to think that Rosie had been here – *here* – only hours ago! In his mind's eye, seeing her: all that soft brown hair, and the wide-apart hazel eyes; and the feature that really got to you – her mouth, that sort of *hungry* look—

Supposed to be keeping this tub off the rocks, for God's sake ...

He'd logged the time of weighing as 0345 G.M.T. And the echo-sounder told him – conveniently, just as he glanced at it again – that they were passing over the shallow spot. One and a half fathoms – perfectly safe, since the gunboat drew only about four and a half feet: and the time now 0354. So now – four hours short of high water at Dover, tide therefore from the northeast – the best course to steer would be ... North twelve west. He passed that up to the bridge, and heard the C.O. tell Ambrose 'North twelve west, Cox'n.'

Only 1100 yards, now, from this point to the La Petite

Fourche buoy – which the Germans had left in place for the convenience of French fishermen, despite the fact that no fishing was allowed at night and that in daylight surely they'd know their own home waters. Not that one would have complained: it was a very useful mark. But – four and a half minutes to it, say. Three and a half or four before they'd spot it from the bridge. He checked the sounder: fourteen fathoms. The Brisante shoal would be close to starboard.

'Pilot – broken water starboard, cable's length—'

'The Brisante. Fine, sir.'

Particularly in confined waters like these he always began to worry if he didn't know precisely where he was at any given moment. Good on Messrs Kelvin Hughes, he thought, for their echo-sounders. Shallowing here now – twelve fathoms. As he'd have expected – or rather, hoped . . . It was as well not to be too confident, never to pass up a chance to check, confirm. Belt and braces . . . They'd see the buoy in about one minute.

He wondered whether Rosie was in her safe house by now. Getting big eats and a soft bed in some farmhouse, perhaps. Penalty for harbouring her, for Christ's sake, being death. Truly fantastic people, those Bretons.

She was, too. As well as being so easy on the eye. Recalling his initial sight of her in Dartmouth yesterday: her curvy little figure making that blonde Wren who'd been with her look like something you'd hang a sail on.

'Pilot – Petite Fourche coming up fine to starboard.'

'When it's abeam, come round to north ten east.'

Course for Lizard Head. (Course to be made good actually north eight east, but for another half-hour you had to take into account the coastal tide.) Hughes had decided that since it was odds-on that M.G.B. 600 would be used for a follow-up trip in two or three nights' time, necessitating a quick turn-round, it would be best to make for the flotilla's advanced base at Falmouth, a distance of only a hundred and ten miles. If for some reason they were required to return to

Dartmouth, they'd be told so in plenty of time to adjust the
course halfway across: not before that, because wireless
silence couldn't be broken until you were far enough
offshore not to risk compromising the L'Abervrac'h pinpoint.

Voicepipe: he answered it, and the skipper told him 'La
Fourche is abeam, altering now.'

'Aye aye, sir.' He logged it, the time and the change of
course. The boat was corkscrewing, with wind and sea
slightly abaft her beam. The motion was having its effect on
him, too, and he glanced round to check he had his bucket
handy: chiding himself for not admitting to Rosie, when
she'd confessed to being a rotten sailor, that he wasn't
entirely immune himself. Hardly anyone was, in fact. Time
– 0357. Hughes would keep to this slow speed and silent
running at least until they'd passed over the Libenter bank
– which the echo-sounder would pick up, in a few minutes.
Ben leant over the chart, his eye following the coastline of
the Presqu'ile Sainte Marguerite to the point where Rosie
would have got ashore. The nearest marked village would be
Broennou: but they probably wouldn't be stopping that close
to the coastline. Landeda possibly – a larger centre, about
four miles inland – or one of a number of other villages,
those further inland not marked on charts of course, where
the locals were actively pro-Resistance.

She might lie up for a day, he guessed. Or perhaps not,
since the longer an agent stayed in any one house the greater
the risk to his or her hosts. Stories filtered back: during his
year in that Naval Intelligence section he'd heard enough of
them to be constantly bewildered by the courage of people
who in other respects could be described as 'ordinary'. And
Rosie being one of them now was – staggering. It wasn't
easy to keep thoughts and images of her out of mind. Even
now – watching the echo-sounder for the edge of the
Libenter shoal . . .

'Stop both outers!'

Urgent tone: and a second later, abrupt cessation of engine

noise. Plenty of sea-noise, though, the thuds and creaks of her pitching, banging around, rolling becoming wilder as the way came off her. It was virtually a reflex action to check the position on the chart, and a relief in seeing there were no rocks within half a mile. The tidal stream being from the northeast, she'd be drifting no closer to that nearer group either. He'd logged the stop-engines order and the time; keeping an ear meanwhile to the voicepipe.

'Two of the buggers ... Number One, warn the guns – pay 'em a visit, would you – tell 'em to hold their fire.'

They normally would – would wait for the 'fire' buzzer – but if some enemy suddenly loomed out of the darkness at close quarters and a gunner had reason to guess the bridge couldn't have seen it, he'd be wrong *not* to let rip.

'Losing steerage-way, sir.'

'All right, Cox'n'. Into the voicepipe then: 'Pilot.'

'Sir?'

'Two armed trawlers will shortly be crossing our bows from east to west. I'm going to lie doggo if they'll let us. Come up if you like.'

He could get a compass bearing on the loom of the Ile Vierge searchlight, he thought: and a position-line later from the QH. In any case there'd be nothing useful to do down here.

Cold night wind with spray in it. Pitch dark. Looking for Ile Vierge – about three miles to starboard; they had a searchlight on it with its beam sweeping constantly at sea level ... *There* – like a lighthouse flash only slower in its traverse, a dome of reflection for a moment or two in the sky above it. Hughes told him, 'Saw the first one in silhouette against it.' Ben had his own glasses on them, then: small, stubby ships plugging westward into wind and sea. The M.G.B. rolling like a cow and swinging her forepart downwind, no way left on her now. Hughes called over, '*Wouldn't* it be nice to give 'em a big surprise!'

Taken unawares, the trawlers wouldn't have stood a chance. At speed, coming up from astern on a parallel course and passing at close range, opening up with everything you had, blasting one as you swept past it and then the other, and perhaps dropping a shallow-set depth charge as you whipped across the leader's bows: short and sharp and deafening, two dead trawlers burning as they sank.

If only . . .

But you couldn't afford to compromise the L'Abervrac'h pinpoint. No Royal Navy gunboat would be this close to the Brittany coast for any purpose other than a clandestine landing or pickup. You'd have destroyed two armed trawlers but you'd have lost the use of the pinpoint, compromised the *réseau* ashore and left a dozen airmen stranded.

Shepherd arrived back in the bridge, having to claw his way to its forefront, the way she was throwing herself about. 'They all have the message, sir.'

'Cursing, no doubt.'

The enemy ships were passing probably less than three cables' lengths to the north. Range of five hundred yards, he thought: if one had been setting a range at all. They'd be steering to round the Pointe de Landunvez and as likely as not carry on down to Brest. Beside him the signalman, Crow, was being sick: it reminded him that he wasn't feeling all that marvellous himself. Hughes admitted 'Wouldn't've seen 'em if it hadn't been for that light behind 'em at the time. *Might* have, but . . .'

He'd dried his glasses and put them up again. Hughes was telling Shepherd, '– so close they'd have seen us too . . .'

And still might. The gunners fore and aft, crouching at their weapons with itchy fingers, would doubtless be hoping they would. They were intelligent men, knew the priorities of the job and that its value was a lot greater than the sinking of a couple of armed trawlers – but this was still a gunboat; by rights she ought to use her guns occasionally.

Not on this occasion, though. The range was still opening, chances of action lessening with every passing second . . . Ben shared the signalman's bucket briefly but effectively, then lurched over to the binnacle to take a bearing on that light.

5

The change of rhythm as the train slowed woke her to the fact that this was Rennes coming up. Getting on for halfway. Or a third of the way, at least. The small man at the far end of the seat facing hers was on his feet, stretching and yawning; he muttered, either to himself or to his neighbours, 'This'll be a boring affair. If my guess is right, we're in for another search.'

Small, balding, with a small black moustache. Guillaume: a pal of Vidor's. He and Rosie had arrived at Landerneau together early this morning but they'd embarked separately and since then ignored each other. His journey had nothing to do with hers, but he'd told Vidor he'd keep an eye on her. In other words, if she was arrested in the course of one of the railway checks London would hear of it, she wouldn't just have disappeared. She'd commented, over breakfast in the doctor's house at Lannilis, 'Fat lot of comfort *that* provides', and Vidor had mumbled with his mouth full '*Don't* get arrested, that's the answer.'

The engine was blasting off steam as the train clattered over points: a marshalling yard, a couple of acres of criss-crossing lines with a backdrop of blackened and roofless warehouses or engine sheds. Courtesy of the R.A.F. or U.S.A.F., no doubt. The line curved away from it, to the left, and suddenly this was the end of a platform sliding past.

Guillaume was probably right that they'd be examined again here. She'd already seen one group of soldiers stolidly watching the train's windows as it huffed past them. Earlier checks had been made at Landerneau where she'd embarked, and then at St Brieuc. More Germans: and *milice*, brown-shirted French Fascist paramilitaries. Guillaume grumbled – on his feet to stare out past her at the platform – 'They'll be making a meal of it here, *that*'s for sure.'

When Vidor had told Nick Ball on the island that there was a security clampdown around Brest, she'd wondered whether they'd be moving her further east – to Morlaix for instance – to join the train well outside the net. But she'd realized then, talking to Vidor about it during the crossing of the sandbar, that she hadn't been thinking straight. With a cover story that started her off from a farm near St Saveur, how would she have explained embarking at Morlaix – when Landerneau was just up the road? By French country standards, just up the road. Actually she'd told them at the Landerneau check that she'd cadged a lift up on the milk wagon: *the* milk wagon, from *the* farm, as if they were the only ones in France and as well known to her questioners as they were to her.

At St Brieuc, police had checked passengers' identities but only glanced inside one piece of luggage in every six or eight. They'd have been looking for black-market goods – not only the real racketeers, but ordinary people who'd been visiting friends in the country bringing stuff back to Paris for their own consumption or their families'. Through half-closed eyes now she saw the group approaching this carriage and climbing in, a little further along. The German in plain clothes was the one who counted. S.D., or Gestapo – equally unpleasant, overlapping in their activities so that they were often in competition, but both answerable to Heinrich Himmler. This one had three gendarmes with him – in kepis and dark blue tunics – and in case anyone made a run for it there was the backup of soldiers in groups all along the platform. Steam hissing, shouts mostly in German. She put her head back and shut her eyes. To get to Landerneau and catch this so-called express she'd have needed to be on the road before daylight: in any case the train's dusty warmth was soporific. With so much noise around her she'd hardly be sound asleep, but she wouldn't be bright-eyed and alert either.

In fact she wasn't. Alert – she had to be – but not bright-eyed. After crossing the sand there'd been several miles more of foot-slogging before they'd arrived at a farmhouse where the doctor from Lannilis was ostensibly visiting a sick child. They'd been given coffee and bread in the kitchen, then Rosie and Vidor had been taken on into Lannilis in the doctor's charcoal-powered car, Rosie slumped in the back with a rug over her, and Vidor in front. If they'd been stopped the doctor would have said she was a patient – Vidor's young sister – whom he was taking to the infirmary. Léon had stayed behind with the two French passengers, who must have had some other form of transport coming for them. Saying goodbye to her, the little one had kissed her hand.

'Tickets and papers!'

A police sergeant. Other policemen further along the carriage were doing the same thing. This one had black hair and a moustache, brown eyes with bags under them. Guillaume had his documents ready in his hand, but the sergeant was currently examining those of an old man in blue serge, pot-bellied and with a neck like a turkey's. He'd embarked at St Brieuc. The sergeant grunted, pushed the papers back into the old man's hands, nodded to a French naval N.C.O. sitting opposite him, and ignored Guillaume again – this time in favour of two middle-aged sisters who'd spent the whole journey whispering to each other. There was another naval man on Rosie's left.

The plain-clothes German had been strolling this way down the central corridor, keeping an eye on the progress of the search. He'd paused in the gangway now, taking a look at each of them in turn. Rosie met his gaze for a moment – blue eyes in an annoyingly pleasant, boyish face – and glanced away quickly from the beginnings of a smile. He picked on Guillaume then: snapping his fingers under the small man's nose, Guillaume tilting his head back with his eyebrows raised – but of course complying, surrendering his papers. He muttered to the man opposite him, 'At least they're getting on with it . . .'

'Indeed we are.' The German was looking at the luggage in the rack: 'This yours?'

A fat, heavy-looking briefcase: Gladstone bag, one might have called it in English.

'Get it down, open it.'

Guillaume sighed as he stood up. Rosie felt sick. She couldn't look that way any more. The sergeant growled. 'Ticket and papers.'

She had them in a large, crumpled envelope in a pocket in her coat: had to half rise to pull the coat down. Trying the wrong pocket first. 'Oh, Lord . . . Ah – here. Sorry – I was half asleep.'

'Where's the child this belongs to?'

She stared at him for a moment; then comprehension dawned. 'Oh, my *God*. I *can't* have—'

'Lefèvre, Jeanne-Marie . . . And – Lefèvre, Juliette, a J2 card?'

'My daughter – I just took her to her grandmother, on the farm. God, they'll *need* it, they'll—'

'What's this?'

The S.D. man – if that was what he was. The sergeant showed him. 'Two ration cards. One's a J2. Says it's her daughter's.' Staring down at Rosie: she'd begun to cry . . . 'What age is she?'

'Three and a half. Oh, I'm such a *fool*!'

'Return ticket – to Paris.' The S.D. man passed it back to her. 'You say you've left your child on some farm?'

'With her grandmother. I am a widow, I need to earn a living – and this person in Paris, a sort of cousin – well, he has a job for me, I *hope*—'

'All right.' He gestured – he'd heard enough – and the sergeant dropped the papers in her lap. But the German had turned back ... 'What's this cousin's business?'

He was looking at her suitcase, on the rack roughly at his own eye level. Rosie protested, 'Not *exactly* a cousin—'

'What sort of job does he propose to offer you?'

'He is a *parfumeur*. He hopes to be able to employ me as a sales woman.'

He stared at her for a few more seconds: then turned back to Guillaume, who had the opened briefcase beside him. 'What's in this?'

'Business documents – and my own overnight essentials. I'm a representative.'

'Representative of what?' Fingering the top edges of the papers, flicking through them ... 'What business?'

'Veterinary products – for horses, cattle, sheep, pigs and poultry. Head office is in Paris. Your Ministry of Commerce people know me.' A shrug ... 'Indirectly, they employ me.'

'Well. Lucky them.' He winked at the naval men as he said it, and they both laughed. A glance at the sergeant: 'Finished?' The search was moving on into the next section. Rosie muttered, dabbing at her eyes, 'I'm such an *idiot!*' Her hands were shaking as she fumbled the papers back into their envelope. One of the two sisters told her, 'You've only to pop it in the post, when we get to Paris. I'm sure your mother won't let the baby starve, meanwhile.'

'Mother-in-law. And she already has it in for me.'

'But my dear girl, that's *normal*!'

Chuckles and smiles all round. From Guillaume, a particularly warm smile. In the bottom of his briefcase were several packages of plastic explosive which he was to deliver to a *réseau* leader in Auteuil. It was not improbable that if it hadn't been for the fuss over ration cards the S.D. officer might have searched the case more thoroughly and found it.

God bless you, Marilyn ...

Whatever you had to carry with you – Guillaume's explosive, her own radio and the money – was the quickest and deadliest giveaway. Guillaume's cover was probably quite genuine, and she'd got away with her story three times now – without even having to produce Louis's letter, which if there'd been any doubts should have convinced them. But if either of their bags had been looked into – well, you could forget such niceties as cover stories.

It meant the difference, in a matter of seconds and by some nauseating individual's whim, between staying alive and free or being taken away to an extremely unpleasant death.

There were bigger issues than that, too – objectively speaking. As the train pulled out of Rennes she was thinking – her head back again, eyes shut, pulse-rate gradually returning to something like normal – that in Guillaume's case they'd have found the P.E. and perhaps aborted or postponed some sabotage operation; but there'd have been wider effects too, depending on Guillaume's knowledge and connections and whether or not he gave way under torture.

She thought most people did, unless they were lucky enough to have a propensity to faint in the early stages. But you didn't know until the time came how you'd make out. It was a persistent anxiety: when Ben Quarry had said something about 'the bravest of the brave', for instance, the doubt had flared . . .

Vidor's advice was simple but good, she thought: just don't get arrested. What they'd have scuppered if she *had* been – if they'd looked inside *her* suitcase – well, a lot of things. For instance, there was the basic, long-term task of restoring an effective S.O.E. presence in and around Rouen, and the more immediate one of setting up arrangements for reception of two para drops. These had been pre-planned so as to minimize exchanges of signals; times and locations had been fixed, all that was needed was Rosie's OK to Baker Street after she'd alerted the recipients, who'd then listen out for the BBC broadcasts.

Then – in collaboration with César, of course – the reconstruction of the *réseau*. Sorting out Baker Street's doubts about Romeo – ideally, getting him flown back for vetting – and the recruitment of sub-agents and couriers, establishment of safe houses, letter drops and so forth. Secure radio communications too, obviously, so that further drops could be arranged in due course. And on top of those S.O.E. functions was the job she'd taken on at the request of S.I.S., and which Maurice Buckmaster despite his own misgivings had admitted was 'a matter of huge importance' – to acquire intelligence of the Germans' plans for deployment of their much-vaunted 'Secret Weapons'.

Research, manufacture and trials were known to be in full swing on the island of Peenemunde on the southern Baltic coast. One rocket had gone wild, landed on the Danish island of Bornholm, and photographs of it taken by a Danish naval officer and passed to the local Resistance had reached London. More recently a French agency – Amniarix – had amplified earlier reports including the fact that a Colonel Walther had been made responsible for selecting and constructing launching sites in the Pas de Calais and Seine Maritime *départements*. He'd not only set up his headquarters in Amiens, he'd taken on Jacqueline Clermont, alias 'La Minette', as his girlfriend.

Which was where Rosie came in ...

'The urgency's quite obvious.' Buckmaster, in their talk in his flat two days ago, had had no argument with S.I.S. on that point. 'Jerry knows as well as we do that before we can put an invasion force across the Channel there has to be a very large build-up of men and material here in southern England, and if he can deploy his damn rockets soon enough – well, it could make it impossible for us. For an invasion to be mounted at all. Which is unthinkable ... Therefore, the sites have to be located so that the R.A.F. and the U.S. Air Force can hit them and keep on hitting them. Plus sabotage on the ground, which of course *will* be our pigeon. That's all clear as day, Rosie, and it obviously is an absolutely top priority – nothing could be more so. But it's still S.I.S.'s job, not what *we're* for. This is my point: part of the reason they're passing the buck to us is that we have people like you in the field, and my guess is they haven't. Not in that region. Things may have been going to pot worse for them even than they have for us. And what you have to bear in mind, Rosie, while you're pulling their chestnuts out of the fire for them, is that the Germans can't be unaware of our interest in all this. So for God's sake—'

She'd said it for him: '—be careful. Yes, I will, sir. I'll be *very* careful.'

Railway stations could be traps. One technique for an agent travelling alone and having reason to believe they might be looking out for him or her was to tag on to a family party or other group, try to look like part of it. But at Gare d'Austerlitz – the train had been diverted, would normally have come into Montparnasse: you didn't query such things, which were often due to bomb damage or to sabotage – as they drew in she decided against this. She had a suspicion that the German plain-clothes officer might have stayed on the train – he hadn't been on the platform when they'd pulled out of Rennes – and he might remember that she'd been on her own. Better therefore to *remain* alone. She had no reason to suspect that they'd be looking out for a female agent. But – for instance – what if 'Romeo' *had* been turned, told them 'Angel' was on her way?

There'd be a check for black-market stuff here anyway. If you were carrying half a dozen eggs, or a chicken, for instance ...

'Madame?'

She glanced round, and the younger of the two sisters asked her, 'Do you have a place to stay, in Paris?'

Hesitating, while she thought about it. She wouldn't know until she'd seen Louis ...

'I'm not sure. It's most kind of you, but I'm hoping my cousin will have made arrangements for me.' She looked round again as Guillaume climbed down to the platform. He shifted the heavy case from one hand to the other, and raised his hat about a centimetre: just that, no word: she'd called

'Good luck, monsieur!' but he was on his way, probably hadn't heard. Back to the sisters, then: 'It's very kind of you to suggest it—'

'Well – if you find you do need a bed for the night, we're in Vincennes. You take the Metro Porte Dorée. Here, look – take this.' An envelope – she removed its contents – addressed to Mlle Hortense Velestier, at an address in Vincennes. 'You'd find the number in the book. We'd truly be very happy – *any* time . . .'

'You're most kind.'

So she *had* joined a group – and no pretence about it, all on the up-and-up. They were walking towards the barrier with a straggle of others around them and Guillaume's grey trilby still in sight ahead. One of the sisters was a widow, the other unmarried; the widow had a son at medical school. They both thought that to work for a *parfumeur* would be heavenly: 'All those glorious aromas – and perhaps a little bottle going begging now and then?' Shrieks of hilarity, while getting their tickets ready to hand in at the barrier. Rosie saw Guillaume being arrested, at that moment. He'd passed through, and she'd had only a swift impression of two large men in plain clothes moving to intercept him: whatever was going on then was out of her range of sight, but having passed through the bottleneck, surrendering her ticket, it was exactly as she'd envisaged – and dreaded: the man who'd questioned them on the train was holding Guillaume by one arm, and the other was crouching to search the case that had plastic explosive in it. The sisters darting glances over their shoulders as they passed: Rosie heard 'Black marketeer, perhaps . . .' She was thinking – sharply aware of disaster, that one arrest almost always led to others – that with luck 'Louis' would be able to warn the *réseau* in Auteuil – so they could scatter, vanish, or at least stay away from whatever parcel-drop or safe house Guillaume might have known of – and also notify Vidor, for Christ's sake . . . The widowed sister was shaking her head: 'Oh, the poor man, the poor man . . .'

Dead man, she thought. He'd know it, too.

'Now don't forget – we'd truly be delighted—'

'You may well hear from me. Thank you *very* much.'

'And good luck with getting that job, my dear!'

She let them go on ahead, down into the Metro. Feeling sick again: in dark contrast to the flood of relief she'd felt for herself and Guillaume when they'd seemed to have got away with it at Rennes. Cat and mouse, though: or as Ben would have put it, cat and *bloody* mouse. Oh, Ben . . .

He'd be back in harbour by this time, she guessed, his image in her mind as she paid for her ticket at the *guichet*. And the gunboat's, tied up alongside that old steamer, with the backdrop of green hills and woods. Vision of paradise . . .

There were Germans on this platform too. Grey-green uniforms, rifles, packs, helmets, shaven backs to their thick necks. So obviously better fed than most of the crowd filtering around them.

A train had just pulled out, northwards – the way she'd be going, two stops to Bastille. The kind-hearted sisters would be changing there, eastward for Vincennes, while she changed to the same line but in the opposite direction. Other travellers packing in around her: if any of them had been watching, following, she couldn't possibly have known. There *could* be someone following: if for instance the man on the train had had some reason to suspect that she wasn't as naive as she'd seemed. Guillaume had thought *he* was in the clear, after all.

She and Guillaume might have exchanged one look too many?

Her mental snapshot of him with the German's hand clamped on his arm was still sharp-edged in her brain. Rattling through Hôtel de Ville, Louvre-Rivoli. Drab fellow-passengers uninterested in her, uninteresting in themselves, keeping themselves *to* themselves. Leaving Tuileries, she decided to break her journey at the next stop – which would be Concorde – to make certain she wasn't being tailed.

If she was, she was doomed anyway, but she didn't have to lead them to Louis's door.

Concorde. Thinking about Vidor, to what extent *he'd* be in danger now. In a crowd of others, making her way up to the daylight. Wondering whether she might be only wasting time ... But time wasn't a major factor, in this predicament. *Potential* predicament – for all of them except Guillaume. In that sense it *was* very much a factor – in relation to getting warnings out to the others. Please God, Louis would have means of contacting them.

Meanwhile, it would have looked more natural to be taking a stroll on this enormous *Place* if one had not been carrying a suitcase. As Guillaume would have been a lot safer without *his* luggage. Thoughts constantly returning to him ... This vast open space was as good as you'd find anywhere for present purposes, though. Wandering unpredictably across it – then vaguely back again: bicycles everywhere – more bicycles than there were pedestrians – and *vélo-taxis*, pedal-powered rickshaws ... Of course, if they'd guessed you'd eventually be going back into the Metro, they'd let you take your exercise and then pick you up again.

So *don't* go back in there?

It was only two Metro stages to the Rond Point. Or one stage beyond that, probably – the Clémenceau station. Easy enough walking distance anyway, especially after sitting in that train all day.

Walk, then, up the Champs Elysées. Resting for a minute first on a stone bench at the corner. Turning her face away from the Nazi banner and flags on what had been the Ministry of Marine: preferring to visualize the guillotine out there where it had stood a hundred and fifty years ago: the bloodthirsty crowd, thud of the blade, cheers for each spouting of blood, day after day ... The human race didn't change much with the passage of the centuries, remained just about as foul. Walking on – turning her back on that image too – up the Champs between green open spaces where anti-aircraft batteries were camouflaged and most of the fine old houses had been requisitioned – to the Rond Point, where she crossed to the other side of the avenue and paused to glance back before continuing. Nobody was following her. She hadn't expected there would be, but there were other lives than hers at stake. Getting into the commercial part now. Progress seemingly so *slow* ... After another age, over a crossing which she thought might be the Rue Clémenceau. Street signs in German, black lettering on white. Too soon, she guessed, to be the Rue la Boétie. She was limping a bit – not all the time, but whenever some piece of grit got into the wrong place in her shoe, but there were no benches around here; if she'd sat on her suitcase she might have attracted attention, looked like some sort of down-and-out, would *feel* conspicuous even if she wasn't ... There was a lot of passing traffic, a significant proportion of it military. Possibly all of it, give or take the limousines of high-powered collaborators. Civilian vehicles were mostly *gazogènes*. The limp reminded her that César was lame, that it would be a way of recognizing him. Otherwise all she knew was that he was fair-headed, blue-eyed and about five-nine. The clincher, anyway, would be the business of two coffee cups in front of him and both spoons in one saucer.

Tomorrow, maybe. If she could get straight on down to Rouen.

The larger intersection she was coming to now might – touch wood – be the one. A kiosk on the corner was smothered in collaborationist newspapers and magazines, some more notorious than others including even *Le Matin*, on which Maurice Buckmaster had once worked; as well as *Signal* and *Au Pilori* – about the vilest of all, with its vicious anti-Semitism. And *La Gerbe*, which ran it a close second. She was already in the approaches to what had been one of the most sophisticated of shopping areas – and still was, for Germans, who had the exchange rate heavily loaded in their favour. Thinking of Guillaume again: she shivered. Psychologically, she knew, a lot of this feeling of dread came from imagining oneself as being in his shoes. Passing a packed restaurant: tables all over the broad pavement, customers even standing in the spaces in between them. Roar of conversation. It was *Le Colisée*, she'd heard of it ...

Rue la Boétie. At last. Although from here on the directions weren't entirely clear in her mind. She'd hadn't thought of finding her way to the Maison Cazalet – Louis's establishment – as calling for any great effort of memory. God knew, the memory cells were crowded enough ... But to the left here, she thought. Or maybe – the next one, this looked – unlikely ... Try the next. And if that didn't look right either – well, if you got to the end – Rue du Faubourg St Honoré – you'd have come too far. Two more cars passed, both German. And from some distance, what might have been police whistles. She told herself, Not *my* business. Dozens or even hundreds of Parisians would be reacting (or non-reacting) in the same way: cover the ears, avert the eyes ...

Guillaume again: herself one of a horde of people passing by, ignoring it.

But what *else*?

This looked more like it, now. There'd be another turn a short way down: she wasn't sure which way, but with luck it might be visible from the corner. Rather tucked away, they'd told her, but not far from this corner, in a setting of some elegance.

There. Between two antique shops – handsome old houses actually, converted at street level into shops. One of them was boarded up, but next door to it – Maison Cazalet.

An old woman, bent almost double, was coming towards her on this side of the road, and on the other a German officer and a girl in a flowered dress were gazing into the window of the antique shop. Moving on now, to gawp at whatever Pierre Cazalet alias Louis had on display. There was nobody in sight who was noticeably static, as a watcher would tend to be. That pair – the German and the girl? There were plenty of windows, of course, and doorways. She started down the road – on this side, not Cazalet's: you couldn't do much about windows, especially since experienced observers tended to sit well back from them.

What might be happening to Guillaume, she wondered. Their usual practice was to leave a prisoner alone and without food for a day or two, to weaken his or her resistance, raise the anxiety level before starting the interrogations. But in his case they might not wait. He'd been about to deliver the P.E. to someone here in Paris, and they'd know that that person – or those persons – would be around now and might not be later on: certainly would not be once the news was out.

Chances were they'd have started on him already.

The hobbling woman wasn't all that old. Just crippled. They'd passed each other: but two off-duty Boche soldiers were approaching from behind there, the way she herself had come. She saw them when she glanced back at the cripple, who was muttering to herself – cursing the soldiers, perhaps, her first sight of them as they'd appeared round the corner. Rosie went to the kerb, to cross the road: if those two overtook her they'd be likely to try to engage her in conversation. She knew from her own experience that they tended to, especially when you were alone and in an uncrowded street like this one. Better to stay clear of them: and to seem to be going somewhere, not just loitering – luggage or no luggage. The opening gambit would be an offer of assistance: smirking at each other, meanwhile. The Master Race, she thought: may they all rot in hell. Well, they would, if there was any justice: and if there was such a place as hell other than the camps, cellars and gas chambers in which they created it for their victims. She'd stepped into the road just before a Wehrmacht staff car swept round the corner, coming fast straight at her. A man on a bicycle shouted a warning as he swerved his bike, mounting the pavement just behind her; the car's soldier-driver impassive and an officer in the back craning round to stare at her as if *she*'d been to blame.

Damn French, jay-walking. Not disciplined, as we are...
She was conscious of her own utter loathing of the *bloody*
Master Race. Careful not to glance round when one of the
soldiers behind her shouted something – shouting after the
speeding car, safe in the knowledge that he couldn't be heard
by the officers inside it, and probably to impress *her*. She
supposed that he'd be totally unable to comprehend that
even if amongst his own people he might be thought of as
a thoroughly good fellow, to any practising human being he
was simply a trespasser in a country where even the pigs
were more civilized than him and his compatriots, every
single one of whom was by his mere presence an aider and
abettor of practices that were utterly obscene.

She'd reached the other pavement, knowing she had to
take a grip on her emotions, which might otherwise show
when she looked at any German. Reminding herself that she
was Jeanne-Marie Lefèvre, worrying only about her child
and what she'd use for money if she didn't get this job ...

She paused at a jeweller's window – to let those two get
out of sight before she started back towards the Maison
Cazalet, also to use the glass as a mirror, confirming to
herself that the doorways on the other side still had no
loungers in them. She'd made sure before starting to cross
the road that this side was clear. The two German boys had
gone out of sight around the corner. There were a few other
pedestrians in the street, two cyclists and a *gazo* Renault. No
visible dangers, anyway. She limped towards Louis's place,
pausing to look in through plate glass protected by an iron
grille and seeing that he sold other things as well as scent.
Rather beautiful silk squares, expensive-looking handbags.
Germans for the use of, she thought, pushing the door open.
Or their lackeys. Who else would have that sort of money,
in the Paris of 1943?

Well – *she* would. She had a million and a quarter francs
in her suitcase, she remembered.

A petite brunette with a stylish hairdo and a skimpy black
dress, double strand of pearls glowing against smoothly

tanned skin, was looking at her rather doubtfully from behind the glass counter. They sold crystal here too: there was some on display inside it. And Lalique. The air was heady with perfume. The girl was pretty and very carefully made up; her uncertainty, of course, stemmed from Rosie's rather dowdy appearance.

'Mam'selle?'

She smiled. 'It's Madame, actually.'

'I beg your pardon, madame. May I—'

'I have an appointment to see Monsieur Cazalet. I'm his cousin, Jeanne-Marie Lefèvre.'

'You're Louis, of course.'

He nodded. Downstairs, in front of the girl, she'd called him Pierre and he'd called her Jeanne-Marie. He was of medium height, plump and with wavy dark hair – perhaps a little too dark to be natural. About fifty, she guessed. Full, curving lips, brown eyes narrowed by the squeeze of flesh around them. A pale blue silk handkerchief protruded from one cuff of a beautifully tailored silvery-grey suit.

In anything like normal life, she thought, I'd run a mile.

'And you're Angel. Do you happen to have my letter with you, by any chance?'

'Yes. Here . . .' He'd led her to this first-floor sitting room, which was furnished with antiques, mostly she thought Louis Quinze. The painting above the fireplace looked like a Cézanne. He'd asked for the letter as positive identification, she imagined; somewhat less than positive, in fact, since anyone impersonating her might very well have acquired whatever papers she'd had with her. She told him, 'There's one urgent matter. Do you know someone called Guillaume?'

'I would think at least a *dozen* of them, my dear!'

'This one was with Vidor. He and I came on the same train – separately, of course. I'm sorry to say he was arrested at the Gare d'Austerlitz.'

'Oh. *Oh* . . .' Then a sharp glance: 'Austerlitz?'

'There was a diversion. I don't know why.' She added, 'I
know what was in his briefcase, and that he was taking it to
someone in Auteuil. He and Vidor were discussing it this
morning over breakfast. On the platform they'd made him
open it and one of them was riffling through it while the
other kept a grip on poor Guillaume. I'd say they had a fair
notion of what they were going to find. Boches, of course,
plain clothes, one of them had joined the train at Rennes.'

'Aren't we lucky that you saw it.' Cazalet reached to a
white telephone. 'I want Toutou – at once, please.' Nodding
to her as he put the receiver down: she was wondering who
or what Toutou might turn out to be: the word's English
equivalent would be 'bow-wow' or 'puppy-dog'. Cazalet
was saying, 'Very lucky indeed, my dear, that you were
there. Otherwise – great heavens . . .'

There was a silver-framed portrait, on a side table, which
looked as if it might be of Hermann Goering. Autographed,
by the look of it. But too far away, and close behind
Cazelet's shoulder, she couldn't stare at it too hard. Anyway
– it couldn't be . . . The door opened behind her: 'Want me,
boss?'

'Come in, Toutou. Shut the door. My dear, I present
Toutou. Toutou, this is my young cousin, Jeanne-Marie
Lefèvre.' He was watching her, amused by her surprise as
Toutou came into her field of view. In fact, filled it. He was
about six foot six, and he'd have had to turn sideways as well
as stoop to get through most doors.

Facially, not unlike the filmstar Wallace Beery, she
thought, as an enormous hand enclosed hers. A rather
charming, genuine-looking smile . . . 'An honour, mam-
'selle . . .'

'That's enough flirting, now. Listen to me – I want you to
take a message to Auteuil, immediately. You must memorize
it, nothing can be written down . . . Why might you be in
Auteuil, though? Hardly to attend the races . . .'

'To visit that one who mends china?'

'Of course. Excellent. In fact—' He paused, glanced at

Rosie. 'My dear – would you excuse us, just for a few moments? Come, Toutou . . .'

He led the colossus through to an adjoining room. Very sensibly, she thought. One should *not* let the left hand know, when it didn't need to. She was rather uncomfortably aware of knowing too much already. On the other hand, while the cat was away . . . She got up, went quietly to the side table for a close look at that portrait – which *was* of Goering. The smirking Reichsmarshall was in a white uniform festooned with decorations, and the scrawl across the bottom right-hand corner read – in German, of which she had only a smattering, but enough to make this out – *To Pierre, the best wishes of his friend Hermann.*

Crikey. But it would help, she realized. Might help a *lot* . . . Fairly staggering, all the same. A door through there had opened and shut, and now a telephone tinkled. Toutou on his way, she guessed, and Louis calling Vidor. He'd have some coded way of passing on the bad news, probably through an intermediary with whom he did legitimate business. Something of that sort. Glancing at the portrait again: Louis was certainly – something special . . . She crossed to the window – further out of earshot – and stood looking down into the street: at pedestrians, cyclists, *gazogènes*. Thinking about Vidor and his *réseau* and whether the arrest of Guillaume and the chance that he'd talk might force them to split up, or at least temporarily suspend their operations. In which case, what about the airmen who'd be there by this time?

The gunboat flotilla did use other pinpoints, as they called them, besides the island at L'Abervrac'h. Four or five others, Ben had said. So obviously there'd be other *réseaux* at work in those other places; the airmen might be shuttled along to them, she guessed.

Unless Guillaume was only used as a courier, didn't know much?

But he knew Vidor, for God's sake . . .

'My dear – *profuse* apologies.' Cazalet closed the door silently. 'But it's all taken care of now. Thanks to you.

Come, sit down. I've told them to bring us some tea and cakes – you'd find room for some, eh?' The arch smile faded ... 'Some suggestions for you now, though. Unless you have any better alternative, my sister Béatrice would be enchanted if you would make use of the spare bedroom in her apartment. It's not far from here, and you'd find it comfortable enough. Tomorrow, you see, I must tell you a thing or two about this perfume business. If you're going to represent us out there in the wilds, eh? A day is as much as we'll need, I'm sure. So – if you agree – two nights at my sister's place – and we'll go out for a meal together, there are still restaurants worth visiting – and they let me in, I'm tolerated – friends in high places, and so forth' – he'd thrown a glance at that portrait, obviously well aware that she'd have seen it – 'well, anyway, day after tomorrow we'll put you on the train to Rouen. I have an address there for you – a most charming family, very well disposed. You won't want to stay with them for ever, of course, but—'

'You're the tops, Louis.'

'Oh – my dear . . .'

'I'm very grateful.' She changed the subject. 'What will Vidor do?'

'Vidor.' He shrugged. 'Really, I have no idea. Except that he'll make his own assessment ... You barely knew Guillaume, I think?'

'I didn't know him at all.'

'No. Nor did I. But Vidor does, of course – or did ... It's for his judgement, eh?'

6

Sailing time was set for 1700, two hours earlier than it would normally have been, to allow for an expected deterioration of the weather. Destination L'Abervrac'h again: the dinghies were to be at Guenioc by 2359 G.M.T./14, i.e. midnight tonight, Wednesday 14th July. Bastille Day: more importantly, the last night of the present moonless period.

Dinghies plural because they'd embarked a second one to allow for the number of escapers. This had been decided when the anticipated number had been twelve: now it was seventeen. Vidor's signal that he had the airmen ready for pickup had reached Baker Street yesterday evening, and Hughes had had his orders by scrambled telephone within the hour. M.G.B. 600 had been on stand-by – refuelled, watered and provisioned – since her arrival here in Falmouth on Monday afternoon.

Ben had shaved his beard off, as he'd promised Rosie he would. Not that she'd have given a damn whether he did or didn't . . . More usefully, he'd also cleaned off his charts: the ones in most frequent use were getting dog-eared and discoloured, but they'd survive another trip or two. In his plot now – early afternoon, alongside the Coastlines wharf, the flotilla's usual berth – he was doing his homework, checking in the Nautical Almanac and filling several pages of his brown-covered navigator's notebook with data on tides, tidal streams, depths, and rocks' heights above water hour by hour from midnight to 0400.

Weather prospects weren't good. The return trip from L'Abervrac'h on Monday hadn't been more than average-rough, and there was only a light wind at this moment; but according to the forecasters the worst was yet to come. The gale was still out there in the Atlantic, only hadn't moved east as fast as they'd expected; Monday's blow had been just a curtain-raiser.

Last night in the Bay Hotel, where he and Don Shepherd had gone with Hughes for a quiet pint – leaving Ball on board as duty officer – Ben had suggested that he should take charge of the second dinghy.

'Obvious bloke for it, aren't I? I mean, damn-all to do once we've dropped the hook. Eh, skipper?'

Hughes had agreed. 'You did some at Praa, didn't you?'

Praa Sands, in Cornwall, was where they all practised beaching dinghies through heavy surf – turning dinghies on to their beam ends often enough too, before getting the hang of it.

'Give him something to do, won't it.' Shepherd nodded through a haze of smoke. 'Especially with no girls on board this trip. Find time *very* heavy on his hands.'

They'd have no passengers, or cargo. Last night another of the flotilla – M.G.B. 318, an older boat, 'C' class – had landed some agents at the Grac'h Zu pinpoint, thirty miles east of L'Abervrac'h, and for the time being there were no more in the queue.

'Ready for sea, sir.'

In her bridge, P.O. Motor Mechanic Harvey, who pre-war had been part of a motor-racing team, touched his cap to the solicitor from Ross-on-Wye. All four engines were running, warming through, had been doing so for the last fifteen or twenty minutes.

Don Shepherd climbed into the bridge. 'All hands on board, sir, dutymen closed up. Take off the backspring?'

'Yes, please.' Hughes returned the salute. 'Let go aft, while you're at it.'

With the midday news broadcast Vidor's code-phrase had gone out: *Le père de Gilles est assez vieux.* He'd hear it again this evening; he and Léon would then begin moving their seventeen airmen over the sands to Tariec.

Shepherd reported, 'All gone aft, sir'; Hughes moved the port outer telegraph to slow ahead. 'Starboard ten, cox'n.' Turning her stern out into the stream by pivoting her on the forespring, a hemp rope running from her stem to the jetty abreast her stern.

'Ten of starboard wheel on, sir.'

Hughes moved that telegraph to stop, then both outers to show astern. 'Midships. Let go for'ard.'

Backing off the quay: with only the shoreside berthing party who'd let go the ropes and wires to see them leave. Ben checked the time: 1702. Not bad ... Mental reservation then: if the weather doesn't fall *totally* to pieces ... On the upper deck the hands were falling in, fore and aft, Ball up on the bow and Leading Seaman Mollison, the second cox-swain, with the party on the stern. Hughes had crossed to the starboard side to see the fore-breast and spring flop away. He glanced round: 'Stop both outers.'

'Stop both outers, sir ...'

The stern-way came off her almost immediately, in the run of the ebbing tide. Hughes said, 'Slow ahead outers. Port fifteen.'

P.O. Ambrose flung the brass wheel around ...

'Fifteen of port wheel on, sir!'

'Outers slow ahead.'

Gathering way, then, and swinging her bow towards the exit. Four destroyers lay at anchor out there, some trawlers and M.F.V.s this side of them. A barrage balloon was being wound down very slowly, slanting away from the wind. Blue sky, wisps of fast-moving white cloud, flecks of white on the sea out there in the channel. Ben was thinking about seeing it in a frame, how it might turn out if he had canvas here, and paints: he knew exactly how he'd *want* it to turn out.

He went down to his plot. After she'd cleared the bar

– on all four engines by that time – they'd go to action stations and test-fire the guns, then at cruising speed relax to what was known as the second degree of readiness, with only the Oerlikons and the point-fives manned, for anti-aircraft defence. He'd be piloting her then through a departure point four miles south of the Lizard – the D3 buoy – on to a course-made-good of south five degrees east for L'Abervrac'h.

Jotting down figures on the edge of the chart ... At a cruising speed of twenty-two knots the trip would take five hours, so ordinarily you'd have sailed at 1900. Allowing for foul weather and having to reduce speed – even to half-speed, possibly, say halfway over – you'd need all of the extra two hours. Two and a half or even three, he thought, might have been a better bet, but the skipper had reckoned this was playing it safe enough.

As the roar and clatter of the guns petered out, he was wondering where Rosie was at this minute. On the last trip she'd told him that although she'd been warned about it she'd almost jumped out of her skin when they'd all let fly.

What she'd really been scared of, though, had been whatever lay ahead of her in France. There'd been moments when he'd seen and heard the tension in her. The most fundamental kind of bravery, he thought: to be frightened half to death and still go ahead.

She was bloody marvellous, that girl. Truly and absolutely bloody marvellous.

Extremely secretive, though. He still didn't know her name, or where her people lived in England. When they'd been talking – here, in this plot – and she'd side-stepped all such questions, he'd told himself that it didn't matter, because he knew how to get in touch with her now – through the S.O.E. office in Baker Street. But he'd realized since that he wouldn't know who to ask for, or what name to put on a letter. And you could bet they wouldn't hand out any information unless they were sure you already had it.

Birds of a feather, you might say.

The only name he could put on the envelope would be ROSIE. And even if it got to her, she might well decide to maintain the wall of secrecy he'd first run into eighteen months ago.

In the Wellington, near Hyde Park Corner, at a fairly early stage in the evening. Might have been at the New Yorker, in fact ... Anyway, he'd given her his own story, about this terrific break he'd had – getting back to sea – and about the time he'd spent in Paris pretending to be an artist, all that – and then it had been her turn to expound on whatever these troubles were that needed drowning: other than S.O.E. having turned her down, which he'd known about already. She'd been reluctant to tell him any more, even at that stage: she'd been worried that she might become maudlin and weep all over him. He'd urged her, 'But you're welcome to. Any time ... come on, we had a deal, remember? Gets worse, anyway, if you bottle it up – well-known fact, Rosie ... Please, let's hear it?'

So she'd told him about her husband having been shot down and killed only a day or two before this, and her need to escape, make a new life; and that since she was a fluent French-speaker – bilingual, she was as French as she was English – she'd had this thought of joining S.O.E. for some time, only hadn't done anything about it because her husband hadn't wanted her to. Which was understandable enough, Ben had thought, who would? But with the shock of her husband's death, in a mood of desperation she'd come to Baker Street to offer them her services and had been told – in so many words – that she wasn't the sort of recruit they wanted.

'Doesn't make sense, Rosie.'

'Wasn't only Johnny not wanting me to. I felt he needed me there when he wasn't flying. I mean it was obvious, he really *did*.'

'Yeah, well—'

'You think that's normal? I mean, like he'd need a mother?'

'Oh, surely—'

'Surely, yes. Girls, all over. All over *him* – or vice versa. I was only the one he had pegged down, the one who – well, ironed his shirts too ... Listen, it would've been all right if he'd stayed alive, would've *come* all right – God knows how, but – given the chance, I mean, a year or two—'

'You'd have made it come right.' He nodded. 'Sure you would. I'm sorry, Rosie. *Damn* sorry.'

'He was still a bastard ...'

And she was a very mixed-up sheila, he'd realized. Or perhaps more accurately, a sheila in a very mixed-up state. Maybe the bloke in Baker Street wasn't such an idiot after all.

And should have stuck to that decision, he thought now – with the gunboat banging along at twenty-two knots, slamming across a low swell with a slight chop on it and the white spray sheeting, brilliant in the sunlight – she might have settled for some job where she could have used her French and *not* had her neck on the block every minute of every day and night.

If she'd have accepted such a job, of course, which quite likely she would not have.

After she'd talked about her husband for half an hour or so, embarrassing herself by shedding a few tears now and then – well, it might have been the result of his own conscious efforts but anyway the tone of it all had changed and they'd found they were having a party again, instead of a wake. He'd asked her – in the Gay Nineties, he thought this must have been – 'What's the rest of the story, Rosie?'

'Isn't any rest. Told you all that matters.'

'Well, where's your home, for instance?'

Shaking her head, metronome-like. Already fairly squiffed. But so had he been: although there and then he hadn't been giving much thought to that aspect of it. She'd told him – flatly, as if this finished it – 'I'm here, 's all.'

'But when you're home – family—'

'Home's where the heart is, didn't they tell you?'

'So where is it?'

A shrug . . . 'God knows.'

'Well.' Nodding. 'Glad *someone* does.'

'Does what?'

'Ask no questions, eh?'

'And be told no lies. I swear – no lie shall pass my lips.'

'Some lips, Rosie . . .'

The repeat of the broadcast about Giles's father's antiquity came after the overseas news broadcast. Vera Lynn's now familiar rendition of 'We'll Meet Again' had been interrupted for it, the signalman remarking to Ben as he passed through the plot on his way below, 'I could tell her what we'll meet again. Dinner and tea, that's what.' It was blowing up, and the boat was making hard work of it, down to twelve knots by this stage.

Might turn out all right – just – if it didn't get any worse. Touch wood . . . You did need to be in there, at anchor and with the dinghies inshore, right on the dot. Two dinghy trips, in bad weather – cavorting in like corks, then struggling out against wind and sea with a load of passengers to slow you down . . .

Three hours' work, he thought. Not less.

She was already rolling and pitching like something in a fairground. As much roll as pitch, and heavy jarring impacts as she drove through it, testing her hull-strength ten times a minute, with the green seas lifting to be smashed and sent flying back – solid, some of it bursting like truckloads of bricks against the forefront of the superstructure – this plot – and sheeting over and into the bridge, a fair proportion of it dropping green on the watchkeepers' heads and some of the rest swamping over the sill and down the ladderway so that the plot's deck was also running wet. The skipper and Don Shepherd would be wet through up there, despite their goon-suits. So would the lookouts – who'd also man the Vickers G.O. machine guns in any sudden emergency. In these sea conditions and fading light it would be sudden all right, any enemy you ran into would be at point-blank range.

He was glad they didn't have Rosie on board this time. It was a factor he'd thought about before, on previous bad-weather crossings with agents to land: that they'd have enough to contend with even landing in good physical condition, let alone weak and empty, exhausted by hours of sickness.

Wouldn't have wanted that for Rosie.

Didn't want her anywhere *near* this business. Certainly not right in the heart of it, as she was. Compared to what she was doing, he thought, he might have been a bus driver ... Glancing round as someone lurched up beside him, grabbing for support against a particularly savage roll. Nick Ball ... 'Some summer, this!' He was dressed for the bridge, goon-suited, had paused for a look at the chart – clinging to the edge of the table, Ben making room for him, the gunboat at that moment hard over to port, bow-down and shuddering, foam sluicing over ... 'Would you believe it – July, God's sake?'

'Not dinghy weather, is it?'

'Oh, we'll be all right, don't worry about *that* ...' This was the expert reassuring the novice ... 'Where're we at now?'

'Here. Give or take fifty miles. By the way,' – he reached for his notebook – 'we'll be on a rising tide – see, couple of hours after low water – our friends'll have made tracks – huh?'

To get back to shore over the sand before the tide covered it. The Frenchmen would put their party of airmen on Guenioc, and nip back while the going was good.

Ball was at the ladder, clinging to it: her bow was up and she was surging forward ... He yelled agreement: 'Beating the tide, *and* before it's a full gale.'

Hughes called down, 'Plot!'

At the voicepipe: 'Plot, sir.'

'I'm reducing to revs for ten knots, pilot.'

Christ ...

*

He'd adjusted the course to south twelve west, to counter the tidal flow and wind from the same direction. He was navigating by dead reckoning based on a QH position half an hour earlier; the QH had chucked its hand in since that last gasp of usefulness, disliking the rough treatment it had been getting, and he was watching the echo-sounder now, hoping that it would soon tell him they were crossing the Libenter bank: if this didn't happen within a matter of minutes he'd know he'd brought her too far west and could be running into trouble. He'd thought that from the bridge they'd have picked up the loom of the searchlight from Ile Vierge some time ago, but they hadn't – which could lead to the same conclusion. On the other hand visibility was next to nothing, Ile Vierge was – *should* have been – nearly four miles away, and it was conceivable that the searchlight might not have been in operation.

Running on only the outers now, silenced and making about eight knots. Engines not only silenced by the Dumb-flows but partially drowned out by the noise of the weather and the gunboat's violent motion. Vomit-stink: which didn't help much, tended to create a vicious circle. He hadn't succumbed, so far. *Don't bloody think about it.*

Fourteen fathoms under her.

They were going to be an hour late at the R/V. At least an hour. Hour and a half, maybe.

Five fathoms, suddenly. It could mean he'd boobed, was driving her into God only knew what . . .

Breathe again. Back in eleven fathoms – and there *was* a small shallow patch just to the north of the Libenter. So now – watching the sounder, praying that it wouldn't pack up too . . . It had been known to, in conditions of this kind. Twice, in fact, both times at crucial stages in an approach.

Six fathoms: another abrupt shallowing. And – astonishingly enough – just about perfect!

Sheer luck. Not that anyone need know it. Correction, though: it wasn't *all* luck: more like a combination of dead reckoning plus instinct and experience – and an absence of outright *bad* luck. Still, a hell of a relief ... And another memory of Rosie, how he'd muttered despairingly to her that night in fog-bound London, *Oh, fine navigator I'll make!*

Not that one would have done any better now, in those circumstances. Fog so thick you couldn't see a yard – which of course was what had kept the Luftwaffe away that night.

Ten fathoms. The course couldn't have been much better. Should have sailed at least an hour earlier, though. His own suggestion of an extra half-hour wouldn't have helped all that much. He leant to the voicepipe: 'Bridge!'

Skipper's voice: 'Yes, pilot?'

'Sixteen hundred yards to Petite Fourche, sir. Should see it fine to port.'

'The buoy, perhaps. Probably not the rock – all broken water.' Ben heard him yelling to Shepherd to look out for either. And of course it didn't matter about the rock as long as the buoy was still on station.

Sounding now – sixteen fathoms. It matched the figures on the chart, near enough. The bow soaring – and falling away to port before Ambrose up there jammed on the rudder to bring her back.

'Plot!'

Back at the voicepipe: 'Plot ...'

'Petite Fourche buoy fine to port, half a mile.'

'Right on, sir.' No surprise in it, though. Since that sudden shallowing he'd known pretty well for certain where they were. 'When it's abeam, alter to due south.'

That would still allow for the tidal flow. But you'd need to stay clear of shallow patches from here on, patches she'd float over with room to spare in a reasonably calm sea but which tonight mightn't be far under her keel when she was in the troughs.

Corkscrewing, meanwhile. Weather on the bow, Atlantic swell running in on the quarter.

'Plot – Petite Fourche abeam. Coming to due south.'

'Grande Fourche next, sir. Fine to port again – if visible.'

Rock, not buoy: in fact rocks, plural. He thought they'd be visible – like shellspouts, seas shattering themselves against them and pluming up stark-white against the blackness. Grande Fourche, and then the Brisante. When the Brisante was abeam they should have Guenioc in sight, and to the south of it – in the usual anchorage or perhaps a bit closer in – there might be some small degree of shelter.

At the first attempt the anchor didn't hold. They had to haul in a few fathoms of the grass line while Hughes brought her in a bit closer to the island to try again, and by the time it was holding they'd drifted back southeastward by about half a cable.

The problem was the weed. There was a lot of it about and you had to drop the hook where the sand was bare or nearly so; in pitch darkness it was a matter of trial and error. Ben was on the bridge while this was going on, in a goon suit and Mae West – as the dinghy's crews were; Ball, who'd gone aft to see to the preparations for launching, came back for'ard.

'Bad news, sir. Second dinghy's compass is U/S.'

'Oh, Jesus . . .'

It was Ben's responsibility, technically; a compass came under the heading of navigational stores, and he was navigating officer. He'd left it to Ball simply because he hadn't thought beyond the fact that Ball was boat officer, and the compass would have been supplied to them with the second dinghy. They were ex-R.A.F. compasses, portable and luminous: and this wasn't, Ball told them – wasn't luminous. Or had lost its luminosity. Was therefore useless. (You couldn't possibly use a torch – even if you'd had a spare hand for one – on account of the German lookout posts on shore. You didn't even show a burning cigarette-end.)

He told Ball, 'I'll follow you – stem to stern, if possible.' To Hughes, then: 'All we can do, sir. We'll get cracking, soon as—'

'Anchor seems to be holding, sir.'

Shepherd, returning to the bridge. *Seeming* to be holding was about as good as you'd get, with no visible shore features on which to take bearings and check for any drag.

'I'll give you a lee, starboard side.' Hughes added, 'You're aware of the time factor, uh?'

His way of saying *Don't waste any*.

The dinghies had to get away pretty well together, so they could stay in sight of each other. Shepherd came aft to supervise the launching – eight sailors, four to each boat, manhandling them over the rail in the pitch darkness and down to the sea with as little crashing against the gunboat's side as could be managed.

Two Jacob's ladders had been rigged – Mollison's work – so the crews could embark simultaneously. Ben's oarsmen were Abercrombie, a New Zealand farmer's son and Davidson, a Londoner.

'Over you go.'

Down into a cockleshell that was trying to smash itself against the side ten times a minute: the sea's rise and fall was six or eight feet. Oars, and Ben's scull for steering, were to be passed down once they were embarked. Hughes meanwhile had the starboard outer running slow astern to hold his ship beam-on to wind and sea and give the boats a lee. The effect wasn't all that noticeable, but no doubt they'd have been worse off without it.

Course to the beach would be about north five east. The island had been visible from the bridge, through glasses, as a black hump extending over about fifteen or twenty degrees, but you couldn't see it from the deck and certainly wouldn't from the dinghy. You'd be relying totally on Ball's compass and on keeping him in sight.

Davidson called, 'Ready, sir!'

He climbed over. 'See you, Don.'

He *thought* he'd heard 'Sincerely hope so' but the wind had whipped it away. Down the ladder then, transferring into the dinghy as it came to the top of its vertical movement,

hopping directly into the sternsheets at the centreline as it
started down again, the sea sucking away from the M.G.B.'s
side, seething white: from his seat in the stern he was
craning his head back to look up for a sight of the oars being
passed down: as they were now . . . 'OK, sir?'

His scull: and the crewmen had their oars. A yell from the
other boat as it swung broadside-on, Ball already on his
way.

'Shove off, for'ard!'

Bloody lunacy. But necessary, of course. And no time for
saying prayers – even if anyone would have listened to them.
Which wasn't very likely . . . 'Give way together!'

His own scull wasn't for steering yet, he was using its
loom to fend off. Then, clear of the M.G.B.'s side, he slid it
out over the stern and into the slot in the transom: the two
sailors in unison putting their weight on their own oars,
driving the little boat curving up a wall of sea to crash bow-
down into an abyss beyond it. Ball's dinghy was visible only
when they were both well up: it was imperative therefore to
stay close, or you'd lose him.

'All right, you blokes?'

Too bad if they weren't . . . Heavy spray was bursting over
but the boat wasn't shipping much. Incredibly . . . The built-
in buoyancy, of course, and the skill of designers Messrs
Smyth and Nicholson. *Rolling* wasn't the word for it,
though; flinging herself from one beam to another every
couple of seconds wasn't bloody *rolling*. Scull in steeply and
most of his weight on it, forcing the stern around as she'd
sheered off course – he was on to the need for it very
quickly, the need to keep Ball in sight. In a surround of black
water streaked with white his view of Ball's dinghy as this
one shot upwards again was of some blacker object,
shapeless but recognizable – just – with the white of the
oars' emergence showing up only through their regularity.
There was comfort in the recognition, after each short period
of anxiety when you didn't have a hope of seeing anything
at all: and acute awareness that if he lost Ball he'd *be* lost.

Having no mark to steer by, *nothing* except darkness, no way at all of knowing which way into it you were pointing.

'Doing fine, you blokes!'

Lashing spray flung it back at him. Knees jammed against the boat's sides, the scull's loom under his left arm with the right hand grasping it, left hand available some of the time for holding on and the dinghy doing its best to make that impossible, throw him out. He was glad in one way that he didn't have a compass, which he'd have had to be gripping between his knees. Tall order – next to impossible, lacking Ball's experience – jolting, explosive *crash* as she hit the bottom of a trough, sea frothing up to about gunwale height, oars' blades dipping and driving her slanting up the next one – lacking Ball's expertise, which up to now perhaps one hadn't fully appreciated ...

Searching the darkness ahead – in panic for a moment – his eye caught the glimmer of a light just briefly, out to starboard ... Probably a false impression: ignoring it anyway, needing to find the other dinghy ... All right, so you had the weather on the port side, this blow straight out of the Atlantic, but regrettably it wouldn't be enough to steer by, not within say thirty degrees ... Christ, where—

There. Slightly to starboard. He put his weight on the scull to edge her round: roller-coasting, and juddering from the impact, but the two oarsmen working with the steadiness of machines.

There *was* a light there. Ship, or on shore. Shore, he guessed. Farmhouse window – or one of the German lookout posts?

If it was fixed, and stayed there, it *would* be a mark to steer by. Not with any accuracy, but as a rough guide: by keeping it at that angle to the boat's fore-and-aft line you'd know you were going in more or less the right direction. *If* it was fixed, though, and stayed switched on, and visible. Couldn't watch it – Ball's dinghy was what you had to watch – or rather look for ... Now – lifting again, bow up almost vertically then tilting over while the boat was carried rushing on the crest,

on an even keel for a change and travelling at what felt like
enormous speed, and the other boat suddenly in easy sight
against a background that showed it up: surf-line, beach-
line ...

'Nearly there, lads!'

Ball had explained: with the seas racing up on the beach
not at right angles to the coastline but slantwise, the tactic
should be to approach the nearer end of it and then swing the
boat's stern to the weather at just the right moment to ride
in on a roller which you'd have selected. Because if you
went straight in with the sea on your beam or quarter when
you got into the surf you'd be rolled over: a lesson learnt by
trial and error in those frolics on Praa Sands ... The light
was still shining: one quick search in that direction, justified
by – well, anxiety ... Eyes back to the other dinghy then:
clear to see, travelling from left to right: Ball had made his
turn, was being swept into the thunderous chaos of the surf.

So here *we* go ...

Turning her, as she lifted. Digging the blade in, leaning on
it hard, forcing her round as a big one came rushing ...

'Oars!'

Meaning, stop rowing. They had done – oars across their
knees, the men both stooped forward ... Balancing act, too,
swaying against the motion of the boat, but the work was all
Ben's now, holding her stern-to, while the wave carrying her
in to the beach flowed on under, melting into the boil of
surf.

'Boat your oars!'

Otherwise they'd be smashed ...

Scraping of sand under her bow: then she was out of
contact with it again, lifted and driving in. A heavy jolt, then,
impact under the keel, her forefoot – on sand quite solidly,
but still driven ...

'Hi, there, Navy!'

Dark figures wading to them through the surf, yelling over
the noise of it and waving. Another American voice: 'Are we
glad to see you guys!'

'Hey – not Krauts, are you?'

'Sorry we're late.' Davidson and Abercrombie were out of the boat, one each side, joining the airmen who were hauling it up. Ben got out too. An English voice yelled 'Cripes – we going in *this*?'

'Safer than you'd think, cobber . . . Senior officer here?'

'Guess that's me.' Yank: tall, about Ben's own build. 'Charles Hansen – major, U.S. Air Force.'

'Ben Quarry, lieutenant.' Ball had come to join them, trailed by the group who'd met his boat and hauled it up. Ben told the major, 'This is Nick Ball, sub-lieutenant. He's the fellow that counts, small-boat genius . . . Major, are there still seventeen of you?'

'Yeah. Half in each boat, eh? Oh – here's your senior British officer – Tom Bristol, squadron leader.' Ben shook hands with him 'Should get a move on, if you're ready. Two trips: first one I'll take four and the sub here'll take five; we'll be back in about an hour and take four each. OK?'

'Whatever you say. Australian – right?'

'Couldn't miss it, could you?' Thinking about that light, narrowing his eyes into the darkness, looking for it. It should have been visible from here – *if* it was still shining and in the same place . . .

It was. So that was fine. The major was telling the crowd of men around him, 'Nine of you, this time. Five in that boat, four in this. I'll wait with the next crowd. Get to it, fellers.'

The light was still there, its apparent flickering due probably to the distance and the conditions between here and there. Bearing near enough due east. Struggling back on this first return trip – the rowers having a much harder time of it, fighting out with the weather broad on the bow and Ben's scull needing all his strength right from the start to hold her on course, and four Americans crouched on the dinghy's bottom-boards – he had the light somewhere near abeam all the way. It had to be a couple of miles away, and the distance from shore to ship was only about 250 yards; the bearing couldn't have changed by more than a degree or two between shore and ship.

His first sight of the gunboat came after he'd seen Ball alter course sharply into the wind to run up alongside. Hughes had been ready for them, had her lying across the wind again to make the transfer of passengers easier. He'd have been counting off the minutes, Ben guessed. They'd left the island just after 0200, and it was now 0250. Twenty minutes – roughly – ship to shore, and forty-five shore to ship: they had a barely adequate hour now in which to get back to the beach, embark the rest and bring them out – and from Hughes' angle to have them on board, boats out of the water and anchor out of the sand by 0400.

It wasn't a stipulated deadline, but no-one could fail to be unaware that even with this heavy overcast, any later than that you'd be looking for the first flush of dawn.

As would the Germans in their coastal defence positions.

Ben's Yanks were directed to the ladder, and hauled on board. Abercrombie was then relieved by A.B. Bright, a Gosport man, and Davidson by 'Tommo' Farr from Port Talbot. Real name Jimmy, nicknamed after the great Tommy Farr who a lot of people thought should have been given the decision at his world heavyweight championship fight with Joe Louis in '37.

Ball pushed off, Ben followed, as before. Anxiety over the time element was ameliorated by the comfort of having the light still there. If he should happen to lose sight of Ball he'd have at least some idea of a course to steer. He'd thought about using the wind direction for the same purpose, but it wouldn't have helped much, particularly as it seemed to be backing and veering from one minute to another between southwest and northwest: how it felt, anyway – which was what counted.

In the sea, as much as on it.

Same routine then at the island: Ball into the surf-line first, then Ben well clear of him, and airmen wading into the surf to meet them. They'd separated themselves into two

teams and were ready to embark; the dinghies had only to be
turned round, to battle their way out again.

Time: three-nineteen. Ben's passengers were the American major, the R.A.F. squadron leader and two sergeant-
pilots. Two each side of the boat, steadying it and ready to
push off and jump in. Ben told them, pointing in Ball's
direction, 'Let him away first. He has the compass.'

'You don't?'

Shouting, over the thunderous booming of the surf . . .
'Borrowed boat, this one. Came with a duff compass.' To his
crew then: 'Oars forward!'

They couldn't start rowing until the passengers were
inboard: taking the dinghy out a few yards first, foam boiling
up thigh-deep. Ben yelled, 'All *right*, get *in*!' A wail like a
seagull's shriek, to his own ears and above the surrounding
din: and they *were* in, the dinghy beginning to swing away
– with the danger of being rolled over – but OK then as the
oarsmen put their weight into it. Ben looking for Ball's
boat . . .

There. Thank God . . .

Scull in, ruddering her round to get on to Ball's port
quarter. Easier than following directly astern, with the
rowers' heads and shoulders blocking one's view some of
the time. He'd realized this on the last trip out to the ship and
had felt stupid for not having caught on to it before.

The light was still there, with its fast, infinitessimal
flicker. Then as the dinghy plunged into a trough, nothing in
sight at all, only the stroke oar's regular lunging to and fro
and the white flashes of broken water, a wave's white-
fringed crest overhanging, threatening . . . Rolling hard to
port as he steered her round to climb it: telling himself *Be
alongside just after four. Won't have been bad going, for an
amateur* . . .

Riding high again then: but he couldn't see Ball's boat.
Down in a trough of its own, he supposed. Then, watching
for its reappearance, he realized suddenly that the wind was
well abaft the beam, quickly wrenched the scull's blade

outward to haul her round ten or twenty degrees to starboard: the fact occurring to him that if you let that happen too often, or steered ten degrees off course for say one minute, Ball would by then be a long way out of sight: also that in terms of steering by the wind direction as one felt it, twenty or even thirty degrees this way or that was as good as you could hope for.

Find that light . . .

Smell of vomit in the wind. The last lot had been sick, too.

There. Close to the beam – where it belonged. So – OK. Now find Ball.

Not immediately, you wouldn't. Falling bow-down again, black water lifting like a wall ahead. Just hang on, no panic . . .

Because of the existence of that light, no panic.

Shooting up again: the dinghy practically standing on her transom – and trying to pay off as the wind hit her bow. He'd checked that: and the oarsmen were performing miracles. No pauses, no mis-strokes: in *these* conditions . . . Still couldn't damn well see Ball, though. How long since he last saw him? Much *too* long – that was for sure . . . Sweep-oar well out to starboard again, his weight on it . . . Bloody hell, though, the law of swings and roundabouts had to apply here, surely, at least *some* of the time you'd have to be well up simultaneously – see each other?

If you were in visibility range at all . . .

Check on the light again.

Couldn't find it . . .

Had to be there. Less than a minute ago it had been in sight, on the beam. Even if – well, if you were say forty degrees off course – which theoretically was – well, Christ's *sake* . . .

No light anywhere. Switched off, or covered? He'd searched all round – an acknowledgement in itself of having little idea which way he had the dinghy pointed.

But he hadn't. Hadn't a bloody notion . . .

7

In Rouen, Rosie woke with the dawn: on a bed like corrugated iron. It would be why she'd woken this early, she supposed, opening her eyes to a grid of pinkish light between the slats of shutters which Marthe Bonhomme had warned her last night not to open, unnecessarily advertising the fact they had someone living in their attic. She'd been about to open them in order to let some air in: in the top of the old house the summer heat was trapped under the low, sloping ceilings.

It would be a damn sight less comfortable in Dachau or Ravensbruck, she reminded herself.

Happy thoughts, in the delicately pretty light of dawn – and a delicious aroma of baking bread. This was a bakery – the ground floor was – Boulangerie Bonhomme, in Rue de la Cigogne.

Wondering about Vidor. Whether he and his *réseau* were still functioning or whether he'd have shut up shop at the news of Guillaume's arrest: in which case, what might have happened to the dozen airmen who should have been in his charge by the time he'd had that news? She guessed that he'd have seen at least that operation through, counting on Guillaume's holding out for the prescribed forty-eight hours. Might even have decided to hang on and chance it – depending on how he felt about Guillaume. If you could *ever* be certain: even about yourself, for God's sake ... But – odds-on, she thought, that he'll have got that lot on their way. In which case they'll be on board the gunboat – now, this moment, on its way back to England, having cleared the French coast before first light. Thinking about that, she was visualizing Ben in his little chart-room, stooped over the chart, his face half-lit by the light from that gooseneck lamp and the other half of it in shadow: this serious, *intent* Ben . . .

She could say now that was where and how they'd met. If she saw him again, if he had a leave and she invited him and they came to stay in Buckinghamshire. Wouldn't have to tell her mother *We met by chance one evening and finished up in bed* . . .

Thursday, this was. One of César's days to be at the Café Belle Femme. He was to be there on Tuesdays and Thursdays from 11.15 to midday, and she was to arrive at 11.25 sharp; he'd be expecting her at exactly that time, would take no notice of anyone showing up at say 11.23 or 11.27. He'd be alone at a table with two cups on it – and there'd be the business of the spoons . . . A cardinal rule in all rendezvous arrangements was that you stuck precisely to the times: if the person you were meeting didn't show by the deadline, you didn't hang around.

What she had to decide now – because she'd been too tired to think straight last night – was whether to keep the rendezvous today or leave it until next Tuesday. Factors involved in the decision were – in favour of going along – that he might have been waiting for her two days a week for the past fortnight or so, that you were supposed to make contact as soon possible after arrival, and that important S.O.E. operations might be held up until the two of them did get together. Or the three of them, if he'd decided to take a chance on Romeo. But the contrary argument – the alternative of giving it a miss today – was the fact she had these other tasks which he didn't have to know about – namely (a) getting the message out about the parachute drops – which was extremely urgent – and (b) starting some kind of ball rolling with Jacqueline Clermont. It might make a lot more sense to get (a) done with and (b) under way while she was still so to speak a free agent.

They really did need to know *now*, about the drops, to have time to prepare for them. Each reception involving at least half a dozen men, and transport, and having caches ready – pits dug, or whatever. None of which *she* needed to know about. She had only to tell them where and when, and the code-phrases to listen out for. There was a good chance – she reached down, touched the attic's boarded floor – that passing it all to one individual in the village of Lyons-la-Forêt might take care of both drops, saving her a certain amount of time and pedalling.

She'd have to travel by bicycle. Louis might not approve of this as a means of transport for the Maison Cazalet's representative, but she'd be able to explain it easily enough, if called upon to do so. New to the job, no money, having to economize at least until she'd started earning some commission. She'd take the radio with her, of course: a clear priority was to get a signal off to Baker Street reporting her arrival in the area and notifying them that the safe house in Lyon had been taken over by the Gestapo. This would be at Louis's request: they'd been upstairs in his house on Tuesday discussing the ins and outs of the perfumery business when he'd been called down to the shop and had come back up ten minutes later looking worried: 'I have had bad news, Jeanne-Marie. A *planque* in Lyon, Pension d'Alsace, is now a mousetrap. Several arrests.' He'd put a hand on his diaphragm: 'You know, it makes me ill to think of it. Really *ill* ... but you could help us with this, please – if you're going to be talking to London soon?'

So the contact with London was a priority, because of the Guillaume business, and consequent doubts of the security of more than one *réseau* and their pianists' operations in the Paris area ... And actually it was a strong point in favour of meeting César this morning. He'd have to know – later – that she'd made that signal, so he'd know she'd been here, and in reporting her arrival she'd be bound to include *No contact made as yet with César or Romeo*. If she'd deliberately avoided making contact, he'd justifiably want to know what she was playing at.

So go ahead and meet him? Tell him frankly that she had a job to do this weekend which wasn't strictly his business, and that she'd be available to him full-time as courier/pianist by say Tuesday?

Best solution, probably. He mightn't like it, but it could save later complications.

Telling no lies . . .

She made her own reconnaissance of the town, and before eleven had located the café and the hairdresser's, having asked strangers here and there for directions – advisedly *not* having asked the Bonhommes, as she'd intended, before setting out from the bakery. What she had not found as yet was a bicycle shop: which was odd, seeing that the streets were full of bikes; you'd have thought they'd sell them on every corner. Could have asked Raoul Bonhomme that, she supposed, without giving anything much away. Might ask him later, if she still hadn't found one – or unless César had been here long enough to know.

Or Romeo, if she met him. He'd be the best bet by far, for local knowledge. *If* she met him: which was a decision best left to César.

She was on the Quai du Havre now, on a stone bench, resting her feet as well as killing time, and resting her eyes – behind sunglasses – on the Seine's smooth-flowing surface. Flowing from left to right, on the ebb, swirling around the massive stone supports of the Pont Jeanne d'Arc. This was the Rive Droite; she had the sun climbing to her left, its reflection dazzling on the water even through the glasses, which had been a present from Louis.

A sense of peace here – antiquity, continuity . . .

As far as the river was concerned, anyway, and the ancient streets through which she'd been wandering for the past two hours or so. Ornately decorative stone frontages on some of the wider streets and squares, heavily timbered lath-and-

plaster enclosing the winding cobbled lanes, some so narrow
that in places the overhang of upper floors just about shut out
the sky. The centuries had washed through them, leaving
them unmoved. Picturesque, all right: but she'd soon begun
to appreciate that cobbles weren't all that good to walk on,
in French cardboard-soled shoes. Bloody agony, in fact.
She'd eased one shoe off and was massaging that foot, her
thoughts moving meanwhile to the desirability of finding
somewhere else to live. Through César, perhaps.

Marthe Bonhomme had invited her to get her own
breakfast when she was ready for it. There'd be coffee on the
stove and this morning's bread on the table. Her husband
would be at work in the bakery – from as early as four a.m.
– and she'd be in the shop from about seven-thirty ... 'But
tell me, will you be out all day?'

'Well ...' At close range, looking back into the rather
small, brown eyes: 'I expect so ...'

The query had still been there, an invitation to tell her
where she'd be going or what she'd be doing. Natural
curiosity, probably, but it was coupled with a certain
edginess which Rosie understood now but which at the time
had reminded her of that insistence on keeping the shutters
closed – when in fact there was no reason she should *not*
have been staying here. Her cover was really very sound:
young widow with a child in its grandmother's care, the
need to earn a living and some distant cousinship with a
well-known Parisian who was prepared to give her this
chance – and who happened, incidentally, to be a chum of
Reichsmarshall Hermann Goering, as well as other bigshots.
Jam on the bread and butter: repulsive as it might be from
some other points of view ... Admittedly, if the Gestapo had
been tipped off that an S.O.E. female agent would shortly be
arriving in this city, or that one might recently have arrived,
they'd be looking at every new face; but the Bonhommes
knew nothing about that – about Guillaume, whose arrest
was the factor imposing this special danger.

At the time of Madame Bonhomme's warning about the

shutters, there'd also been her strange question: 'You don't walk about at night, I suppose?'

Rosie had laughed. 'Not usually.'

'No.' A brusque gesture. 'There's a bolt on the door. You'll lock it, will you?'

Presumably her husband did walk about at night, she'd guessed, and when he'd unexpectedly joined her in the kitchen this morning the suspicion had been more or less confirmed.

'Did you sleep well, Jeanne-Marie?'

Nodding, with her mouth full. The bread was really something. 'Well enough, thank you.' She'd added. 'It's very kind of you and your wife to let me stay here.'

'Ah. It's our pleasure.' He'd dumped himself at the table, rather too close to her for comfort. Squat, with arms like a weight-lifter's dusted with flour, and a strong body odour ruining the scent of the bread. A sideways smile: 'Mine, anyway.'

For 'smile', read 'leer'. She'd shifted her chair – making room for him, it didn't have to be taken as a rebuff . . . 'Only for a few days, of course. Until I find somewhere of my own.'

'Yes. That's wise. Sorry to have to say so, but—'

'It's a fact of life.'

'Unfortunately.' He'd shrugged. 'You're a smart girl, Jeanne-Marie.' The leer, again. 'We could be good friends – hunh?'

He'd reached over, to squeeze her shoulder. Warm, heavy hand, unpleasantly clammy through the thin cotton of her blouse. It was one of several articles of clothing which Louis had found for her – or the tarty little assistant in his shop had. They'd tarted *her* up, to some extent – clothes, the shoes, make-up, sunglasses, a smart new holdall as well as the sample-case – in which there was room for her radio under a cleverly fitted false bottom – and a change of hairstyle. Louis had arranged for a young male friend of his to come to the house to cut and set her hair yesterday, before he himself had taken her to the Gare Saint Lazare and put her on the Rouen train. The hairstyle was fairly disastrous, she thought, but didn't want to offend Louis by mentioning it. He'd explained in some embarrassment and with repeated apologies throughout the period of transformation that in his business a degree of sophistication was *de rigueur*, perhaps especially so for a representative of Maison Cazalet; and she'd been more than ready to go along with it, through awareness that the Gestapo and/or S.D. might well be looking for the young woman of rather homely appearance who'd been on the train from Brest.

If Guillaume had heard enough, and had remembered, been able to describe her, he might have been – or soon would be – induced to tell them all he knew: or even to select items for them which might be less close to his heart than others.

One's life was *always* in other people's hands. As it was now to some extent in that slob of a baker's. In the kitchen earlier this morning she'd moved her chair a second time, not giving a damn whether it offended *him*; he'd shrugged as if to some invisible audience – *these girls, how d'you ever know?* – and poured himself some coffee. Telling her – almost as if he'd read her mind on the other subject – 'Not that we'd worry, ourselves, in the normal way of things. But – fact is – we have a daughter – married, but she often visits – and she's – well, doesn't share our own view of – of the situation generally. D'you understand me?'

Louis couldn't have known they had a daughter who was pro-Nazi. Married to a collaborator, probably. To a German, even. It would be as well to make sure he *did* know, as soon as possible. Although thinking ahead – as one had to, every minute of the day – if the girl walked in right now it wouldn't necessarily be disastrous.

It would have played into this bastard's hands for her to seem worried, anyway.

'Is she your only child?'

'Sadly, she is. We had a son – Etienne – but he was killed,

in a road accident. He was working for your cousin, Monsieur Cazalet. He may have told you?'

'No.'

'Well, he was extremely generous to us, at the time, although he was in no way – responsible ... That's why – *anything* we can do for him ...'

So that was the connection: she'd wondered what it could be. Louis assuming he'd have these people's loyalty, in return for the 'generosity': which must have been in the nature of a hush-up, she guessed. Having, she told herself, a nasty mind ... But she liked Louis, didn't let herself think about it.

Eleven-ten: time to make a move. The Café Belle Femme faced into the Place de la Pucelle, which was only a few minutes' walk from here, just this side of the old market. Plenty of time, therefore: but she'd have a good look at the place before breezing in there. If there'd been another café within sight of it she'd have been there now, watching the Belle Femme for any sign that *it* might have become a mousetrap: signs like Germans in plain clothes ... Anyway – twenty minutes on this hard stone had been quite enough: her feet had had as much of a rest as they were going to get ... As she got up, and picked up the sample-case, there was a tramp of heavy boots, and raucous voices: a group of German soldiers, eyeing her as they passed along the *quai*. One of them made some remark and several glanced back at her, sniggering. All shouting at each other again, then: reminding her of how strongly she disliked their ugly, brutal-sounding language. Her loathing of it obviously stemmed from its various associations in her mind, but it was a reaction as instinctive and immediate as the hackles rising on a dog's back.

Fear was a part of it, of course. A mental and sometimes actual shiver at the thought of physical contact or even proximity. Dangerous, potentially. She'd reminded herself just in the last day or two, at some point, not to let her feelings show. That lot had gone on, anyway; she was crossing the road to walk up Rue Jeanne d'Arc towards Gros Horloge: wouldn't go that far, would turn left in a minute into Rue aux Ours. She'd memorized a lot of the street names earlier on, had the geography fairly clear. She went back to thinking about the Bonhommes again, and the fact she'd left all that money in their attic. She'd really had no alternative: and it should be safe enough – in the new holdall, which had a strong padlock on it, and with their reliance on Louis. The fact they were still in touch with him did rather suggest that it might be a continuing reliance. Chalk and cheese, otherwise. Left here now: Rue aux Ours. Time – eleven-sixteen ... No doubt Madame Bonhomme would be having a good snoop up there, but she'd hardly go further than that, risk killing the golden goose.

All the same – the sooner one moved, the better. At the core of her uneasiness, she realized, was the near certainty that they'd crack under pressure. Even a threat or two might have them grovelling.

That was it. And Louis did need telling.

Rue de la Vicomté ... Over it, slantwise, and Place de la Pucelle was just around the corner – a sizeable square, with the café directly across from the imposing Hôtel Bourgtheroulde – iron gates leading into a courtyard, and ancient carvings in the stone, but utterly ruined now by a swastika banner above the gates. Fine place for a rendezvous, she thought, ironically: there'd be Boches in the café too, as like as not. But – on second thoughts – since it was such a scruffy little place, there might not be. They tended to patronize cafés which they'd taken over for themselves – *verboten* to the French and of course offering far better food and drink.

Eleven twenty-one: César should have been there six minutes, would be expecting her in another four. Well – three and a half ...

The visible tables were outside, under a striped awning. Six or eight of them occupied. And there were two uniformed Germans at one. Only two men sat alone – one fat with a mop of dark hair and one ancient, with none. She'd passed by fairly slowly: and there was nobody even faintly resembling him ... Might be inside, of course: despite the sunshade there was a reflection on the glass making it impossible to see through. Have to go in there, anyway. Not really expecting to find him, now: he'd surely have been outside where she could have seen him and where he could have seen her arriving. He wouldn't have sat inside the café in order to keep away from those Boches, either: he was an experienced agent, would be aware that the best way to avert suspicion was not to give a damn if they practically sat in your lap.

Like using a café right opposite a building they'd taken over as some kind of headquarters, she thought. Recalling also her day in Paris, dining with Louis at Maxim's, which had been full of them, also a surprising number of well-heeled collaborators. Louis being one of that fraternity, of course: several of them had exchanged warm greetings with him.

She turned at the next corner, and started back. As a matter of routine, looking for any tail. César wouldn't have blessed her for leading the bastards to him. But there'd been no tail all morning, and wasn't now. *Gazos* passing, a *gazo* van unloading vegetables: then as she reached the café three nuns in line abreast, their eyes downcast. The fat man showed surprise at seeing her again, looking at her with interest as she passed between his table and another: she was in the doorway then, a grubby old waiter with a tray pulling back to let her into the contrasting gloom and the smell of floor polish.

No customers at all, in here. Only a woman behind the counter, drying coffee-cups and looking ill.

Not floor polish, she thought. Rotting cabbage.

'Twenty gaspers?'

Wordless, reaching into a drawer for a pack. 'Gaspers' was right: whatever label they carried, there'd be a minimal content of real tobacco in them. These were at a black market price as well. 'I don't know – might have a coffee, while I'm here.'

'At a table, then. Waiter'll take your order.'

He'd take a tip, too. 'D'you have a telephone?'

'There. You'll need a *jeton*.'

'Well – not immediately. I'll see . . .'

She decided against the coffee. Emerging into the brightness, getting some looks up and down from several men including the two Germans. Deciding against coffee not because it would be *ersatz*, made out of acorns, so they said – you got used to that, when there was no alternative – but because these people had seen her pass and then come back, and if she sat down now one or other might try his luck – thanks to Louis's tarting-up efforts. She didn't want any complications.

No César, anyway. The fat man was the only one by himself now. But some refreshment, now she'd thought about it, might go down well. Find another café, relax and think this out. She hadn't doubted that he'd be there: had been ready for something like 'Well, about *time* you showed up!' Blue eyes, fair hair, a year or two short of forty: she'd had him pictured in her mind, expecting to recognize him immediately . . . Entering the old market square now – Place du Vieux Marché – where five hundred years ago the English had burnt Joan of Arc – and starting to work it out, assess her position and prospects *without* César . . . Her first thought on realizing that he wasn't there had been that she was off the leash at least until Tuesday next, could get on with her own business. Then the familiar worry – which nagged whenever a fellow-agent wasn't where he or she should have been – whether he might have been arrested. This had flashed through her mind between the doorway and the counter, and the ensuing reflex – resulting in her asking about a telephone – had been that she might ring the contact number she had for Romeo.

That *did* need thinking about.

It would come under the heading of clutching at a straw, she realized. In the absence of the one colleague on whom she could totally have relied, turning to the next best thing.

Even knowing it might turn out to be the next *worst* thing. Maurice Buckmaster's drawl, last Sunday: *If he's a traitor, your cover'll be blown the minute you contact him* . . .

So why even think about it?

She spotted a place on the north side of the square: Brasserie Guillaume. The reference was to William the Conqueror, not to the one who'd been in her thoughts these last few days. This road, in fact, was Rue Guillaume le Conquérant.

Another shabby little dump. But they'd have the *ersatz* coffee – alternatively watery beer, and possibly some kind of apéritif – if this was a licensed day. And if it was a good day, something to eat. Sometimes there'd be black-market stuff on offer – under the counter and at a crazy price of course, and they wouldn't offer it to anyone they didn't know. But there were a few tables out on the pavement here too, and there were some women among the customers, which seemed to her to provide a measure of – security, of a kind . . . She crossed the road – from the market-place, dodging bicycles and a horse and cart – and found a table at the back, where she'd have the rest of them in her sight.

Including a man reading the collaborationist newspaper *Je Suis Partout*. One of its leading lights – might have been either the proprietor or the editor – was a friend of Louis. They'd met in that Paris restaurant and embraced, but Louis had told her who this was and she'd hung back, managed not to be introduced. Shy little country cousin . . .

Forget Louis – who so successfully and usefully played both ends against the middle. Think about Romeo. Putting the sample-case with the Mark III in it under the table, between her feet . . . Romeo, who *might* have been turned. Reasons for that suspicion being – one – that he'd survived when all the others in his *réseau* had been arrested, and two, that he'd been that group's pianist and parachute drops he'd called for in his signals had fallen straight into German hands. There was no *proof* of treachery, but the details of the drops would only have been known to him and to the *réseau*'s organizer – who *had* been arrested.

Correction – one other possibility: the Resistance people who were to receive the drops would have known all about them, and *their* group might have been penetrated, or informed on.

'Mam'selle?'

She ordered coffee, and the waiter – stooped, pigeon-chested – confided in a whisper that he still had a little garlic sausage to offer but wouldn't have for long. Otherwise there was only turnip soup. She ordered sausage, with bread. It was what everyone else here was eating, she could see. Could smell, too. Even out of doors.

Back to Romeo, though. *Why* get in touch with him?

First and foremost, for any news of César: there was no other way she'd get it. Second, whether there'd been any instructions from Baker Street. They'd told Romeo not to transmit, until further orders, but he'd surely have been listening out. Third, to ask him where she might get hold of a bicycle without paying a fortune for it. And lastly to arrange to meet him – next week, and perhaps depending on whether César had shown up by then – in order to try to make up her mind about him, part of that process being to ask him to agree to making a trip to London to be vetted. 'Debriefed', was the euphemism. If he was straight, he'd accept the invitation, otherwise he'd either refuse or initially express willingness and then come up with reasons for delay.

If he *was* working for the Germans, though?

Well. She wouldn't mention the Bonhomme establishment: or that she was looking for lodgings elsewhere. Wouldn't say what she wanted a bicycle for, or name any place, day or time for a rendezvous next week. All he'd be getting was the fact that 'Angel' was now in Rouen – and that 'César' apparently was not – if he hadn't known this already, which he might have – and that she'd be calling him again some time next week.

The *imperative* of taking him on trust to this limited extent

was the hope of finding out what might have happened to
César. She had to know, and so did Baker Street.

She reached down for the sample-case, and went inside,
bought a *jeton* and went over to the telephone – stopping the
waiter to tell him 'I'll eat in here, please. *That* table.' Then
she was dialling a number she'd been carrying in her head
for the past week.

'Bistro Suisse.'

Male, and grumpy-sounding, probably quite old. She
asked him, 'Is Martin Hardy there, please?'

'Hardy,' pronounced the French way: 'Ar-di.'

'Who wants to know?'

'Well . . . *He* knows me as Angel.'

'Does, does he?' A grunt. 'Gets around, that one . . . No,
he's not here.'

'D'you have any idea when—'

'Might be in some time, I don't know. If he's in town, of
course.'

'Well – he could call me – if it's in the next hour, say?'

'Give me the number.'

She read it out to him, off the sticker beside the *jeton* slot.
'I'd be most grateful, monsieur, if—'

Gone. Hung up. She did the same. Thinking, *Bistro Suisse*
. . . She might try to find it, be there when he arrived. She
wouldn't know him but the proprietor would speak to him
and then he'd go to the telephone and she'd see him getting
a dusty answer, hanging up.

Achieving what, though? A person's looks might preju-
dice you one way or the other, couldn't *tell* you anything.

She'd got to the table which had her so-called coffee on
it but no sausage yet, was about to sit down when the phone
began to ring, behind her. She went back to it quickly, driven
either by intuition or by wishful thinking, and with a wave
to the girl behind the counter – who in any case hadn't
moved an inch.

'Yes?'

'Angel?'

'Who's this?'

'Can't guess, my darling?'

'No. I can't. Look, I'm going to hang up—'

'No, please . . . I'll tell you. Since you have a pretty voice – call me Romeo?'

'Ah. Well . . .'

'Interested, eh? Makes two of us . . . Can we get together – right away? Make the fur fly a little, maybe?'

'Any news of César?'

'No. None.' A two-second pause . . . 'Anyway – three's a crowd—'

'He can't be in town.'

'As far as I know, he isn't. *Can* we meet, right away?'

'Actually, I'm afraid not. Not before next week.'

'Next *week*! How can I possibly wait *that* long?'

'Well – you might try taking cold baths?'

'How can an angel be so cruel!'

'You tell *me* something, if you would. Where can I hire or buy a bicycle at a reasonable price?'

'Easy. Garage I use. I have a *gazo*, see. Marc Pigot – tell him I sent you. In an alleyway off the Rue Bras-de-Fer. He does cycles as well as cars, does have some for hire, I know.'

'You have a *gazo*, you say?'

'Have indeed. I'm a travelling salesman, darling. Come to think of it, why bother with a bicycle—'

'I'll call you next week.'

'Which day?'

'I don't know. When I'm back. Sorry, but—'

'Back from where?'

'Next week. You're full of questions, aren't you?'

'But I may not be here! I'm a businessman, I can't sit around all day just in the hope—'

'We'll have to chance it, that's all. I *am* sorry.'

She hung up.

He must have been there when she'd called, she realized, and the man who'd answered had given him the option of not calling her back. Instant cut-out. And then any monitor on this line would have thought the subject was *l'amour*, a blind date in prospect – introduction by courtesy of the absent 'César', perhaps – and she'd been playing hard to get.

Which she had, of course. And so far, so good ... Break the ice at Chez Jacqui this afternoon, find the garage afterwards. Back to the Bonhommes then – by bicycle, with any luck – and make an early start in the morning. With some food to keep one going, en route. The Bonhommes seemed to have plenty to spare. The barter system, she guessed: bread – which like everything else was rationed – in exchange for whatever else they'd want.

More than you'd get here, anyway. A plate of scraps – to be washed down with *cold* ersatz coffee now. Her thoughts drifted back to César – whose absence was convenient in a way, in the short term and for her own immediate purposes, but still worrying ... She had enough of these rather pressing tasks to keep her busy for the time being, but by Tuesday, say – what if he wasn't at the Belle Femme *then*?

To start with, tell Baker Street. She'd have to get out of town again to do it, and that would be her third transmission. The first – tomorrow – would report her own arrival, that she'd been in contact with Romeo but not yet with César, and that Louis had heard that a safe house in Lyon, Pension d'Alsace, was in German hands. Then tomorrow night or the day after, after seeing this Resistance character in Lyons-la-Forêt, a signal confirming that the drops should go ahead as planned.

Romeo had sounded all right, she thought. She'd been left with a reasonably good feeling about him. Although how one could possibly tell, from a brief and flippant exchange like that one, might have been hard to explain. Perhaps that flippancy was the key: a traitor might have tried harder to express concern for César, for instance.

Actually, he'd played it rather well. Brash salesman on the make. She sat back, lit a cigarette, thinking that she'd call him next after the Tuesday rendezvous with César. Knowing rather more clearly where she was by then: even – touch wood – where César was.

'Want anything else?'

She glanced up at the waiter. 'Such as?'

'Well.' A shrug. 'There's some cheese . . .'

'No. But tell me – how would one get to Rue Bras-de-Fer?'

Rubbing his jaw. Muttering, 'Bras-de-Fer . . .' Then a nod: 'Hold on.' She saw him talking to the cashier: getting her bill at the same time. A shadow filled the doorway suddenly, blocking out the sunlight: a big man, civilian clothes, standing there with his hands in his pockets, staring in. His face was too dark to see, against the light, but she sensed that he was German: a type like those at the station who'd arrested Gullaume.

He was still there. Staring at *her*?

She was acutely conscious of the sample-case under the table between her feet, with the radio inside it.

Could they have traced that call?

Telephones were anything but secure. Baker Street's advice was not to use them. But *they*'d given her Romeo's contact number. And she'd cut it as short as possible . . .

The waiter was tapping his own forehead as he came back to her: muttering 'Of course, of *course* . . .' And the room had brightened, the doorway was empty, unobstructed. Not that it would be wise to count chickens . . . The waiter put down a grubby piece of paper with pencilled figures on it, told her 'It's in the direction of the Gare Rive Droite, more or less. From here you'd – well, straight up Rue Jeanne d'Arc. Quite a step, mind you: Or are you cycling?'

'No—'

'Well, keep on to where you cross Boulevard de la Marne. Sort of curve to the right and then left, more or less: there's a fork, you can go up either Boulevard de l'Yser – then Bras-de-Fer's on your left – or Rue de l'Avalasse—'

'In which case it's on my right.'

'Precisely . . . You pay at the counter, mam'selle.'

It was only a short stroll to Chez Jacqui. Just as well, considering the trek she was in for later. It would be only one-way on foot, of course, as long as this Pigot had a bicycle for her.

But now – Jacqueline Clermont, alias 'La Minette' . . .

A soldier – German – was staring at her, as she paused outside the brasserie, getting herself orientated. She turned away, dropped the stub of her cigarette and put her toe on it, then crossed the road and started across the old market – past the monument marking the spot where Joan had been burnt at her stake. She'd read somewhere that when they were burnt in that way it wasn't as horrible as one might imagine, that they suffocated in smoke before the flames got to them. Might depend on the direction of the wind, she guessed. Picturing it: the devout, self-justifying executioners in a circle around the roaring flames, the nineteen-year-old girl's face perhaps still visible above them.

Screaming? Praying?

For *their* souls, perhaps.

Slanting over to the right, into Rue de la Pie. Passing more swastika banners and a German lout on guard at a centuries-old stone doorway. Burn *him*, she thought . . .

But would you? Even one of *them* – if you had the chance? *Could* you?

Probably not. And they'd regard that as weakness. They'd burn *you*, all right.

Rue de Fontenelle. It was a long, narrowish slot of a street between uneven half-timbered frontages; Jacqueline Clermont's hairdressing *salon* was on the other side and down towards the river.

8

The street door clicked shut behind her, and the dark girl fixing a stout, blonde woman's hair glanced round expectantly. There were two other customers, both under driers. Rosie's first thought was that Jacqueline Clermont in her former, part-time employment wouldn't have needed to exert herself exactly to get *any* man into bed ... The smile was fading, though: as if she was surprised to see a face she didn't know. Taking in Rosie's looks – clothes, hair, and the sample case.

'Be with you in a moment. If you'd take a seat?'

She was an inch or so taller than Rosie – after allowing for higher heels. Long black hair swept back: elegantly slim neck. Full mouth, eyebrows arching over wide-set slanting eyes. You could see her mother's Italian blood in her, for sure. She was about Rosie's own age. She'd reached to touch a bell-push; it rang on the other side of a curtained doorway, and almost immediately a younger girl – contrastingly ordinary-looking, in a pale blue smock identical to her employer's – came pushing through it.

'See to Madame Dettrier please, Estelle.'

'Yes ... Was I too long?'

'No, it's all right ...' Stepping back. 'We'll give it just five minutes.' She left the blonde one – might have been a touch-up job done there, Rosie thought – and came over to her, smiling. 'Sorry to have kept you waiting.' Sensational figure, under the smock: Rosie felt envious. Also, that this was somehow unreal: you'd discussed her, thought about her, made your guesses and built tentative, possibly far-fetched hopes around her, and suddenly here she was – asking 'You'd like an appointment?' Getting a closer look at Rosie's hair ... 'Yes. Well ... But it'll be next week, I'm afraid.'

'You must be good, to be so busy.'

'At the end of the week I do tend to be. Busy, that is. It's when everyone wants to come, and I close on Fridays at midday, open again midday Mondays. Monday afternoon, I might fit you in. Or Tuesday?'

She had her appointment book open and a pencil poised: glancing round to check on what was happening behind her. Rosie told her. 'Tuesday'd be best. But there's another thing – I mean I do want something done about this mop, but also I'd like an opportunity to tell you about our range of perfumes – Maison Cazalet, in Paris. The perfumes originate in Grasse of course, but—'

'I did wonder what you had in that little case. But frankly, my dear, I rather doubt—'

'Only a few minutes, just to tell you about them, let you try the samples?'

'We could talk about it when you come in, I suppose.' She shrugged. 'Can't very well stop a customer talking, can I?' Another glance over her shoulder ... 'God knows there are times one would like to.' A smile: 'Tuesday morning?'

'Could it be early?'

'Nine o'clock?'

'Perfect. We might come to a sale-or-return arrangement. If you were interested. Monsieur Cazalet's concern is to have a stockist here in Rouen, another perhaps in Amiens—'

'Amiens!' The blonde woman let out a snort of laughter. 'You might help her *there* – eh, Jacqui?'

'I might, I dare say.' An upward movement of her eyes indicated that she'd heard this kind of thing before, and that it bored her. Rosie looked at her hopefully, waiting to hear what the Amiens connection might be – apart from Colonel

Walther's headquarters being there, which would also account for this business being closed at weekends, in the absence of its proprietor. 'La Minette' added, 'We'll talk about it when you come. Would you like to leave the samples here meanwhile?'

'Oh, no, I couldn't—'

'I thought for your own convenience. Dragging that heavy-looking thing around ... But – Tuesday at nine.' Pencil poised again: 'May I have your name?'

'Lefèvre. I'm a widow. On the other business, by the way – if you wanted a reference, the parfumeur – Pierre Cazalet, in Paris – he's my cousin. I have his card here ...'

Now for the long hike up to the garage. With a lingering thought in mind of Johnny – having mentioned her widowhood and seen Jacqui's little conventional frown of sympathy – her thought was of the remoteness of her image of him, the 'previous-existence' quality which the world they'd inhabited more or less together had now acquired in her memory.

It could have been a film she'd seen. Dashing fighter-pilot, playing fast and loose in his spare time. Wife waiting for him *really* to come to earth: resentful, but ever-hopeful. Sucker ...

Back up into the market square first, and across it. Germans all over, more of them than there had been earlier. She crossed the lower end of the square more or less diagonally, into the Rue Rollon and then turning left in Place Foch. Thinking about Jacqueline Clermont, how nice she'd been to her. Whether she *could* at heart be pro-German ... More Nazi banners down to the right besmirched the vast grey frontage of the Palais de Justice, which being the local Gestapo prison was hardly named appropriately, in present circumstances. It had been mentioned in her briefing by the S.I.S. people: in the Middle Ages it had been home to the parliament of an independent Normandy. Some comedown, she thought. She was in Rue Jeanne d'Arc now, and the front

of the Palais was out of her field of view. It fronted in fact
on Rue aux Juifs – 'the Jews' road': unless they'd renamed
that one by now. She glanced at the near end of the building
– grey, massive, threatening, with a sentry guarding a small
side door where Germans were passing in and out under that
foul emblem. Gaolers, interrogators, torturers? It was like
coming across a wasps' nest: you knew what it was because
of the wasps going in and out. She thought again of the
dramatic contrast – the crude brutality of those creatures
against the elegance of the girl she'd just met.

Perhaps she shut her eyes, pretending it was someone
else? Might be nuts about the bastard, too. Might under the
veneer of charm be an enthusiastic supporter of the Third
Reich. Or – like most of them – backing what she thought
was the winning side.

The next crossing was at the Rue des Bons Enfants. She'd
been in it at one stage of her wanderings this morning, had
passed a picture-theatre plastered with swastikas and notices
to the effect that it was reserved exclusively for the German
soldiery. *Soldartenkinos*, they called them.

Over that road now, trudging on, the sample-case already
about twice as heavy as it had been.

Would you like to leave your samples here?

Peculiar, really – even at its face value, only trying to be
helpful. In the event, who'd have been waiting for her at nine
o'clock on Tuesday? And then – imagining it – César at the
café, worrying about where *she* could have got to. Might never
have got to know, either. You'd simply have disappeared, into
that chamber of horrors. As so many had already, in every part
of France. Reports from former detainees in Fresnes prison –
which as well as housing ordinary criminals was a stopover for
those en route to the death camps in Germany – had provided
answers in some cases.

Rue Thiers. A wide one, this. She had to wait while a
convoy of four cars and a truck – petrol-driven cars,
therefore Germans – drove past quite slowly, only one or
two of the occupants turning their heads to stare at her.

Boche V.I.P.s being shown the sights, perhaps. All motorcars had been requisitioned; to run even a *gazogène* you needed a permit. There were some exceptions: doctors were entitled to retain their cars, for instance, and some farmers their farm vehicles. And Romeo – and Louis – who'd mentioned that in Paris there were about 7000 licensed private cars, which gave one some idea of the extent of collaboration.

Still a lot of Rue Jeanne d'Arc ahead of her. The damn case weighed a ton: she was changing hands quite frequently. Thoughts of Jacqueline Clermont again; that quick warmth, spontaneity – as if they were friends already. Extraordinary: but *very* promising ... Another crossing: Rue du Baillage. With a church off to the left ... She paused halfway across for another military vehicle: a Mercedes, khaki-coloured with insignia on its mudguards, a soldier in the front passenger seat staring at her as it passed rather slowly from left to right.

Juddering to a halt. She'd only heard it happening – the brakes abruptly jammed on – looked back to her right now to see it swerve in to the kerb and stop. Doors flinging open.

Christ. Christ, *please* ...

Out-of-focus awareness of other pedestrians quickening their pace, turning abruptly to cross the road, pretending not to see. Along to her right, though, green uniforms stopping to watch. A yell, then: 'You!'

They were waiting for her to go over to them on that side. An officer – quite young – and a sergeant. *Abwehr*, she guessed. At closer range she saw she'd guessed right.

'Put that down. Your papers, please.'

She set the case down, rather carefully, and the sergeant snatched at it. She told him quietly – as evenly as she could – 'It contains glass. Please be careful?'

'Glass?'

She'd got her papers out, handed them to the officer.

'Samples of perfume. I represent the Maison Cazalet, of Paris.'

The young man was flipping through her papers. The

sergeant put the case down flat on the pavement and applied his thumbs to the catches.

'Oh – you'll need the key—'

He snatched it from her. She thought she wasn't visibly shaking, but she could hear her heartbeats, feel them like fast internal hammer-blows.

Breathing wasn't too easy either.

One fastener clicked up, then the other: he pushed the lid back. The lieutenant asked her, 'Where were you going?'

'To hire a bicycle.' Past tense, she'd noted: as if she was no longer going anywhere. She nodded northward, the direction of the Rive Droite railway station. 'Place I heard of – if I can find it—'

'All right.'

She had her papers back. Had managed not to look down, to where the other one had the case open. She did now, though – *had* to – and saw him poking among the scent bottles in their little wool-lined niches with a blunt fore-finger: he had the price-list in his other hand, must already have had a look at it. Glancing up: 'Want some for your girl, Herr Leutnant?'

A frown: and a suggestion of a bow to her. 'Thank you, madame. It's routine, you know.'

A *polite* one . . .

Dry-throated, and feeling the coldness of all-over sweat, shutting and relocking the case, which the sergeant had left lying there open . . . She saw them climb back into their Mercedes and start away, on the move even before the slam of the second door. She got up: with the case locked again, heavy at her side. Disorientated, for the moment: she'd been in another world – or the anteroom to it. On her sore feet again now, getting herself together . . .

A sort of curve to the right, the waiter had said. Then there'd be a fork. This was the Boulevard de la Marne, all right: and the waiter's 'sort of curve' was easy, only a matter of following the pavement around yet another ancient monument, a tower, crumbly-looking stone rising sheer from the cobbles. Looking for the fork, one branch of which would be Boulevard de l'Yser. Stay on this side, for the time being. Heart still thumping. If that sergeant's thick fingers had probed just a little bit more cleverly she'd have been in the back of the Mercedes now with cuffs on her wrists. You had to put it out of mind, though. A near-miss, but a miss was as good as a mile. What was more, the sample-case had stood up to inspection. She'd crossed one small transverse road, and now a second, was about to ask for directions – from an old woman who looked as if she might have lived here all her life and might not for much longer, meanwhile despite the summer warmth was wearing a blanket with armholes cut in it – when she saw the half-obliterated road-sign: Boulevard de l'Yser. It was actually a continuation of Boulevard de la Marne.

Five minutes later, on her left and leading off from an open space where various roads converged – some unnamed *Place* – she found Rue Bras-de-Fer.

None too soon. Or as Ben Quarry might have put it, none too *bloody* soon. It was strange how he kept coming into her mind – even at a time like this – considering that for something like eighteen months all she'd done was try to forget him, his very existence ... She was taking long, slow breaths, still needing to slow her pulse-rate.

'Monsieur Pigot?'

She'd found big double doors that had once been painted green but showed only small traces of it now. Remnants of posters, too, stuck there and since torn off, and the timber's lower edges rotted away. One door was open: peering into semi-darkness she could see several vehicles crammed in close to each other and – close-to – a man in overalls working on a lorry's engine. The light from a caged bulb on a wandering lead was causing him to narrow his eyes, squinting at her as if he had only partial vision. Which would hardly be surprising, for anyone who worked for long in that half-light.

Quite an old man. Thin white hair, face narrow and pointed, like a whippet's.

'Help you?'

It was pleasantly cool, inside.

'I was told I might be able to hire a bicycle – or buy a second-hand one. Monsieur Pigot?'

'In his office.' A jerk of the head. 'There.'

At the back – a lit window, yellowish and cobwebbed. She murmured thanks as she edged round the old man, getting a strong whiff of horse manure as she did so – from the body of the truck, not from him as she'd first imagined. He was straightening, one hand massaging the small of his back: he'd put the light in its cage on the roof of the cab, and in turn was getting a good look at her as she squeezed by. It occurred to her that this might be stupid, risking herself in here: if he'd gone to that heavy-looking door now and shut it, she'd have been trapped.

Paranoia, she told herself. Occupational disease. It could on occasion save your life, admittedly, but still had to be kept under some degree of control.

The profile of the man in the office wasn't exactly reassuring, either. A long, pointed nose, deepset eyes, two or three days' growth of beard and a grim set to the mouth. She'd pushed the door open, rapping on it as she entered, and he was staring back at her from the other side of a littered desk. The light came from a lamp on top of a wooden filing cabinet – it also had a kettle on it – and there were some shelves, a telephone on the wall, and a pin-up of a provocatively posed, half-naked black girl on a door behind him. Cupboard door, probably. No window or skylight: just that lamp.

Faint but definite smell of urine. Perhaps that wasn't a cupboard after all.

'Yeah?'

He was less appetizing full-face, she thought, than he'd been in profile. Deathly pale, under the patchy stubble, and looking at her as if he hated her.

'Monsieur Pigot?'

'What if I am?'

'I was told you have bicycles for hire. I need a good strong one – I could buy one, if it wasn't—'

'Who told you?'

The eyes in their pits lingered on her sample-case.

'Someone called Hardy. His first name's Martin, I think. *Do* you have bikes for hire?'

'Might have. I don't sell 'em.' He pointed with his head: 'Take a seat.' A wooden chair: she sat down, glad to rest her feet, and put the case down beside her. The chair wobbled, if you let it. Pigot was poking around among the junk on his desk, and eventually found a notebook.

Thumbing through it, to an empty page . . . 'Your name?'

'Lefèvre. Madame Jeanne-Marie Lefèvre.'

He wrote it down, very slowly.

'Address?'

'I haven't one yet, I've only just arrived in Rouen. But I'll be in touch with your friend – Hardy – if for the time being you'd take that as an address?'

'Where's he hang out?'

'Don't you know?'

'Barely know the man. But you must, surely?'

'As it happens, I don't.'

'Then how'll you be in touch with him?'

She shook her head. She had the feeling she was being interrogated and that he wasn't telling the truth. If he *was*, then Romeo had lied about keeping a *gazogène* here. In which case it was conceivable that she *had* walked into a trap. She glanced round – as if out of curiosity at her surroundings – and was relieved to see a rectangle of daylight out there – the door still open – and a nearer glow where the elderly mechanic was still at work.

'Listen – I'll give you an address when I have one, but I'm going to be out of town this weekend. That's why I need a bicycle. How I'd contact Hardy – the simple answer is I'm bound to run into him.'

'Don't you even have a telephone number?'

'If I had, there'd be no problem, obviously.'

'Perhaps not ... Would you be taking the bike far?'

'Quite a distance. I certainly don't want one that's going to fall to pieces.'

'Would you want a panier on it?'

She nodded. 'And a carrier behind the saddle.'

He wrote that down: taking an age, with his tongue showing between discoloured teeth. She thought he might be simple: she'd already been here about ten minutes. He was sitting back now, studying what he'd written as if the accomplishment impressed him. Eyes on her, then: and a movement of the narrow head, towards the sample-case. 'Selling something?'

She frowned, holding his stare.

'My occupation, monsieur, is hardly your concern.'

'Oh, isn't it? When you want me to let you take a valuable machine away with no security, no address, no damn-all?'

'I could pay a deposit. Would that satisfy you?'

He seemed to be thinking it out. As if it might be some new idea. Shrugging, then: 'With no address, it'd have to be the full value of the bike.'

'All right. If it has to be.'

'But why the secrecy? If you're selling something you have to tell people what it is – eh?'

'I don't like being interrogated, that's all.' She shrugged. 'All right – I'm a *parfumeuse*. I represent Maison Cazalet, of Paris. Monsieur Cazalet happens to be my cousin. If you or anyone else cares to check with him, go ahead. Meanwhile, can we get this settled?'

'Think you'll make any money, flogging scent?'

'I *intend* to, monsieur.'

'Do, do you?' The faint smile improved his looks considerably. 'D'you know what they use for perfume in the countryside around here?'

'I can guess. In fact I can smell it from where I'm sitting. But there's Beauvais, isn't there – and Amiens – Neufchatel, even.'

'That far, by bicycle? Why not use the train? Heaven's sake – in one weekend? Where d'you think you'll be selling your perfume on a Sunday, anyway?'

She reached down for the sample-case. 'I hadn't expected either to cover the whole area in a weekend – I didn't say this was a selling trip, did I? – or that just to rent a bicycle I'd have to put up with this – grilling.' She shifted the chair round, on the point of standing up.

'So now you don't *want* a bike?'

He was probably a bit crazy, she thought. Shaking her head: 'Not if it means sitting here much longer. On the other hand, if we've finished with the questions now—'

'You'll pay the full deposit?'

He'd glanced to his right, into the garage. She agreed – not in the least keen to have to start trudging around the town again – 'Yes. If I have to.'

'*I* have to be sure of you, you see. My questions weren't intended to be personal. Bikes have been known to vanish, you know.'

'May I see one – what choice there is – before we settle on it?'

Looking that way again. 'I suppose ...' Hesitating again. 'You see, not knowing anything about you – well, all right, you've given me that reference now, but—'

'For God's sake,' – her voice had risen – 'If you have the full value of the thing—'

The door opened behind her, startling her for a moment. The mechanic, she supposed – then saw in a glance over her shoulder that it wasn't.

'Bravo, Marc. Took me longer than I—'

'Madame Lefèvre.' Pigot, performing introductions: at this point she'd barely seen the newcomer – but she'd guessed, suddenly ... Pigot confirmed it: 'Martin Hardy.' Smiling like some dogs can smile, showing the stained teeth. 'My apologies, madame. I'd promised if you came before he got back—'

'Romeo?'

He chuckled, offering his hand: 'Your very own, my angel.'

She felt stupid – and annoyed – not to have foreseen this ... She was looking at a man of about fifty: dark eyes, a seamed, tough face and a lot of greying, unkempt hair. Short of breath, telling her jerkily, 'I was here a couple of hours waiting for you, had to see a guy then in the port. Anyway – you're still here, all's well.' He pushed some of the rubbish aside on that end of Pigot's desk, and perched himself there. 'I'm sorry about this. But you were a bit standoffish earlier on, weren't you?'

He had a smile that started in his eyes then spread through all the creases in the face. He'd know all about it, would have seen its effects often enough before, she thought. Johnny had had that sort of smile – not the same, by any means, but one he'd been able to switch on when he'd thought it would serve some purpose. She'd shrugged. 'Didn't suit me to meet you yet, that's why.'

'I know. And I'm sorry. My excuse is I've been waiting a damned age, for one thing, for another if anything unpleasant happened to either of us before we'd met – well, there are enough loose ends already, don't you agree?'

'I suppose you have a point there.'

'Didn't you suspect I might be here?'

'No, it didn't occur to me.'

What *had* occurred to her, she was remembering, had been to find the Bistro Suisse and get a preliminary look at him without his knowing it. So – sauce for the goose, Rosie ... She added: 'Perhaps because we're supposed to be on the same side, it didn't.'

'Well.' Hands opening defensively. 'I *have* apologized.'

'You said you're a salesman?'

'Agricultural machinery. Sell it, also maintain it, fix it – on site, usually on the farms. Second- or third-hand, all of it – all we can get. Not a bad racket though – gets me around, eh?'

*

Her first impression had been that he was wearing an ill-fitting suit, but in fact the jacket didn't match the trousers, and neither fitted him.

'You're Mauritian, they told me.'

'Am indeed.' That smile again, briefly. 'Both parents Mauritian, but my paternal grandfather was a Scot. So I read engineering at Edinburgh.'

'Well, *naturally* . . .'

'I like you, Angel. So glad. One doesn't always, does one? Tell me, what is the position with our leader?'

'César.' She shrugged. 'Wish I knew.'

'You must have some means of contacting him?'

'Oh, yes.'

She glanced away, into the dark cavern of the garage. Pigot had gone 'to give old Roger a hand', but more likely to leave them on their own, having first wheeled out a bicycle and given her a receipt for a week's hire which she'd pay later. She'd demurred at having this conversation with Romeo here in the garage, suggesting instead that they might go for a walk together; he'd commented, 'You don't trust me at all, do you? Think there might be a microphone planted here? Well, you're right to be careful. I don't know if you've worked in the field before—'

'Yes, I have.'

'Good. But the thing is, we're safer here. There are excellent reasons that we shouldn't be seen together – if we can help it . . .'

Thinking of the *Abwehr* men in the Mercedes, and remembering that the Germans might be on the lookout for a female agent arriving in Rouen, she'd agreed with him. It had been no sacrifice to give up the idea of walking any further than she had to, either.

(Buy a pair of the wooden-soled shoes, she promised herself. The cardboard ones she had weren't going to last much longer anyway. She'd seen the wooden ones in Paris: they weren't clogs, the soles were sort of hinged, articulated.)

She'd said 'Yes', and no more than that, to his question about making contact with César ...

'All right. You have a way of contacting him, but you aren't letting on. And he isn't here yet – you know he isn't, so you must have tried to communicate with him. Only thing is, how would *I* get in touch with him if you got yourself arrested meanwhile?'

'You wouldn't have to. He'll have the same contact number for you that I had.'

'Ah. That's all right, then. Or will be, if he gets to use it.' If César hadn't been arrested, that had meant. Romeo added, 'I suppose I'm not allowed to know what you'll be up to this weekend?'

'Sorry, no. If it's any comfort, I won't be telling César about it either. Wouldn't be telling him now if he was here, I mean. Smoke?'

He took one. 'So you've some independent brief with which you don't need help ... Angel – in the general run of things, I accept that your caution is entirely proper. But in this instance – present circumstances – isn't it all the more so because I'm on Baker Street's suspect list?'

'Are you?'

'Stands to reason that I would be – and that you'd know it. They'd have warned you. And obviously you wouldn't tell me any more than you had to. The fact is, things fell to pieces here – quite suddenly. Drops were met by Boches, and the others of my *réseau* were –' he'd lit her cigarette, now his own – 'were rounded up. Some may be dead by now. And yours truly being the only one not taken out of circulation would suggest to Baker Street that I'd betrayed them all. Correct?'

It wasn't easy, this. She nodded. 'Probably why I was told to invite you home for debriefing.'

'Debriefing, my foot. Third degree, more like. But – I welcome it. Please. Whenever they like, and the sooner the better.'

'I'll see about setting it up, then.'

'You'll be transmitting? Well, of course—'

She nodded. 'Have to.'

'Take care, Angel. I've been warned off – as you'll know.
The Boches *might* have broken my code – it would account
for the drops going wrong – but I can tell you they were also
homing in on me. I'd been using a bell-tower a few hundred
metres from here, and – you know the routine, long-range
bearings give them the position within about twenty miles,
then the detector vans arrive, narrowing it to say three or
four, and finally the portable sets – goons prowling around
on foot with packs on their backs, trying not to look obvious.
Didn't get to that stage, because I spotted the vans – saw 'em
before when I was in Orléans, trucks with canvas hoods to
hide the gear – and I shifted away damn quick. Shortly after
that was when London told me to shut up, and I was glad to,
believe me ... Incidentally, all I've had from Baker Street
recently has been to expect you and César – that you'd
contact me – no, that *he* would.'

'That's right. I was supposed to leave it to him. To that
extent I've disobeyed orders. But since he's not here – it was
assumed he *would* be ... D'you feel like telling *me* what
happened – those arrests?'

'You mean explain my non-arrest.'

'Including that, obviously.'

'Obviously ...' He sniffed. 'From my point of view you
might say *fortunately*. To put it mildly. And thanks largely
to Max – our organizer, at that time. Anyway – there's a
highly clued-up S.D. man around – only a sergeant, but he
seems to pull a lot of weight – name of Clausen. The rank
thing might be just camouflage: if so it'd be his idea, he's up
to all the tricks. I haven't met him – thank God – but I've
seen him: good-looking guy, women like him and he uses
that – so I've heard ... Well – as far as I've been able to piece
it together, he made his breakthrough with a French couple,
sub-agents recruited locally, name of Sariet – René and
Huguette. René worked as a courier and Huguette ran their
flat as a safe house mostly for escapers in transit. Clausen

got his hooks into René when a girlfriend he'd had in Dieppe informed on him. He'd been using her apartment regularly, but he'd got fed up with her, he was trying to put an end to it, and she shopped him. Enter Clausen, who had him pulled in, and mentioned in one of their cosy chats that Huguette was going to bed with our Max, in the Sariets' house, whenever René was on his travels. He also told him it was Max, not the girl in Dieppe, who'd informed on him. Clausen would only have had to refer to him as 'your *chef de réseau*' – I don't think he could have had any way of identifying him until then. If he *had* known who he was he could have arrested him without all this shilly-shallying, obviously. But it would have been quite believable, that story – lover boy's motive having been to put hubby out of the way for good and all, d'you see? The only doubt – if I'd been in René's shoes it would have seemed a large one – was that surely the organizer would have anticipated René getting his revenge by turning *him* in. And actually it would have been right out of character for old Max, he's not – or wasn't – such a damn fool. But René swallowed it, apparently – sexual jealousy can blind one to much the same extent that sexual passion can – and I dare say he didn't know Max all that well – anyway, he gave Clausen his cover-name, address, telephone number – whatever he had. Oh, and another flaw in this is that if what Clausen had said was true he could surely have picked Max up *chez* Huguette any old time. Perhaps he gave René some reason for not having done so. Not *having* the address, perhaps, until then, only knowing it happened at *a* safe house. Something like that. What he did – there's no doubt of *this* – he had the Sariet residence staked out, leaving Max on the loose while the others walked into the trap. Escorting shot-down airmen, maybe – but he nabbed them all in such short order my guess is he might have used the first as a stool-pigeon to lure the rest on. Then Max – before he could get the news and leg it.'

'But you weren't lured in.'

'I never went near that safe house. Never had. No reason to. I was a courier as well as pianist but I never acted as escort to escapers. The Sariets didn't know me, nor did the other couriers. All they could have divulged about me was that the *réseau* had a pianist-courier code-named 'Toby' – that was my tag before this all blew up. The only person who actually knew me, you see – where I lived, what I looked like, what my cover was – was Max himself. Everything went through him – thank God – and when he vanished I didn't run for it, for the simple reason that I trusted him. Wasn't wrong, either – God bless him.'

She nodded. 'Yes.'

'Mind you – with all respect to him – respect and admiration – I'm not counting chickens. For instance, they might have left me loose so they could pick up any new agents coming in. You, for a start.'

'Thought for the day, that.'

'I wouldn't put it past Clausen. It's partly why I suggested we shouldn't be seen together if we can help it. And to be honest, why I'd be very glad to have the break you're arranging for me ... Although it *has* been some while now. If I'd been under surveillance I think I'd know it by this time.' A pause, then. Looking at her. '*Think* – couldn't be sure ... You're very attractive, Angel. I guessed you might be, from your voice.'

'As you mentioned, over the telephone. Misleading for any crossed lines, but let's keep it for that – please?'

A shrug. 'I was only paying a compliment – an honest one—'

'Your friend Pigot is a sympathizer, is he?'

'More than that. They killed his girlfriend. Looking for her brother. He was in a group that blew up the railway near Vernon, the Paris line, someone identified him and – well, he was on the run. So they took *her*.'

'She didn't—'

'He's still alive and kicking, so – no, she didn't.' Then – with his eyes on hers – as if reading her mind – 'It can be done, you see.'

'Yes.' She looked down at her hands on the table, thinking that by exceptional people it could be done. Recalling Ben Quarry's phrase, 'the bravest of the brave'. *Very* exceptional people, she told herself. And until it happened—

Not until. *Unless.*

She looked up. 'What else is there?'

'Well – you'll get in touch next week, you said. Whether or not César's joined us by then?'

'Probably on Tuesday.'

The doubt was whether she'd be able to arrange for the reception of both drops through that one individual in Lyons-la-Forêt. If she found she could, she might get back to Rouen on Sunday. Otherwise there'd be another day pedalling, another meeting, *then* a whole day cycling back. Monday – back here Monday night. Could be a tight squeeze: arrangements for the drops did have to be con-cluded – that was the priority – but it was almost as important that she should be here on Tuesday morning to keep her appointment with Jacqueline and then – perhaps, and please God – the rendezvous with César.

'Will you be at your bistro on Tuesday?'

'I'll be – around. I don't just sit there – for anyone to walk in on me, God's sake. I wasn't there when *you* called. They call me – elsewhere – I either call back or I don't.'

'It'll be early afternoon, most likely. If you're not there I won't leave a message, I'll try later – or on Wednesday.'

'I'll be there. One point, though – about this trip you're making. You know, I've been around here quite a while, I visit all the farms, they all know me. Well – we don't want to be treading on each other's heels – right? In the longer term, we must coordinate our efforts, d'you agree?'

She nodded. 'But with luck it may not be long before you're flown out.'

He was offering her a cigarette, but she'd only just stubbed one out. He muttered, lighting his own, 'I'd like to be out *today*. .Believe me – *soonest*. But I'd also like to see some drops set up before that – to know it's happening. As soon as possible – *if* it's possible, now we have you as pianist. They had good reason to shut me off the air, but the shutdown's not good for any of us – the boys out there need the stuff, they'd be using it if they had it. As well as stocking up for when the great day comes. They'll begin to wonder what use we are to them, why they should risk their necks passing the airmen through to us, for instance – when it's so *very* dangerous not only for them but for their wives and children.'

'Yes. I know.'

'Get a drop set up soon, d'you think?'

'I don't see why not. You've had requests, have you?'

'Half a dozen.'

'In which areas?'

Quick smile – through a screen of smoke … 'I'm supposed to answer *your* questions?' Drawing another lungful … Then: 'Fix up my trip to England, Angel, I'll park *everything* in your lap.'

She couldn't push it. She'd have liked to have known, because of the drops that were already organized. When she met the man in Lyons-la-Forêt she wouldn't know about any requests *he* might already have passed to Romeo, for instance. They'd know each other, you could bet on it: in fact his reticence now might be aimed at embarrassing her, to pay her back for keeping *him* in the dark. She couldn't argue the point, either, without telling him where she was going and what for.

He was telling her – she'd been ready to leave, but he'd started in on it – about the present state of affairs in and around Rouen, including the fact – regrettable but not surprising – that the majority of the population were still primarily interested in getting by, which meant taking damn good care not to get involved in 'subversive' activities.

'Mind you, having their men shipped out to the work-camps hasn't pleased them. Serve 'em right – they've seen the Jews shipped out – men, women, children – and not lifted a finger. Well – *helped* with it, ordinary gendarmes did

most of the rounding up. And denunciations from the public
... But there *is* a suspicion here and there that the Germans
may not win. Invasion in Sicily, defeat of the Afrika Korps
... The Boches taking over what was the Zone Libre hasn't
made them any more popular, either. Stalingrad – that's a
big thing. People aren't certain any more – and they'll get a
lot less so, more and more anti-Nazi – *potentially* so, at least
– as Allied successes mount. The weathervane factor, eh?
Pretty soon they'll wake up to the fact the Boches *can't* win
... How long before the invasion here, any idea?'

'None at all.' She added, 'Thank heavens.'

He nodded, knowing what she meant. With that kind of
information in your skull you'd be a walking bomb. Romeo
added, 'What they're harping on now – the Boches, in all
their news-sheets and every time one of 'em opens his
mouth, is this "secret weapon" story. To counter so-called
"defeatist" attitudes, they're claiming that once they get
these magical weapons into action – any time now –
England'll be wiped off the map. And so forth.' He changed
the subject. 'Didn't bring any money, I suppose?'

She thought fast again ... 'César'll have some.'

'After you give it to him, you mean?'

'What?'

'Not that it matters, who brings it. I assumed you would
have because I know you've come from London, and if the
same applied to César you'd have arrived together.'

'I don't know *where* he's coming from.'

'If he doesn't show – which God forbid – well, they'd
send you someone else, I suppose. And if I'm getting out I
won't need any, in any case. Tell you the absolute truth,
Angel, getting out is what's mostly on my mind, right now.'

There was one thing still on hers, in terms of immediate
practicalities: where she could move to, leaving the Bonhommes. The best thing would be to bid them farewell in the
morning, having some other place lined up in which to hole
up when she got back; and the immediate question was
whether to risk asking Romeo for suggestions.

She'd be putting herself very much in his hands, if she did. She could imagine how aghast Buckmaster would be, at her even considering it. Or anyone else, for that matter. Marilyn: she could visualize the raised eyebrows, the expression of incredulity...

Fact was, her instincts told her he was straight. And since César, on whom she'd been relying, was conspicuous by his absence and might well remain so, where the hell else would she get advice?

It was a bit more than instinct, anyway. He *looked* about as trustworthy as an old crocodile, but there were things he'd said and others he hadn't: and the way he devoured cigarettes, with that slight shake in his fingers – his nerves were shot, he genuinely did intend to accept Baker Street's invitation.

She took a breath. 'One thing. I need to move from the place I'm staying at. I was sent there, didn't just take pot luck, but they have a daughter who's pro-German and makes a habit of dropping in, apparently. Can you suggest where I might go?'

If he wanted to shop her he'd have plenty of opportunity, she told herself, even *without* knowing where she lived.

His dark eyes were thoughtful.

'Mind if Pigot knows where you'll be?'

'Why should I – if he's one of us?'

'Anyone who knows anything about you adds some risk. I'm surprised you're asking *me* – in present circumstances.'

'You could give me away without knowing any more than you do already. Knowing where I'll be living – could make it easier, I suppose, but that's all.'

'You've given it some thought, then.'

'Of course.'

'Well. I'm encouraged.' He got up out of Pigot's chair, called into the gloom: 'Marc – spare a minute?' He stayed there until he saw him coming, then turned back. 'He's consumptive, by the way. That's how *he*'s avoided the labour camps. Also they accept he's useful here – like me ...

Oh, Marc, sorry to bother you—'

'Who's bothered?'

'Your friend Ursule – might she have a room free, d'you think, for Madame Lefèvre – a few days, perhaps longer?'

'I'll call her.'

'Money no object, of course.' He winked at Rosie. 'But don't tell her that.' Pigot was dialling. Romeo murmured, 'It's on the Rive Gauche. She lets rooms, mostly to girls who – well, who ply a certain trade. It's not a brothel, mind you—'

'How reassuring . . .'

'She inherited the house, decided to let rooms, it was how it turned out, that's all. She's taken people in for us before this, quite often – transients, you know . . . She's a widow, husband killed in '40, son about seventeen in the S.T.O. – know what that is?'

She nodded, listening to Pigot . . . 'Ursule – it's Marc here. I wondered – a young lady, friend of a friend, she's looking for some place to live – I'm not sure for how long, but could be you'd have room for her?'

She wondered again if she wasn't insane. It was too late anyway for second thoughts. Hearing Pigot murmur into the phone, 'I think right away – but hang on—'

'Tomorrow morning. I'd leave some luggage. Take the room from then – if there is one.'

It sounded as if there might be.

Take the money to the country with her? Or leave it in the locked bag at this house of ill-fame, whatever . . .

Or *here*?

Here, in this garage. In the new grip with the padlock on it, which she could bring here on her way out of town in the morning. Leave the money in that, and borrow something from Madame Bonhomme for her essentials over the weekend. A rucksack would be best. Easier to manage, especially as she'd have the sample-case as well.

She interrupted: 'Marc – Monsieur Pigot—'

'Hey, wait, would you?' Scowling round at her – back to

his old self for a moment – with a hand covering the mouthpiece: 'What?'

'I'd like to take the room from Monday. Not tomorrow. If I could leave some of my stuff *here* until then?'

He turned back. '*Chérie* ...'

Meeting Romeo's unsmiling gaze: disturbingly aware – as he was too, she could read it in that dead-serious look – of how irretrievably she was putting herself in his hands. He'd know where she'd be living: knew also that she'd be coming here early tomorrow and that she'd have the radio with her, and probably – as he'd already guessed – some fairly large sum of money.

She thought, *In for a penny* ...

Pigot hung up. 'She'll expect you Monday.'

9

Vidor told Ben Quarry on the Friday evening, in a farmhouse loft half a mile from the village of Broennou, 'I cannot pretend you are – how to say it – what we are *needing*, at this moment. But,' – he shrugged – 'we will do our best, of course. One difficulty is we're short-handed, in the present situation.'

'Could we lend a hand?'

Vidor – scrawny, with thick dark hair but blue-eyed – he was a vet, the only one in this region – stared at him, thinking about it. Nodding, then. 'Perhaps. Yes. I think . . .'

The 'present situation' being that the *réseau* was under threat – as he'd been explaining, and as Léon had mentioned briefly in the small hours of the morning on Guenioc island but hadn't wanted to elucidate – through the arrest in Paris of one of its members, a Frenchman who'd left on the train from Landerneau this last Monday, along with a girl agent who'd landed from M.G.B. 600.

Rosie.

Vidor had known her as 'Angel', but it could only have been her. He felt the shock like a kick in the balls. Blinking at the Frenchman for a moment before he found his voice. '*She* wasn't arrested – was she?'

'No. Fortunately.'

'Would you know, if she had been?'

'The report of his arrest originated with her. She was free then, for sure.'

He let his breath out slowly, thinking *God Almighty*. Imagining the sheer horror of it ... Vidor was saying, about the one who'd been arrested, 'A tough guy, fortunately.' Tapping his head: 'Tough *here*. But it's not the only problem we have, not at all ... Anyway – there's work to finish quickly, and I appreciate your offer, Lieutenant.' Glancing at the two sailors: 'These two speak no French, eh?'

'Not a word.' They were shaking their heads, Bright asking Farr 'Parly voo, monsewer?' Ben added, 'Let me tell you, we're a darn sight more grateful for what you're doing for *us*. Glad to help any way we can.' He added, in his own Australian-accented, fractured French – Vidor had been using French-accented English, slightly less fractured – 'After we've had some rest, if that's OK. Be more use to you then.' Then on a double-take – reminded by the tension in the Frenchman's weathered face – 'That arrest's not all, you say?'

'No. Unfortunately ... But I think only you, Lieutenant. The language problem, you see. Perhaps very difficult – dangerous, could be ... Yes. It's a pity, but – you alone.' He nodded. 'You sleep now, someone will come for you in the morning. Before sunrise, perhaps I myself.'

'Whatever you say.' He saw the point, more or less. If they were stopped and questioned they'd stand no chance at all of passing themselves off as locals: whereas he just might – to a German's ears, anyway.

'What's the rest of it, Vidor?'

'The rest ... Well – the number of Boches we have here suddenly. Too many, still more arrived today. We had something of the sort around Brest just recently, and I *hope* it's the same thing spreading this way, *not* Guillaume. But—'

'Guillaume?'

He wasn't thinking straight yet. They'd had this colossal meal – served shyly by the farmer's young, very pretty redheaded daughter, name of Solange – eaten it like famished goats, really did need to get their heads down for a few hours. *Then* – whatever ... Vidor was at the door – or hatchway, more like – glancing back at them: 'It will be all right, don't worry. Get some sleep. A few hours, I'll be back.'

He'd heard the gunboat leaving. Probably the worst moment of his life. Well, it was: *still* was, in memory. The stuff nightmares were made of.

It had been Farr – stroke oar – who'd heard it first, then there'd been thinner, wind-whipped shouts from seasick men in the dinghy's bow. They'd all been listening then, even Ben with his damaged hearing trying to sort out the bearing of that deep growl of engines as M.G.B. 600 moved out from her anchorage. She'd have to be on a northwesterly course, to clear the island: but *where* ... Competing noise from wind and sea was confusing: especially when you were half-deaf anyway. At one point he'd thought she might be coming straight towards them, sparking simultaneously the fear of being run down and the hope of being spotted and picked up: but the sound had faded quickly, leaving him with an appalling sense of failure, personal and professional ignominy.

All wind and sea noise, total darkness still, the dinghy throwing itself about: forcing himself to decide, through the shame of it, what the hell came next.

Well – bloody obvious. Get back to the island. If you could find *that* ...

The wind would have to be coming in over the port side – port bow, if such accuracy were possible. But they could have been forty yards out, or four hundred. Even steering that sort of course relative to the wind direction you could miss the island altogether, if during all this floundering around you'd been carried further down-wind than you'd reckoned.

He didn't think they could have been. He thought he wouldn't have heard that engine-noise so clearly if it hadn't been damn close. She'd have been on outers only, at low revs and silenced, and there was a *lot* of surrounding noise.

So hold this course now. Guessing at Hughes' state of mind: having already hung on longer than he should have, and with dawn not far off, the absolute necessity of having his ship well clear before first light. No option, he'd *had* to start out: but even so, leaving three of his own men and four passengers, he wouldn't be feeling exactly jolly.

Bright had yelled something, and Farr had half-turned his head, shouting an answer. All of their weight and strength combined in driving the boat up out of a trough, more black water slopping over here in the stern and the white stuff stinging, ice-cold: hitting the crest then and toppling, beginning the long fall bow-down but for a few seconds in the full force of the wind – where it took all *his* strength on the sweep-oar to keep her from broaching-to ... Farr had shouted 'Surf – right ahead!'

Meaning, Ben had thought, *somewhere* ahead. Probably Guenioc, but it could also have been one of the other islands, or rocks. When you were lost, you were lost: and when you couldn't see a damn thing and didn't have a compass, 'navigating' amounted to little more than hoping for the best. But tell *that* to these guys, who'd thought they'd be on the way home to England by this time: *would* have been, but for the bloody Aussie's fuck-up – was how they'd see it.

It was the truth too. How *he* saw it. Should have had a compass that worked, to start with – *he* should have seen to it that they had – and lacking one he should have had a grass line linking the boats. Not in tow, but in touch . . . He saw the island – the high white rim of surf, and a blackness behind it darker than the night – when they were already almost *on* it. The dinghy was lifting again and in a fresh rush of horizontal movement surging forward, Ben's weight on the sweep-oar again holding her against that tendency to wash round to port. Forget wind direction: keeping her stern to the sea was all that mattered. White water boiling gunwale-high as she scooted through it – stern up again, then, bow down – a savage jolt as the forefoot hit sand – only momentarily, thank God. If she'd stuck harder she'd have pivoted and capsized, there'd have been nothing he could have done about it – but she was lifted off in the next second, rushing on and then striking again – solidly enough but at a better angle, with a harsh grinding of sand under her flattish bottom all along her length. Bright and Farr were shipping their oars and leaping out one each side to steady the boat as it drove on, lightened by the loss of two men's weight: the passengers were out then too, helping to drag her up the beach.

There'd already been a faint lightness in the sky above Presqu'ile Sainte Marguerite. He was checking his surroundings while the others carried the dinghy up well out of the sea's reach. The beach was steeper here than at Nick Ball's landing place. If those were rocks to the right, he guessed they'd only just made it, the eastern end of the island. Sheer luck – if this *was* Guenioc. Touch wood, it had to be – with about the optimum chance of being taken off, he guessed, by Vidor and company. The only other island of comparable size was Tariec, which for any protracted stay would be uncomfortably close to the mainland lookout posts.

One thing was certain, anyway. This had been the last night of the moonless period: there'd be no gunboats calling in the next three weeks.

They'd still been only dark shapes here and there. Faces and personalities would come with the daylight: recriminations too, he supposed. So far they'd gone easy on him. Dark shapes, though, and low voices, finding themselves places where they could sit or sprawl. They'd put the boat in among rocks for cover and had climbed higher now, into an area where there were patches of low scrub. Bristol, the squadron leader, had suggested to the American – Hansen – that although they were the senior men in this party, Lieutenant Quarry knew more about the place than they did and it would make sense to accept his guidance.

Ben had shrugged, in the dark. 'Gluttons for punishment if you want more of *that*', but Hansen either hadn't heard him, or ignored it, agreeing with Bristol, 'That's good thinking … Let's have your views on our situation and prospects. Lieutenant. You'll have been here a few times before this, eh?'

'Never put a foot ashore – but yeah, I know the area – know *about* it. Enough to say we'd better keep our heads down, and not move around any more than we have to. Not in daylight anyway. Smoking'd be dangerous too. Well – down in the holes, those clefts, I suppose – but in daylight only; at night they'd see any match flare, and we'd have had it. If this *is* Guenioc there are German coastal defence positions there, there, and there – not to put too fine a point on it, roughly spitting distance.'

'We had to pass between two of 'em on our way down to the beach.'

'I suppose you would've.'

'Prospects, then?'

'Yes … Well, the gunboat – Hughes, my C.O. – will get a signal off to base as soon as he's far enough out to break wireless silence. With sea conditions as they are, he won't be making more than about twelve knots, so – four hours' time, say. Then London'll get on the air to the Resistance here. This evening, I'd guess, they can't listen out all day and night, only at certain times. By midnight, anyway, they may know we're here.'

'You say they may – not they *will*?'

'If they aren't listening out tonight, don't get any message—'

'But chances are they will, eh?'

'Let's hope so.'

'Right. So then, what?'

'Well – the long and short of it is this moonless period's finished. There'll be no gunboat pickups in the next three weeks.'

'Christ …'

'Truly have dropped you all in it, haven't I?'

'Sticking to practicalities' – Hansen again – 'they'll come

for us – the French will – say within a day or so – and hide us another three weeks – right?'

'Back to square bloody one.' Bristol's mutter was barely audible over the surf's roar. 'Spent the last fortnight cooped up—'

Ben cut across him: 'The moon'll be a limitation, for the French. We could get ourselves over to Tariec in the dinghy. I suppose – but another factor's the tide, for that slog across the sands.' He was thinking it out as he went along. 'We're stuck here for today, anyway. I suppose they might get to us – *might* – tomorrow night. I mean tonight – it's already tomorrow, isn't it?'

'Even with a moon, you're saying, they'll come out for us?'

'When it's set – *no* moon – why not? Can't be certain when, mind you – they might have other jobs on hand. The moon, though – should be well up before sunset, and set an hour or two after midnight. If they were ready to move between then and dawn – first light . . .' He checked himself: 'No – pre-dawn, *this* sort of time. Wouldn't want to cut it too fine.'

'If *they* can, why couldn't a gunboat?'

'We're here, on the spot. It's not like starting from more than a hundred miles away, with the approach from sea at least an hour, hour and a half say, in easy sight from shore, then another hour or two getting out again.'

'Right . . .'

'Wouldn't take Einstein, would it?'

That had been the other sergeant. Ben added, 'I'm assuming, meanwhile, this *is* Guenioc . . .'

It was. As dawn's pinkish light flooded the mainland and the sea, the scattering of islands, half-tide rocks with the sea sporadically pluming up above them, he'd identified all the landmarks. Tariec, for one – about the same size as this and halfway to the mainland coast, directly in the path of the rising sun. Then in more or less full daylight he'd found the container of weapons which Ball had stashed here two nights earlier. It was in a crevice and covered with loose stones and sand, but one corner had been visible. Ball and his boat's crew hadn't done a bad job, at that, considering they'd been working in the dark.

Come to think of it, the French might well be coming out to collect the stuff, some time soon. He'd mentioned this to Bristol, and the squadron leader had asked caustically. 'How soon? A week?'

With no food, no drink either – unless it rained. Bristol – rather froglike features under two or three days' stubble – had asked him, 'What's the distance to Tariec, from that end?'

'Seven hundred yards, roughly.' Visualizing the chart, which was pretty well imprinted on his memory. He could have drawn it quite accurately if he'd had a pencil and a sheet of paper. Wasn't a very experienced small-boat man, that was all – not without a bloody compass, or any mark or light ... He told Bristol, 'Less at low tide – more sand to cross, less rowing ... Low water'll be about ten, say. So eleven a.m. tomorrow, and the sand between Tariec and the mainland's passable about two hours each side of low water. So if by some miracle – like getting over to Tariec after moonset tonight—'

Hansen had joined them. Ginger stubble on a tanned face, ginger crewcut ... 'How about we do that. Then all we have to do after is look like we're gathering seaweed. God knows what for ...'

'Manure on their fields.'

'Huh. Learn one every day, don't you? But we wouldn't have the gear – forks, buckets, so forth. And coming, we had a guide, farmer's daughter, knows where the mines are. Gerries have laid mines along the shore there, do you know that?'

'Yes. There's always a guide laid on. Wouldn't risk it without one. Another problem'd be where we'd go – people around here are all strongly pro-Resistance, they say, but we might still knock on the one and only wrong door. Least, *I* might ...'

*

He'd spent most of the day asleep or dozing. Hunger gnawing, thirst too: asleep, dreams were mostly of food and drink. You had to keep out of the sun, finding shade among the rocks – because of the thirst factor, let alone the scorching. In intervals of wakefulness when he wasn't studying the weather – wind dropping, sea still rough but a lot less so than it had been – he thought mostly about Rosie. Half dreaming, on and off – on his back, on sand in a fissure between walls of rock – hearing his own voice that night in the London fog, *Fine navigator I'll make!*

She'd laugh, when he reminded her of it and told her about this balls-up. If he ever did get to tell her.

Bloody *have* to . . .

He knew – or thought he did – why she'd kept her distance, all this time. Because in the cold light of day – not the dawn, which had been beautiful, truly and seriously marvellous – later, getting-up time, *splitting*-up time, as it turned out – sober and by the looks of her as hungover as he'd been himself, for some reason she'd been critical of him for not having dossed down in the bath. Some fiction in her mind that he'd told her he was going to – which was plain barmy, would never have occurred to him . . . And she'd said – repeated – words to the effect that she'd never behaved that way in her life before. She'd remembered how it had been in the dawn, he'd guessed, and it had shocked her. Thrilled him, shocked her . . . She'd told him, effectively, that she wasn't that sort of girl, that what he was thinking about her simply wasn't damn well true, she was *not* like that – meaning she was not an easy lay, round-heeled, a pushover, etcetera, and ignoring his own fervent protests that it was most certainly *not* the way he thought of her. Might as well have been talking to a brick wall, though; and since then she'd kept her distance and silence, he guessed in the belief that if she'd agreed to see him again he'd have assumed she was ready for more of the same.

On those lines, anyway. That morning she'd paid no

attention to anything *he*'d said. He'd been on his knees at one stage, imploring her to listen, hear this, believe it ... She'd been *very* mixed up. Stood to reason – her husband being killed so recently, for one thing. Oh, God *yes* – she'd called his name. In the dawn – making love, the best he'd ever known it, really he'd learnt then how it *could* be – she'd called him not Ben, but Johnny.

The others were being very decent about all this, he'd thought. Not a word of blame. Although he, no-one else, was responsible for the fact they weren't in England by this time. *And* they were hungry and very, very thirsty.

Hansen's only comment had been 'Guess it could've happened to anyone.' He'd added, 'Nelson, even. Right?'

'Nelson would have made sure he did have a compass.'

Bristol, then, pointing skyward – he seemed to have got over his sulks – '*I've* been lost – up there. Had a compass all right, still got lost. Couple of times, to be honest. Anyway, you got us back on terra firma – which I can tell you I for one was glad of – to put it mildly.'

'Hear, hear. If that's life on the ocean wave—'

'You can have it.' McDonnell, sergeant-pilot, formerly of Cork City, agreed. Reminding his friend Dunlop, 'Spewed all over me, you bugger ... Sure they won't come back for us, even *with* that bloody thing?'

Meaning the new moon, a pale sliver well up and visible even this early – as Ben had known it would be. He told him no, not a chance. Three weeks ...

'*Here*?' Tommo Farr, the Welshman ...

'Always swim for it, couldn't we?'

'Where to?'

Chat: most of it pointless: only maintaining contact, confirming to themselves as the light went that they were all in the same hole together. Whys and wherefores and whose fault it was hadn't seemed to come into it – except for A.B. Bright musing at one stage, 'Beats me Mr Ball didn't stick close. Seeing as he had a fucking compass and he knew we didn't.'

'Had his own hands full. The same problems *we* had.' Ben had added, 'I was supposed to stick to him, not the other way about. Only wish now we'd had a line between us. A grass would've been the thing.'

'Could've been awkward, that, sir.'

Welsh intonation, through the darkness. Then Bright's mutter 'Not *this* fucking awkward.'

The true answer, Ben thought, was that he shouldn't have been looking for lights on shore, should have kept his eyes fixed on Ball's boat.

Squadron Leader Bristol came from Nettlebed, in Oxfordshire, Charles Hansen from Michigan, McDonnell was an Irishman and Sergeant-Pilot Dunlop was from Blyth, Northumberland. He and Hansen were the only married men in the party: the American had got himself tied up, as he put it, only a few days before leaving for England.

'Wish you hadn't now, do you?'

'Hell, no.' Then second thoughts: 'Well – *some* ways, maybe. Like right now, I guess ... You have a girl or two, Aussie, do you?'

'One, that matters.'

'And where's she?'

'Good question ...'

He'd wondered, while most of the others slept, where she might be, and doing what ... In fact she'd been in Rouen that Thursday night, her second night at the Bonhommes' bakery in Rue de la Cigogne, but of course all he'd known was that she had to be somewhere in France. Picturing her in his mind – and trying to understand *himself*, how he'd not thought about her much in the last year or so, then happened to glance up at the old paddle-steamer's rail, and – *incredibly* – there she'd been, and he was in it up to his eyes again.

The noise of the surf had a regular pattern to it, when you'd been listening to it for a while. What seemed at first to be a continuous roar had its separate components: the explosion and rush of each heavy sea crashing in, its thunder up the slope of the beach dissolving into a hiss of withdrawal just seconds before the next one ... The wind was down, he realized. By morning there'd probably be only a swell breaking on the beaches and very little white elsewhere.

Very little food, either. In fact none. No water either – and that was a lot worse. Bloody serious, in fact. But – tomorrow night – touch wood. If Vidor didn't show up then – well, just have to chance it, get ashore, moon or no moon. Licking cracked lips – and trying not to, trying to put thirst out of mind. How long could a man last without even a sip of water, he wondered?

'Quarry. Hey, Quarry ...'

'Huh?'

Hansen was crouching beside him: a shape in the darkness identifiable only by that Yank accent. Others were moving too, though: there were movements and voices in the background.

A *French* voice?

Dreaming ...

No moon, now. Early morning, therefore. Hansen telling him, 'Frog with a boat, Lieutenant, come to take us off.'

Sitting ... 'Vidor?' He called in French – what *he* called French – 'Is that Vidor there?'

'No. It's Léon ... Who's that, someone speaks French?'

'Damn little ...' He switched back into it, though – such as it was ... 'I'm Lieutenant Quarry, from the gunboat, M.G.B. 600.'

'You have a peculiar accent, you know that?'

'Pure Australian.'

'Ah. Well, never mind ... But listen – there are seven of you, that correct?'

'Yes. We've our own boat too.'

'OK. We'll use it. That's good – we have to take the guns, you see, the container. In your boat maybe, and tow it. Get over to Tariec now while it's dark enough, and later they'll come with a cart – for the *algue*, eh?' *Algue* meaning wrack, seaweed. Léon had climbed up to him: a man of about his own height, shaking hands with him and then more perfunctorily with the others. Ben tried his French again: 'I'd thought the best we could hope for was tomorrow night.'

'I was coming for the container anyway. There's trouble – we have to shift a lot of stuff – a lot more than *this*, I tell you. But there was a message about you so I brought the larger boat.'

'What kind of trouble?'

'Maybe none. *Could* be, that's all. Let's get a move on, hunh?'

They'd made it to Tariec, and hidden the dinghy high and dry and under a heap of rotting seaweed. Léon had stayed with them, watching the tide fall, and in mid-morning they'd seen the cart and a team of seaweed-gatherers coming out over the sand. They'd brought a barrico of water in the cart, also some bread and dried fish. The container had been loaded – on the blind side of the island – and the seven foreigners had climbed in too, under a covering of seaweed which had become heavier and wetter during the cart's slow transit back to the mainland, five Frenchmen – four plus Léon – sporadically tossing forkfuls of the wrack in on top of them, for the benefit of any watching German soldiery.

Then off the beach, up steeply on to a farm track, the men's shoulders at the wheels to help the poor old horse. Earthy Breton language . . .

At Broennou – at this farmhouse, on the edge of the coastal village, which had one of the German gun-emplacements immediately to the south of it – there'd been an ambulance waiting, a *gazogène* conversion which if its driver had been questioned would allegedly have brought the old farmer home after he'd had treatment for his gammy leg – he was *very* lame, his daughter Solange seemed to run the place – and the four airmen had transferred to it. There wouldn't have been room for more than three in the hayloft, so Ben and his two seamen were to stay here while the others were taken on to some other billet. Léon had shaken hands with everyone again, and disappeared, and Vidor had turned up when the three of them had been finishing an enormous tureen of fish, turnips and potatoes. It had been brought up to them in the loft by Alain – a boy of about sixteen with a mongoloid look about him, dribble on his chin – and ladled out into bowls by the daughter, Solange, who came up with Vidor. She had a shy smile and green eyes, spoke no English at all but seemed amused by Ben's Australian accent. Vidor told them when he arrived that she sometimes acted as a guide through the minefields on the foreshore.

The boy wasn't any relation. The farmer and his wife – Solange's long-dead mother – had taken him in years ago after his own family had thrown him out.

Vidor explained – in the dawn, riding bicycles side by side through deep, stony lanes – 'Our caches of munitions have to be moved to other locations as soon as possible. If we had more men we'd do it all at the same time, but we're too few for that. So your offer to help's most welcome.'

'Because you've lent some for this sabotage job?'

'Exactly.' He'd mentioned it last night. 'All happening at once. As always.'

'The action's at Brest, you said?'

'*Near* Brest. A factory at St Renan. They make periscope sections for U-boats.'

'Worthy cause.' He nodded, stooped over the handlebars. 'I'm definitely *for* that.'

'Unfortunately there's always a reaction. Hostages, so forth. One doesn't mount such an operation without the best of reasons. But this one was planned weeks ago. So happens, it could have a beneficial effect – for *us* – if some of the troops they've been deploying here were withdrawn to police the St Renan district, after this. The Master Race sometimes act like headless chickens, you know?'

'Why should the next-door *réseau* need your people?'

'Because of the security clampdown in their area. It's made complications for them.'

'Ah. Suppose it would. Although from what you say you're getting a similar state of affairs here now ... Can you tolerate another question?'

'Why not?'

'Couldn't this factory be hit from the air?'

'It could. But there are houses close all round it – very close. Bombing's not always so accurate, is it? Our way, explosives are placed on the machines or in them, it's certain – and families living nearby aren't hurt.'

'Except for the reprisals?'

'You see, we can't give in to that. We'd be living on our knees. What they *want*, the bastards.'

'There'll be a guard on the place, presumably?'

A grunt. 'Such things will have been taken into account.'

'They'll have their throats cut, you mean.'

'Well – could be *greater* tragedies ... Turn to the right here.'

'I see what you meant about not needing *us* here, just at this moment.'

'Never mind. I'm grateful for your help. Anyway, if they withdraw some of their soldiers it won't be so bad. Depends – I think – on whether or not this infestation is connected with the arrest of Guillaume. I hope *not* ... But he was carrying explosive with him, you see. Figure it to yourself – if they get to believe there's a dump on this small neck of land – a farmer with a cache on his place, say – if they take his wife and children, shut them in the barn and tell him they'll put a match to it. Huh? If *you* were that farmer?'

'Christ ...'

'They've done such things before. And look – if for instance our man is able to hold out – in Paris, Avenue Foch or Rue des Saussais, wherever, poor sod – but if they only know he was here or nearby, it would be enough. Or of course if they break him. They haven't yet – if they had they'd have been here. He may be dead ...'

'Meanwhile you move the stuff anyway.'

'Certainly. We ourselves could disperse at short notice.

Join the Maquis, for instance. Those without wives or children anyway, it's much easier for us. But the rifles, machine guns, mortars, ammunition – we've all risked our necks for it – so have you, *your* people – and one day – soon, please God—'

'Hey, look—'

Lights ahead. Car or lorry, facing this way. It was stationary, by the look of it. Waste of its battery: it was virtually daylight now. Vidor said, 'If it's police or Germans – act dumb.' Peering ahead, slowing slightly but not by much. 'I'll talk for both of us. You're my assistant – Félix, all right?'

The only Felix he'd ever heard of was a cartoon cat.

'I've no papers, if—'

'I'm on my way to castrate a donkey. I need you only to sit on the animal's head while I do it. You're a bit slow on the uptake – you don't articulate too well, either.'

It was a *Wehrmacht* troop-transport. Lights burning but no-one on or in it, and no barrier on the road. But there was a cottage – farmhouse, maybe – set back to the left, a light glimmering in an upstairs window – candle or lantern maybe . . . A shout – German-sounding, but some way off, from the direction of the house. Vidor gritted, 'Keep going. We're in luck.' That they hadn't left even a driver with the truck, he must have meant. Vidor put all his weight on the pedals, pushing the bike along hard, Ben doing the same although he'd dropped in behind him, about a length between them. Passing through the aura of the transport's yellow lights: then Vidor was out of it, and so was he: there'd been no more shouts. Vidor glancing round: 'Made it. Left fork in a minute.'

He was easing off, and they were coming to the fork. Tall hedges overhanging, cutting out enough light to put the clock back by an hour or so. Side by side again: Vidor told him, 'That *was* lucky. For *us* . . . This is a slightly longer route, a way *they* won't take.'

'Pointing the other way – wasn't it?'

'Nothing to stop them turning. When they've finished whatever they're doing at the Demorêts. It won't be just a social call, for sure.'

'Farmers, are they?'

'They raise ducks and turkeys. Damn it, I can guess what the swine *may* be there for . . .'

The shot came sharp as a whipcrack – rifle-shot, therefore – from somewhere behind them. A single shot, then a pause, and then a rattle of automatic fire, its echo fading into what sounded at first like a dog's howl but resolved itself into a human scream. A woman – in horror, despair, extreme of pain . . . Imagination played its part: the scream had been cut short and one envisaged a blow, a rifle-butt . . . Vidor shouted 'Keep going. I'll come back, later. Christ Almighty . . .'

He fell silent – more or less – and Ben kept quiet too. It wasn't time for comment or for questions. Being out of one's element and having an enquiring mind – as well as fairly acute anxiety – one tended to ask too many, anyway. Uphill stretch here, legs aching from strains they weren't used to . . . Vidor burst out with it suddenly: 'They have a son who escaped from a work-camp in Germany, arrived back here in the middle of the night – a month or six weeks ago. It happens often enough, I may say, I know of several who've done it, but this Demorêt lad – Youen, that's his name – was lying low at home instead of going to join the Maquis right away. If he's still there – Christ, his parents face a death penalty for harbouring him, even. How d'you like that – for "harbouring" your own son?'

'Where's the Maquis, that he'd have joined?'

'All over. Mountainsides, forest areas – wild parts, not easily accessible. Some bands are several hundred strong, others much smaller.'

'Do the Boches leave them alone?'

'Go after them sometimes. Sometimes they send their French units. *So-called* Frenchmen.'

This had to be Landeda now, though. A scattering of houses and hovels thickening considerably ahead. Church

spire ahead too, with the sun behind it like a skewered
orange. The garage was on the outskirts of the village, was
all Vidor had told him: having done enough pedalling for
one morning, he hoped it might be on *this* side of it.

Vidor muttered, 'Didn't *have* to be looking for the
Demorêt boy, though. Could be just taking pot luck. Some
ways, that could be worse ... Incidentally, we're going to
have to move you anyway, before long.'

'Is there a connection?'

A grunt. 'As much as anything, it is the strain on such a
small *ménage*. Food and cooking, for one thing – Solange
doesn't have many minutes to spare, in her days. Not really
the resources either. But mostly, it's bloody dangerous for
them – *and* too close to our islands, eh?'

To Guenioc and Tariec, he'd have meant.

'So you'll move us – where to?'

'I don't know yet. But if they're going to start searching
isolated farms like the Demorêts' – Jesus Christ ...' Then:
'Sorry. But they're such good people. The best. Or they
were. You know, I can't believe it – that we actually *heard*
it ...' And after another pause: 'Might not be easy for us to
stay in business here, the way things look.'

'The pinpoint?'

'It's – a possibility. One has to be ready for such
contingencies.'

'Would you get out, yourself?'

'No. I've my job here. I mean the farms, the animals.
Léon has his too – he's a farmer's son but he has a boat,
spends most of his time fishing and potting for crabs and
lobsters. And Luc – our radio man – he has his own job too
– works in the café – he'd stick around. Well – touch wood,
if we were left alive and free, in this hypothetical situation ...'

'As you see it, it *is* only hypothetical, then.'

'It's as I say – to be ready for it – for *whatever*—'

'Another thing I was going to ask – what about our boat,
down there?'

'It's still there. Well covered. The best place it could be, right now.'

'But if they found it—'

'Then it's curtains.'

'Couldn't we land it – in that cart, under seaweed?'

'You'd need to hide it somewhere ashore. Anyone would know at a glance it's not a local boat. Not easy to hide, either. Break it up – that's possible ... But the best way is the next moonless time, next gunboat visit – you take it with you, eh?'

'If there *is* another gunboat visit here. And it stays hidden for a fortnight.'

'Exactly. One can only – keep one's nerve, say one's prayers ... Down here now, we've arrived.'

The garage was at the bottom of a short cul-de-sac. It was a rickety-looking barn made of tarred planking: wide doors standing open, semi-wrecked vehicles dumped all over about half an acre of dockweeds. Vidor freewheeled down the pot-holed slope and straight in, calling as he dismounted 'Anyone home?'

'Ah. It's you.'

Ben followed him down, and in, dismounting. Preparing to be introduced – as the village idiot, no doubt, more or less incapable of speech. He could guess what had put that in Vidor's mind – the boy at the farm, Alain. And he'd be looking the part well enough, he guessed, in the old farmer's ancient gear – patched work-trousers, torn jacket, a sweater with holes in it and one sleeve mostly unravelled. The girl had brought this lot to him, at Vidor's request. He hadn't shaved for a couple of days either. Must look bloody marvellous, he thought: stand me in a field, keep *all* the crows away ... Vidor was shaking hands with a shrimp-like, elderly man in clean brown overalls. Long chin, small hooked nose, wisps of grey hair plastered across his scalp. Vidor introduced them: 'Paul Durand ...' Jerk of a thumb: 'Call this one Félix. He's kindly offered to help. Doesn't talk much French and he has no papers – keep him out of sight, eh?'

'No French and no papers. Gift from the gods, I *don't* think.' The little man hadn't shaved much lately, either.

'I do talk *some* French.'

'What sort of accent's that?'

'Would you believe Australian?'

They heard the lorry then: firing on no more than three cylinders, backing down the slope – and finally, into the barn. The man at the wheel, craning round to look backwards, could have been a farmer. Durand called 'Jacques, come here!' in a high, noise-penetrating yelp, and a boy in oily dungarees appeared, still chewing, from some nether region. Vidor and the lorry driver were shaking hands, and the driver – a big man with a large belly – was telling him, 'A lead off one plug, is all. Others are oily anyway, but I want 'em that way, we'll break down again at Bodilis, see . . . How's it with you, then? Boches a bit too thick on the bloody ground, aren't they?'

'When we passed, they were paying the Demorêt place a visit. There was some shooting.'

'Bloody hell . . .'

'I'm going back there – snoop around—'

'Well, for Pete's sake—'

'From the back, across the fields. I'll be like a mouse.'

'Yeah. Mice get caught, remember.'

The inspection-pit, immediately behind the lorry, was stacked with rifles, Sten guns and ammunition. The boy Jacques was prising up the boards that covered it, using an iron bar. Vidor explained to Ben, drawing him aside, that the old man – Durand – would busy himself now with the malfunctioning engine, at the same time keeping his eyes open for unwelcome visitors, while Ben, the driver and the boy would load the cargo into the back of the lorry, then rope a tarpaulin over it and on top of that spread a load of scrap-iron.

'That lot there. For the railway siding at Landivisiau, supposedly – en route to the Ruhr, they send whole truckloads when they have them full. But you'll be stopping en route at a church where the *curé* has a tomb open and ready for this lot, he's expecting you. The lorry'll have more engine trouble, young Jacques'll be working on it while you unload. But listen – there'll be another transfer you can help with tomorrow – the last, thank heaven – so best stay here tonight – in Durand's house – over there. He'll give you a meal and a bed. I'll see you tomorrow. Meanwhile I'll try to move your men from old Brodard's place. I think that's wise ... See you tomorrow, anyway.'

'By then will you have had news about the action at St Renan?'

'Before that. This morning, I expect.'

He put his hand out. 'Good luck.'

'Same to you. And thanks.'

Calling *au revoir*s to the others, then, Vidor wheeled his machine out into the slanting early sunshine. Ben wondered as he went to work what the hell would happen if Vidor – the king-pin in all of this – ran into trouble at the turkey farm, got himself shot or arrested. Stooping to grab the rope handle of an ammo box: thinking *Bloody chaos* ...

10

At Lyons-la-Forêt, a German army car with a general's flag on its bonnet drove in through the entrance to the Hôtel de la Licorne; as soon as it was inside, the wooden gates were pushed shut, a trooper with a slung rifle emerging just before they actually closed, to mount guard outside on the pavement. Either the general had the hotel to himself and meant to keep it that way, or he was joining others already in there. A staff conference, or somesuch. Or a party. Whatever it might be, it was an obscenity, in this peaceful, beautiful old French village.

There was another inn, Rosie saw – Le Grand Cerf – fifty metres farther along and on the same side as the Licorne. Might as well use that one, she decided.

She'd only known of the Licorne, but a pub was a pub, what the hell ... Outside it, she propped her bicycle carefully at the kerb. It was a relief to be off that saddle, too. She'd been on it for about the last eight hours, for Pete's sake ... Without hurrying now, she untied the strings which had been holding her sample-case and the tatty old leather-and-canvas bag which Madame Bonhomme had lent her, and took them with her into the Grand Cerf, passing under the big inn-sign of a stag with enormous antlers. It was a very old, half-timbered building, its plaster nearer yellow than off-white.

Gloomy, inside. Small windows, low ceilings, dark paint-work. Coolish, anyway. Two old men in a corner, staring at her, their eyes on her as she entered but then shifting – like lizards' eyes, she thought – to watch the approach of a waiter – barman, whatever he might be. Wooden-soled shoes loud on the bare boards . . . 'Help you? Want a room?'

Having seen that she had luggage, of course: reasonable question, therefore. He was a squat, plump boy, smooth-cheeked, wearing a striped apron over shiny-seated serge trousers. She shook her head: 'I don't know. I'll tell you later. Meanwhile I'd like a long, cold drink. Lemonade, d'you have?'

He nodded. 'Anything to eat?'

'D'you have a sandwich?'

'Sausage?'

'Fine.'

She sat down, and lit a cigarette, fully aware that she could well have done justice to a proper meal, but for the time being only needing something to keep her going. She'd only come in here to ask for directions and in the course of doing so to leave a reason for (a) being in Lyons-la-Forêt and (b) visiting that particular individual – who might in fact offer her a meal. But if anyone had any interest in her presence here, an enquiry here might satisfy them.

It had, really, been a hell of a long bike-ride. The hardest bit had been right at the start, a long, steep climb southeastward out of town. She'd taken the quieter, country route – out through St Aubin and Montmain, more of a lane than a road, but actually more direct and for someone on a bicycle just as fast – or slow – as the main road past the airfield at Boos. It was a Luftwaffe station now, of course, with Junkers 52 transports in and out all day, every day. She'd seen one this morning, from the road she'd been on. At that early stage, on the fairly open and straight section between St Aubin and Epinay, she'd stopped several times to look back, to see whether she was being followed. With Romeo in mind, primarily. He *had* seemed to her to be sound enough – as far as you could ever tell – and she'd thought his story held water, but only an idiot wouldn't hedge her bet, in all the circumstances.

He'd been *very* keen to know where she was going.

But then again, wouldn't anyone, in his position? Especially as this had been solely *his* territory for quite a while?

No-one had followed her, anyway. No *gazogène* starting and stopping, a man with a mop of grey hair behind its wheel, keeping her in distant sight. There'd been no roadside checks either: rounding each corner she'd been ready for it, but – her lucky day, it seemed.

Romeo, though . . . Having all that time on the road, alone and with time to think it all over, she'd admitted to herself that she found him attractive. Recalling the tentative advance he'd made – not just the compliment, but the tone and his expression at that moment – and that she'd been surprised, slightly indignant even, to have such an approach from a man she'd met only an hour before and who was old enough to be her father. But – with hindsight – that might be most of the attraction, she reflected. Being completely alone, scared stiff inside her shell: then suddenly here's a friend, someone to lean on – in César's absence – and one with a certain charm, at that . . .

As well to recognize it, she thought. Ensure it didn't affect one's judgement.

If it hadn't already?

Baker Street would know by this time that he was willing to take a vacation. She'd diverted from her route shortly after passing Epinay, pedalling up a track through sparse woodland, then hidden her bike in the ditch, fought her way through brambles and nettles and strung the Mark III's seventy feet of cotton-thin aerial wire over gooseberry bushes, coded the message, put on her headphones and – after getting a 'go ahead' from Sevenoaks – tapped it out. By this time it would have reached Baker Street by dispatch rider. *In contact Romeo but César was not at R/V 15th. Louis reports Pension d'Alsace in Lyon has become mousetrap. Romeo accepts invitation to home leave, please send pickup details soonest*. Finishing the transmission, she'd asked the

Sevenoaks operator whether there was any message for her, but there hadn't been, and she'd signed off.

The gooseberries were delicious.

It had been a very hot day, as well as a long, hard one. She knew she'd be as stiff as a plank when she woke up in the morning. *Where* she'd be waking – in a bed or a ditch, for instance – time would tell. A bed was always preferable not only from the point of view of comfort but because when you'd slept in a ditch you usually looked as if you had. Beds tended to be closer to sources of sustenance, as well. If the man she'd come to see proved inhospitable she might well come back to this pub.

'Here you are,' – the plump boy's eyes flickered towards her wedding ring – 'Madame.'

'Thank you.'

'Come far?'

She nodded: glancing round, and seeing that the two old peasants were listening. 'Far enough ... Does your father own this place?'

He shook his head as if regretfully. 'Uncle.'

'You're local, anyway. Perhaps you can help me. To start off with, I need to find the school. Is it right in the village?'

He'd glanced at the old men, then back at her. 'Where you turn up from the main road. Other side of it – grey stone building, and you'll see the yard ... Teacher, eh?'

'No. I'm not a teacher.'

'Sorry. Just that we don't get many strangers here, these days.'

'I have a small daughter. She'll need to go to school – not yet, but soon enough – and the *professeur* might know of some possible foster-home locally. I don't want her in Rouen when the bombing starts again. I suppose you don't know of anyone?'

He didn't. She finished her lemonade, went out and got back on her bicycle. She'd been looking for the right-turn up to the village, not to her left, where he'd told her the school was. Not that it mattered – a couple of hundred yards, and downhill at that.

*

'Madame Lebrun?'

A nod. Skinny little woman, between thirty and forty: she had an alert, youngish face but there were streaks of grey in her dark hair, which was drawn back tightly into a bun. Rosie told her, 'I'm Jeanne-Marie Lefèvre. I've cycled here from Rouen –' she pointed at her bicycle, which she'd leant against the playground wall – 'actually to see your husband, about my daughter Juliette.'

'Do we know of her?'

'Oh, no. She's with her grandmother at the moment – in Brittany, as it happens. I'm starting a job based in Rouen but with a great deal of travelling involved, and if I could find somewhere – a foster-home, perhaps a family with other children – I could come out and see her at weekends. I really *must* have her closer to me, but not in Rouen, because—'

'You'd better come in.' She called, 'Georges! A Madame Lefèvre here to see you.'

'Madame Lefèvre . . .'

Shaking hands . . . He was a lean man, grey-headed – probably ten years older than his wife – in shirtsleeves and a waistcoat, grey bow-tie. Greyish complexion, too. He'd emerged from a room on the right, into the square, stone-paved hall. There was a strong schoolroom odour – unmistakable, a blind person would have known where she was. Lebrun ushered her into the room he'd come out of: 'I heard you say you'd cycled all the way from Rouen. You must be exhausted?'

'Well – I *am*, a bit . . .'

She'd left her sample-case on the bicycle. But there was no-one around, out there, and it might have looked odd, bringing it into their house with her. Once they knew who she was, it would be different . . . She was glancing round: at hard chairs encircling a round table with a brown cover on it – one chair pulled back, a heap of papers in front of it, a pen and a pot of red ink on a blotter – and sepia-toned photographs of groups and individuals all over the walls.

Above the fireplace, an oil painting of a man very much like this Lebrun except that he had mutton-chop whiskers. The schoolmaster had seen her glance at it: he murmured, 'My dear father. Tragically struck down, alas, in the full flower of his youth.'

'How very sad . . . Monsieur, I apologize for this intrusion—'

'Not at all, madame,' indicating a chair across the table from his own: 'Please . . .'

His wife remained standing, close at his side; he was peering at Rosie over his glasses, waiting for her to begin. He was nothing like she'd expected.

'I think you may have had word in advance that I'd be calling on you. If the name Lefèvre doesn't ring a bell – the fact is, a lot of my friends call me "Angel".'

'Oh.' He took his glasses off. '*Oh.*' Glancing round at his wife: 'Check that the lock's on the door please, Béa.' Turning back to her; without glasses, and suddenly eager-looking, really quite different. 'We *were* told to expect you. A mutual friend from – oh—'

A frown, as if it had slipped his memory . . .

'From Beauvais?'

'Beauvais, indeed.' Smiling at her: 'You're *very* welcome, Angel. Especially if it means we'll at last be getting what we've been asking for?'

'Yes. I'm sorry we've kept you waiting. Various problems – bad ones, I'm afraid.'

'So one heard.' A nod, pursed lips. 'So one heard.'

From Romeo, she guessed. He'd have been asking them to be patient.

'But we're back in harness now. It's set up for next weekend. Two drops, simultaneous, one near Chênes and the other at Hêtre de Bunodières. With a diversionary bombing raid on the Boche ammunition dump at La Haye starting five minutes before the drops. The Bunodières delivery's for the Beauvais *réseau*. They'll complain it's a long haul for them, but it's a field we've used before, and the attack on La Haye will cover theirs as well as yours, so it's clearly to their advantage. Now, the thing is – can you make arrangements for both receptions, if I leave you all the details? Alternatively, could you persuade the Beauvais *chef de réseau* to visit us here? Tomorrow, or Sunday?'

On her way back to Rouen on the Monday morning she stopped in the forest near Sainte Honorine and sent off another message to Baker Street: *Reception of Operations Tractor One and Tractor Two arranged.*

One job done, anyway. They could arrest her now or shoot her dead, those two drops would go ahead and the munitions would be received by those who'd been waiting for them – L'Armée des Ombres, as the Maquis was sometimes called, in whispers.

Army of the Shadows . . .

Pierre Juvier, the *réseau* chief from Beauvais, had come to lunch at the schoolhouse yesterday, arriving in a *gazo* and bringing his wife with him. Both of them large, loud-voiced, complete contrasts to their host and hostess. He was a building contractor and worked almost solely for the Germans now – which explained his having a licence for the *gazogène*, Rosie had supposed.

He'd told her, 'The simple reason is, no-one else is building anything much at this time,' and Madame Juvier had put in 'Call us *collaborateurs* if you like – one has to live, that's all. Why not take *their* money?'

Lebrun murmured, 'And cut their throats in one's spare time, eh?'

'Exactly!' A shriek of laughter. 'Best of both worlds, eh?'

Later on, Rosie had asked him, 'Seriously, it doesn't worry you that some people might regard you as *collaborateurs*?'

'Only the most ignorant. Those who sit on the sidelines – which is the reason they *are* ignorant.' Juvier had added, glowering, 'When the hour strikes, *I*'ll know who was with us and who wasn't!'

The location of the para-drop hadn't worried him at all,

although it was to be about forty kilometres from Beauvais. He'd told her, 'We won't be hauling the stuff that far, in any case.' A heavy arm around her shoulders: 'No problem, Angel!'

Lunch had consisted of a roast chicken, apple tart and cheese, Madame Lebrun explaining that the chicken had been a gift from a grateful parent. Rosie had noticed during her two days and three nights with them that they didn't do themselves too badly, anyway. They had their own laying hens and grew vegetables, and she guessed there was a lot of barter going on. Juvier's contribution to the meal had been some bottles of Rhône wine which he'd told her was reserved entirely for consumption by the Occupying Power.

'Don't ask how it happens *we're* consuming it!'

Their 'shop' talk had been mostly after lunch, some of it in Lebrun's study with a large-scale map spread on the desk, and then strolling in the vegetable garden, Rosie and her host both dwarfed by the hulking Juvier. Rosie had done most of the talking at first, going over the details of the drops and the confirmatory message which the BBC would put out on two consecutive days – twice on the actual day, which weather permitting would be Saturday. The broadcast phrase was to be *Ma belle-soeur est devenue malade*.

'Poor bitch.' Juvier's fat chuckle. He'd had twice as much wine as anyone else. Taking Rosie's arm: 'Thank God for this, my dear ... As a matter of interest, though, what about Le Cocher's crowd? The last drop was to have gone to him, wasn't it?'

She didn't know – hadn't ever heard of 'Le Cocher'. Glancing round at Lebrun, who murmured, 'He's an *ex*-Cocher, now.'

'D'you mean he's dead?'

A nod. Stooping to make a close examination of a cauliflower; there were a lot of the white butterflies about. Juvier asked him, '*Literally* dead?'

'I don't know about literally.' Lebrun straightened, and winked at Rosie. 'Physically – yes.'

'I meant,' – scowling, irked by such pedantry from the schoolmaster – 'you could have said "dead" meaning he was out of it as far as the *réseau* was concerned. Who's in his place?'

'I am, for the moment. But I've told 'em to lie low for a while.'

She'd noticed that Juvier hadn't asked how this 'Le Cocher' person had met his death. Probably in the course of some sabotage operation. Otherwise, why would the others have needed to lie low?

In mid-morning, having started out soon after dawn, she ran into a roadblock at the Le Mesnil-Claque crossroads – about halfway to Rouen. There was a *Wehrmacht* truck parked right on the intersection and police barriers across both the road she was on and the one that crossed it; two farm lorries ahead of her had pulled in and were being searched, and there was another facing this way. At first sight – the immediate shock, that tightness in the gut – she'd murmured aloud *Curses, here we go again* – making a kind of terse non-joke to herself while preparing for the worst – which would start with the discovery of her radio. She'd warned herself over and over during this journey that she couldn't expect to get away with it every time, *all* the time, that a cat had only nine lives, etcetera ... But when she got there, dismounting, a policeman impatiently waved her through. Police were doing the searching, Boches just standing by, and they were checking lorry-drivers' loads and papers, weren't interested in girls on bicycles with all their worldly goods tied on with string.

Marc Pigot told her, 'Sorry. It's gone.'

The case she'd left here, with the money in it.

Staring at him: horrified, thinking *It can't be ...*

Except it *could*. Thanks to her own damn stupidity. Despite having been warned, at that. Oh, *Christ* ...

She'd stopped at the garage on her way into town to tell him she'd pick it up later, and ask what time he'd be shutting. It was three-thirty: she had to get down to the bordello on the Rive Gauche, dump the stuff she had with her and then come all the way back again. On Friday morning she'd brought the case here with her, but only the comparatively short distance from Rue de la Cigogne, and with the other stuff she'd been carrying even that hadn't been too easy.

She'd found Pigot working on a *gazogène* van. The elderly mechanic didn't seem to be here today,

She'd found her voice . . . 'What d'you mean, it's *gone*?'

'I'll show you.' He led her to a wheel-less wreck of an old Ford, fumbled for a key and opened its rusty boot. Standing back, to give her room. 'Gone, see?'

There were other things in there, but not her case. She thought – in shock – *Romeo*.

'Martin Hardy—'

'I put it in here when you brought it – remember? Friday morning, wasn't it?'

Gazing at her: as if more interested in her reaction than his own responsibility. It was simply too frightful: to have absolutely fouled it up, through one's own senseless misjudgement . . . She muttered again. 'Hardy . . .'

'Yeah. There's your culprit.' He was sniggering, suddenly. 'Your chum Martin, *that*'s who!'

'I don't understand—'

'Having you on, that's all. Jesus, you're white as a sheet!'

'So where—'

'Doing you a favour, wasn't he – dropping it off at Ursule's.' Pausing, the smile fading . . . 'Haven't been there yet, eh?'

'*It* had damn well better be there!'

'Well – why wouldn't it?'

A million and a quarter francs suggested that it might not be . . . But the cloud was lifting: in the last couple of minutes she'd been questioning her own sanity, in having trusted him to the extent she had . . .

'Is he in town?'

'Uh-huh. Back tomorrow, he said. When he left –
Saturday – he knew he'd be going right past Ursule's. That's
why . . . Look, I better tell you how to find her place . . .'

The house was narrow and had three storeys, was actually
one half of what a hundred or more years ago had been a
convent. Telling Rosie this, Ursule smiled round at her over
her shoulder – leading her along the top-floor passage, after
all those stairs . . . She was in her thirties, small and rounded,
her hourglass figure indicative of tight stays. Mousey-
coloured hair piled up, with combs in it. She added, 'The
nuns would be screaming blue murder, poor dears.'

'Monsieur Hardy did mention—'

'I bet he did.' A shrug, shake of the small head . . . 'Don't
worry, you won't be bothered. It only happens that – well,
you let one of them move in, she likes it and tells a friend,
and so on.' She stopped at the third or fourth door: the house
had more depth than breadth. 'You won't be the only lodger
who's not a whore, my dear – you can be sure of that. I don't
allow 'em to entertain their customers on the premises,
either. What they do when they aren't here's not my
business, is it?'

'Absolutely not . . .'

'Heavens knows where they do it. I'd rather *not* know.'

It wasn't a bad room at all. Quite large, and simply but
adequately furnished. She noticed this *after* seeing her bag
on the foot of the bed, with its padlock still in place: she
dumped her sample-case beside it, and Ursule put down the
other one.

'It'll suit me very well, I think.'

Except – she was at the window – there was no fire
escape, for quick or surreptitious exits. A metal fire escape
was good for connecting an aerial to, as well. Ursule was
telling her, 'The only meal I provide is breakfast – on the
ground floor between seven and nine. I'll need some ration
coupons, of course, but there's no hurry. If you want other
meals locally, there's a café just round the corner – Café

Saint Sever. It's not bad, not too expensive either.'

Which was more than *she* could claim, Rosie thought. They'd discussed money downstairs, and the rooms weren't cheap. One was paying, no doubt, for a certain discretion – whether you were an agent, or a tart.

Alone, she first unlocked the bag and checked that all the money was there, feeling some shame at having suspected Romeo – except that you had to suspect everyone, until you knew them. And even *then* ... Could have been in Romeo's mind, too, she realized. Convincing her of his integrity: if he had bigger fish to fry?

At a million-plus, they'd be damned expensive fish.

Exerting muscle-power, she forced the sash window up and leant out, taking in the panorama of roofs and chimneys, one church spire in the foreground and – at much greater distance northeastward – that of the cathedral, on Rive Droite. The river wasn't visible. More interesting to her, anyway, was the drop from this window and what other windows might be directly under it: thinking of the aerial wire of the Mark III dangling across them when she paid it out.

There were shutters, though, latched back. If she pushed the wire out between the slats, fiddled the rest of it through and pushed it out to the end ... If the lower windows were directly below this – they would be, surely – it would hang down a foot and a half to the side, not across them. That was the answer. It was fine wire, and black, non-reflective, you'd have to be looking for it to see it.

Not that she was intending to make any transmissions from this room, but she'd be listening out – for details of Romeo's pickup, for instance – and on occasion would need to blip off an acknowledgement.

11

Tuesday: she was at Chez Jacqui a minute before nine: pushing in to find Jacqueline Clermont busy on the telephone – glancing her way and recognizing her, smiling, wiggling the fingers of one hand. Her assistant, Estelle, in the same pale blue smock with the darker entwined letters CJ on the left shoulder, also looking round, from cleaning one of the basins: 'Good morning, madame.'

Jacqui was now holding the phone at arm's length, raising her eyes to heaven while a shrill voice gabbled, like Donald Duck's except that it was female; when it paused for breath Jacqui said quickly, 'Tomorrow afternoon at three, then. Forgive me, I've a *horde* of customers. Until tomorrow.'

She hung up. 'One of *those*. Imagine when it's in here, going on two or three hours. As I think I mentioned ...'

'Earning your living the hard way.'

'And I hope' – a glance at the sample-case – 'you've begun to earn yours?'

Rosie put the case down, beside one of the chairs in which customers could wait. Bright cushions, magazines. It weighed a lot less than it had done: she'd loosened a floorboard under the bed in her room at Ursule's and hidden both the Mark III and the money in there. The board hadn't been loose to start with and didn't *look* loose now.

Touch wood. A vision of Romeo waiting across the street to see her leave. It was less a matter of maligning him than of questioning her own judgement.

Straightening, she shook her head. 'Truth is, I'm pinning a few hopes on *you*.'

'But I did warn you—'

'I know, but—'

'The *real* truth is – forgive me for speaking frankly – well, there must be a small market for your perfumes, but it'd be a miracle if you could live on it. People don't have money to splash out, these days. Anyway, not many. Germans perhaps – French perfumes to send home as presents to their women – *that's* a possibility.'

'Do you have German customers?'

'A few. Not men, of course. But the men window-shop, don't they – and they'd tell each other ...' Checking the time: 'Oh, God ... Look, if you don't mind, we'd better make a start. I tell you what – if you'd like to, you could come this evening, we could talk then?'

'I'd love that!'

'So ... My last customer,' – she opened her appointment book – 'last one should be out of here by – six. Suppose you come at seven? Then we won't be interrupted – upstairs. I can sniff all your lovely fragrances?'

'But that'd be perfect!'

'I'd like it too. Fine, that's settled. Now – here you are. Cut, wash and set?'

'Please.' She sat down: a blue cotton surplice swung, settled around her. Looking up at the clock: 'How long, d'you think? Two hours?'

'About that. A snag sometimes is the power supply. The dryers can be erratic in their performance.'

'I asked because I have an appointment I *must* keep, soon after eleven.'

'We'll step on it, then. But first' – ruffling Rosie's brown hair – 'what to *do* with this?'

'It's a bit of a mess, isn't it?'

'To be frank again, my dear, it looks as if it's been bitten off in lumps ...'

'Well – a young Parisian did it, as it happens – and at the time—'

'Even worse before that, was it? Would you leave it to me, to do what I can?'

'Yes. Please. As long as I can be out of here at eleven.'

'Good-looking, is he?'

'What?'

'Your mid-morning date. Good-looking – rich?'

'It's not that kind of date at all.'

Estelle was on the telephone. Jacqui murmured, 'Don't you *have* a man friend yet?'

'Not in Rouen. Heavens, I only got here last Wednesday!'

'With your looks you should have been beating them off with a stick by Thursday!'

Smiling into the mirror: 'Don't have a stick.'

'You'd need one, if you took yourself in hand, a little. This hair, to start with – OK, we'll fix that – but also make-up – and perhaps a splash of your own scent – and try not to look so worried—'

'Didn't know I did.'

'This job you've taken on, I suppose.'

'Anyway – I'd still be an ugly duckling beside *you*.'

The smile was involuntary – as if she'd touched an electric button. She thought, *Bull's-eye* … following it up with 'I'll tell you honestly – first sight I had of you, I thought *Hollywood would absolutely snap her up*!'

'*What* a happy thought …'

'Must have occurred to you, surely. Wouldn't it appeal to you – if it were possible?'

'*If* …' Scissors were in play now, 'As a young girl, I suppose one might have had such thoughts. Day-dreams. But then – well, the money would be nice, I'd like *that* part of it …'

'You're not married – don't wear a ring, anyway – but I'd guess you *do* have a man friend?'

'Oh, yes.' Her eyes met Rosie's in the glass. 'I do indeed. Talking about *me* now – I start on *your* problems, and—' The street door had opened, another customer arriving … She glanced round: 'Good day, madame.' Calling towards

the curtain, then: 'Estelle!' Back to the customer: 'I'm sorry
– that girl's constantly disappearing ...' Then to Rosie,
quietly, 'Tell you about him this evening, if you're interested
... Estelle, Madame Guertz has come for her wash and set.
I'll attend to the setting myself, of course ...'

The people in S.I.S., Rosie thought, would be patting her on
the back. At this stage, anyway. It was sheer luck, of course,
no skill in it at all, they'd simply taken a liking to each other.
She couldn't have acted it anything like as well: even if the
ulterior motive hadn't existed, she'd have been looking
forward to seeing Jacqui again. Because of the ulterior
motive, though? Without realizing it, liking her because
she'd made it so easy?

Perhaps she – Jacqui – didn't have many friends of her
own here. Result of her German connection? (Connections,
plural: as Colonel Walther's mistress she'd have to consort
with his brother officers, presumably: he wouldn't *hide* her.
It was a reasonable guess that in Amiens her friends would
be either German or French collaborators.)

Anyway, Rosie told herself, the thing would be now to
play it carefully, not push it too hard to try to progress too
fast. Let *her* make the running. If she was lonely – during the
week, at any rate – felt the need of female company ... It
was natural enough that Jeanne-Marie Lefèvre would welcome the contact – as a newcomer to a town in which she
knew no-one at all, *and* needing any help she could get with
the scent-flogging business ... And if she wanted to talk
about her colonel – well, fine, *let* her. It would be perfectly
natural to show interest, too. In the relationship itself and its
history, and what sort of man he was, and from that what
kind of soldiering he did. To Jeanne-Marie politics wouldn't
count for much: the Germans were here, that was simply a
fact of life, her primary interest would be survival. She
might well be envious of Jacqui, and wonder whether she
might not climb on to a similar bandwagon: not through
inclination, not like Jacqui – whose interest in men in

general was slightly obvious – viz. information more or less
admitted by La Chatte to S.I.S. – but because prospects in
the scent business were practically nil and even the ingen-
uous Jeanne-Marie would be beginning to suspect as much,
might well be losing sleep over it.

So let that show. Stir Jacqui's sympathy. Maybe she had
already – it could be part of it.

Eleven-ten now. She was too early to go straight to the
rendezvous at the Café Belle Femme, had strolled up into the
Place du Vieux Marché: unhurried, a lot more relaxed now
that the sample-case had only samples in it. She felt
comparatively *safe*. Papers in order, nothing incriminating
on her, a sound cover-story, if anything slightly enhanced
now by prospects of a business relationship with Jacqueline
Clermont.

She didn't expect César to be at the rendezvous. And to
be honest with herself, she had to admit that at this stage she
didn't need him. The drops were organized, Baker Street
would be making arrangements for pulling Romeo out, and
she wanted to concentrate on the Jacqui business, which had
nothing to do with César anyway.

Except that if he didn't turn up pretty soon you could be
fairly certain he'd come to grief.

She was passing the old church that was dedicated to Joan
of Arc. Its windows were boarded up, the stained glass
removed against the risk of bomb-damage. Imagining
herself kneeling in there in the gloom: *Please, God* . . . There
wasn't time, though: it was eleven-fifteen, and if César was
in Rouen he'd be dropping into a chair outside the Belle
Femme at about this moment, looking for her to join him in
ten minutes' time. So – from the top of this *Place*, eastward
along Rue Guillaume-le-Conquérant: she'd turn down Rue
Jeanne d'Arc when she came to it. Then three blocks and
turn right again.

Ignoring the bloody swastikas. Red for blood, black for
darkness. Look the other way: with that familiar shiver in the
brain . . .

And feeling like that, but able to contemplate an almost genuinely friendly association with a Frenchwoman who shared the bed of one of them?

Because he was the target: for no other reason. And seeing her through the eyes of Jeanne-Marie Lefèvre, not those of Rosie Ewing.

There'd been no bombing here for a month or five weeks, Ursule had told her at breakfast – *ersatz* coffee, bread which might have come from the Bonhommes, plum jam. There'd been several other inmates at the communal table, but no obvious tarts. Ursule had joined her for a few minutes, chatting about this and that: about the bombing, and the damage that had been done. The port was always the target: but of course bombs did go astray . . .

Letting the Allied airmen off the hook of responsibility for it? Rosie hadn't risen to the bait. To accept the risk of being killed in one of their raids, you'd have to be devoted to the Allied cause.

Eleven-eighteen. Turning right into Rue aux Ours. Slowing her pace, with only about a hundred yards to go. This was really only a matter of 'going through the motions'; she could tell Baker Street that for a second time he hadn't shown up, and get on with her own commitments – which would include some more trips out into the countryside: to the north and northeast. Amiens, for instance, Jacqui's colonel's base. She'd thought about this when she'd woken in the night, would have to think about it some more and also talk to Romeo, pick his brains without giving anything away.

Grey-green and buff-coloured uniforms crowding past her. *Doing all right this far, Ben* . . . Over the road, into Place de la Pucelle: pucelle meaning virgin. The Hôtel Bourgtheroulde's ancient stone hideously defaced by that outsize swastika banner. She was at the corner more or less opposite it, with the café just along here on her left, its pavement tables already in her field of view. Three – four – were occupied: one by the fat man who'd been here last time. His bulk and the hunched-together shapes of two elderly women at a nearby table – like two vultures, quick-eyed, furtive, looking up at the waitress who was hovering over them – temporarily screened her view of the customers further back: and she had to look away, there being some danger of Fatso imagining that she was interested in *him*.

Then with the view cleared, another glance that way . . .

Fair hair, and a floppy blond moustache. She hadn't expected a moustache: recent addition, she supposed. Much less than forty, you'd have guessed nearer thirty. Wide-shouldered: leaning back in the chair with one arm dangling, the other hand fiddling with the coffee-cup in front of him. Surprise as it were stopping her in her tracks – figuratively speaking – mentally, psychologically – while physically she'd changed direction to pass between Fatso's table and those women's, on what might have been her most direct route to the café's open, glass-topped doors.

Twin cups on the table, one unused, both spoons in the saucer in front of him. Sipping at his coffee – or making a show of doing so – narrow blue eyes on hers over the cup's rim.

She pulled a chair back for herself. 'César. At last . . .'

They'd left the Belle Femme, after a few mundane remarks aimed at Fatso's obviously straining ears, and were now strolling – limping, in César's case – westward along Quai du Havre. Getting towards the Quai Boulet, in fact. There was a cool breeze off the river, a smell of tar, shipping on the move . . . César was carrying her sample-case for her. He was quite a small man: when he dipped, each time his left foot touched the ground, he came down more or less eye-to-eye with her. She knew – had been told, in London – that the limp was the result of an injury to his left knee during parachute training in 1940, but he'd told her – when they'd left the café and had been heading river-wards down Rue St Eloi – 'According to my papers, a horse fell on me. Caused me to be invalided out of the Army, in '38.'

'French army.'

'Of course.' He was actually quite pleasant-looking, in his own way. Strangely slitted eyes, though. And a bit tense: it showed around the mouth. She guessed he might have grown the moustache to make himself look older. She queried, 'French horse, too?'

He glanced at her – surprised – for a moment before he laughed. Then it was as if he was amused at *her*, rather than at the weak joke: she sensed the beginning of an easier relationship, a slight relaxation. Telling him, 'I was getting worried. Thinking something had happened to you ... Colonel Buckmaster asked me to give you his regards, by the way.'

'Oh. That's – nice.'

'Did you run into problems, on your way?'

'You could say so. You could say – a marathon ... Look, shall we sit here?'

One of the stone benches: there was one every fifty yards or so, and this one was unoccupied, an old man having just got up from it and shuffled to the riverside.

'A marathon. I'll tell you about it. But – Angel – we've a lot to be getting on with, haven't we? To start with, what's your cover here?'

'*That* is.' Nodding towards the sample-case, which he'd put down on the paving between them. 'I'm representing a well-known Paris *parfumeur*. Maison Cazalet. I'm calling on hairdressers and such people – anyone who might be interested – and those are samples.'

'*Is* there a Maison Cazalet?'

'Certainly there is. Pierre Cazalet, who heads it, happens also to be a personal crony of Reichsmarshall Hermann Goering. How d'you like that?'

An intent stare, while he absorbed it. He could have been an Englishman, she thought. If it hadn't been for the moustache, anyway. An Englishman would have clipped or shaped it; this droopy thing was definitely French.

'You're telling me he's a friend of the Reichsmarshall –

therefore presumably accepted as a *collaborateur* – and he's provided you with this cover?'

'He's also supposed to be a cousin of mine. Helping an impecunious young relation – I'm a widow, you see, I have a small daughter whom I've left with my former mother-in-law while I try to scrape a living.'

'This man's *really* your cousin?'

'Of course not. But it's good, isn't it? I'm working quite hard at trying to sell the perfumes – not full-time, but enough to make it *real* ... It's almost flawless. As long as Louis himself stays in the clear, of course. And with friends of that calibre—'

'You referred to him as Pierre – that's his code-name, "Louis"?'

'Yes.' Studying him – the sun's reflections from the river's moving surface flickering in his brilliantly blue eyes. His French was slightly stilted, she'd noticed, had a degree of correctness that suggested a language learnt, not grown up with ... She asked him, 'And *your* cover?'

'I was about to ask whether you've made contact yet with this Romeo, so-called.'

'I have, yes. All right, I'll—'

'No – I'll give you my story first. Have our backgrounds straight, and go on from there ... This is a bit of a tear-jerker, I'm afraid. At its roots quite similar to my own true origins – Father's business in Dieppe – and Rotterdam, we spent a lot of time in Holland, I actually spoke Dutch before French although I *am* French ... I was never in the family business, straight from school to Saint-Cyr. Name of Rossier, by the way, Michel Rossier – and your name?'

'Jeanne-Marie Lefévre.'

'Lefévre, Jeanne-Marie. And you're a widow. OK ... Well – I married a girl from Rouen and we spent a lot of time here – all my leaves from the Army, weekends and so forth. But she's dead – some time ago, in a road accident – and now *I*'m for it – I've only six months to live.' He tapped his chest, the region of the heart. 'Six months is an estimate – could be less, could be a year, but that's the prognosis.'

'Commiserations.'

'Thank you. I'm – er – older than I look, you realize.'

'Yes. You certainly don't look – forty, is it?'

'Thirty-eight.'

'Certainly *don't* look it ... Why are you in Rouen now, though?'

'I'm spending my last six months in the place where my wife and I were so happy. I've enough money to live on – living carefully, of course. Which reminds me, Angel—'

'Yes, I've brought a million francs.'

'A *million* ...'

'It was decided that to set up a whole new *réseau* from scratch—'

A quick nod ... 'Where's the money now?'

'Hidden with my transceiver. I'd be delighted to be relieved of it – the money, that is.'

'This evening? At the Belle Femme?'

'If you like.'

'It's where I'm living, you see.'

'*Living*?'

'I have a room on the top floor. They know my story – I only want a quiet life, some cognac when they can get any – black market prices of course – you know ...'

'I'll bring you the cash this evening, then.'

'Do you have any immediate financial needs yourself?'

'Not at the moment. But Romeo does. I told him you'd be bringing it, so—'

'Right. Let's talk about Romeo ... By the way –' his hand rested on her forearm – 'the first job I'll have for *you*, Angel, is to tell London I'm here and getting down to work, and a few other rather important things as well. In fact important and quite urgent.'

'Tomorrow, if you like. Have to pump up my tyres, that's all. Bicycle. I'll only be transmitting from outside the town, you see. Baker Street's orders – because of the other interceptions – if that's how the information about those drops got out. In any case it doesn't seem like very safe ground here, I think it's a wise precaution. Have they given you all the background?'

'That the former *réseau* was infiltrated, drops went wrong, all of them were arrested except this Romeo – *that* background?'

She nodded. 'So London aren't all that sure of him. They want him back, to debrief him.'

'Ah . . .'

'Didn't you know it?'

'That he'd have been under suspicion is obvious. That's why I asked you about him. Have you met him, or only spoken?'

'Met him. I believe he's straight too – as it happens. But going back to what you were saying – I'm to tell Baker Street you're here, etcetera – fine, I'll do that. But the thing is, my orders are to transmit as seldom and as briefly as possible and never from the same place twice. And never from Rouen itself. Well, obviously another fairly urgent job is to get out into the country and make contacts for future drops. Make up for lost time. Romeo made this point – that our Resistance friends are beginning to feel let down. I'll get around mostly by bicycle, anyway – longer distances by train, I suppose – I can be on my way to Amiens or Neufchatel or wherever, to sell scent, and I'll make whatever transmissions you want en route.'

'Very well.' His eyes were on the river. Downstream, quite a large ship was being turned around by tugs. César told her, 'May have to send it in more than one transmission. Twelve hours and some kilometres apart, perhaps. Up to you, Angel, that's your department. But – so much to sort out, isn't there – of one kind and another . . . What you've just told me – no transmitting from Rouen, all that – I agree, it's wise—'

'Romeo was warned off the air altogether, at the crisis time, and it still holds, because of the risk his code's broken – but he told me he was only too pleased to pipe down, the direction-finders were homing in on him. He saw the vans.'

'Lucky for him.'

'He's very experienced, very cautious. They got close to him in Orléans once, apparently, he's alert to the technique.'

'What I was going to say – apart from transmissions, to receive signals *from* London—'

'Yes. I'll arrange listening-out schedules. Haven't done so yet because you weren't here and I didn't know what might have happened to you, it seemed better to keep my head down. But with this next transmission I'll suggest I listen out three nights a week, from there on. I've already reported my own arrival, by the way – and that you weren't at the café last Thursday, and I'd contacted Romeo. Oh, and that he was willing to be picked up, please arrange ... Come to think of it, I'd better get back to them pretty soon on that anyway.'

'I'd like to meet Romeo soon, too.'

'Well.' She hesitated ... 'They'd hardly send him back to this *réseau*, would they? And he may be leaving us quite soon – they were anxious to have him back, and now they know he's willing ... It's possible he'll want to keep his distance. As I said, he's *very* cautious.'

'Where's he living?'

She didn't answer at once. People passing slowly, staring at them ...

Eventually: 'I don't know where he lives. Didn't press him to tell me, either. He attributes the fact he wasn't rounded up with the others to having been careful to stay away from them. His only *réseau* contact was with the Organizer – someone called Max. He trusted him and no-one else, and evidently it paid off. That's why I have some doubt—'

'You telephoned him, did you, at the number we were given?'

'Because you weren't here.' She nodded. 'Otherwise I'd have left it to you. But he might have known what had happened to you – and there was no other way I'd have found out – could have waited for ever!'

'Yes.' Rubbing his jaw, eyes on the river ... 'Yes, I understand that. And I could get in touch with him myself, I have that same number. Obtained it – also the routine for my rendezvous with *you* – from a man code-named "Fabien", in Lyon. He was arrested that same day – which is what sent me on my travels, instead of coming here. But – back to the point – Romeo – rather than I do it, you might arrange for him to come to the Belle Femme with you this evening?'

'I'll try to. I'll come with the money anyway.'

'It's a question of recognition, mostly. Easier if you bring him. And if he's in need of cash?'

'Yes. I'll try.'

'Where are *you* living, Angel?'

She pointed. 'Over there, Rive Gauche. I only moved in yesterday. Before that I was living over a baker's shop – a family to whom I was sent by Louis – my employer – and I must warn him somehow, they have a pro-German daughter, it's not all that safe.'

'So where—'

'Best way – well. If you go over Pont Corneille – up Rue La Fayette, and turn left at the church – Saint Sever, that is. It's a boarding-house: yellow shutters, you can't miss it.' She shifted her position: the stone seats weren't ideal for lengthy occupation. 'I have a telephone number I can give you ...' She shut her eyes: '*Damn* ...'

'Something wrong?'

'It'll have to be early, this evening. Six, six-thirty?'

'Make it six. What is it, a later appointment?'

'With a hairdresser, to talk about perfume. In her working hours she's too busy. Then I have to get back before curfew—'

'What time's that, in this town?'

'Ten. Used to be nine, but—'

'Six to six-thirty would be fine. You and Romeo, I hope ... Angel, if you'd like something to eat now – we might find some place not too far ...'

*

On the whole, she decided, she was glad to have him here. From Buckmaster's description she'd expected someone tougher and older-looking: but those inner qualities would no doubt reveal themselves, in times of need. His presence would complicate things for her, a little; although she was beginning to wonder whether she hadn't been somewhat over-confident, mightn't eventually need him to lean on – again, thinking of him in Buckmaster's terms ... Not that she'd change her mind at *this* stage, on that issue: S.I.S. had wanted her to play it solo, and she would – touch wood: but her hopes might have been raised *too* high by Jacqui, her own view of the prospects there sparking excessive optimism. As well as feeling comfortable about Romeo – *contrary* to Buckmaster's advice ... In better perspective now, she could see there was still a long way to go with Jacqui and that if she wasn't very careful, very patient – as well as continuing to be lucky – it might well blow up in her face. Jacqui had worked with 'La Chatte', for God's sake – in one particular capacity – and was now a German officer's mistress. The Boches had known of her connection with La Chatte, had arrested her as well – La Chatte almost certainly having shopped her. And they *must* have turned her: or she in turn had informed on La Chatte, got her own back. It was potentially a minefield: on top of which Romeo would be leaving soon – possibly within days, less than a fortnight anyway, since the Lysanders of the Special Duties Squadron only flew in and out of France when there was a moon, and this present one had no more than a fortnight's life left in it – after which there'd be *only* César to turn to, if things went wrong.

She wondered if he was married. By the age of thirty-eight, you'd guess so. On the other hand, that bit of his cover-story might be real.

He'd had a fairly hair-raising time, getting here. The collapse of the *réseau* in Marseille to start with, a pattern of events not dissimilar to those which Romeo had described as having occurred here and in Dieppe: César had been sent there to pick up the pieces, as it were, before coming to set up a replacement network here in Rouen. Security of communications in the Marseille area being about as uncertain as they were in Rouen, he'd been told to visit a resident agent in Lyon, code-named 'Fabien', who'd give him instructions about making his contacts here, the rendez-vous with 'Angel' and a telephone link to 'Romeo'. It was the first time he'd heard of either of them. In fact he'd been dead lucky, as far as the timing had worked out: having arrived in Lyon and booked in at a safe house, Pension d'Alsace – Rosie had recognized the name and tried to interrupt, but he'd ignored her and she'd desisted – he'd called on this 'Fabien', an elderly character who dealt in silk. He'd spent no longer with him than he'd had to – five or ten minutes – and then returned to the *planque*, and later that same evening a young girl had arrived in a state of panic to tell them that Fabien's premises had been raided and the old man arrested simultaneously at his home. There'd been a cache of Resistance weaponry in his warehouse, apparently. It would be a matter of only an hour or two at most before the pension was honoured with similar attentions – the owner/manager was Fabien's niece, and he was quite frail, couldn't be expected to hold out for long against inter-rogation by Klaus Barbie's team – and a complication had been that in the pension were three U.S.A.F. aircrew who were to have been collected in a few days' time by a courier from an escape pipeline channelling escapers over the Pyrenees and out through Spain. (The route by which Rosie herself had got out a year earlier, as it happened.) So, César had taken them under *his* wing – by train to Montauban, where he'd had a contact, thence to Perpignan to leave them in the care of a Spanish bar-owner who had a link to the Pyrenean group, code-named 'Switchback'.

'The delay was in establishing my own identity. I could have been a German – *agent provocateur*, Gestapo agent or what-have-you. I've been taken for a German more than once, as it happens. I look like one, eh?'

'Hardly ... Well, I suppose at a pinch ...'

'And from the years in Holland my French has some slightly different intonations, so I've often been told. You must have noticed?'

'There's a very faint – well, it's—'

'Didn't arouse *your* suspicions?'

'Until you told me about Rotterdam—'

'But that itself could be a ruse. It was what they thought in Montauban – until I was able to convince them, thank God. They'd have killed me, otherwise.'

'How would a Gestapo agent bring American flyers with him?'

'They might have been taken from some prison camp, for that purpose. Might be a good dodge – eh?'

'Perhaps.' She shrugged. 'What I was going to say just now, though – the news that Pension d'Alsace in Lyon had become a mousetrap reached Louis – in Paris, my employer – when I was with him.'

'Ah. *Did* it, now.' Gazing at her: then a nod ... 'So he'll have passed it on. Good. Having no access to a radio myself, I asked the Spaniard – as soon as he got to Perpignan—'

'I passed it to London myself, last Friday.'

'Small world, uh?' The smile faded. 'Did you tell them about Fabien too?'

She shook her head. 'Never heard of him, until now.'

'So we'll include it in your next transmission. Tomorrow – on your bicycle?'

'If that's what you want.'

'It's what I want, Angel.' A nod; blue eyes resting on her. 'It's definitely what I want.'

She was earning her pay today, all right. Romeo, when she rang him from the Brasserie Guillaume and invited him to join her there, flatly refused.

'But I *have* to see you!'

'My darling, I'd like nothing better, believe me.'

'Well, then—'

'Not there, that's all. Especially if you're in *that* mood . . . How about Marc's place, in half an hour?'

'It's so far . . .'

'It's also more private. I can send him out – be on our own. Unless you're saying you only want to *talk*—'

'No. No – all right. In one hour, though, there's something I must do first – new shoes, actually – these are practically worn out already, and—'

'Use your bike, for heaven's sake!'

'I'm going to, but I'll have to go back and fetch it. Say an hour and a half, in fact. All right?'

Then César at six, Jacqui at seven. Full day . . .

She bought a pair of shoes at a shop in Rue Gros Horloge, using about three-quarters of the money she had left and most of the coupons supplied by both Marilyn and Louis – whom she had yet to contact, incidentally, to warn him about the Bonhommes' daughter. The articulated wooden soles took a bit of getting used to, but at least the soles of her feet, already bruised and hurting, were protected from the cobbles. She was keeping the old cardboard ones to use as bedroom slippers.

Get some cash out of César this evening, she thought. Or extract it from the quarter-million earmarked for Jacqui and which César didn't have to know about. Better to get it from him, though. The shoes sounded like clogs: she'd noticed it before, the loud clack-clacking other women's made, but when it was your own feet doing it you found yourself trying to tread softly.

She got to Ursule's, finally, met no-one on her way up to the room, found the money and radio where she'd hidden them and transferred the former to her sample-case. The bicycle was in a back-lobby off the kitchen: she wheeled it out, and joined the hundreds of other cyclists on the streets of Rouen St Sever. Right, then, into Rue La Fayette: having difficulty in keeping the still smooth wooden soles from slipping on the pedals.

By the time she reached Rue Bras-de-Fer, either she'd got the hang of it or the wood had roughened. But she'd wear the old ones for long rides like tomorrow's, she decided, as long as they held together.

'Well, Romeo . . .'

In Pigot's office, he glanced from her to the clock, 'Only a quarter of an hour late, not bad . . . Anyway – is it that your boy's arrived, or that he hasn't?'

'He's here.' Massaging her feet. 'He wants me to bring you to meet him at the Café Belle Femme at six this evening.'

'What for?'

'Well –' she looked up, across the rubbish on the desk – 'reviewing his troops, I suppose. He's all right, incidentally, I quite like him.'

'*Quite* like him?'

'All right, I like him. But having only met him this morning . . .' She shrugged. 'You want some money from him, don't you?'

'Not now, no – not if I'm due for the magic carpet. In view of which I'm hardly one of his troops, either. With all respect to him, and best wishes for his success, etcetera—'

'Be easier if you *did* come.'

'You had the money anyway, didn't you?'

'What's that got to do with it?'

'Reminding you that I'm not a complete idiot, that's all. Just because this fellow snaps his fingers—'

'It's not like that at all. What harm is there in just saying hello to each other?'

'The same as there might be in meeting you at your brasserie or anywhere else where there's a crowd. I told you – I might have been left free deliberately – as a stalking horse, you might say. Or – listen – suppose some of the small-fry were turned and let loose. You can just about bet on it, some will have been – turned, anyway. Families as hostages, if necessary. But even without that . . . Obviously they knew of my existence, I was their pianist, for Christ's sake – and for all I know one or more of them might have had a sight of me – seen me with Max, for instance, guessed it was me? *I* wouldn't have known ... Well – I can't live underground like a rat, life has to go on and I have my job – but I don't loaf around town, either. Don't meet pretty girls in brasseries, or newly arrived agents in cafés. Your new friend wouldn't thank me if they'd kept me under surveillance until I led them to *him*, would he – on his first day here?'

It made sense. They *would* have a damn good idea that sooner or later S.O.E. would put in a new *réseau* in place of the one that had been rolled up, and they'd have applied all the brainpower they could muster towards setting the scene for a repetition of that clean sweep. She'd known it, obviously – could have written a thesis on it – but in this instance her awareness of the danger had been primarily in the context of Guillaume's arrest – what he might tell them about the girl on the train when they pointed a red-hot skewer at one eyeball, for instance.

Romeo was saying, 'Tell him for me, please. I want to get away – for my own sake, I've had enough, I don't mind admitting it – and meanwhile for *his* sake I'd be a damn fool to go near him. Got a cigarette on you, Angel?'

'Of course. Here ...'

'No news of a pickup yet?'

'No.' She leant forward, to the flare of his match. 'I haven't been listening out. I'm going out of town again tomorrow, though, I'll be using the radio and they may have news for us. In which case –' exhaling a stream of smoke – 'if it was urgent I'd come back right away, but otherwise I'll be back in two or three days.'

'Long trip, is it?'

'Well – I'd like some advice on that, please. Introductions, too – northeast of here – Neufchatel-en-Bray, and the Amiens direction. The most useful Resistance contacts we have in those areas, the really key men – you'd know them all and how I could find them, wouldn't you?'

'With what in mind? Some secret brief you weren't letting on about last time?'

She shook her head. 'The usual, what drops are wanted, and where.'

'But I can tell you that – enough to be going on with, anyway. As I mentioned—'

'You *wouldn't* tell me, I seem to remember.'

'Oh.' A shrug. 'You put my back up a little, that's all. But you're getting me out, and I don't want those people let down. Their sake, our sake, sake of killing fucking Boches . . . I beg your pardon—'

'It's all right. Listen – I'll gladly take over those requests for drops. And I'll see they get them – wherever. But I still want to talk to key men up that way, where I said. Even in Amiens itself – or beyond it. Ideally, leaders or *a* leader who'd see the word was passed on – as far as Calais, even. That's not impossible, is it? *Réseau* to *réseau*, word of mouth?'

'Not impossible.' He smiled: that special one, the slow spread of it . . . 'But not *quite* "the usual" either – huh?'

'Not quite . . . Well – it *is* – with an extra dimension added, that's all.'

'Same as last time.'

'No. *Not* the same. But if you could give me names and map-references—'

'Better than that, Angel. *Much* better. Listen – I could take you – introduce you. Be with you when you get an answer about my pickup, too, incidentally . . . You see, it's time I visited up that way – my work, legitimate, I *have* to. Anyone asks, you're a girl I brought along for the ride. What do you say?'

12

In mid-week – Wednesday, when Rosie was leaving Rouen in the Neufchatel-Amiens direction – Ben was still hanging around the Landeda garage and Durand's nearby bungalow. The transfer of the second cache of weaponry – to a builder's yard at the village of Locmélar – had been cancelled early on Sunday morning, Vidor dropping in at breakfast-time to tell them that a road-block had been set up overnight about a hundred metres from the yard's entrance. So the move was off, until further notice, and the cart that would have brought the stuff here for transfer to the lorry would not be coming. He'd also told them that the Germans who'd raided the Demorêts' turkey-farm the night before had arrested the son and his father and shot their dog when it had attacked one of them.

'It was still there. I had to force my way in, old Mathilde was still hysterical and she thought I was one of them coming back to get her. I took the dog out, buried it, more or less hauled the neighbours over to take care of things for her.' He told Durand, 'The Taupins.'

'*That* pair . . .'

'They're not the sort to risk their necks, that's all. They told me they'd heard nothing, seen nothing – then admitted the Boches had been to their place first, and they were asking about weapons dumps – had they ever been asked to allow their farm to be used for it. The Boches know them, obviously, know they wouldn't have the guts to risk it, so the

question was only had they been *asked* to. For all I know,
they may have said "try next door". The Demorêts had been
knocked about, all right – not the old woman, far as I could
tell, but there was blood splashed around that wasn't the
dog's.'

'Wouldn't trust either of the Taupins a centimetre.'
Durand's little eyes, as sharp as gimlets, aimed upwards at
Vidor ... 'Maybe we shouldn't move your final load at all.
If the sods are poking around they'll watch the roads too,
won't they?'

Vidor had nodded. 'Maybe.' He asked Ben, 'Yours went
all right yesterday, did it?'

'We weren't stopped anywhere.'

'Good.'

'The tomb wasn't empty, though. Disintegrated coffins,
skeletons lying there grinning at us.'

'What'd you do – grin back?' He'd mimed it – raising a
non-existent hat: '*Messieurs – mesdames* ...' Back to the
subject, agreeing with Durand: 'This last lot we *could* leave.
It's one of the best hidden.' To Ben again, explaining, 'It's
as much the people whose land it's on as the material itself
that concerns us. Even after it's moved – signs it *was*
there ...'

'I suppose ... But listen – d'you think the pinpoint's done
for?'

'Not necessarily. It *may* be. There have been no moves
down there – not on the beaches, or visits to Tariec or
Guenioc ... Land there for five minutes, they'd find the boat,
of course ... We have to hang on, wait and see, eh?'

'Are the fly-boys happy to – those four? Under cover
somewhere near here, are they?'

'Yes – and no.' Vidor put a hand on his shoulder. 'We
have them close by, yes, but they're not willing to wait,
when it's so uncertain. They – well, I wasn't going to
mention it, but I'm taking them south – today, *now*.'

'South ... Meaning—'

'Bordeaux. Leaving them with an escape *réseau* there,

they'll be taken from there to Hendaye and over the Pyrenees. I think they're wrong, perhaps, but they say why wait here – two weeks for the moonless period, then maybe no gunboat anyway. We'd have then to move them – and you – to the Grac'h Zu pinpoint – at short notice, if we've waited too long before it's decided ... You wouldn't want to lose this pinpoint if it can be kept, would you?'

'No. But you're shifting those four despite – as you've said – patrols, roadblocks, all that?'

'I can do it. Southwards, it's possible. And to be honest, where they are this minute is not so safe.' A shrug. 'Where *is*? But a few days, I'll be back. *Maybe* move you three then to Grac'h Zu, but – look, I admit, *that* might not be easy – anywhere along this coast. No point pretending it *will* be easy, Ben.'

'What about your St Renan business?'

'That's the *good* news. All wrecked, people heard it miles away. Only thing less good is one of our boys has had to hole up there. Place is alive with Boches and *milice* – well, *would* be. Life complicates itself sometimes, eh?'

This was the last Ben had seen of him. His final words, saying goodbye, had been to repeat that when he got back he'd see about moving Messrs Bright and Farr from the Brodards' place to somewhere further from the coast. 'And you. But you see, if they're searching farms like the Demorêts' – who knows?'

'You do, I hope.'

'I hope, too. But – the way the cat jumps, isn't it?'

'You don't want me to join them at the Brodards', meanwhile?'

'If you insist – I suppose ... But an extra mouth for Solange Brodard to feed – whereas it's no hardship for the Durands ...'

Having more time than he needed for speculation – four days and then a fifth, nights in the bungalow and days at the garage helping out, when there was any odd job he was

capable of helping with – he'd thought through all the
possible alternatives if there was *not* to be a pickup here.
Well, there'd be radio exchanges with Baker Street and St
James', and presumably – as Vidor had suggested – they'd
have to *try* to get to Grac'h Zu instead. Difficult or not, you
wouldn't want to spend *another* month here. From his own
point of view the most important thing was to make sure
Bright and Farr got out all right: *he*'d dropped the poor
buggers in it.

Early that Wednesday, trundling out of town northeastward
in his *gazo*, Romeo flicked a cigarette-stub out of the
window . . . 'So he wasn't pleased.'

Referring to César, to whom she'd had to explain last
evening at the Café Belle Femme that he'd declined the
invitation to join them.

'Putting it mildly, he wasn't. He was damned angry.'

Gazing out at forest off to the left of the road, with a wide
area of felled trees between here and there: she had her radio
in the sample-case and a message to send off to Baker Street,
when they'd put a few kilometres behind them. The *gazo*
was no speedster.

She shook her head. 'I gave him your reasons, but they
didn't help much. To be honest, I rather sympathize with
him. Sorry, but—'

'You're entitled to your view.'

'Two things, mainly. It's fairly obvious the Boches do *not*
have you under surveillance. As you said yourself, if they
had you'd have been aware of it by now. You're no idiot—'

'Flattery now!'

'—just bloody obstinate. But the other thing – the fact
you're leaving us, or that we hope you are, doesn't affect the
issue at all. You've been here a long time, and he's new to
the place, you could be a big help to him. He'd *still* like to
meet you. Won't you change your mind?'

'I'll think about it.'

She could sense that he hadn't meant that, but still

persevered. 'It could make a big difference – to us here, what you'll be leaving behind, I mean. All the contacts you've made, for instance – we'll be recruiting sub-agents, obviously, couriers – starting from scratch – you could save us weeks and possibly some blunders. And as for contacts out in the countryside—'

'Over a table in a crowded café – in how long, all this – half an hour?'

'Yesterday's meeting would have been simply to break the ice, which is now of course thicker. It'll take a lot more breaking than it might have. But *please*—'

'Does he know I'm escorting you on this outing?'

'No. But he does know you were giving me introductions. All of which I'll pass on to him, of course, when we get back.'

'Thinks you're on your bicycle, does he?' He saw her nod. 'So why – you think he wouldn't like it that I'm making it easier for you?'

'He might not. I think in his shoes I'd want to satisfy myself about you – not take someone else's word. After all, he's responsible—'

'But since I'm happy to pass on to you everything I know – isn't that as good as passing it on to him?'

'*Why* me and not him?'

A chuckle . . . 'You're prettier. At least, I *imagine*—'

'This is quite a serious matter, Romeo. For all of us.'

'Perhaps I should explain myself more clearly. Try to understand this – please . . . If he'd been the first to arrive and he'd contacted me as you did, I'd have been dealing with him, not with you. One needs *a* contact, right? Isn't that why you got on to me? But only *one* contact, Angel – that's my personal philosophy, I believe it saved my life this last time and I'm sticking to it. That's the fundamental – in my position, or for that matter in yours; it's the same thing. I really do commend it to you. But it's obviously a different kettle of fish for an Organizer. He's got to know us all, he's – the ringmaster, isn't he? Well – all right, when you called through to the bistro I did have an alternative – I could have stayed clear of you – of *both* of you – could have gone on the air to Baker Street and told them I want out, please sir. But they aren't trusting my transmissions, they told me to keep off the air, remember? And maybe they're right, maybe my code *was* being read . . . Smoke?'

'Thanks.'

'That's why I needed you. Or César – either one. Because especially in the context of setting up drops or pickups they'd have ignored any requests that came from me, wouldn't they?'

'Might have, I suppose.' Holding a match for him to lean to with his cigarette, before she lit her own. Knowing damn well they'd have ignored him. In the eyes of Baker Street, he was a traitor until he convinced them that he was loyal.

They weren't going to be reassured by hearing that he'd refused contact with César, either, but it was included in César's message which she was carrying in her shoe already coded. She didn't have to mention this to him, it was simply her job to send it, César's orders. Romeo would have to explain that to them, as well.

They could be right, she realized, about him, *She* could be wrong. If she was, she was now in about as exposed a position as an agent could be. On ice, so to speak, to be picked up when they judged the time was right, when in their view she'd served her purpose – such as, for instance, leading them to César last evening. If they'd been watching her they'd have *him* on ice too, now. They might also – if one continued with this unpleasant flight of fancy – have tailed her from the Belle Femme to Chez Jacqui in Rue de Fontenelle, and thus know that she'd spent a couple of hours there last night. Then it wouldn't take the S.D. or the Abwehr or Gestapo long to connect hairdresser Jacqueline Clermont with Colonel of Engineers Hans Walther.

So you'd have let S.I.S. down as well as S.O.E. By following one's own so-called instincts, ignoring the experienced Maurice Buckmaster's authoritative advice. Rosie's head swam: shutting her eyes, exhaling smoke . . .

'Are you all right?'

Anxiety, in the creased, greyish face – which he'd shaved carefully, this morning. She smiled: with a quick intrusive vision of Ben, that beard he'd promised to shave off . . . 'Quite all right, thanks.' She added, 'Thoughts from far away.' On impulse she pulled the window down and tossed out the half-smoked cigarette: movement of any kind serving as a release from inner tension, there'd been no *reason* to discard the thing . . . Looking back at him, at his really rather impressive profile, thinking *I still do believe he's straight.*

Imagining Marilyn asking her sardonically *Is that how you tell – by their profiles?*

But she *had* to believe it. It was the only answer to such flares of panic – which she'd known in the small hours of the night often enough, but hitherto had avoided in broad daylight . . . Looking back at him quickly as he suggested, 'At Quincampoix – if we turn up to the left there – there's a smallish wooded area that might suit you for your solo.'

'I was going to ask you – all right if I use this car's battery?'

'Of course. I always did.'

'I'll leave mine in your box of tricks then – OK?'

Saving battery-life to start with, and weight in the sample-case as an extra dividend; his 'box of tricks' was a crate packed with spare parts for on-the-spot repairs to farm machinery.

He muttered – to himself as much as to her – 'Must admit, I'll be damn glad to have my own future decided.'

His pickup, he meant. The hope was that they'd have it for her, at the end of her own transmission: place, date and time for a moonlight assignation with a black-painted Lysander from Tempsford in Bedfordshire.

César had asked her yesterday evening, 'Did you come in by Lysander, Angel?'

He'd cooled down, by then, got over his annoyance at Romeo's non-appearance, and she'd given him the money, which had seemed to raise his spirits. They'd been upstairs, in his room under the eaves. It was quite large, furnished as a sitting room as well as bedroom, and attractive – in a slightly gloomy way, with its ancient timbers and uneven floor. The brass bedstead – it was wider than an ordinary single bed – had items of clothing scattered over it, some of which he'd thrown there in the course of clearing two chairs so they could sit down: he'd pulled his own up to the oak table and laboriously counted the million francs.

'One million.' Sitting back. 'You'll need some of this, I imagine.'

'Yes, please. I'll be away at least three days, I'd guess.'

'That long?'

'Longer, if I stop in Amiens to sell perfume. Which I should do, really. But it's a large area anyway, a lot of ground to cover. Depends of course how many individuals I have to see.'

'You must have some idea of that, from whatever Romeo's told you – if he's supplied the introductions?'

'Yes. But one contact can lead to another. I'll be looking for what you might call key men – who'd deal with lesser fry, save us a lot of legwork – pedal-work, rather. And time – and come to that, exposure.'

She wasn't certain he'd understood her, on that point. It was pretty well what one might call the Doctrine According to Romeo: not to have your name and number in more address-books, so to speak, than was strictly necessary. César had been barely listening, though – still thinking about money, how much to give her.

'Here you are, anyway. Keep you going for a day or two, I hope!' He'd handed her a 50,000-franc note.

'Take a bit of changing.' Looking at it uncertainly … 'Well – I suppose I could say my cousin Pierre gave it to me as a float …' She'd nodded. 'Yes. And my hairdresser friend would change it for me, I dare say.'

'Otherwise, if you delayed your departure by a few hours, in the morning *I* could—'

'No – thank you, I'll manage.'

'I'll change a few notes elsewhere, anyway.' He wrapped the rest of it up again. 'We won't starve, *that's* for sure.' He'd become almost jolly, certainly more relaxed. He might have been worried about money, she guessed. Amongst other things. It was hardly surprising that Romeo's refusal of cooperation had annoyed him, when he had a whole network to recruit and organize and no contacts at all.

'That was a lot of cash to have been carrying around with you.'

'Yes. Terrifying.' She'd smiled at him. 'I'm glad to be shot of it.'

That question, then: 'Did you come in by Lysander, by the way?'

The thing was, one simply didn't ask such questions. Didn't ever want to: no agent wanted information he or she didn't need, about a fellow-agent. For similar reasons you didn't use real names – even if you'd trained together, knew each other well.

She'd hedged it ... 'I had a long, trek, believe me. Via Paris, as you know. Our lords and masters don't give much thought to one's convenience, do they?'

It was a fact, they didn't. It was primarily a matter of what transport was available at that particular time. When a Lysander came in for Romeo, for instance, it might bring with it one agent destined for Nice and another for Bordeaux. César had agreed with her: 'They don't, do they?' His eyes stayed on hers, though, as if he'd been about to repeat that question – if he had, she'd probably have given him a straight answer – but he must have remembered the convention and decided to contain his curiosity.

She'd assured him – by way of changing the subject – 'I *will* talk to Romeo again.'

A nod: 'Please do.' Then – as if it had only just occurred to him to ask – 'Incidentally, what name does he go by, in Rouen?'

'Heavens. I don't think I know. I've just called him

"Romeo". And when I telephoned—'

'You could find out, perhaps?'

'Well, of course. I will ... But you can understand him – just ... If you see it through his eyes, I mean. He's certain that he's only walking free now as a result of having kept himself to himself, and now his feeling is that he's only got to survive another week or two and he's – you know, away and clear. He's been here a long time – and recently all on his own—'

'Hardly the point, is it? I *need* his help: advice, information, his views on various things. *We* need it. All right, he'll tell *you* what in *his* opinion is all the information and background we may need – but damn it, *I* want to question him, get the scope and kind of detail *I* want!'

'Yes. I'll ask him to think again.'

'Don't ask him, *tell* him. He works for S.O.E., doesn't he?'

'Yes. Yes, of course.' She let it drift, for a moment or two, let him settle again. Glancing round, then: 'This is a nice room you've found, César.'

'Not bad, is it? And look here – it's also a much better place for us to meet and talk than any more public venue. Right? But in the course of doing so, one must realize that the proprietor and his staff are bound to arrive at – well, their own conclusions, about our – er – relationship. Much as you may find that – er – distasteful.' He'd got up: limped to the nearer of the two low windows, stooping there almost double to peer out. Continuing, after a pause: 'The fact is, it would give us very convenient cover. That's my point. If you wouldn't mind – well, not discouraging them in that belief. It would allow you to come here at virtually any time of day or night. In fact – in practical terms, Jeanne-Marie—'

'I think we have it made, actually.'

'Huh?'

He'd straightened, turning to face her. What she'd guessed he'd been about to propose would have been more or less par for the course – certainly not unheard of. The unusual aspects were that he'd have got round to it so

quickly – almost before they knew each other – and, judging
by the run-up – so perfunctorily ... She told him, 'The place
I'm living at – where I told you, on Rive Gauche – well, it's
a rooming house, and apparently quite a few tarts live there.
The proprietress told me they go out to meet their clients
elsewhere, she won't allow it in the house. So as I'll be
coming here quite a bit – I'd guess it's common gossip, that
address – these people here can *think* that's what I come for
– if they want to.'

'Oh. Well.' Flat tone. 'Good, that's—'

'There *is* a man in my life, Michel.'

'Of course.' A couple of quick blinks ... 'I'd have been
amazed if – if there were not.'

She wondered again whether there was a woman in his.
Not asking, because (a) she didn't want to show what he
might take as personal interest, (b) one *didn't* pry into
fellow-agents' private lives. Thinking also – again – about
Buckmaster's description of him: whether perhaps when
crises arose – like getting those fliers out of the safe house
just in time, for instance ... She nodded: 'Anyway – it *will*
make things easy.' Checking the time: 'Did you say you'd
written down the message I'm to send tomorrow?'

'Yes. I have it here.' Still slightly pink, he went to a locked
briefcase on the bedside table. Murmuring with his back to
her: 'The small fortune you've brought me can go in here for
the time being. Until I find somewhere more secure ... Ah,
here it is. Better make sure you can read my scribble – and
if there's anything else we should be telling them, at this
point ... Angel? Jeanne-Marie?'

She was at the window, crouching where he'd stooped,
gazing across the Place de la Pucelle at the Renaissance
splendour of l'Hôtel Bourgthérouide, fouled by its swastika
decoration.

'Filthy bloody thing ...'

'What?'

'*That*.' Pointing. '*That* obscenity. And those disgusting
creatures ... God, how I *loathe* them!'

She glanced round. He'd stopped in the middle of the room, a slip of paper in the fingers of one hand and an expression of astonishment on his face. She smiled: 'Sorry. Letting off steam. Pure self-indulgence.'

Twenty minutes later she'd told Jacqueline in her flat above the shop, 'I just nearly had a pass made at me.'

'*Nearly*?' Jacqui smiled at her across the room, pouring two glasses of Pernod. She had cognac there as well. 'One a minute, I'd have guessed. Was it a Frenchman?'

'Oh, yes—'

'Well – as long as he's rich. Which would make him a *collaborateur*, of course ... Here you are now, Jeanne-Marie. To you and me, let's be great friends, huh?'

'I'd like that.'

Jacqui had perched herself on the fat arm of a duck-egg blue sofa. 'Sit, if you like. I do whenever possible. Worn-out feet are an occupational disease, for hairdressers. But for you too, I suppose, tramping around. No, please don't look at this furniture, it's only what I could scratch together ... Tell me about your Frenchman?'

'He's not *my* Frenchman. And what I'd sooner tell you about are these perfumes.' Gazing at the dark girl, half-smiling: then frowning, as if on a double-take: 'When you asked was it a Frenchman – you're implying it might have been a German?'

'That would be the obvious alternative, surely. Some of them are really quite nice – if you give them half a chance.'

Rosie sat down. 'I'd rather not. I dare say there are some decent ones, there must be, but—'

'Listen. You talked about Hollywood. If I ever did go there, d'you think I'd take a janitor for my lover? Oh, it's a silly question – illustrative, that's all. You go for a man who can look after you – don't you? A *winner* – right?'

'The man friend *you* mentioned—'

'Certainly. Good guess. And I'll tell you, if ever there *was* a winner—'

'You don't really think the Boches are going to win?'

'They *are*. I *know* it!'

Rosie looked down at her sample-case, conscious of having come further in about three minutes flat than she'd have expected to in a week – even a month. Aware also that she was walking on eggshells: but simultaneously driven to capitalize on this, not waste it ... She heard herself saying, 'We should be talking about scent.' Looking up at her. 'Safer subject?'

'How, *safer*?'

'Well. At the moment, you're by far my best prospect not only as a customer but as an entrée to the trade here. I've rather left it, in the hope you'd be my starting point. Apart from selling some scent for my cousin and making some money, we'd get on rather well, I'd thought. But I don't want to sit and hear about the Germans winning, Jacqui.'

'And *I* wouldn't want to think of them *not* winning. If it turned out that way, I'd be done for.'

'Why? How d'you mean?'

'Well, I'll tell you. Then you can leave, if you like, shake the dust from those attractively small feet. I'd sooner you didn't, I *would* like to be friends, but – if that's how it takes you ... What I was saying – well, I'm fully conscious of being surrounded by people who – frankly, who despise me. That's simply a fact of life – as of this moment, and in this place. So don't think that your disapproval comes as a surprise to me. A disappointment, yes.'

'All right.' She shrugged. 'None of my business, let's say.'

'Because you want to sell your damn scent, you say that.' A nod. 'OK. If there's one I specially like, I'll give you an order. As long as you don't mind the fact it'll be paid for by a German.' She swivelled on the sofa's arm, slid down inside it. 'Let's see what you have. Might be easier if you sit here, closer?'

'All right.' She hadn't moved yet, though. 'Only—'

'Don't *want* to sit closer?'

'I'm sorry that I've offended you, that's all. Certainly I'd like to sell some scent – but not even for a *huge* order—'

'You won't get that, don't worry!'

'I was thinking of your stocking them – sale or return, cost you nothing. But – Jacqui, d'you *really* want the Boches to win? *I* can imagine no prospect more horrible!'

'Less *want* than – it's necessary to my survival, to put it bluntly. But then again, I happen to be rather well informed, and what I've heard is *extremely* reassuring.'

'From reading' – Rosie had noticed a heap of newspapers and magazines – '*Je Suis Partout*, *La Gerbe*, *L'Illustration* – all that bullshit about Hitler's "Secret Weapons"?'

'Well, Jeanne-Marie.' Lazy, cat-like stare ... 'How odd that you should mention *that*. Perhaps you're more astute than you realize. Not for calling it by that vulgar word – in fact very far from it ...'

'Frankly, I don't think it's particularly astute to go on about secret weapons when we have solid facts such as the English and Yanks being in Sicily and obviously soon will be in Italy – having driven the Boches and the Italians out of Africa – and the Russians making mincemeat of them. Berlin and other cities being pounded from the air day and night—'

'You realize this is subversive talk?'

'Are you going to report me?'

'Oh.' A smile ... 'Perhaps I should, but on the whole—'

'Whisper it across a pillow?'

The smile had vanished. 'One can share a man's bed without—'

'—sharing his thoughts, or letting him into yours?'

A frown ... 'You're less sophisticated than I'd thought you were, Jeanne-Marie.'

'Quite possible. But I'm not talking about me. If that sounded like a sneer, I'm sorry – I'm *thinking* as a *friend* ... At least, a would-be friend. Look – all right, I'm prejudiced. But I take your word for it, yours is a good one. But you said yourself – about people despising you and you'd be done for. You *think* it'll turn out right for you – but whatever they

tell you or he tells you – well, he would, *he*'s not likely to
indulge in "subversive talk", is he? – but there's a *lot* of talk
around – in Paris, anyway – of an invasion here soon.'

'They won't invade. They won't be able to.'

'Are we back to the mythical "Secret Weapons"?'

'It's no myth, my dear.' Jacqui reached for Rosie's near-
empty glass. 'Believe me. I *know* it's not.'

They'd told her in her sessions with S.I.S., 'If you avoid a
subject too consistently, it gets to be obvious you're
avoiding it. Where it would come in naturally, *bring* it in.
And another maxim: When it's something you'd disapprove
of – you in your rôle as Jeanne-Marie Lefèvre, that is – don't
be afraid to dig your heels in. That way you're *real* – huh?'

She thought she'd followed both those precepts closely
enough, in that opening round with Jacqueline.

Romeo's deep voice on her left: 'It's your mouth. That's
what it is.'

'What?'

A leap in space and time: from the apartment in Rue de
Fontenelle to this *gazo* bumbling northeastward, by this time
about halfway between Isneauville and Quincampoix. A
straight, rather narrow road: locked in her thoughts, she'd
been only vaguely aware of a long stream of military
vehicles thumping past them, heading towards Rouen, and
Romeo deferentially hugging the right side of the road to
give them room.

He'd muttered once, 'I don't *ask* for trouble.'

The column had passed now anyway.

'What did you say?'

'That I've discovered the key to a problem that's been
bothering me. What gives you your singular attractiveness.'

'I'm happy for you that you've resolved it.' She laughed,
delving for her cigarettes. 'Want one of these?'

'Well – why not . . . They're under-the-counter, I imagine?
Mine are. At a price, I can get you all you want . . . Turning's
here, we'll go left – rather than all the way to Quincampoix.

Come back down there afterwards – sort of a circle, save a mile or two.'

'You know your way about, evidently.'

'Visiting farms, you get to know all the small lanes. What I was saying – that mouth of yours. It gives a man ideas.'

'That what does it?'

'Definitely. Oh, don't worry, I'm not confusing myself with the other Romeo!'

'Romantically – if that's the word – I'm rather tied up already, as it happens.'

Shades of César. One should wear a badge, perhaps. Certified member of the No Thank You Club ... He'd surprised her, though. She put a match to her cigarette – as he slowed for the turn, giving a cyclist time to get past it, coming this way ... Exhaling smoke and remembering Ben telling her – it had been at the bar in the Wellington, if she could trust that blurred snapshot in her memory – 'You're the most compulsively attractive sheila it has ever been my privilege to get pissed with.'

She'd laughed. 'You're pissed, all right!'

'True. No denying it. But listen – it's your mouth. Looks like it can't wait to start kissing. No, this isn't a come-on, I'm simply *telling* you ...'

Romeo shifted gear, starting the climb towards the woods. 'I was stating a fact, Angel, that was all. It's been a puzzle to me. You're not what I'd call conventionally beautiful, but—'

'Compliments are always welcome.'

'The best word for it might be "compulsive".'

'Might be codswallop, too.' Out of the corner of her eye she was aware of him looking at her. Watching for a reaction, no doubt. The old grafter ... She turned away, drawing deeply on her cigarette.

Amazing, though. Even the same words he'd used.

Similarly limited vocabulary?

Jacqueline had told her after their third Pernod – she'd changed the money for her, first holding the fifty-thousand note against the light to check that it was genuine – 'You could snare one of your own, you know. I could introduce you to one who'd – no, don't shake your head, he's *very* charming, comes in here quite often—'

'For a wash and set?'

'Silly. Actually, he's been away – *weeks* now. And I'm not sure I *would* let you have him, on second thoughts—'

'I wouldn't deprive you, Jacqui.'

She'd told her by that time – Jacqui had – that her German lover was a colonel of engineers, a very intelligent, attractive man who happened to be in an extremely important and influential position, had his own operational headquarters in Amiens and a luxurious apartment nearby.

'Where you spend your weekends.'

'Except when he's in Berlin. He has to attend conferences there from time to time.'

'Why not live there – in Amiens? Why here, and —'

'Because he says this is more discreet. Also during the week he's working flat-out, and moving around a lot. Actually he's busy at weekends too, sometimes.'

'People here know about your Amiens trips, don't they? That pseudo-blonde, heavyweight customer, for instance.'

'*That* old bag.' Jacqui had sniffed. 'Butter wouldn't melt, you might think. The hell it wouldn't ... With her and her kind it's jealousy, nothing else. Others – well, when I go out with Hans in Amiens – to a restaurant, for instance – or *here* for that matter, even on my own – I get that staring routine – you know?'

'Hostile?'

She'd nodded. 'From total strangers. Of course, I ignore it. Try to, anyway. Try not to think about it either. Only now and then – in the night, you know?'

'Yes – I do.'

'Well – I *should* ignore it, because in the long run – she who laughs last—'

'Ever get threats?'

'Since you mention it. And for my business I have to be

in the phone book, unfortunately. It's – not pleasant, sometimes ... But it *is* good to have someone like you to talk with, Jeanne-Marie.'

Her story was that she hadn't been looking for any man, either French *or* German: it had simply happened ...

'He's married, of course. And I swear to you, I did *not* – initiate it. But what the hell –' smiling, tossing her hair back – 'he's nuts about me, he's also rich, he has a big structural-engineering business in Germany – and just think how much structural engineering there'll be when this is over – huh? – with all the bombing that's going on? It makes him laugh out loud sometimes, just to think about it! And he's *nice*. All right, you hate Germans, but if you *met* him, Jeanne-Marie ...'

She strung her aerial wire over branches, clipped the power-supply to the *gazo*'s 6-volt battery, and settled down in the ditch with the transmitter in her lap and the headphones on. Romeo meanwhile was leaning back against the offside of the van, smoking, with a long view both ways, up and down the lane.

She got the go-ahead from Sevenoaks, and started rippling out the dots and dashes. It was quite a long transmission and she played it fast.

César now on station. Delay was due to his Lyon contact Fabien being arrested shortly after their meeting and before Pension d'Alsace raided, César then escorted US aircrew from the pension to escape réseau Switchback at Perpignan. Romeo refuses contact with César, will deal only with Angel, citing personal security as his reason and awaiting instructions for transfer to UK. Would appreciate despatch of replacement courier soonest. Requests for drops in Neuf-chatel-Amiens region currently being collected and will follow. Meanwhile intend listening watch Sundays Wednesdays Fridays midnight to 0200 GMT starting Sunday 25th. Message ends. Out.

It was about as long a transmission as she'd have wanted

to make: but not all *that* over-long, and she had no real fears of her new code being crackable at this early stage. They'd had months in which to work on Romeo's. She switched to 'Receive', waited with a message-pad resting on the set and a pencil poised, and within a minute Baker Street's signal came stuttering in; five minutes later she was in the van decoding it while Romeo coiled the aerial wire for her. He'd disconnected the set from the *gazo*'s battery first, and slammed the bonnet shut.

'Well?'

Half in, half out, surveying the road uphill and down, and as much as was visible of the surrounding countryside. There wasn't another person or vehicle in sight, but if they *had* been surprised now they'd have been necking. Earlier, it would have been a breakdown. She glanced up, told him, 'Thirtieth. Friday – nine day's time. 0130 G.M.T. Hold on ...'

He slid his thick body in, pulled the door shut. Muttering 'Nine days. Nine bloody days ...' Then: 'Where? Where, Angel?'

'Give me a minute, God's sake!'

'Sorry.' Drumming his fingers on the wheel. 'Sorry ...'

Finishing, she handed him the pad. 'Can't be far from where we are now.'

He was to be picked up by Lysander in a field – its grid coordinates were supplied – in a high, wooded area between Hêtre le Poilu and Carrefour du Chatelet.

'You're right. Not far from Bellencombre. Oh, I know it, it's a field we've used before – *no* distance from here ... Long trip out of Rouen, mind. One-thirty G.M.T., that's—'

'Midnight, French time.'

'Angel – we'll stop next at Bellencombre.' He tapped the map. 'There's a *gazo* depot, I can change the cylinder.'

'Want to check on the Lysander field, do you?'

He nodded. 'As well to be sure they haven't littered it with rocks, since the last use. I heard of that happening once. Imagine it ... But anyway it's two birds with one stone, we have a man to see at Ardouval, eh? After that cross-country to Mesnières – see it, Mesnières-en-Bray? And from there a backtrack to Neufchatel. All right?'

She was following it on the map – his own map, a legal one, pencil notes of his customers on the margins.

'Yes. All right.'

'I'll get rid of this. Hang on. Boy, oh boy . . .'

He was excited – elated – his large hands clumsy as he ripped off that sheet and a few blank but indented ones under it. Climbing out, he dropped the ball of paper at the roadside, crouched to put a match to it – the third match did it – then crushed the ashes under his heel. Another visual check in both directions before he eased himself back in behind the wheel – slamming his hands down on it and chuckling suddenly, turning to grin at her . . . Like a big, grey-headed schoolboy, she thought – a schoolboy in the state of mind which she remembered had been known to her and her friends as 'term-enditis'. She smiled back at him, thinking what a very nice man he was: he leant to her, kissed her cheek. 'Come see me off, will you, Friday week?'

13

Saturday, late afternoon: they were coming into Rouen from the northwest, having detoured that way in order to send off the last of the requests for weapons drops from the countryside near Yerville. It had been Rosie's fifth transmission since that one on Wednesday: six in all, and by this time at least five of them would be in Baker Street and decoded.

Romeo's murmur, on her left: 'We haven't done at all badly, Angel, you know?'

Glancing her way ... She'd been fiddling with her bra on that side, where she had the suicide pill. When she'd sewn the pocket into this one she'd left an edge which had now become scratchy. The other bra, which she'd washed on Tuesday night and left in her room at Ursule's to dry, was the second she'd done and she'd managed it more neatly.

She'd agreed – massaging that shoulder instead – 'A lot better than I'd have done on my own, I'll tell you *that*.'

They'd given the bastards plenty to chew on. The *Reichssicherheitshauptampt*'s long-range radio direction finders would have picked up all her signals, the first from that place just north of Rouen, then four from the Neuf-chatel-Amiens area and today's from west of the Rouen-Dieppe road. Six transmissions in four days. She could imagine the behind-scenes activity: cypher experts burning the midnight oil, detector vans deploying around Amiens – ready to lock on to further transmissions which wouldn't be forthcoming – and wires humming between the various Security departments. A new pianist at work, a hitherto unknown hand and code prefixes: obviously a new *réseau* in being, in place of the one they'd smashed. If they'd been as thorough as they were cracked up to be, she thought, they'd have had checkpoints on all these routes by now, stopping every vehicle and searching it for the radio. After all, the previous *réseau* had been based in Rouen – why not assume the new one would be, and that the pianist might be on his or her way home?

In these four days they'd been stopped only once: the other side of Neufchatel, on the second day. *Milice* had checked their papers and asked the usual questions, only glancing casually into the back of the van and then releasing them. Romeo had muttered, as he'd put the *gazo* into gear and got it moving, '*Eight* days to go ...'

He'd warned her, this morning, that the heat would be on now.

'You could say you're in a minefield – which is a basic, permanent situation, you could always tread on one any minute –' a gesture, hands momentarily off the wheel, simulating an explosion – 'but now there'll be snipers too.' A shrug. 'If there weren't before – who knows? I mean they'll be out looking for you – for this pianist, they have a target now.' Then, after about a minute, 'I'll feel bad ducking out on you, Angel.'

'Don't be silly.'

'I'd recommend my system to you, incidentally. Staying clear, I mean. Other than César, of course. Like I worked with Max? Worked for *me* – eh?'

'They'll probably send a new courier in the Lysander that comes for you, though. He and I'll have to know each other.'

'Not to know where you live or what you're doing. Not to hobnob with you either. Persuade César. Everything through *him* – pianist otherwise on her own. Other way of putting it, you're *his* pianist.' Glancing round at her, scowling ... 'Stay *alive*, Angel!'

Last night, Friday, had been spent in a forester's house near Ardouval. Their second visit – it had been their first port of call on Wednesday and while they'd gone on eastward the forester had arranged for Resistance colleagues from Londinières, Evermeu and le Mesnil-Réaume to bring their wives to this social gathering. Only an hour or two before the party got together Rosie had listened to the BBC's Overseas News broadcast and heard the pre-arranged message *Ma belle-soeur est devenue malade*. The timing had been perfect: she'd been able to tell the men around the table, 'You may be interested to know there'll be two drops tomorrow night, and a bombing attack in the same area as a diversion. Believe me, we *are* back in business.'

Romeo had been looking at her with an eyebrow cocked. This had been the first he'd heard of the Lyons-la-Forêt operations. Rosie had murmured, 'Tell you later.' Then looked from him to a *réseau* leader who'd leant towards her across the table to make some point.

'Yes, monsieur?'

'Certain other groups have been given priority over us, have they?'

She'd known this one was a communist; the forester had mentioned it. And his comment, she thought, was typical. Cooperation as long as his own group got what it wanted, but not a hint of friendship or gratitude, only suspicion that maybe they could be getting more. She'd told him – all of them – 'These are drops that were asked for some time ago and arranged before I left London, obviating the need for radio exchanges which might be intercepted. But there's no question of priorities – it's first come, first served. This is a new start, and the requests you're making now will be among the first that I'm transmitting ... However – I have another subject to raise now. The Nazis' so-called "Secret Weapons". Have any of you any knowledge of construction work, or survey teams at work – German-led, possibly organized from Amiens – in connection with rocket-sites, in your districts?'

'What form of constructions might they be?'

A big man: a farmer, name of Duclos. She told him, 'Concrete, some sort of ramp pointing towards the Channel. There'd also be huts, accommodation for technicians and military guards, storage and so on. They'll need to connect power-lines and telephones – which could be easy sabotage targets, incidentally. Probably a barbed-wire perimeter.'

'How many such sites?'

'We don't know. Could be hundreds. But for our purposes, they've got to be located so our bombers can hit them, knock them out or at least delay construction. Otherwise the danger is of heavy and continuous bombardment of the south of England, even to the extent of making it impossible to mount the invasion we're all waiting and praying for. That's unthinkable, you'll agree.'

They'd agreed, all right.

She'd had to let Romeo in on this line of enquiry. He was with her all the time, had to be, and in any case she felt sure of him now. She'd told him about it – this end of it, the field research, nothing about Jacqui or her colonel – right at the start of the trip, on Wednesday night in the house of a woman schoolteacher in Neufchatel. Romeo had dossed in the living room, and Rosie had shared the teacher's bed. And there'd been several meetings similar to last night's, at which she'd collected requests for weapons drops and asked for reports of rocket-site developments. The research was to cover a wide area – from Amiens, the word was being passed to *réseaux* as far away as Arras and Lille.

He'd asked her this morning, soon after they'd got on the road, 'Two drops tonight, you mentioned?'

'Should be.' She'd touched the wooden dashboard for luck. 'Catch that same broadcast later, I hope.'

'In the area of Lyons-la-Forêt – both of them?'

She'd stared at him: and he'd chuckled ... 'Where you went last weekend, wasn't it?'

'What makes you think so?'

'I was called upon to give you a reference. Friend of mine

telephoned, asked whether I'd ever heard of an angel who
rode a bicycle. He thought a real one might have used its
damn wings, he said.'

'Play your cards close to your chest, don't you?'

'Don't *you*?'

'Georges Lebrun, I suppose.'

'That's the fellow. More to him than you'd guess at first
sight. Dry old stick, eh?'

These *had* been well-spent days. She'd even managed to
visit shops in Neufchatel and Amiens, offering the Cazalet
range of perfumes. In one, an effeminate Belgian had sniffed
at each sample, gone into raptures over some of them and
promised to send an order direct to Paris. He had a friend
who was a friend of Pierre Cazalet, he'd mentioned, and
she'd thought, *Small world* . . .

She'd been doing some hard thinking about Jacqui.
Another item from the advice she'd been given by the people
in St James' had been that there were often situations in
which you had either to take a risk head-on, or bog down and
get nowhere. 'A tide to be taken at the flood' had been the
relevant quotation, and it seemed to her entirely apposite to
the present situation, vis-à-vis Jacqueline Clermont: the
basics of it being (1) that she couldn't know how much time
she'd have – realistically, this did have to be faced – and
(2) that as things stood at the moment she did seem to have
an exceptionally good hand to play.

So – forget those earlier qualms, push it along now.

See César on Sunday, she thought. It would be too late
tonight. Call him this evening and arrange to meet tomorrow,
and see Jacqui on Monday if possible. She'd be in Amiens
until then. Call in at the shop: an excuse for dropping in
might be to tell her that her willingness to stock his scents
and toilet waters had been passed to Pierre Cazalet, who was
delighted and would be writing to her shortly. Actually Rosie
hadn't done anything about it yet, but she'd give him a call
early in the week. Tell him about the Belgian, too – make the
old dear's day for him.

*

They'd done a lot of talking – on the road, mainly, but also practically all night on the one occasion they'd shared a room – Thursday, on a farm near Foncarmont, where as well as conducting S.O.E. business he'd mended a tractor. He'd slept on the floor on a mattress of folded blankets, and she'd had the couch, which had probably been less comfortable. In the course of hours of sporadic chat, she'd asked him what had got him into S.O.E.

'The same as everyone else. I was recruited. Fluent French and sterling qualities – isn't that it?'

'But you were over here in the first place – I mean, to *be* recruited.'

'Sure. Came by boat. Big one, very tall funnels, French boat. Oh, the *Pasteur*.'

'To England?'

'France, then England after the debacle ... D'you know Mauritius?'

'Hardly. *Heard* about it.'

'It's the loveliest place on earth. Come visit us one day, eh? Meet the wife and children.'

'I thought you told me she'd run out on you.'

'*New* wife. I told you the old one skipped out, that's true. Incredible, don't you agree?'

'Absolutely.'

'Yeah, well ... She went with this French guy, to Réunion. Kids are in Mauritius though, with my sister.'

'And this new wife—'

'Some lucky girl got a big surprise coming, uh?'

'Oh.' She'd caught on. 'My, *hasn't* she!'

'It's a pipe dream. You have to live on something, eh? What does your man do, Angel – *your* new one?'

'He's in the Navy. Thought I'd told you ... But he's also an artist.'

'Painter? Good one?'

'I don't know. Haven't seen any of his pictures yet. Did I tell you he's Australian?'

'Don't think you did. But look here – Mauritius is on the way to Australia – if you come round the Cape, that is. You and he might stop off sometime, eh?'

'Lovely idea . . . You'll definitely be going back there, will you, after all this?'

'Oh, sure. My kids . . .'

Then – out of the dark, after a minute or two of silence – 'He's got to be a *very* good man to deserve you, Angel.'

One of the things she'd remember all her life, she thought, as the *gazo* carried them through the Bois de Guillaume. Not only what he'd said, but that gravelly voice out of the surrounding darkness in which they'd both been very much aware that any such continuance – survival, to enjoy it – could only be a hope, never an assumption.

Pigot wasn't in the garage, but Romeo had a key to the wrecked Ford's boot; he extracted an old wireless-set and plugged it in, in the office. He checked his watch: 1915 Greenwich Mean Time meant 1745 Central European Time, and it was now 1754.

'Just made it, Angel. If we're lucky.' In time, he meant, for the messages that would follow the bulletin. He lit their cigarettes: as an essential preliminary, she supposed – fretting, slightly . . . Twiddling knobs then, getting atmospherics as well as bursts of the usual jamming, and finally Bruce Belfridge's voice, thin at first – summarizing, repeating the headlines. Palermo had fallen to Allied forces, Mussolini was thought to be on his way out, Allied bombers had hit Rome.

Lost it again, in the jamming: the bit that mattered. Adjusting the tuning, microscopically . . .

Bernard vient d'acheter un complet neuf.

Good for him: but that would be news for someone else. Not that it mattered if she and Romeo missed out on theirs – as long as the others got it, Lebrun in Lyons-la-Forêt and Juvier in Beauvais. They'd have heard it last night and alerted their reception teams, would probably be with them now, straining their ears for this confirmation.

The broadcaster's voice broke through a lot of crackling: '– *est devenue malade.*'

Rosie murmured, 'There ...'

Watching Romeo, who was still crouched over the wireless, glancing up smiling as the repetition came '*Ma belle-soeur est devenue malade.*'

She cycled through the town to Ursule's. Romeo had given her the rations that were left – some stale sandwiches and an apple – and she might be able to make tea in Ursule's kitchen, she thought. Ring César first, though, get that over. She was very tired suddenly, the exertions of the past few days catching up on her.

Jacqui's money was all there, in the cavity under the floorboard, and she put the Mark III in with it, brushing dust over the board when it was back in place. The radio's next use would be tomorrow night, the first of her listening-out routines; Baker Street might have some responses to her requests for drops, by then.

Really, one *had* achieved quite a lot.

She went down to see Ursule – who reminded her that a week's rent was due, but agreed she could use her stove to boil a kettle – then went out to the telephone in the hallway. It took a few minutes to get Monsieur Rossier down to the Belle Femme's telephone.

'That you, Jeanne-Marie?'

'I'm back, Michel darling. Ringing just to let you know all's well. How are you, sweetheart?'

He'd grunted – surprised, for a moment ... Rock of a man not all that quick on the uptake, she mentally noted ...

'Will you come here – *now*? We could have something to eat?'

'Oh, I'd love to, but—'

'Uh?'

'Michel dear, it's so late!'

'*Late*?'

'The curfew, darling. And by the time I've cleaned up and changed – *have* to, I've ridden about a hundred kilometres today – frankly, I'm exhausted!'

Two tarts on their way out stared at her as they passed. Skinny legs under short skirts, wooden shoes clacking on the linoleum. All the lads would be in town of course, tonight. César was agreeing reluctantly, 'All right – so come tomorrow. As early as you like, but you could lunch with me here, or—'

'Can't wait. *Lots* to tell you, darling …'

'Went well, did it?'

'*Very* well. Except I missed you—'

'Anything about our mutual friend?'

'Yes, it's all fixed.' The tarts were in the doorway to Ursule's apartment, and one of them was listening. And over this telephone line, *anyone* might be listening … Rosie told him, 'Don't worry, darling, I'll—'

'Talking to him tonight, d'you expect?'

'I don't know. Might try, later. Anyway—'

'He's got to be told, hasn't he – as soon as possible, surely. And perhaps now he'd consent to talk to me – might join us tomorrow, if you asked him nicely?'

'I'll ask him – *if* I get him.'

'Another thing is I'd like a list of the new customers you've found. The whole business. When you can?'

The idea was highly unattractive. But she agreed – 'All right. If I can stay awake that long.'

'It doesn't necessarily have to be done tonight, Jeanne-Marie.'

'All right. I dare say … But Michel – darling – I really *must* go and have a bath, while the water lasts. So—'

'It's finished, honey!' The tart in the doorway had called this to her. Adding – by way of explanation – 'It's Saturday, after all!'

She sighed, turning away. 'Michel?'

'Who was that?'

'Just another – inmate. Says there's no hot water left.

Look, I'm going to run – it may not be *completely* cold. See
you tomorrow?'

She did all her chores before turning in: including a repair
to the bra that had begun to irritate. Laundering it then, with
other 'smalls'. The thought in her head meanwhile of having
to put all those Resistance men's names, addresses and other
particulars on paper appalled her. Names on bits of paper
could be death warrants. If she were stopped and searched
on her way to the Belle Femme in the morning, for instance
... There was a sense of treachery involved, simply in
risking it. Not only those individuals' lives, but their
families' as well: and they were paying her the compliment
of trusting her, for God's sake ...

She wrote slowly, unwillingly. By the time she'd finished
she was so tired she could hardly think straight. Preparing
for bed, finding the suicide pill on the bedside table where
she'd put it before starting the sewing job: she barely
remembered having put it there. The rice paper was intact
but discoloured, somewhat. Sweat. All the long, hot days.
Might *not* be such a marvellous idea – if it got really soaked.
If sweat had the same effect that saliva was supposed to
have?

Marilyn's voice: *Bring the beastly little thing back with
you – uh?*

She'd dropped off – almost. Perched on the edge of the
bed: jerking awake again, and pushing herself off it – to
attend to the window: light off first, then drawn back the
heavy blackout curtains – she already had the sash window
pushed right up, not only for air to breathe but with thoughts
of the bombing raid on La Haye, the chance of hearing it.
Straight-line distance being roughly twenty-five kilometres
– thirty at most.

Conditions were good, for the bombers and for the drops.
Very little wind, no cloud that she could see, stars paled by
a nearly full moon. Leaning in the window, her head and
shoulders out, gazing up at it: thinking of it as a bombers'

moon tonight, and that next weekend when it would be only about half the size it would serve as a Lysander's moon. Thinking of which led her to that question of César's – but there'd been no *danger* in it. A breach of the convention to have asked, but – she could hear it in her memory, an entirely conversational tone, and he'd made no attempt to return to the question when she'd hedged.

Exhaustion bred paranoia.

And the remedy for exhaustion was – bed.

And sleep. Like the surf on that dark beach – washing over her, washing her into dreams conjured by her last waking thoughts. Distant drumming of exploding bombs, flames reflected in the sky, and a few miles away – she'd got there herself, somehow – in the forest clearing with other dark, wordless characters grouped here and there, pinpoints of red torches marking the extremities of the dropping ground, and one torch unmasked, white, flashing the recognition signal into the sky. Lebrun, that was – his pale face upturned to the moon, the torch aimed at a single oncoming aircraft – black, twin-engined, blasting over in its own welter of deafening sound and the containers spilling out, 'chutes opening as the noise peaked and immediately fell away. Gone: but the loads swinging earthward, men standing back staring up to catch sight of them in mid-air before each crashed down shaking the hard-baked ground and was then surrounded by the dark shapes desperately bundling the masses of material and lines then humping the containers into the cover of the wood and to whatever transport they had waiting – a farm-cart, coal-lorry, forester's tractor with a trailer ... Rosie woke in the morning – having heard nothing, slept without moving from the moment her head had sunk into the pillow – with the thought in her mind that Lebrun would have seen to it, surely, that the villagers were warned: a whisper of unknown origin, family to family. She *hoped* they'd have managed that.

César hadn't heard the bombing either, but he'd heard *of* it.

By breakfast time everyone in Rouen had heard that the target had been a *Wehrmacht* ammunition dump at La Haye, part of which had blown up: there'd been one extremely loud explosion, apparently. It was also said that there'd been considerable loss of life. The younger son of the house, Gaston, had told César this when he'd brought him his morning *ersatz* coffee.

'We're less well informed, on Rive Gauche.' Rosie had attended Mass in the Saint Sever church, breakfasted late and got to the Belle Femme in mid-morning: she'd been shown up to Monsieur Rossier's room by the other boy, Emil. 'All we heard was there'd been a raid somewhere east of here.' She added, 'Let's hope the lives lost were all German.'

César stared at her for a moment. She added, 'Not only as a worthwhile end in itself, but it doesn't help *us* much to have our own people killing Frenchmen, does it.'

'No. No, of course not.' He changed the subject. 'Did you get hold of Romeo?'

'Sorry, no. Being Sunday – and having no idea where he lives. Catch him tomorrow, I expect. His pickup's set for Friday night, by the way – Lysander, a field near Bellencombre. If you've got your map—'

'Bellencombre . . .' He went over to the briefcase which he kept locked, and opened it. He was wearing lightweight khaki trousers and a white open-necked shirt. Barely thirty, she'd have guessed – let alone the forty or so they'd said he was. He came limping back, opening the map. 'Show me.'

'Here. It's a clearing in woodland, quite high. The R/V's set for midnight, French time. I'll go out there that day and be on hand to meet the new man – if they send one. I'd guess they will – wouldn't you?' He'd nodded; she went on, 'The *réseau* leader there is a forester by name of Plumier, lives at Ardouval.' She put her finger on the map again. 'I spent a night in his house, he'd got some of the others together so I was able to kill several birds at one go. Did the same in a couple of other places too. Saving legwork – and time on the road is time one's exposed, isn't it?'

'You've thought it all out.'

'Well. Common sense, really. Anyway this isn't my first deployment, Michel.'

'No. Of course . . .'

Looking at her as if she fascinated him. Although why she should have was a mystery. He was a far more experienced agent than she was, by all accounts. *And* Buckmaster's blue-eyed boy. She thought, *Perhaps it's my damn mouth again* . . . Telling him, 'The other places I had several together at once were Neufchatel and a village just south of Amiens called Dury. The king-pin there is a cattle dealer by name of Mattan.'

'As I said, Angel – although you didn't exactly enthuse – I need to have all the names and details. If anything should happen to you – and with Romeo out of it—'

'I know. I just hate putting names on paper. To be honest, I didn't much like having to talk about it on the phone, either. Also I was – exhausted.'

'I realized that. As to telephones, though – well, you're right, but – frankly, Angel, speaking as a *very* experienced agent – one can put too many obstacles in one's own path. Obviously, one doesn't articulate certain words . . . Huh?'

It was true, she thought, as she remembered their conversation, that it *could* have been some business subject they'd been discussing . . . She shrugged. 'Anyway – here it is.' Unrolling yesterday's *Le Matin*, which she'd picked up at Ursule's, and flattening the curled sheets of paper which she'd had inside it. 'Item one, copies of all the transmissions I made. This on its own gives you most of the story, really.'

'Let me see.'

She sat back, reached for a cigarette. 'Want one?'

A quick shake of the fair head: impatient, eager to read the stuff. The moustache still looked silly. When they knew each other better, she thought, she'd pick a good moment to suggest it didn't really suit him. Or that he'd be handsomer without it . . . He was engrossed in the material she'd given him, narrow eyes sliding to and fro, diverting now and then to check a location on the map.

Finishing, he glancing across at her. Looking surprised – or admiring, or both . . .

'This is a *heck* of a lot of munitions they'll have coming in.' Glancing down at the pages again, flicking through them . . . 'What, a dozen different groups here?'

'Eleven. It's been some time, remember, since they had anything. And the closer we get to the invasion the more they're anxious to stock up. Incidentally, there'll have been two drops last night, under cover of the La Haye bombing.'

The slit eyes glared at her.

'Last night? Last *night*, Angel? Drops *you* arranged?'

'Not exactly. London did, before I came out. All I had to do was tip the boys off to be ready for it. I did that the weekend before you arrived.'

'And decided not to mention it to me?'

He looked angry. Really *very* angry: you could see it growing in him. She shook her head, holding his stare. 'It was done. On Colonel Buckmaster's orders. If you'd been here when I arrived – but you weren't, I simply got on with it. I'm sorry – perhaps I *should* have told you about it – but really, what for? Never occurred to me, I don't think.'

'Never occurred to you . . . Jeanne-Marie – I'm the Organizer here. Remember? Don't you think I should know what's going on? Are you working with me, or are you an independent operator?'

'Now you're here, I work with you. Under your direction. Obviously.' She exhaled smoke. 'Goes without saying. But why you should be – as furious as you *seem* to be—'

'Furious . . .' Still glaring . . . 'Yes. Also – *amazed* . . . I'm your Organizer, for God's sake, I *insist* on being informed of every damn thing that goes on here! What you do, or intend doing, or are told to do by London—'

'Michel, listen.' She'd got up, was standing at one of the windows, her back to it. 'Let's understand each other . . . I work under your orders – now. Before you got here I didn't

– obviously. I was under orders from Baker Street. What's more, I was trained – as you must have been too, and both of us must have practised this in the field – not to provide people with information they don't need. I certainly don't want any *I* don't need . . . All right?'

'Well—'

'Romeo's case is relevant, isn't it? He's proved something – by distancing himself from all the members of his former *réseau* except the Organizer he's alive although the rest of them are dead – or may wish they were . . . I think I'd like to work in much the same way – contact with you, no-one else. We could work like that, couldn't we?'

He sighed, passing a hand across his eyes . . .

'Yes, we could. I'd have no objection to that at all. But sit down, Jeanne-Marie. And let's *calm* down. As you say – we *must* understand each other. I'm sorry – you took me by surprise – you'll admit it's unusual for an Organizer to be told *after* a drop takes place . . . I still think you *should* have told me. I take it, incidentally, that you'll be following up, to check they got it all?'

'No need.' She shook her head. 'If anything went wrong, I'd hear. Anyway – here's the next instalment.' A second sheaf of notepaper: she pushed it to him across the table. 'The last two names on this are last night's recipients. I met them both in Lyons-la-Forêt, in the schoolmaster's house – as I said, the weekend before you arrived. I was looking for you here that Thursday, of course, and you *weren't* here so I went ahead. Lebrun is the schoolmaster. Mousey little man, but he's right on the ball.'

He was lost again, absorbed in her notes. His insistence on having it all on paper was justified, she'd realized, in a way. Usually you'd make one contact at a time, or at most two or three, and commit them to memory; she did happen to have an exceptionally reliable and capacious one. But César could hardly have managed this lot without having notes to refer to when he needed.

'You won't leave that screed lying around, I hope?'

'What?'

Still reading ... Glancing up then, a finger at the point he'd reached. Blank for a moment, before it sank in. 'No – of course not.' Eyes down again. Rosie watching him, her cigarette nearly finished, holding the stub between fingertip and thumbtip to get the last of it. Sounds of a brass band out there: some Boche parade. They were inclined to dress up and goose-step through the towns which they infested, on Sundays.

Music certainly *not* the food of love, she thought. More a cacophony of hate.

He'd finished. Shuffling the sheets together, folding them; his hands shaking slightly, she noticed. Glancing up at her then, hesitating – as if he was getting himself together ... 'Last night's bombing was intended only as a cover to these drops, you said?'

'Three birds with one stone. Hitting the Boche ammo dump at La Haye would have been a worthwhile effort anyway, I'd have thought. But listen, Michel – I've another thing to tell you about. Before you complain of being left in the dark again. When I met these people I wasn't *only* collecting requests for drops and suggestions for dropping-fields and so on, I was asking them for something in return.'

She told him about the rocket-site research. Not mentioning Colonel Walther, of course, only the fact she'd asked for reports on any survey operations or construction work.

'In fact this isn't S.O.E. business, Michel, it's S.I.S. Maurice Buckmaster agreed they could use me for it, and he suggested I should let you in on it if I felt I needed help. S.I.S. on the other hand made it clear they'd rather I kept it to myself.'

'Buck's the man *I'd* follow. He's a great guy. Truly is. Did I tell you he came to my wedding?'

'I don't think so.'

'In Dublin?'

'Well – no. But—'

'It's where my wife is. She's there now. Out of the

bombing, thank God ... But are you saying you've found you do need my help?'

'No. No, I'm not.' She added – with a quick smile, softening it – 'Thanks all the same ... It's only that we're sure to get messages coming in about it, I don't want to have to keep them from you, so it's best to tell you. It's my personal brief, though, there's nothing for you to do.'

'All right ... They'll cooperate, will they?' He touched her notes. 'This bunch?'

'It's very much in their interests, isn't it?' She nodded. 'And not only them – every *réseau* to the north and east, right into the Pas de Calais.'

'They're passing the request along – that it?'

She nodded. 'Some reports may go direct to London, of course. That's what I've asked for, hope for. But we're likely to field at least a few here too – *if* anything of that sort's happening.'

'Yes. Yes – *if* it is ... Anyway – as you say, it's your personal brief, so – just keep me informed. Primarily, in case anything happened to you – and there'd be pieces to pick up ... Meanwhile, Angel,' – he patted her notes – 'I must say, you've made a *flying* start ...'

14

The moon was about full. Ben rode stooped low over the handlebars, using the shadow in the deep lanes close to their hedges, hugging the wrong side when that was the dark one: he was retracing the route by which he'd come with Vidor eight days ago, having to think hard to remember the twists and turns. Slanting right now where another lane came in from the left: somewhere ahead there, this straight bit, was where that truck had been stopped, the Demorêts' farm.

Seemingly deserted now. No glimmer of light, except the moon's on glass. Tall, straight trees like mourners: you'd expect owls, the flutter of bats, that scream ... Pedalling on – legs pumping, heart pumping too, breaths harshly audible in his one good ear ... Boche patrols were more frequent than they'd been a week ago, Boches thicker on the ground all over this peninsula and its immediate hinterland; Madame Durand had told him that she'd heard they *were* searching for weapons caches. Perhaps for the one cache which Vidor had decided should be left where it was. So what changes of survival this L'Abervrac'h pinpoint might have, God knew.

And if chances of getting to Grac'h Zu still weren't good: well, what the *hell* ...

Sweating, in the distinctly cool night air. A wind off the Atlantic being the cooling factor. Sweating internally too, though, over what might have happened to Bright and Farr.

He remembered having wondered a few days ago how things might be without Vidor holding it all together. And that was the situation now: or seemed to be. Germans all over – one team had paid a visit to Durand's garage, two days ago, had poked around, fortunately not amongst the debris in the yard amongst which Ben had been crouching, hearing their contemptuous remarks and questions to old Durand, addressing him in bad French and the tone you might use to a dog if you didn't like it – this had been Ben's first close brush with them, and foremost in his mind had been that in his scarecrow outfit he'd undoubtedly be treated as a spy, however strongly he claimed to be a serving naval officer.

For 'serving', he thought, read 'bloody useless'.

The home team, during Vidor's absence, had been doing absolutely nothing. Only conversing briefly in whispers when they met, exchanging whatever scraps of gossip or information there might be: who'd been arrested, whose place had been searched yesterday or last night . . .

A couple of hours ago Durand had told him, his back to him as he climbed down from his breakdown vehicle – 'There's bad news and there's worse. How it goes, these days – eh?'

He'd towed in a broken-down BMW *gazo*, nose-up on the truck's hand-operated winch. It looked like scrap, but there were plenty like it on French roads. He'd been to Plouvien to collect it, had intended stopping in Lannilis on his way back, to lend an ear to whatever was being said, if anything. He might have been there for hours, if anyone had offered him a drink, but obviously they hadn't. Ben had been at the back of the garage, keeping an eye on the wide-open doors – as he knew he had to, had been doing for a bloody week now – and not expecting the little *garagiste* back before dark.

Which it would be pretty soon now anyway.

He got up on the truck's tail. 'Not bad news of Vidor, I hope.'

Vidor had left on Wednesday, escorting the flyers to

Bordeaux via Rennes and Nantes; he'd reckoned on two days each way and maybe one day in Bordeaux handing them over. Back Monday evening at the earliest, therefore, and any news of him at this stage might well have been bad: *very* bad, then, for anyone around here. Everything hung on him: he was the mainspring of it all.

Durand turned his head, and spat. 'Wouldn't be word of him yet. Couldn't be . . . OK, then, turn her down.'

Ben had the brake off the winch: he began winding it down. Durand told him, 'First thing is there're more fucking Boches around – Lannilis and here – than there was even last week. In the café there even – stiff with 'em . . . OK, that does it.' Jerking chain loose, to unhook. 'Other thing is – well, I got this from Luc's sister—'

Luc being Vidor's radio operator: they kept their transceiver in an attic over the café, Vidor had mentioned, used it sometimes for chatting to Baker Street even when the café itself was full of Germans. Luc and his sister both worked there, behind the bar.

Durand straightened. 'Come to think of it, might be a headache for *you*, this one. She told me – Hélène Vannier did – they raided the Brodards' farm, see, and—'

'*Brodards*'?'

Where Bright and Farr were still holed up . . .

'—he's dead, poor bugger. They're calling it – according to Hélène – heart attack. Couldn't talk more then; like I said, they're in there thick as fucking cockroaches.'

'My men are there – she didn't say—'

'No. Didn't.' The little man was rolling himself a cigarette. 'I just thought of that, too. Only spoke about ten seconds, mind you—'

'—how it happened – or whether the daughter's—'

'Fuck-all. Like I said—'

'Look, I'm going. Soon as it's a bit darker. Christ, should have gone *days* ago!'

'Then you'd've been bagged too. Time to gimme a hand with this, have you?'

There was going to be a damn great moon in any case. But he *should* have joined them long before this, would have if Vidor hadn't advised against it: and being an intruder here, a liability to them in the first place, he'd felt obliged to cooperate. Durand had even warned him again now – his little eyes beady as a lizard's flicking over him – 'Do better to stay put. I tell you, the sods are all over . . .'

Damn right, they were. He'd just heard them – petrol engine, and the rumble of its tyres on the rough road: glancing back, swerving out into the middle of the lane as he did so and then correcting so quickly that he'd almost come off . . .

Talk about bloody fools. Right in the middle then, in full moonlight – only for a couple of seconds, but the driver'd have to be stone blind not to have seen him.

Had seen him. Shifting gear, *revving* . . . Ben in an edging of black shadow about five feet wide pedalling flat out. Uselessly – putting every ounce of his weight into it but also knowing it was pointless effort, they'd overtake him anyway and couldn't be anything but German – this time of night, and a petrol-engined vehicle – one of their damn patrols . . . Teeth clenched, the old bike rattly under him, engine-noise louder every second. Oh, Jesus . . .

A swathe of moonlight lay right across the road ahead, too. He'd be floodlit again . . . He realized then, though – there'd be a gap in the hedge, gateway: faint hope, therefore – coming up *now* . . . He swung into it, into the brilliant moonlight, off the bike then and carrying it with him, trotting: it wasn't actually a gate, but an old bedstead filling the gap. He lifted the bike, flung it over into the field, and followed. The bedstead had barbed wire on it, which in other circumstances might have been painful. He picked up the bike and pushed it into the hedge – not exactly hidden but not in plain sight either – hearing the truck braking, wheels locking, ploughing up loose stones: he was running by then, back the way he'd come, in the field – the field side of the hedge, its moonlit side. It might have been instinctive to

have gone on the way one had been going: he hoped –
vaguely, although mainly acting on impulse, having to
choose one way or the other – they might more naturally
search that other way. Or into the field, directly away from
the lane. A small field, triangular, with trees in it – fruit trees,
he guessed. They might think he'd have gone *that* way –
across it, directly away from the road, using the trees'
shadow for cover from this *bloody* moon.

Most people would have, he supposed.

Should have, probably. He flung himself down flat and lay
still, virtually *in* the hedge. Hearing shouts in German: and
the truck backing up . . . Germans were already in the field,
though – they'd have jumped down as the thing braked,
come running back . . . More shouting then, and he guessed
they'd found the bike.

Should have gone straight over, using those trees' cover.
Lying flat in lush, deep grass close to the hedge's roots, he
saw more soldiers climbing over, the moon bright as a
searchlight on them. Torches, too: with which to probe into
hedgerows, do doubt. Any minute now. Telling himself
caustically *another* triumph for Benjamin bloody Quarry.
Probably his last, at that. What to do – jump up and run, and
get shot in the back, or stand up and surrender, get shot or
hanged a bit later?

Hang on, though . . .

Fanning out, into the field. Torch-beams fingering in the
shadows, and the rest all floodlit anyway. Sudden racket of
beating wings as a roosting pigeon broke out: torch-beam
shining up there, into that tree. *Might* have climbed up into
a tree, he thought: except it would have been such a bloody
obvious thing to do. Scaring the birds too, dead giveaway.
But seeing a climbable tree with no moonlight penetrating,
one might have.

Be feeling bloody stupid now if you had, old chum. Not
having thought of them having torches . . . He turned his face
down, into the grass, in case the moonlight might catch its
comparative pallor where beard didn't cover it. Thinking then,

So far, so good, *not* so fucking stupid. This far, anyway. *Only* this far: things might change dramatically when they finished messing among the trees. Unless there were easy exits from the field on that other side, in which case they might extend the search in that direction. It was probably what *he'd* do, he thought, in their jackboots ... On the other hand they might not be so dim-witted as not to consider the possibility that the fugitive had come this way. A few might be detached from the main party, on the off-chance ...

More shouts. He'd never liked the sound of that language. Not in men's voices, anyway. He turned his head the other way, towards the hedge, and woke up to the fact that he was looking *through* it. That background of brilliance was the moon's illumination of the lane's centre and left-hand side.

Hedge therefore penetrable?

Problem being that if it proved not to be, or to be penetrable only with great difficulty – it certainly wouldn't be *easy* – one might make enough noise and disturbance to draw the bastards' attention. But – shrugging, mentally – might do that just lying there, too: so what the hell ... Then – as he started worming round, to try his luck – second hazard: if one or more of them had been left behind, to watch the lane ...

Good chance they hadn't, he thought. Once in this field a searcher might well look around, see this long hedgerow and decide *Best take a shufti along there, lads*, but just off the cuff he'd hardly expect his quarry to double back *into* the lane ... He was still hearing shouts from somewhere out there in the field or on its far side, but the sounds of his own laboriously slow progress were louder, in his one good ear. Head-first, worming, thrusting a way through, aware that the tunnel he was making would be visible – at close range anyway – to any searcher.

Unless they attributed it to foxes or badgers ...

Nearly through. He'd be emerging into the shadowed side of the lane, fortunately. Stay in it, turn and creep back to the left, the direction from which one had come?

Might get away with it ...

At least, if another patrol didn't come along too soon.

But they'd still be between him and where he had to get to. A detour might be a possibility, but not knowing the country at all well – only the way he'd come with Vidor, and even that without much certainty – mightn't be all that simple.

Across the lane, through the other hedge into the field *that* side?

He was through now, anyway. Crouching close to the hedge, well inside the band of moonshadow and watching to his right for movement around the troop-transport – which was what it looked like. Tail lights glowing like red eyes.

Glow of a cigarette, beyond them – on the roadside, *this* verge.

Bloody hell ...

If one moved out into the moonlight, even if that Kraut was facing the other way – into the field, where the action was – and one made the smallest sound, sent one stone skittering – well, he'd be looking *this* way, and the next thing would be a bullet.

Sit tight, wait for them to go away?

A shout – from mid-field, by the sound of it – and the one with the cigarette was moving. Into moonlight, showing himself – the truck had hidden him until now – he was there for a few seconds, motionless as he drew hard on the cigarette then dropped it and put his foot on it: a soldier, slim-bodied under his helmet, which in the moonlight and a streak of shadow gave him the look of some kind of mushroom: then he'd moved again, vanished into the recess of the gateway.

So – *move*. Baboon-like, stooped double so his fingers brushed the ground: into the moonlight without pausing or anticipating – either a shout or shots – then diving flat again, still floodlit but against this other hedge: and in nettles. Lying still for a moment – facing into the hedge, listening hard, his own heart's thuds astonishingly loud ...

Snatches of distant German exchanges, despondent or angry-sounding.

Giving up?

If so, they'd all be thronging back, to that gateway and their transport: might as an afterthought make a recce along that hedge and find the hole ... Really, might *well* ... He began to fight and wriggle his way into *this* hedge: discovering immediately that what it had over the other one was brambles. Wondering again what might have happened to Farr and Bright: who were in whatever hole they *were* in through nothing but his own cock-up – and whom he should have rejoined days ago ...

Through. In a shallow ditch, with multiple lacerations and more nettles. Clothes, such as they were, doubtless in ribbons. Bright and Farr had at least been wearing uniform, he remembered; if they'd been arrested they couldn't legitimately be shot or hanged as spies. Not *legitimately*, they couldn't ... He began to crawl – in the band of moonshade, up this side of the hedge towards the truck. To get on that side of them, en route to the Brodard place: having no idea how long they might hang around here. Might be about to leave, might not, might only be regrouping to search in another direction.

Why go to such effort, though – for one bloody cyclist?

Looking for some individual, perhaps – Vidor for instance – and reckoning this might be him? Or if they were here to find munition caches – which was the generally accepted theory, certainly Durand's and his wife's, in various conversations with friends who'd dropped by to swap gossip and guesses – they might reckon any peasant on the road after dark might be connected with such activities, would therefore be worth slapping around a bit, for information?

Might be, too. *This* peasant, for one. Could lead them to a cache, too – that tomb where the skeletons lay grinning.

Extraordinary business ... Be hard to find anyone in Brisbane who'd believe it. He froze, listening: a German had shouted, was answered by another at roughly the same distance. Several others then, in chorus. Could be calling it off, could be changing direction. *Back to the road, boys, search the hedgerows, both fucking sides . . .*

From the other direction – his left – a vixen screamed. And much closer – really *very* close – the German driver hawked and spat – so close-sounding you could imagine you'd felt the spray of it – then yelled some question into the night. Could have been something like *Got him, have you?*

Crawling on. Having considered staying put, and decided against it. Toss-up, either way, but there was relief in movement. Remembering – quite inconsequentially – Durand telling him that an acquaintance of his had been beaten to death by *miliciens* in Brest. Then one of the truck's doors slammed, and a second later its engine started: he changed his mind, stopped and let himself down flat again. If they were leaving – he crossed fingers on both hands, lay still, patient . . .

Would *Rosie* believe this, even?

Getting to the Brodard farm took another hour – keeping off the roads, following them on the field sides of their hedges. Only one vehicle had passed in all that time – coming back this way, the Landeda direction, might have been the same truck coming back.

Vixens were up and about and vocal, by this time. He'd heard owls too.

The gate at the start of the track up to the farm seemed too dangerous an approach, when for all he knew there might be Germans around. He ducked under wire instead, followed the track up on the dark side of a thorn hedge. An odour of pig: the sties were off to his right, up-wind. Not that there was a lot of wind. The Brodards' goats would be in the barn. Geese were another matter: if they weren't shut up he knew they could be a bloody menace. If they were anything like Australian geese, they could.

The old man was supposed to have died of a heart attack, Durand had said. So there hadn't necessarily been any

shooting, or other mayhem, and presumably the daughter –
Solange – and the mentally-retarded boy, Alain – would will
be around.

Please God. *And* Bright and Farr – please . . .

Hope for the best. Nothing else one *could* do. But if the
Krauts had been here and found those two they'd surely have
arrested the others as well, for sheltering them. The girl,
anyway, – mightn't bother with Alain. But thinking of the
bastards taking Solange – who was very young and rather
pretty, with those green eyes and the little shy smile – gave
him the same sort of queasy feeling that he got whenever
he'd thought about Rosie and what *she* might be facing. You
had to take off your hat to anyone in that line of work, male
and female, but the girls were so *terrifyingly* vulnerable, he
thought.

This place might well be deserted. Not a glimmer of light
anywhere. Well, there wouldn't be, they wouldn't be
wasting oil or candles at this time of night . . . The turf was
rock-hard underfoot, and the moon halfway down, throwing
long shadows. He had the barn in black silhouette against it:
that was where the lads would be, if they were here at all.
Although the closer he got to this, the less hope he had that
they *could* still be here.

Germans might have taken possession? Knock on the
door, have it opened by some Kraut with a Luger pointing
at your head?

No transport in the yard, anyway. That was a good sign.
If there'd been Germans here there would have been, surely.
Couldn't be under cover, either – the main barn's lower floor
was full of hay and stuff, and the other one was where they
put the goats at night.

Try the house first, *then* the barn . . .

The dog began to bark: and immediately the geese were
in full cry. They had an enclosure behind the goat barn. The
dog was an Alsation cross, name of – he got it, Marco. It
should present no problem – beyond sounding the alarm, as
it was doing now – since they kept it chained. The racket was

still bloody alarming, though: knowing how far sound carried in the surrounding peace and quiet. It would be somewhere near the house: he wasn't sure, had only heard it barking and whining when he and Vidor had set off from the barn: this time it must have heard him climbing the gate, where the hedge ended. The paddock was now behind him, orchard at its top end – pig-sties and the small barn up there too – the bigger barn to his left and the house some way to the right of it. Marco – Ben could see him now, flinging himself against his chain and barking blue murder – close to the front door, you'd never get to that door if he didn't want you to.

'Marco. Hey, Marco. We're old pals, Marco – remember?'

Seemed he didn't.

Glimmer of light, though: at an upstairs window. Just a flicker, then it had gone: but the window was being opened ... 'Marco!' Girl's voice. Solange ... 'Quiet, Marco!' Then – as the dog obeyed, more or less – 'Who's there?'

'I'm Ben Quarry, Solange. Ben. Royal Navy – the Australian?'

'*L'Australien?*'

'Right! I went with Vidor, remember?' Ben started walking towards the house. 'He's away somewhere, he left me with the Durands – the *garagiste* at Lannilis. I just heard you've had trouble – Boches here, and your father—'

'Wait. I'll come down.'

Seconds later, he saw the glow of an oil lamp in the open door: a yellowish pool of light on this shaded side of the house, her figure bulky-looking, hunched, as she unhooked the dog's chain and moved it to another tethering-post. He'd been moving closer meanwhile, towards the door: seeing at shorter range that the shapelessness was due to an old coat she'd thrown on over her nightgown. Hair wild, her face under the light white as paper, eyes like dark holes in it.

She could have been *old*, in that moment ...

'Solange!'

'Are you hurt?'

Holding the lamp high, to throw light on *his* face. He told her no, only scratches, brambles and so forth. 'But *you*, Solange—'

'Your face is all blood!'

'Never mind that. I'm so *sorry* – your father—'

'Oh. You heard.' A breath like a gasp ... 'But Alain also—'

'They killed *Alain*?'

'Yes. Come inside – Monsieur Ben ... Is that right – *Ben*?'

He followed her in, and she put her lamp down on the table. This was the kitchen. Pushing the door shut ... 'Solange – what about my two seamen?'

'Gone. Luc took them.' She was up close, examining his face, then getting him to show her his hands – which if anything were worse. Shaking her head as she turned away. 'I'll draw some water.' Luc, he was thinking – Vidor's man. Thank God for *him* ... Relief was huge – even if it was only partial. He asked Solange as she worked the pump, 'When did Luc come for them?'

'Oh – the day before ... There's hot water on the stove, don't worry, I'm going to mix it.'

'That's about the *last* thing I'd—'

'They shot Alain in his head. He rushed to attack one who – oh, he was – you know, twisting my arms, and – to make my father tell them things – and another had brought in Alain, he went for this one who was hurting me, and the man shot him. *There*. And my father died in that chair – that one. He had his eyes on me and his mouth open – trying to speak but as if he'd swallowed his tongue – and he just fell forward' – pointing with her head again, twisting round from the iron stove – '*there*.'

'*I'll* do that.' The enamel bowl – lifting it, transferring it to the table. In this poor light you'd barely have known that her hair was red. And she looked as if she hadn't slept for a week. Tattered old tweed coat hiding the figure which he

remembered had had Tommo Farr's eyes out on stalks ...
'Let me do this myself, Solange. Only scratches. Fuss about
nothing. Really.'

'Sit down, eh?'

Where her father had sat. He obeyed her, for some reason,
and she started work on him, using a sponge and frowning
with concentration while she dabbed and wiped and the
water turned pink then red. 'Your French has improved,
Monsieur Ben.'

'Glad you think so. Been getting a lot of practice ... Not
Monsieur Ben, please, just Ben. You know, I think you're
marvellous?'

'For what?' A shrug. 'Life must go on.' Her expression
tightened. 'For some of us.'

'Running the farm all on your own.'

She shrugged again. 'Not everything gets done that should.'

'I'll help, anyway, now I'm here. Just tell me what and
when, and—'

'I think you should stay inside. They could come again.
They're searching, still. I think they were satisfied we have
no weapons here, but – one can't be sure, there seems to be
no system one can comprehend.'

'What makes them think there *might* be weapons cached
around here?'

'I don't know. Maybe someone said something. Mostly
what they ask about is explosive. But – it's what's happening, that's all ... Will your boat come in again?'

'God knows. Up to Vidor to fix it with London, one way
or the other. I'd guess not, though.'

'He'd move you to some other place along the coast.'

'I suppose ... D'you know where Luc took those two?'

'I think to Lannilis – the café where he works.'

"Patronized by Boche soldiers?'

'Yes. I don't know. Better not to know, Ben ... You look
better now. If you want to finish for yourself, take off your
clothes and – you know, the rest of you—'

'Yeah. Please. You're *astonishing*. To think about me and

my silly little scratches, when—'

'I feed the goats too, eh?'

A laugh. He laughed with her. 'Well – OK—'

'I'll draw some clean water.'

'No. I will.' She'd been patting him with a scrap of towelling: he took it from her. 'Forgive me asking, Solange, but what's happened with your father's body, and Alain's? Only thinking that if there's anything I could help with—'

'They came for them. I ran to our neighbours, the Faubiers, and they came, and Jacques Faubier went to Landeda on his bicycle. So then the doctor, and Marcel Legrand – for the *pompe funèbre* – and the *curé*, also our own police, two of them, they're not bad fellows ... And I've sent word to my sister – I *hope* she'll come—'

'You have a sister.'

'Yes – Lucinde. She's married, lives near Plouermel. Oh, I do *hope* she'll come!'

'I'm sure she will. But now, look here.' He was on his feet: she had her hands on the bowl, about to take it, to empty it. He put one of his on her forearm: 'Leave this to me, now. I'll stay down here tonight – if I may, if you'd give me a blanket or something – and move to the loft tomorrow – if that's a good idea. But you get some sleep now. You're a fantastic girl, Solange, you really are ... And – look, must be a nightmare – but it won't be for ever. You know? Maybe this sister of yours'll—'

She was in his arms, suddenly. He'd seen the tears coming, the breakup – break*down* she must have been holding off. Her face was hidden against his shoulder now: arms locked round his neck: pressed against him, shivering inside the shabby old coat: sobs like gasps, like fighting for breath ... He heard himself murmuring while he held her – patting her, like calming a frightened horse – 'Solange ... Solange, honey – nightmare now, but it'll come all right, you'll see. Listen – Solange, listen – if the gunboat does come, how about we take you to England with us?'

A child, in misery. *Anything*, to comfort her.

15

On the Tuesday, she put her cards on the table with Jacqui. She'd been intending a more subtle approach, but she saw that flood tide suddenly, and as it were took a header ... Motivated partly through having had – and *still* suffering from – an edgy sense of *now or never*, anxiety to have the S.I.S. operation up and running irrespective of what might happen afterwards. Romeo's partly concealed state of nerves was one factor, the alleged six-week life of pianists was another, and this morning, when she'd been leaving Ursule's, she'd thought they had a tail on her. Wheeling her bike out across the pavement, she'd noticed a male cyclist in the entrance to an alleyway that was a short-cut to the Café Saint Sever: he'd been leaning against the corner with his bike propped beside him, and when he'd seen her she'd had a clear impression that he'd been startled – as if it were her he'd been waiting for and she'd caught him napping. Glancing away then – taking a long look down into the alley in which she knew for a fact there was nothing except dustbins and sometimes a scrawny cat or two, and in which he hadn't been showing any interest until she'd appeared. A youngish man, wearing a grey cap and a striped pullover, overall blue trousers with braces ... Her intention had been to ride up to Pigot's garage, in search of Romeo: instead she mounted, without another glance at the man in the alley, pedalled along to the church and up to Rue la Fayette, over the Corneille bridge, and dropped in on a chemist in the Rue

des Bonnetiers, where a girl assistant had told her she'd like
to stock the Cazalet perfumes but that it was entirely up to
her father, who last week had been away in Dijon, where his
sister lived.

Father still wasn't back, she told Rosie this morning. Try
again in a day or two. He was supposed to have retired, but
he kept the reins firmly in his own hands. She'd shrugged:
'Doesn't make life any easier.'

Outside, there was no sign of the man in the striped jersey.
Either she'd been wrong about him, or he was a pro. There
was another shop she'd been thinking of having a go at, in
Rue des Béguines: not a very hopeful prospect, and rather
out of her way, but a good alternative to the risk of leading
him – them – to Marc Pigot's garage.

Might miss Romeo, she realized. But that would be the
worst of it. She'd made no arrangements for the day, other
than to see Jacqui this evening. César had gone by train to
Amiens to see one of the Resistance men whom Rosie had
met last week and who'd expressed interest in setting up
certain sabotage operations. He'd had some ideas which
César wanted to discuss with him; also, Baker Street had
approved all the weapons for which Rosie had asked –
they'd told her so, on Sunday night – and he'd be passing
this good news on at the same time.

So – back on the bike and down to Rue Saint Lo, and past
the Palais de Justice. Grey, grim, and in one's imagination
– one's vision of the activities inside it – frightening.
Swastikas were swift flashes of colour in the corners of her
eyes as she glanced left and right at the crossing, the Place
Foch – trying not to see them at all ... Joan of Arc's place
of execution on her left, then: and passing the Brasserie
Guillaume she saw that same man – striped jersey, grey
peaked cap, workman's trousers – on the pavement outside
the café. Although he was standing with his back to the road,
reading a menu or a price-list on the post against which he'd
leant his bicycle, the sight of him gave her a jolt.

She got no more than a vague promise of *future* interest

at the other shop. As much as she'd expected ... Emerging, checking that the coast was clear while replacing her sample-case in the pannier, she decided to go back to that brasserie. Reminding herself that it was always better to look potential dangers in the face, than to run scared; this bogey-man might not have the slightest interest in her, and if she could convince herself of this she'd have a better day. If not – well, at least she'd know better than to go within a mile of Pigot's place. As it turned out, he wasn't there – neither inside nor outside. At least, not visibly. She treated herself to a so-called coffee, while from a nearby table two young Germans eyed her, smiling nervously and muttering to each other behind their hands, and she decided – more or less – that the fact she'd seen him twice had probably been coincidence. Rouen wasn't such a huge town, after all, and this square was more or less its centrepiece.

She still played it safe, though – wandered around trying to do business here and there, spent some time on a bench down by the river, had a lunchtime snack at a café near the cathedral, and didn't go to the garage until mid-afternoon. Pigot was there, but Romeo wasn't: he'd been there during the forenoon but wasn't likely to be back.

So that was that.

She was at Jacqui's at seven, bringing a bottle of Hermitage which César had presented to her – 'To compensate for my bad humour yesterday. I think we'll make a very effective team, Angel, you and I. Don't you agree?'

She'd told him yes, no question. There was no reason they shouldn't either. She wasn't exactly mad about him, but they were here to work together, therefore *had* to get on, in the interests of the job.

Jacqui raised her glass: containing wine of her own, not the Hermitage, which would be better for at least a few days' rest. 'Here's to us, Jeanne-Marie.'

Rosie echoed, 'Us ... Hey, this isn't bad!'

'Shouldn't be, either – seeing as it's reserved for the

precious *Wehrmacht*.' They were eating veal with a sauce that had brandy in it, and turnip which she'd mashed and fried. She put her glass down, and Rosie told her, 'You really don't do at all badly, Jacqui, do you?'

'The veal was a present too, I admit. But in general it's my own earnings I live on, I assure you. At weekends, certainly, I've no bills to pay, and that's a big help, but otherwise –' she pointed downstairs – 'the business has to pay, or I'd starve. Hans lent me the capital to set it up, mind you ...' She sighed. 'Why I tell you so many secrets, Jeanne-Marie, I can't imagine!'

'I suppose there might not be many people you *can* – well, let your hair down with.' She shook her head. 'God knows, I talk to myself, half the time ... But – the subject of money, Jacqui – does get to be a headache, doesn't it?'

'For *you*, you mean?'

'Well – so far, the way I'm *trying* to earn a living—'

'I'll do what I can to help you, there, but—'

'I'd sooner talk about *your* problems. You say he set you up here. And helps, one way and another. And – well, you *like* him, obviously, but—'

'I like him very much!'

'—but you really *need* him, don't you? While on the other hand – I keep thinking about it, Jacqui, what you were telling me, having to put up with the malicious telephone calls, and people staring at you when you're out—'

'I can put up with it. For the time being. I think I said – she who laughs last?'

'Jacqui, listen. You must know as well as I do that at the very least there's a *possibility* the Boches will lose this war. A possibility – agree?'

'I suppose. If one looked on the blackest side—'

'Brightest, I'd say. And I'm certain – *certain*, Jacqui – that *we* are going to win.'

The dark head tilted ... 'We?'

'The Allies, say.'

'To you, that's *we*?'

She shook her head. 'It's the plain truth, I'm sure of it, and consequently I'm very concerned for you. One thing about having only oneself to talk to all day is there's time to think ... And thinking about *you*, Jacqui, I've concluded that you're an extremely *kind* person – you've been very kind to me, anyway – who's being misled – misleading yourself, to some extent, to be quite frank – and – Jacqui, look, if the people around here who know this German's your lover and hate you for it – that's the way it is, uh? Well, my God – what's going to happen to you when the Boches are driven out?'

'If that *were* to happen—'

A bell rang. Doorbell. She had a forkful of turnip halfway to her mouth: she held it there, her head slightly on one side, listening ...

'I can guess who this is.' Getting up. 'He's been away, and he was due back about now. In fact I heard, this last weekend ... Listen, if it *is* him, he's a German sergeant – Gerhardt Clausen, one of their – well, Security people. The one I mentioned I could introduce *you* to, as it happens – he's actually very charming, and—'

'I don't *believe* this!' It felt like having a very, very bad joke played on one ... 'Honestly, Jacqui—'

'I tell you he's *nice*!'

'You're going to ask him to come up?'

'Well, I may have to – I can't be *rude* ...'

Romeo's voice in her brain – telling her *Highly clued-up S.D. man, name of Clausen ... Only a sergeant, but he carries a lot of weight ...*

Jacqui repeated from the doorway, 'May *have* to. Just calm down, Jeanne-Marie, he's just a perfectly ordinary—'

'*Much* rather *not* meet him. For the best of reasons, Jacqui. Please – if you can possibly avoid it ...'

The man who broke up the *réseau* here. Romeo again: *Good-looking guy, and he's up to all the tricks. Women like him – and he uses that.*

Please, God ... Because it could blow the whole damn

thing. To be seen with Jacqui, and by this Clausen of all
people: if she was going to work for S.O.E., the last thing
one could afford – or that *she* could – was a known
association. One skittle sending all the others flying: and if
she saw that, she'd refuse the job. She wasn't all that green,
she'd worked for La Chatte, for God's sake....

Which would account for her knowing Clausen?

A door downstairs banged shut, then she was audibly on
her way up – talking nineteen to the dozen ... '—so it was
a splendid weekend, Gerhardt, every minute of it. Well, as
you know, I *live* for the weekends ... Now, then, here she is.
Jeanne-Marie, I'd like to introduce a good friend – Gerhardt
Clausen. Gerhardt, this is Jeanne-Marie Lefèvre, who's
extremely sweet except she's so determined I should stock
and sell her damn perfumes—'

'So—'

He'd spotted her wedding ring. She'd seen him register-
ing it.

'Madame Lefèvre. Enchanted.'

Wavy dark hair with an edging of grey at the temples,
deepset eyes ... He was in civilian clothes – smart ones, at that.
A light barathea suit, cream shirt, blue tie. Looking up at him,
she managed a small smile: 'My pleasure, monsieur.'

'Actually, sergeant. Not that it matters – my job permits
me to go around disguised as some kind of human being.'
Easy smile, fluent French. 'You've not been in Rouen long,
I think?'

'Cognac, Gerhardt?'

'Oh, but you're an *angel*!'

'No. Not long.' Answering his question, she looked at
Jacqui – addressing her then, as the shy Jeanne-Marie
Lefèvre might well do, seeking her friend's support ... 'And
if I can't do a better selling job than I've done so far I won't
be here much longer!'

'But things will pick up, I'm sure. With that one's help,
eh?' He nodded towards Jacqui, who was pouring his drink.
'She's a great girl, I can tell you. As well as the most

beautiful in France . . .' He took the brandy, swirled the glass
in his cupped palm. 'Black market? Business must be good,
Jacqui!'

'It was a present – as you'll have guessed.' The cognac,
they were talking about. She pointed: 'So was that veal.'
There was a challenge in the statement, and in her expression as she'd glanced at him. Explaining to Rosie then – for
her – Rosie's – benefit, perhaps also for her own, following
some instinct that it might be better if in Clausen's eyes she
shouldn't have told her too much about herself – 'I have a
friend – a man friend – in Amiens, who's extremely
generous. That's why I'm away at weekends mostly. And it
was Gerhardt who introduced us.'

'I see.'

Looking down at her folded hands: *being* Jeanne-Marie
Lefèvre . . . Shy, and surprised at her new acquaintance
having German friends, but less shocked or disapproving
than impressed . . . Clausen meanwhile concentrating on
Jacqui: it was fairly obvious, despite his superficially good
manners, that he'd counted on finding her alone and was
more than just disappointed that he hadn't.

Which was fine. And natural – the way Jacqui was looking
at this moment, and the way he could hardly take his eyes
off her . . . Then she'd murmured something very quietly,
and he'd laughed: Rosie heard him mutter, 'Very well.
Twenty-four hours. No – twenty-*two* hours, I'll *just* manage
that . . .' Turning to include *her* in the conversation then:
'I'm sorry – interrupting your meal as well as whatever vital
matters you're discussing. My apologies, madame . . . Jacqui
– *tomorrow* evening?'

He might have introduced her to Colonel Walther, but in
doing so evidently hadn't exactly cut *himself* out of her life
. . . Rosie wasn't actually listening to their conversation at
this stage – Jeanne-Marie wouldn't have; wouldn't have
wanted to be seen as eavesdropping, anyway – but she was
getting snatches of it – a reference to Amiens, and to Berlin
then: and a squeak from Jacqui suddenly – 'You're going

when?' Rosie looked up, saw her hand on his arm and her eyes startled . . . 'A *permanent* transfer?'

'I'm sorry. But – yes, on Friday. I'm only back here to clear up. Not *my* decision, my dear, I wouldn't *volunteer* to leave this place!'

Meaning – obviously – 'to leave *you* . . .'

A minute later he tossed back the last drops of his brandy, handed the glass to Jacqui and was kissing Rosie's hand. She could feel the sweat breaking out on the palms of her hands and her own racing pulse – current thought-processes to some extent aimed at beating all that, a kind of internal whistling in the dark, but then making it worse when the thoughts took their own direction – for instance, as now, that in any get-together in the Palais de Justice he'd be considerably less courteous. . .

But he was leaving Rouen, apparently. Here to say goodbye – in whatever form the farewell might have taken.

'I'll just see him safely down the stairs, Jeanne-Marie—'

Hearing her own complacent 'All right . . .'

Incredible. An S.D. sergeant – with God only knew how many S.O.E. scalps on his belt already . . . Although, she thought – alone, lighting a cigarette with shaking fingers – maybe she hadn't carried it off too badly. At any rate, he'd seemed to take her at face value. *Now*, she could let her pulse slow, relax in the cold sweat . . .

Jacqui came back. 'It's a blow that he's leaving. For good, too, this time. As you said, one hasn't such a wealth of friends here . . . I don't want to eat any more – do you, now it's cold?'

'No. But it was terrific, Jacqui, thank you.'

'So what did you think of him?'

'Oh, well.' She shrugged. 'As you know, I don't—'

'You don't like them. And I suppose – *in principle* . . .' Wry smile, as she accepted a cigarette. 'What if you hadn't known he *was* a German?' She leant to the single candle, sat back leaking smoke . . . 'What would you have thought of him, then?'

'You'd *like* me to say I thought he was madly attractive.'

'And you don't?'

She drew hard on her cigarette: still *needing* it . . .

'Jacqui. I wonder – how frank we can afford to be with each other.'

'Come again?'

'Could we agree to say exactly what's in our minds, d'you think, with the understanding that nothing's passed on to what they call 'third parties'?'

'As far as *I'm* concerned—'

'Good. It's a deal. And the answer to that question is I can't imagine taking him for anything *but* a German . . . Tell *me* something? How you met him, and how come a sergeant introduced you to a colonel in another town?'

'Very long story . . .'

'Well, let's get into it gradually. As it happens, I know quite a bit of it, and I can guess at most of the rest. But you see, Jacqui—'

'What are you talking about?'

She shook her head. 'First things first. Number one is – believe me, I *am* your friend, and I've a lot to offer you. No, I really have – wait, just hear me out . . . For instance – this is the big one, really, we were starting on it when your sergeant friend arrived, if you remember. I was asking you – the way people here feel about you, how you think it might go for you when the Boches are licked?'

'*If* they are.'

'I say *when*. But go on.'

A silence: staring . . .

Hostility? Fear?

'What *is* this, Jeanne-Marie?'

'What might they do to you?'

'Tear me in pieces? That what you want me to say?'

'Reasonable supposition, anyway. So how would you like some cast-iron insurance, a guarantee nobody'd lay a finger on you?'

Staring again . . . 'Jeanne-Marie – are you some kind of—'

'A word to the Resistance that you're working for us is all it'd take, Jacqui. I could arrange it pretty well immediately.'

'My God, you *are*!'

'There'd be no danger—'

'Are you kidding?' Shaking her dark head, eyes wild. 'How about a word from *me*, to—'

'Jacqui – don't threaten me. I know the risks here. I'm counting on your intelligence – that you'll see what I'm offering you – in a minute ... No danger to *yourself*, I'm saying. It'd be known to only a couple of people here, and of course in London. We'd want you to do something for us – obviously, we aren't thinking of telling lies for you, if you *don't* help us ... But I'm putting a lot of trust in you already, aren't I? You *could* inform on me – to that Clausen person, for instance?'

'How *can* you take such a chance?' Her hands opened. 'Unless you're raving mad?'

'I don't believe you'd shop me. But in any case it's important enough that I have to take the risk. Besides, I genuinely like you, the thought of the mob getting their hands on you when our armies drive these bastards out is – sickening ... OK, so I'm grinding my own axe too – wanting your help. You may not realize it, but you're in a position to give us absolutely *vital* help ... Well – here we go – don't faint now, Jacqui, but it's to do with your Colonel Walther's rockets.'

'I guessed. Ten seconds ago. And you're asking the impossible, my dear ... Look, I *won't* inform on you, but I *couldn't*—'

'That's what's known as a knee-jerk reaction. Listen ... Why we need this information is that if the rockets were deployed and active before we can mount an invasion – well, at that point the south of England'll have to be packed solid with troops, transport, guns and so on, and the ports crammed with ships. If there was some kind of continuous bombardment—'

'No invasion.' Jacqui smiled. Still short of breath, though.

'So no defeat of Germany. What are you selling me?'

'We'd still win, Jacqui. Take longer, that's all. Delay it all while we smash the rocket sites. Or enough of them. What we *want* is to smash them before they get into action – so there's no such delay – and to do that we need to know where they are, or will be.' She'd lit a new cigarette – Jacqui's was still going. 'This is where *you* come in. And you see how important it is – so *you'd* be equivalently important to us, and we'd look after you . . . Wouldn't be so difficult for you, would it?'

'You think not?'

'Doesn't he leave papers around, and maps? Don't you hear things – where he was last week, or where his teams are going next?'

'I suppose . . .'

'You wouldn't have to use a radio, or contact anyone, or even pick up a telephone. I'd come to you for a hairdo once a week, and you'd give me whatever you'd got. Verbally, or on paper if you like. Verbally's the safe way, if your memory's up to it. No risk at all. Not like it was when you worked for La Chatte, huh?'

'Oh.' A shrug . . . 'You know about her, then.'

'Lord, yes. Well, she came to London, didn't she?' Rosie glanced in the direction of the sideboard. 'D'you think we could both use some of that cognac?'

'My God, *couldn't* we . . .'

'But La Chatte – yes . . . I know quite a bit of your background, as it happens. Father French, mother Italian – right? Accounts for your lovely colouring, of course. You really are beautiful, Jacqui, Sergeant Clausen wasn't exaggerating in the least . . . But your father was drowned, wasn't he – air crash into the Bay of Biscay in – 1925? And your mother remarried – to an Italian, and when last heard of they were living in Rome . . . Thanks – I think I *do* need this.'

Jacqui sat down again, sniffing at hers . . . 'I can't get over the *risk* you're taking.' She nodded towards the phone. 'One short call to Gerhardt, for instance – or a word to him – you heard, he'll be here tomorrow night—'

'And gone by Friday. I'm glad of that.' Rosie put her glass down. Nodding, breathing smoke ... 'What I'm offering you, you see, is a whole package of long-term benefits. One – insurance against what's bound to happen to you when the Boches are beaten. You know it *would* happen – in my contention one might say *will* happen – whether or not you ratted on me now. OK, I'd be dead – Ravensbruck's where they've killed most of us, so far – but there'd be a hellish time in store for you, too. Or, suppose you were right about them winning – you aren't, but *suppose* you were – you'd have lost nothing, because nobody's going to know anything about this. You can take that as a promise too. In fact the Boches *won't* win – the only reason you can't see it is you're stuffed with all their propaganda – but obviously you'd continue your relationship with Walther – you'd have to, that's your special value – and when it's over you'd not only be safe, you'd be a patriot. Oh, and also,' – she raised a forefinger – 'you'd be of independent means. Walther or no Walther.'

She saw *that* strike home. She'd known it would. Jacqui had been lifting her glass towards her lips: she'd frozen, holding it there.

'How d'you work that out?'

'Doesn't a quarter of a million francs sound like independence?'

'Quarter-million ...'

'Right.'

'Who'd pay it – and when?'

Rosie sipped brandy. 'You'd have it – well, not tomorrow, Clausen'll be here tomorrow ... Thursday?'

'Can I *believe* you?'

'Better than a free sample of scent, isn't it?'

'The scent thing's all baloney, obviously. But – this money—'

'Not baloney at all. It's what I'm in Rouen for. I'm going to try hard to make a go of it, too.'

'S.O.E., are you?'

'S.O.E.? What's that?'

'All right. All right . . . Jeanne-Marie, are we talking about a quarter of a million in cash?'

'Absolutely. Be a useful nest egg, wouldn't it? It's not just a bribe, incidentally, we realized you might need it. If Walther ran out on you – well, I'm sure he wouldn't – but if Clausen arranged for his transfer to the Eastern Front, for instance—'

'Now *look*—'

'Such things have been known. Although Clausen's going to be out of it now, isn't he . . . Did La Chatte pay you well, Jacqui?'

'Oh – no, not so well.'

'You were going to tell me – about you and Clausen, and Walther, weren't you? Tell me I'm on the right track now – it wasn't Clausen, was it, it was a man called Bleicher, who trapped La Chatte. And he was Abwehr, not S.D. . . . But is Clausen a chum of his?'

'They worked together, at one time. Some other place—'

'Bleicher caught La Chatte – and she must have shopped *you*—'

'Perhaps without knowing. He's clever – like Clausen, they're birds of a feather, that's the way they work . . . What I know for sure is Mathilde-Lily was arrested – yes, by Bleicher – and she agreed to work for them. She used her radio to London, giving information *they* wanted her to give.'

'What about you, though?'

'I never worked for them. I was arrested, Bleicher asked me a lot of questions – about her, not about me, I wasn't important to them as she was, I was only her employee. And at that time I was sure she'd betrayed me, so—'

'You told them all you knew.'

'Well.' A shrug. 'Most.'

'And Bleicher became your lover?'

'What gives you that idea?'

'Just guessing . . . mostly . . . But when you came here, he put his friend Clausen on to you – personal favour, or professional cooperation, or both – and – as you said, through Clausen you met Colonel Walther.'

'Gerhardt was looking into Security for him, then – when Hans was setting up, in Amiens. And – there was some socializing, some parties – he's supposed to be only a sergeant, but that's not how they treat him or how he lives.'

'All the same, Walther took you over.'

'If you want to put it that way. Although Gerhardt—'

'—stayed in the wings. Yes, I – imagine. Mind you, La Chatte *really* slept around, didn't she?'

'I hope you're not suggesting—'

'I'm talking about La Chatte. She slept with Bleicher, didn't she? Amongst others?'

'This is an interrogation, Jeanne-Marie!'

'Sorry. More a matter of comparing notes, really. It's as well to be on the same wave-length – for you to know *I* know the background, or most of it . . . I must say I'm immensely relieved that Clausen's leaving. If you and I are going to do business, Jacqui.' She leant forward to stub out her cigarette; in the same movement, glancing at the clock and realizing that if she was going to beat the curfew, she'd have to run.

A better idea, then . . .

'Jacqui – would it inconvenience you dreadfully to let me spend the night here?'

'Spend the night?'

'Curfew-time approaching, long way home—'

'Oh. Well – no, of course. We can make up a bed for you on the sofa there.'

'Lovely. So no rush, now . . . We *are* going to do business, eh?'

Staring at her. Speechless, thinking about it. Scared of it, obviously, despite the carrots: but wanting them – wanting them too badly to refuse them, Rosie guessed. She suggested – feeling sure of it, also an absolute imperative to make it so – 'Let's talk details, Jacqui . . .'

16

César was back in Rouen on the Thursday morning, and Rosie joined him before lunch at the Belle Femme. In his room, to start with, where they could talk business without looking over their shoulders all the time: the bed littered with overspill from an open suitcase, and the briefcase open too, amongst it. She could see her own notes there, on top, the wads of cheap blue notepaper. He had a lot more clothes with him than she had, she noticed.

He'd met the man in Amiens, he told her, and had been introduced by him to a woman agent of B.C.R.A. – the Gaullists' equivalent of S.O.E. – with whom that group apparently had close links.

'We might do well to cooperate with them, Angel, in these sabotage operations he's planning. Don't you agree?'

'London wouldn't.' As he'd known damn well – surely ... Looking at him curiously – and wondering whether the girl might be exceptionally attractive, which might partially explain the aberration. She added, 'Nor would *their* hierarchy, would it – on past form. But I suppose some specific operation – if there's mutual advantage in it, and she's willing?'

'Oh, she *is*!'

He'd been to Lyons-la-Forêt, after Amiens and Dury, to check on the success of the arms drops. She'd already known of this: she'd spent most of yesterday with Romeo at Pigot's garage, and once again he'd had a call from Lebrun,

via the Bistro Suisse, checking on César's bona fides.
Romeo had confirmed to the schoolmaster that César was
the new boss, but suggested he should tell him politely that
he'd prefer to deal only with Angel. Otherwise there could
be wires crossed and other complications: it was always
simpler to deal with just one individual. Lebrun had said he
was relieved to have his own preference backed up, and that
he'd act accordingly.

César commented, 'As you said yourself, not a very
inspiring sort of chap. But you evidently made a great hit
with him.'

'*Did* I, now ...'

'Only wants to work with you personally, he told me.'

'Well – that's hardly unusual, is it?'

'To be unwilling to deal with the *réseau* leader?'

'It would be more that he'd prefer to have just one contact.
Most do – in my limited experience!'

'Shades of your Romeo?'

She changed the subject: 'This is his last day here,
incidentally – Romeo's. Oh, and by the way—'

'To finish about Lebrun – if I may?'

'Sorry—'

'He asked me to tell you that the drop went off without
any hitch and they got what they asked for. He'd heard that
the Beauvais group were happy too. Wanted me to thank
you. Apart from that, what seemed to have made his day was
news of Mussolini being deposed. I ask you – as if *that*
makes any difference to anything!'

'I'd say it's a straw in the wind – wouldn't you?'

'Well – for the Italians, perhaps ... What were you going
to tell me?'

'That Baker Street's sending us a replacement for Romeo,
in the Lysander tomorrow night. His code-name's Saul. I'll
tell him to contact you here, shall I?'

'Why not bring him?'

'I'd – rather not. As we agreed, Michel – he's yours. He
doesn't have to know where I'm living, and he and I don't

have to mingle. At least, that's how I'd like to have it.'

'I did agree. I know.' He obviously regretted it. 'So we'll try it, anyway. Incidentally, I have the names of two possible recruits as sub-agents – acquaintances of the Dury people. Recruitment has to be our next job, I think.'

'Do these two have B.C.R.A. connections?'

'Not as far as I know. No – I'm sure not, that's just one link Mattan happens to have formed.'

'Shall I ask Romeo if he knows of them?'

'Thank you, but' – the shake of his blond head was immediate, a reflex – 'I don't think I'd want to involve him, at this late stage.'

'You'd like him, Michel. He's a good man. Really is. He's been here too long, that's all, left on his own too long – having had that entire *réseau* cut out from under him – then finding he was under suspicion, for God's sake?'

'Tell him goodbye and good luck for me, if you like.'

'Right. I will.'

'But I wonder if it's really necessary for you to go out there. If he went on his own by bicycle, for instance, he could leave it with that forester – what's his name – Plumier?'

'I'd *like* to see him off. And someone should meet the new man.'

'With whom you don't want to associate?' Slit eyes more open than usual, under raised blond brows . . . 'Eh?'

'I don't want any close or frequent association, or to be seen around together. Particularly the three of us – as you suggested I should bring him here, for instance. I think Romeo's point's a good one.'

'Sticking to the *present* point, Jeanne-Marie – Plumier'll be on hand, surely. He could give our new man the bicycle that Romeo will have used.' He saw her expression, and shrugged. 'All right. It would save time and trouble, but – do as you like . . . Will *you* go by bicycle?'

'Starting that way, but he'll have a *gazo* and pick me up outside the town. We'll rest and I dare say have a meal at

Ardouval – Plumier's house, it's handy to the landing-ground – and Saul can spend the night there and ride in on my bike in the morning. I'll bring the *gazo* back, Saul will report to you here – right? – and in the evening I might stop by and collect the bike.'

'Where do you take the *gazo*?'

'Leave it not far from my lodgings. It belongs to a friend of a friend, he doesn't know what it's being used for and I don't have to meet him.'

'What if you're stopped when you're on the road?'

'I'll tell them the man it's licensed to is my boyfriend, he's lent it to me for a business trip to Neufchatel. I *have* called on shops there, my cover'll hold good . . .' She smiled at him. 'It's all *right*, Michel, I've done these things before, don't worry . . . Did you say you were going to stand me a beer?'

'If there's nothing else. I suppose there isn't . . . Oh – you were listening out last night – well, obviously—'

'Yes.' She was on her feet, entirely ready for that beer. 'The news of Saul was the only item. Nothing more about the drops we've asked for. We'll hear from them when they're ready, no doubt. Next listening routine's tomorrow, incidentally – I'll go on the air when the Lysander's come and gone, confirm that and take in whatever they've got for me. Anything to go out?'

'I'll think about it. You'll be starting early, so – call by this evening?'

'All right.'

He'd shut his briefcase, searched for the key and found it eventually in a trouser pocket, locked it and pushed it into a floor-level cupboard in which spare bedding was stored. He wasn't very security-conscious, she thought. All her notes were in that case, and God only knew what else. At least some of the money she'd brought, for one thing . . . He straightened, kicking the cupboard door shut: 'Let's go . . .'

Outside, the overcast seemed to have become heavier.

The air was still, warm and humid: thunder on the way, she guessed. Good thing too, clear the air . . .

There were no Germans at any of the pavement tables, today. At the next table was a young priest with a woman who might have been his mother. César pulled a chair out for her: bags of courtesy, when he felt like it . . . Telling Emil, 'Two beers, please. After that we'll think about what we might eat.'

'Why not ask him what there is – before anything half-decent's wolfed up?'

Smiling at her . . . 'Hungry, are you?'

'Famished.'

'I'll take your advice, then . . . You know, Angel – you rather grow on a man?'

'You don't say. My guess would have been that up to date you'd found me bossy, obstinate, argumentative, insubordinate—'

'Those qualities *certainly*, but also—'

Chuckling, turning to see Emil coming back with their half-litres of swill . . . Rosie thinking, behind her smile, *We're both doing our best, but really we're oil and water.*

Romeo wasn't going to use his own *gazo*, because if anything went wrong it might have been traced to Pigot's garage. The borrowed one, if anything went wrong, could be reported stolen. He was concerned to leave everything neat and tidy, with no problems of *his* making for those who were staying behind. The *gazo*, for instance, was going to stay put for a while, ostensibly having been abandoned by this salesman, Hardy, who'd done a bunk; arrears of rent would mount in the garage ledger, the van would eventually become his in lieu of payment, and he could legitimately apply to re-register it.

'What matters is Martin Hardy will have vanished. A customer Marc didn't know any better than any other. No connection, no involvement, one perfectly good *gazo*.'

'But I can still use this place when you're gone?'

'Sure. Marc's happy with that. But *only* you. Just as I've kept it to *my*self. And cautiously, you understand. As to Marc – for a friend in need, you can trust him to Kingdom Come, you know?'

He'd have asked Pigot to look after her, she guessed. She could read that between the lines. Not that she'd been looking for anyone to lean on – and if she did have to, César would naturally be the man she'd turn to. Even though he still seemed to be somewhat less well organized than one might normally expect, for a *réseau* leader. The briefcase was a prime example – ten seconds with a screwdriver would have it open.

But as he'd admitted, in that reassuring face-to-face they'd had, he did tend to work unconventionally. And the wife in Ireland – well, one still didn't have to *like* him, necessarily, but he was genuine all right.

And as to carelessness – pot calling kettle black – any nosey landlady or cleaning woman might find this hidey-hole, given a few minutes on her own. And in point of fact, what *could* you do ...

Quarter-million. She packed it into the false bottom of her sample-case, and locked it. Then tidied herself up in preparation for taking it along to Jacqui. The arrangements with her were all agreed and finalized; and she was taking her the money now – ostensibly perfume samples. Jacqui'd leave her customers in her assistant's hands for a few minutes, and they'd go upstairs – doing it now instead of later because Clausen was likely to visit her again tonight. She – Rosie – had foreseen this on Wednesday morning, over a hurried breakfast: 'He's not leaving town until Friday, is he? He'll be with you tonight, and – Jacqui dear, you don't really think he'll stay away from you on Thursday, do you? His last night?'

Her interest in the matter had less to do with Jacqui's pleasures than with her own reluctance to meet Clausen again. She didn't want to push her luck.

'What I think' – Jacqui's big, dark eyes on hers, across the little table – 'is you're a witch. You don't look like one, but—'

'Better watch out, hadn't I? What they burnt Jeanne d'Arc for, wasn't it? But Jacqui – listen ... As we've agreed, I'll come about once a week – to get my hair done or discuss the scent business—'

'And I give you whatever I've collected that weekend. I know, don't worry.'

'But if anything happened to me – suppose a few weeks passed and you didn't see me – well, keep up the good work, don't be put off even if you don't hear anything from anyone for a while. Eventually someone else will come for a hairdo, and say – listen to this, Jacqui – she'll say 'A friend of mine by the name of Rosalie recommended you very highly.' Got that?'

'Yes—'

'Then you can trust her – give her whatever you'd have given me. But only if she's given you that name – no other. OK?'

'Rosalie. Your own name, is it?'

'It's a password, that's all.'

'Well, you look more like a Rosalie than a Jeanne-Marie ...'

Friday. Early breakfast – she got it herself, Ursule had left things ready for her – and she was on the road when the pavements were busy with people on their way to work. Still cloudy: maybe better than yesterday had been, but nothing like good enough.

If it *didn't* clear, and the flight had to be called off, Romeo'd go barmy, she thought – swerving into Rue Saint Sever. The traffic consisted almost entirely of bicycles: it gave one a sense of security – invisibility, just one among so many.

Would make things easy for a tail too, of course. Abundant cover ...

But no reason there *should* be one. Despite the scare on Tuesday. No transmissions had been made from this town;

the heat might be on – all right, it *would* be – but they'd still only be making guesses. The pianist was just as likely to be in Amiens or Neufchatel as here in Rouen. To be on your guard was one thing, she reminded herself, shaking with paranoia quite another.

She rode over the Boieldieu bridge and up Rue Grand Pont, past the front of the cathedral and into Rue des Carmes. Thinking about Jacqui – how right she'd been to force the pace. And how the desk-bound warriors in St James' would be hugging themselves, had they known ... Well, they *would* know, pretty soon: she'd give Romeo a message for them – including the line about Rosalie, which could be of absolutely prime importance.

Some character, she thought, was the lovely Jacqui. And one utterance of hers in their talk on Tuesday night still made her smile when she thought of it – that indignant *I hope you're not suggesting* ... After she, Rosie, had made some reference to La Chatte's promiscuity: saying nothing of the facts that Jacqui was Colonel Walther's mistress and pretty obviously Clausen's too, definitely *had* been Bleicher's: or that most of her work for La Chatte had consisted of 'entertaining' men – which had been La Chatte's own speciality, Jacqui being called in only at times when there'd been more than she could handle solo.

I hope you're not suggesting ...

Jacqueline Clermont, she thought – as she pedalled along Rue Beauvoisine – into whose hands you've now put your life ...

It was a fact – beyond recall. And Jacqui might have whispered in Clausen's ear, last night. No insurance against it, she *could* have. After all, she'd already got the money ...

Place Beauvoisine. She was passing within about a hundred metres of Pigot's garage, at this point. Romeo would be starting out from there in about half an hour. This arrangement had been at her own suggestion, so as not to risk leading any tail to Pigot's. Coming directly from Ursule's – as she'd had to this morning – if they *had* had any tail on her, that was where the tailing would have started. She'd sworn that she'd *never* go directly from Ursule's to Pigot's.

All uphill, from here on. Best time of day for it, anyway – still cool, under the cloud cap. Most of the traffic here – still nearly all two-wheeled – was coming the other way, downhill.

Halfway up, she took a rest, dismounting and leaning against a fence, looking back down at the sprawl of greyish town and its landmarks, and the sweep of river where it showed. Nothing like as pretty today, with no blue sky, no sun's rays to gild the ancient spires.

No tail, anyway. No other cyclists hastily dismounting, no vehicle pulling in.

No brown *gazo* van, either. She checked the time, and got going again – walking, pushing the bike up this steeper bit, mounting again where it levelled. She had the Mark III in her sample-case, and would be using it tonight: she'd intended to in any case, but last evening César had given her a message to send about a special drop of explosives for use by the Resistance group at Dury.

With the B.C.R.A. connections, for instance . . .

He'd be easier, she hoped, as he got into his stride. This far, she could understand – just – he'd have felt like an outsider, needing to establish his authority as *réseau* Organizer. Romeo's refusal to meet him hadn't helped; her own failure to tell him about those drops hadn't either. Silly of her: she really hadn't given it any thought.

There were woods on both sides of the road, here: and she was over the ridge, with a long free-wheeling stretch ahead, when the coffee-coloured *gazo* overtook her and pulled in ahead. Romeo was out in a flash – bulky, mop of grey hair flying – wrenching the rear doors open and then swinging round – grinning – to grab her bike. 'Jump in, Angel . . .'

He'd left the driver's door open, and a passing lorry swerved only just in time to clear it: an old man at the wheel screaming abuse at *her*, to her surprise – and Romeo

laughing as he climbed in ... 'It's a wonderful day, my
Angel!'

'Won't be if you smash this thing up.'

'You're right. As always. As *always*, Angel ... Did you
have a good night? I didn't. Not a bloody wink. Here –
cigarette?'

Isneauville. Quincampoix ...

'Coming up for where you tuned in and got the great
news, Angel. Only last week – well, ten days ... Nothing to
send today?'

'Tonight, after you've gone.'

After You've Gone. Lew Stone and his orchestra. Wasn't
it Lew Stone's, that recording? Would have been some really
seedy bunch of musicians in that dive with Ben, that place
they'd danced. Somewhat groggily, no doubt: but sober, in
a joint like that one, you'd have stuck out like sore thumbs.

No denying ... And left me crying—

'I'll be thinking of you, Angel.'

'Well, I'd hope so!'

'Seeing you too, one of these days.'

'Of course. In Mauritius.'

'Maybe in Baker Street before that, who knows?'

'Never do know, do you?' She touched wood. 'Have you
got friends in London – well, in England?'

'If they're around. Otherwise, have to make new ones.'

'May be a bit tough at first, while Baker Street make up
their minds about you.'

'I know. But I'm not worrying.'

'And now, you're not – tense, at all?'

Sarcasm. He was fidgeting, humming to himself, drumming his fingers on the wheel, had been doing so all the time.
Glancing at her with either a grin or a scowl on his face now
and then, for no obvious reason. Simply – *getting out* ... He
should have been worried, she thought – on account of the
clouds, the doubt about any moonlight getting through. But
the question she'd asked about knowing people – she'd

thought of giving him her family's name and address in Buckinghamshire, in case he might need a temporary home of sorts, escape from Baker Street. But her mother might not cope well with him, she'd decided: her uncle, who had the big house – it was a manor, in a hamlet only a few fields away from the small town of Stony Stratford – would have liked him and made him feel at home, but Mama was something else. She lived in the Lodge, had it as hers for her lifetime, had been installed in it with little Rosie when they'd returned to England after Papa's death. She was a difficult, pernickety sort of woman.

She'd adored Johnny. Probably wouldn't like Ben Quarry at all. If she didn't – well, *tant pis*.

'What'd you say?'

Romeo repeated, 'You got the rocket-site brief nicely sewn up, Angel. They'll be pleased with you.'

She touched wood again. She'd given him the message for S.I.S. about Jacqui; and he already knew all about the field research. But he was right, it *was* sewn up. She agreed: 'I could vanish in a puff of smoke, the reports'd still come in – from the field *and* from Mademoiselle Clermont.'

'Yeah. I realize. But stay out of puffs of smoke, you hear?'

On top of the world, most of the time, but he was still very nervous. Smoking non-stop, and constantly watching the road behind them.

'This time tomorrow, Angel—'

'You'll be in Baker Street answering their stupid questions.'

'Yeah. They overdo it, they'll get stupid answers.'

Rocquemont . . . St Martin . . . St Saens . . .

Then Bellencombre, where they stopped to change the *gazo* cylinder. Bellencombre was on the edge of the forest area, with only a short distance to be covered now, to Ardouval. Still a grey overcast, which worried her, although Romeo seemed confident that on that score there'd be no problem.

*

The Plumiers gave them soup and bread for lunch, and more soup with goat-cheese for supper. In between the two meals they'd rested – Rosie had slept – and also heard the BBC's overseas broadcast, the early one, which had been followed by a statement to the effect that in dry summers many lawns turned brown. That was the right message, and encouraging, although there'd still have to be confirmation – repetition – after the later bulletin.

For an hour or so before supper Rosie and Marcel Plumier played bezique, while Madame Plumier – dark, with a gypsy look about her – knitted, and Romeo sat twitching and occasionally muttering to himself. Getting up, pacing around, sitting down again ... Plumier, thickset and bearded, had been needling him, too: after that first broadcast, for instance, he'd told him 'They can call it off at five minutes' notice, remember. All that gibberish tells us is they're like you – *hoping*.'

Romeo growled to Rosie, 'I'd tell *him* something, if I wasn't enjoying the *salaud*'s hospitality. I'd tell him to shut his ugly face.'

The confirmation came, anyway: at about eight, local time. Romeo did a little dance of joy; Plumier, who'd been playing a game of patience, pushed the cards together and got up. 'I'll round up the boys. Curfew's a problem, got to have 'em here before, see.'

'Where from?' Romeo, glancing over at him ... The forester told him, 'Chantier de Jeunesse – but they'll have snuck down to the village by this time ... We'll be hoofing it from here, you realize?'

'Four kilometres?'

'Nearer three. You were there the other day, God's sake!'

'By road from the south, not on foot through the bloody trees.' He frowned, bowed to Plumier's wife. 'My apologies, madame.'

'Oh, I hear a lot worse than that, often enough, from my dear husband ... Why don't you have a snooze, refresh yourself and kill a bit of time?'

'Doubt if I could. Thanks all the same.'

'He's on edge,' Rosie told her. 'Been waiting a long time, for this.'

'I know. I realize ...'

'Talking about me as if I wasn't here. Or some sort of animal.' Pushing his fingers through his grey hair ... 'Another three hours, eh, before we move?'

'Two and a half, more like,' Plumier's wife told him. 'Prefers to make doubly sure, his nibs does. Getting through the woods in the dark, too, you see.'

'We'll have some moon, though.'

'Perhaps not much.' She shrugged. 'In any case, that's his way.'

'He's a good guy, too. One of the best. Just bloody irritating, when he wants to be ... Angel, how are you doing – so quiet, there?'

'I'm all right. But I'll be glad when you're on your way and calming down.'

'Huh.' He pulled a hard chair up close to hers. 'I'll be sitting up there' – pointing skyward – 'thinking of you and Marcel and this new man coming back here. You in all this – crazy business. You know, just sort of pressing button 'A' and flying out of it – *extraordinary*, really ...'

'Yes. It's weird.'

It was nearly ten before Plumier came back with his two helpers, Michel and Albert from the youth camp – S.T.O., *Service Travail Obligatoir*, a Petainist set-up which sent most of its recruits to work in Germany but also had work-camps here in France – for the lucky few. Michel looked about eighteen, Albert no more than fifteen. They worked mainly in forestry, under Plumier, which was how he knew them. They'd slipped under the wire, they told Rosie, weren't likely to be missed as long as they were back before roll call at six a.m. Madame Plumier made coffee for everyone, and gave those two soda-bread and jam; her husband got out the torches they'd be using – two with red material bound over them, which the boys would use, and his own plain glass, uncovered, for passing the recognition signal. He asked Rosie, 'You do it, eh? You're the expert?'

She was taking the Mark III with her, in a satchel with a strap over her shoulder, so as to get her signal off to Baker Street as soon as the Lysander started back. They'd return to this house then, get a few hours' rest and start early for Rouen. She'd decided to take the new courier to within a few miles of town, then drop him off with her bicycle roughly where Romeo had picked her up. He was going to see her, anyway, it made little difference. They might even know each other. But she wasn't telling Romeo this, since she didn't want an argument.

Van and bicycle were both under cover meanwhile, in a shed behind the house.

'Shall we go?'

Ten-thirty. There was thin, high cloud, but enough moon-radiance getting through it to see by. She told Romeo, 'You were right.'

'Wasn't I, though.' He put a heavy arm round her shoulders. '*Wasn't* I, my Angel!'

The clearing was about a hundred and fifty yards north to south, and for most of its length a lot narrower on the other axis, but irregular in shape – wasp-waisted, and wider at this southern end than it was higher up. The last-quarter moon was in the western sky at an altitude of about thirty degrees, its shape vaguely discernible at times but mostly only the veiled source of this milky half-light. There was virtually no wind: the clouds were drifting very slowly eastward, but although this was high ground, here in the shelter of the beechwood you could barely feel it.

It had been an easy walk, with Plumier leading and following contours more than paths. Since arrival, he and Romeo had made their dispositions; pacing out distances and holding up wet fingers, they'd agreed that the Lysander should be encouraged to touch down close inside the northeast perimeter, on a track of about south-southwest. The two boys, with the red torches, were placed to right and left of this track, slantwise across the wasp's waist, so to speak. The pilot would know he had to land so as to pass about midway between them, with his nose pointing at the white torch which would be flashing the recognition signal from this apex of the triangle.

They were all in position now. The Lysander could turn up half an hour early, if it wanted to.

Romeo muttered, 'Wouldn't mind a smoke, eh, Angel?'

'Best not think about it.'

'You could light a bonfire here – who'd see it?'

He was probably right, at that. Although out of some remnant of self-discipline he *wasn't* lighting up. You chose high ground for a landing-field whenever possible, so that the torches wouldn't be visible from still higher ground in the vicinity. There was none that was any higher around here, and the enclosing woods guaranteed privacy horizontally.

'You were here in daylight, weren't you?' Plumier spoke through his teeth, chewing something. 'Did you see the work we've been doing on that side there, over the ridge?'

'Don't recall it ... We came up from Bellencombre, turned at La Fresnaye and trekked over the crest at Hêtre le Poilu.'

'So you wouldn't have. But what I'm saying – we're clearing there as well. Trees all felled, real big 'uns, and now we're tractoring the roots out. Looks like a bloody moon-scape – in *this* light it'd be fantastic.'

Rosie said, 'Sounds as if you enjoy your job, Marcel.'

He grunted an affirmative. 'Plenty worse. Yours, for instance. But you're right, I do ... Flown in Lysanders before, Martin?'

'Oh God, yes!'

It would be on its way by now, Rosie thought. With the new courier beginning to wonder what he might be getting into. Initially, at take-off, the feeling was always of relief –

the end of the waiting, hanging round. Then you saw the *next* hurdles coming up . . .

'One thing,' – Plumier, talking quietly with Romeo – 'one *small* matter, Martin – who's going to service our damn tractors, now you're buggering off?'

'Don't worry. Chum of mine from Rouen'll be in touch. I gave him my customer-list, and all the records – including unpaid bills, you'll be glad to hear. Name's Pigot – Marc. First-class mechanic and – you know, like-minded.'

'One of your lot, is he?'

'No. But he's blown up a few rail tracks, in his time. An action group with links to l'Armée des Ombres.'

'Marc Pigot. Right . . . Hey – hear something?'

Very faint. But *there*, all right . . .

Rosie said, 'Your taxi, sir.'

'By God, it *may* be . . .'

'Coming towards, all right. On time, too. *Must* be.'

'Better stand by. Martin – good luck, old pal, let's see you again one day.' Plumier called softly, cupping his hands around his mouth, 'Be ready lads!'

A red spark glowed, switched off again. The engine-noise sounded about right, she thought. Also on target, and on time. When they arrived, they arrived suddenly – you'd wait hours, and suddenly it would be on top of you, almost before you knew it. Very loud, already. Still couldn't see it. They painted them black, of course.

'Switch on, you two!' Plumier passed her the white torch. 'Here you are. 'AK' – right?'

'Right.' Straining her eyes into the translucent darkness, filtered moonglow over the dense-black surround of bee-ches: then not waiting any longer, flashing the dot and dash, dash-dot-dash. And again – over and over: ear-splitting noise by this time, and she saw it just as Romeo did, shouting and flinging up an arm. It wasn't landing, though, not on this pass, only racketing over like some great roaring bat not much above the treetops. There one moment, gone the next – checking first, she realized, then he'd bank

around, come in and land. The pilots were all adepts, very
expert. She stopped flashing: he'd have seen it, must have,
would know it was OK to come on in, she'd start again when
she heard him out there on his approach. She felt Romeo's
arm round her shoulders and his bristly face against her
cheek, heard his shout of 'On my way. Bless you, Angel.
Take *care* now!' He'd gone – out of this shadow, loping out
into the middle where the machine would finish its run.
Where the pilot would want him, too. If they could make the
changeover of passengers and get back into the air in say
four minutes, they wouldn't take *five* over it. Or even four
and a quarter. She'd seen it often enough before this.
Plumier patted her shoulder: 'OK?' He was on *his* way too,
to help. She'd had an impression – illusion – just for a
moment – of engine-noise inside the forest. But it could only
have been echoes of the Lysander's racket – which was
building again now, as deafening as before, only this time
meaning business. She had the torch aimed and flashing AK,
AK, AK ... Providing a leading-mark as well as the
recognition-signal.

Volume was being turned right up again. Then it cut. OK
– landing ...

Blaze of light – roar of the Lysander's throttle suddenly
wide open – streaks of light and a machine gun hammering.
Impression of fireworks here and there ... She'd screamed
– pointlessly, of course – '*Romeo*!' He was *in* it – all that
light, the criss-crossing streaks – so was Plumier. And the
boys? *Several* guns firing – some upward, tracer streaming
up searchlight beams like sword-blades slashing at the
treetops: the Lysander out of it, though, its noise reducing
rapidly, leaving mostly the continuing, jerky hammering of
machine guns and one's own shock, bewilderment. *Those*
weren't searchlights, they were headlights, converging vehicles – and in the centre, Romeo. Alone – she hadn't seen the
forester go down, but he must have. Romeo with a pistol in
his hand, taking snap-shots this way and that: then he'd
doubled – staggering forward, trotting as if to catch up with

his own toppling weight: then he'd gone down – a belly-flop – and in the same instant she was blinded.

Searchlight – spotlight, pinning her against the backdrop of trees like an actress on a stage. She was ready for it – more or less. Well – what else? A single shot, then – couldn't have been aimed at *her* ... And no more since that one – only dazzling light and running figures, a lot of shouting. She began to put her hands up, then half-realized what she was doing, lowered them again – facing that brilliance, praying to God they *would* shoot.

17

'You'd do better to cooperate with us. Really would.'

A different one, today – saying the same as the other had yesterday. This one's name was Prinz, he'd told her in his guttural French. Badly fitting civilian clothes, mid-forties, flabby-looking, with a large head and mouse-coloured hair. Could have been Heinrich Himmler's nephew – truly, there was a definite resemblance, even the same pig eyes. He was hunched in a round-backed swing-chair behind the desk, and they'd put her on a straight-backed kitchen-type one, out in the middle of the room – which was almost identical to the one in which she'd been through this same routine yesterday. Maybe *was* the same one. Board floor, no carpet, the desk, two filing cabinets, one three-legged stool in the corner and a common-or-garden shovel propped beside it. She didn't remember those, but—

Shivering: in a warm room. All right, the shakes. Trying to control them. Pig eyes on her for a moment, noting it . . .

The Palais de Justice, she was in. She didn't think anyone had told her – simply knew it. Almost as if it had been inevitable that she'd end up here. Three days now – she was *fairly* sure this was the fourth day – which would make it Tuesday. Midnight Friday into early hours of Saturday had been the disaster in the forest. She'd regained consciousness – or partly had – on the floor in the back of a truck a few hours later – in chains and – well, extreme discomfort – soldiers' legs and boots all round her, German voices, occasional bursts of ugly singing – and must have been unconscious again when they'd carted her in. Small hours of the morning, as she'd imagined it, since – the Place Foch deserted, swastika banner hanging limp over that sombre doorway; she'd have been slung over one of the bastards' shoulders, as she'd envisaged it. But at some stage she might have lost a day. Could have stayed more or less unconscious all of Saturday: and there'd have been no way of telling day from night if they'd left her in the cell, where a caged light blazed continuously, but there was a routine of taking the bucket – the cell's only furniture – to empty it in a lavatory at the end of a stone passage, and there was a ventilator in there through which daylight could be seen, when there was any.

What happened in the forest – *how* it had – her brain swam when she tried to think about it. Romeo *might* have forgotten all that self-discipline of his and told someone – some woman who'd thought he was deserting her?

Or at the Ardouval end: bad security by Plumier – or others close to him – or those boys, or one of them?

César?

The notes she'd written for him. Christ, if it *was* him . . .

Disaster, nothing less.

It wasn't, though. *Couldn't* be. Please *God*, it couldn't!

Did I tell you Buck came to my wedding?

But – she remembered now, the conclusion she'd arrived at – last night or some time, in her cell – they *had* to be reading codes, in this case Baker Street's answer to her request for arrangements to be made for Romeo's extraction. Signals had undoubtedly been intercepted in the previous *réseau*'s time – and Romeo had been blamed for it – and it was *still* happening. Despite complete change of personnel, different codes, etcetera.

She'd assumed her own new code would have been safe at least for a few weeks.

Prinz was still leafing through some file. Some time had passed since he'd spoken.

She wondered where Ben was, what he was doing. One of the mental exercises advocated in the resistance-to-interrogation course had been to concentrate the mind on happy memories and on people whom one loved, admired, or even lusted after. Mind over matter: you weren't here, you were *there*. *That* was reality, *this* only an interlude that was to all intents and purposes illusory, was best thought of as a nightmare from which eventually you'd wake up. The psychologists had to give you advice of *some* kind, of course – but she'd thought even then, on the course, that if they were drilling down into the nerves of your teeth, what the hell difference did it make what you *thought* about?

She'd try it, anyway. Try anything – including prayer.

Although if God gave a damn, would one be here now? Would Joan of Arc have burned? Romeo be dead?

They hadn't laid a finger on her, yet. Not since the early hours of Saturday in the woods, and a few kicks in the truck.

'Didn't you hear me?'

There were handcuffs on her wrists, behind her back. When they'd brought her into Rouen she'd had leg-irons on as well. She'd probably been only semi-conscious even when she'd *thought* she was wide awake. Dazed, anyway, not thinking straight – after the crack on the head one of them had given her. It still throbbed all the time, and when in the cell she'd touched it very gingerly with her fingertips there seemed to be a depression in the bone, where the caked blood was.

Gazing up at the window, over the interrogator's head: telling herself, *Hating them, that's what to think about* ... The window was high up, and small enough not to need bars on it. All one saw was a rectangle of grey sky.

So it still hadn't cleared.

How about the moon – how long before Ben might be back on the Breton coast?

'I hope you appreciate that I'm exercising extreme patience.' Glaring at her: an ugly, sulky child. '*Can* hear me, can you?'

She nodded, and it hurt her head. She said it: 'Yes.' No point in infuriating him: perhaps he'd said something to her and her mind had been elsewhere. It was going to start soon anyway, this was only the work-up.

It was a comfort that the pill was still in its pocket in her bra.

What the criteria would be, though – for getting to it and taking it – was something else. How you'd recognize the end of the road, be certain ... Maybe you wouldn't have to think at all – just *do* it.

'*Are* you deaf?'

'I may be. One of your men hit me. You can see—'

'You are an agent of the British so-called Special Operations Executive—' he'd put that in English, mouthing it with a lot of lip-movement and in that almost comically German accent: they were *all* stage Germans, if you let them be. He was telling her, 'You were caught red-handed, and resisted arrest. You're lucky not to have been shot out of hand. Now listen to me. I've been studying your file – such as it is. It's an S.D. file, and far from complete. For your information, we're not S.D. here now; we're *Geheime Staatspolizei*.' Gestapo, that meant: he sounded smug about it. 'The officer you saw yesterday compiled this, and it tells me next to nothing. About as much as you told *him*, eh?'

'I – don't know ...'

'So you see – my purpose in giving you that information – it leaves a great deal for you to tell us. Of course, our own researchers will be getting to work on it now—'

'I don't remember anything. My head—'

'Let's forget your head. If you think it's painful – well, believe me, you don't know what pain *is* – yet. But – let's see if we can't spare you that. As I said – you'd be best advised to cooperate with us. First – obviously – by providing truthful answers to my questions – which you will do, that's a foregone conclusion – but for a long-term, *complete* solution – you should give serious thought to working *with* us. It would be enormously to your advantage.

In fact it's a privilege I'm offering you. Not only would you remain alive – and what one might call uncrippled – you'd live in comfort and security, be well looked after, have no financial problems – and you'll be joining the winning side. What d'you say?'

'I'll – think about it.'

The forty-eight hours during which one was expected to hold out had already been exceeded: that was a certainty; the only doubt was whether she'd been here three days or four. But how soon after the event César might have had the news, she'd no idea – couldn't be sure he *would* know, even – except that when she hadn't reappeared he'd have contacted Madame Plumier, she guessed – or one of the neighbouring *réseaux*.

Except they'd have arrested Plumier's wife, she supposed. Poor woman . . .

Prinz bent over the file again, flipped over a page or two. Tapping down the text with a pencil-point . . .

'All right.' He sat back. 'Jeanne-Marie Lefèvre – as you call yourself. Let's start on some basic questions. Such as – well, you're a radio operator. You've admitted that. You could hardly deny it, could you, seeing you had the radio with you when you were taken? Incidentally, you damaged it at the time of your arrest, but it's being repaired – you may like to know this, because all we'd really want is that you'd use the transceiver from time to time, under our direction. Not so onerous – in return for so much?'

He might as well have been talking Chinese. Funny – you'd imagined it, woken some nights sweating from the nightmare, but you'd never believed – really, fundamentally – that you'd end up facing the unspeakable, unthinkable; unable realistically to see any hope at all of remaining alive for any length of time beyond it. Knowing what had happened to others: also that once these creatures were sure they had as much information – or as little – as they were likely to get, they had no interest whatsoever in keeping one alive.

He'd sighed, histrionically. 'Very well. Radio codes and checks. Checks, primarily. Codes aren't much of a problem – that rigmarole on the silk thing you had. Our cryptographers'll make short work of *that*. But the checks – you'd have at least two, am I right?'

There were three. The 'bluff' was the one an agent was permitted to divulge – under torture – and the other two were the 'security' and the 'random'. The security check was an individual hallmark, exclusive to each operator, a spelling mistake which had to appear in say the third or the eleventh word of every message he or she transmitted. If there wasn't an error where there should have been, Baker Street would know it was a fake, that the radio was probably in enemy control.

There was a fourth, far more natural check, too – what was known as the operator's 'individual fist'. Styles of Morse transmission were as distinctive as fingerprints.

'Well?'

She stared at him. 'What d'you mean?'

'You know damn well what I mean! Your radio checks – describe them!'

'I – don't think I can.'

'You don't, eh?'

'I think – the blow on my head—'

'Oh. Lost your memory.' He nodded as if that was understandable, and reached to a bell-push. 'Perhaps we can help you to regain it.'

There'd been an interval. Another one had come in, in answer to the bell, and Prinz had absented himself for a few minutes. For a pee, she guessed. Or to rack up her state of fright? Glancing at her as he re-entered ... 'Once you start talking, you won't want to stop. Matter of breaking the ice, that's all.' A pause, watching her: she'd been with Ben, was trying her damnedest to stay with him ... Prinz gestured, then, and this other one – also in civvies, but not an officer – judging by the way Prinz spoke to him – put the shovel down on the floor near her, pulled her off the chair and forced her down on it – on her knees, on the edge of the shovel's blade, so that the wooden shaft tilted upwards.

'We'll talk about radio checks next time. Sit down together with a pencil and paper, easier that way. Meanwhile, to get you started – try *these* questions. If anything, they're more important ... Two weeks ago – Wednesday 21st, Thursday 22nd, Friday 23rd – oh, and one on the Saturday too – there were a number of radio transmissions from differing locations around Rouen and Amiens. Obviously it was you, *your* radio. Were you calling for arms-drops, by any chance?'

'I don't know anything about it.'

'All right.' He nodded to the other one: a big man with an immensely thick neck. He put one foot on the raised handle of the shovel, then his weight on it: the blade was forced up into the sinew between her kneecaps and shinbones.

She screamed.

'How's the memory doing?'

Screaming helped – a little. The big one, keeping his weight on the shovel, stooped and hit her in the face backhanded so that her head snapped back. 'Upright! Not bend forward! Upright!'

There'd be worse than this. It didn't seem possible, but she knew there would be. Think about hating them: of the war ending, nooses round their necks. Jesus *Christ—*

'Any recollection yet?'

'*Upright!*'

Head back, body arched, screaming ...

'Let it down, Riess.'

She fell forward – on all fours. Nobody hit her. The pain was still pumping through her, but dully, like pulsing echoes of what it had been. Prinz asked her, 'Do you want to tell me about the transmissions?'

'There was another pianist—'

'Romeo, d'you mean?'

'Yes – *yes*. He—'

'Again, Reiss.'
'*Up!*'

'They *were* for weapons drops!'

She couldn't stand. On the chair again with her head back, eyes shut where tears had streamed, still trickled. She must have told him, she realized. Hadn't meant to. As if some internal force ... Like pressing a boil, pus burst out. Prinz's voice again: 'You see, when you supply an answer, the pain stops. A *correct* answer, mind you. Are you hearing me? *Look* at me ... That's better. Answer now – are you hearing me?'

'Yes.'

'So much easier, to answer. *Truthfully*, of course. We know enough already, you see, that you won't get away with lies. I told you our information's sketchy at this stage, but that doesn't mean we're stupid. Listen – if you lie to me again, I'll have you whipped. The lie about Romeo, for instance – we know he was told by your masters in London to stay off the air – some time ago, when they were calling him 'Toby'. New *réseau*, new code-name ... But it could *only* have been you. Another point – to warn you, so as to avoid further silliness – and a whipping – we know not only about you – 'Angel' as they call you – but also your new Organizer, César, alias Michel Rossier? By the way, you've been masquerading as a *parfumeuse*, I see ...' He sat back, shutting the file: 'Anyway – I'll have Rossier in that chair, before much longer. All I'm saying now is I'll recognize a lie when I hear one – and you'll regret it, I promise you ... On the other hand – if you'd decide to work with us – no more pain, no tears – isn't that a *far* better idea? Tell you what – would you like some coffee? Or tea – a cup of tea – while you think about it?'

She nodded.

'Good. I'll have one with you. And a cigarette, eh? But – oh, look, just a few things I really would like to clear up first. Just help me on this ... The drops you asked for – now we know it *was* you – where are they to take place, and on what dates, and in each case the identity of the man or men for whom you were arranging it. That's a lot of questions, so – just a minute, I'll make notes as you dictate.'

She heard his chair scrape. And a mutter, 'Then it'll all be cleared away, we can relax.' She shut her eyes again, put her head back and slightly to one side, which at the moment seemed to help it. Clear it, too – seeing that it could *not* have been César – why would they torture her to get information which they'd have had already?

'All right. The names and the locations. Go ahead.'

Thinking of Ben and herself in that London dawn . . .

The best ever. Not only physically, but metaphysically, height and depth of love in its truest, also wildest sense. Like she'd *wanted* it to be with Johnny and at one stage had *imagined* the possibility of it becoming – glimpsed the existence of such a plane and allowed herself the frantic hope they'd stood a chance of reaching it. Then lost him – lost him a bloody age before she'd found Ben.

'You aren't going to start being stupid again, I hope?'

She remembered Romeo saying something like 'So – it *can* be done . . .' Meaning that it was possible to hold out – when he'd been telling her about that girl who'd made it—

'All right. Wasting time here. Riess—'

She'd passed out. A recollection of falling, and of voices shouting at her, then darkness and Ben telling her it was going to be all right, he wouldn't let them touch her again. Nightmare, though, because she'd dreamed *that* – the bit about Ben – and what was real was the solid and immoveable fact that the only way to stop it happening would be to give in and start naming names. Which she could *not* do, ever – irrespective of what they might do to her. It was a law she'd had implanted in her brain for a long time now and couldn't break – at least, not consciously.

So they'd kill her.

Eventually. Well, they *would*. It wasn't a supposition or make-believe, it was fact.

Think of something else. Ben, for choice. Whether he'd
ever hear of this. Probably only of the fact she'd died. Died
in Gestapo hands, maybe. It *did* leak out – had with those
others, anyway. And having old links to S.I.S. – yes, he
would ... She was being dragged along, her feet trailing.
'Giving you a bath, now. Cool you off, eh?'

It *was* a bathroom. Huge brass taps, both of them running,
water thundering in ... And she knew about this one. They'd
been put through it – those who volunteered for it had – in
the resistance-to-interrogation course in Hampshire. She
hadn't actually undergone it but some of the men had.

'That's deep enough.'

Cessation of water-noise. The one holding her up asked
'Want to strip off, or go in as you are?'

She was in a skirt and a blouse, and the blouse was filthy.
But the cyanide pill – in its rice-paper wrapping and the
gelatine that might not be quite as good as new by now – any
lengthy immersion, for Christ's sake ...

But stripping off didn't appeal either. *And* they might spot
it – find it ... The one who'd shut the taps off was grinning
at the big one, glancing back at her: 'Which'll it be?'

'As I am.'

Even if it squashed or leaked, she might be able to suck
the dregs out of the little pocket. When they put her back in
the cell tonight – if they did, if she didn't drown here – once
the handcuffs were off for the bread and water—

'In you go, then!'

At the first bite, they'd promised. Barely time to swallow.

Might all end here anyway: they might go too far and
drown her. The technique involved coming as close as
possible to drowning the prisoner, taking him or her to the
limit: head back, forced under, held under until you
were damn near drowned, then you'd be hauled up and
allowed a breath or two, then down again, under – worse
each time.

Victims had drowned, on occasion – so the instructors had
said: either drowned or suffered heart-failure. The answer

was therefore – ludicrous as it had sounded in those days – in a sense, to *help* them.

If you wanted to live. She didn't, so she'd fight.

'If you want to start talking – let us know, eh?'

Guttural pidgin-French . . .

God, let me drown!

Nearly did, once – in the river, the Little Ouse. Not long after they'd settled back in England. It had ruined a Brownie camera they'd given her for her birthday: she'd been stalking an otter, to photograph it, slipped and been carried into a deep pool. Uncle Bertie, who'd lived on one lung since 1918 when he and his platoon had been caught in German gas, had jumped in and fished her out.

Under. Roaring in her ears, pressure, agony in the damaged side of her head where it was being forced against the bottom of the bath. She'd let her breath go – had to. Nothing like the river: trying to picture Uncle Bertie – who was *not* here this time. She *was* drowning: opening her mouth to shout – swallowing river-water, the current dragging her down . . .

Conscious again – some time later, she didn't know how long. The big one was holding her up by the hair with one hand, using the other to slap her face to and fro.

'You there? You *there* now?'

'Eyes are open.'

'OK. This time, a real good one . . . You *want* to drown?'

Vidor asked Ben, 'Want me to try to get you to Grac'h Zu?'

Staring at him, across the table. This was in the Brodards' house, the kitchen. Ben had been sleeping in the old man's room – since that first night when Solange had slept in his arms with the overcoat over her nightdress and he hadn't slept at all, only lain there wondering about – well, precisely what Vidor had just asked him – that was *still* the crucial question – and how long before Vidor got back, what the hell to do if he did *not* get back . . . Watching the light grow outside, hearing the dawn chorus and the barnyard rooster, then the dog whining and jerking at its chain: and in the morning light, Solange's face as quiet and unstressed as a child's, her soft reddish-brown hair tickling his lips.

Since then he'd slept in her father's room. Because she'd wanted to have him in the house, also because if the Boches came back you wouldn't want signs of occupation of that loft.

He answered Vidor's question with one of his own. 'Are you saying *this* pinpoint is busted?'

'Not exactly.' Hard brown eyes on Ben's: a small shake of the head. 'At least – OK, maybe I'm just staving it off because I don't *want* to give up here ... There again, there *is* a hope – two hopes, if they're real. One, night patrols on the roads seem fewer, and two, still no activity around the islands. Course, that could be bluff. At worst, it's even possible *they're* waiting for the moon – guessing *we* are, *someone* might be ... Another thing though is getting you to Grac'h Zu still won't be plain sailing. No certainty about it. I learnt a lesson the other day, you know?'

He'd had to bring the airmen back, instead of leaving them in an escape *réseau*'s hands in Bordeaux. All four were at the Durands' house now, where Ben had been. There'd been a crisis in the Bordeaux area too, apparently, German infiltration of the group that would have taken the airmen down through the Landes via Bayonne to St Jean de Luz. Getting them back to Lannilis had also had its problems, Vidor had found; he'd decided to return by a different route and had run into the hornet's nest his friends had stirred up with their sabotage operation at St Renan.

Main roads and main railway routes seemed to be the best bet now, he'd concluded. Country lanes and minor branch lines, in coastal regions, anyway, were getting more than their fair share of attention. It followed therefore that transferring across-country to Grac'h Zu might be a very chancy business.

Solange joined them in the kitchen. Early afternoon: Vidor had come out by bicycle, to see they were all right and assure Ben that Able Seamen Bright and Farr – in the Lannilis café, two floors up from the bar-room where the customers included off-duty German soldiers – were in reasonably good shape, though restless – which Ben could well imagine – and to talk about the pinpoints, this one and/ or Grac'h Zu. Time was getting short now, only a few days' life left in this moon.

He'd been back about a week – six days, maybe – from the abortive Bordeaux trip, and had made it back just in time to be present at the joint funeral of Solange's father and the boy, Alain. That had been the last time Ben had seen him. They'd had a brief chat upstairs in Brodard's bedroom, then from the window Ben had watched them setting off – from out in the yard here, the local doctor with his *gazo* – an old Buick, charcoal-burning – and three cousins from some other village – Solange's closest relations, the sister having stayed away – all of them in black, climbing back into the crocked-up old limousine as Vidor emerged from the house with Solange on his arm, and from a mile away the Broennou church bell tolled sonorously across the fields and the salt-swept coast. Ben had sworn to himself he'd paint the scene, one day. The church would be only a grey spiked fragment in the background, but he'd do his damnedest to make anyone who looked at it hear that bell.

The entire village had been present, Solange had told him that evening. But not the sister, the one person she'd really wanted. There'd been some awful row between her and her father a few years ago, apparently, when she'd left the place; Ben suspected – from some remark of Vidor's – that it had involved a pregnancy.

Vidor said, 'It has to be munitions caches they're looking for.'

'How would you guess they'd have known there were any?'

'Oh . . . Well – when our friend Guillaume was taken, was when it started – or soon after—'

'Christ, yes – I'd forgotten—'

'I'm not saying he told them anything. Far from it. I'd guess if anyone could keep his trap shut, he could – and *would*. But he had explosive, and he was on that train . . .'

The same one they'd put Rosie on, Ben remembered. How'd you forget *that*, for God's sake? Vidor added, 'He'd got on it at Landerneau, couldn't lie about that either, they'd see his ticket . . . Ben, you're doing a good job here. Good for this one not to be alone, too. Eh?'

The brown eyes intent, probing. Ben said – relaxedly, glancing from him to Solange – 'She's a great kid. Brave as' – half-smiling, still looking at her – 'some gentle little lioness.'

'That's a nice description.'

It wasn't bad. The green eyes, tawny hair – and her quietness, self-containment. She was remarkably resilient. Age nineteen – and quite alone, with that frightful business still vivid in her very recent memory.

There'd been no mention by either of them of his spur-of-the-moment suggestion about taking her to England. He'd been hoping ever since the morning after that she might not have heard it, or remembered, or understood what he'd tried to say.

Vidor asked him, 'Those the old man's clothes you're wearing?'

'Yeah. The others were in rags. And she'd burnt my reefer jacket – how d'you like that?'

Vidor smiling at her: 'You burnt his uniform?'

'Before he came. I thought if they came back to search—'

'Quite right.' He came back to business. 'Ben, listen. We've got until the weekend – for this moon. I've suggested a decision by Thursday night, between us and London. So – if there's no change between now and then – what d'you say, do we risk it here, or—'

'Vidor.' Solange handed him a mug of coffee.

'I adore you.' He smiled at her. 'Don't tell Pierre, huh?'

Her boyfriend Pierre, son of a local fisherman, had been in a work-camp in Germany for a year now. She'd told Ben she'd almost forgotten what he looked like.

Ben took his own mug from her, told her in Australian, 'You're a beaut, Solange.'

'Oh.' The *shy* smile, that one. 'Sanks.'

Vidor raised his eyebrows: 'Language classes?'

'Well – you know – long, quiet evenings . . .'

'Ah. Yes . . .' Treating *her* to that thoughtful gaze of his: she'd laughed briefly, gone back to the stove. He turned back to Ben: 'What do you say?'

'What change could there be?'

'I don't know. Troop withdrawal, maybe?'

'Not likely, is it? Why *now*?'

A shrug. 'Good question.'

'You're telling me London know there's a doubt, but if you give them the OK, they'll come – so it's our decision?'

'Right.' Vidor nodded. 'Big one, too. You – us – your gunboat . . . Has to be *our* decision – not *mine*. OK?'

She was back on the same chair: if they hadn't tied her to it she'd have fallen off. How long she'd been unconscious she didn't know, but she was still soaking wet, her clothes plastered to her, although the bath itself and a time when she'd believed she *had* been drowning seemed like a far more distant memory.

She could see the outline of her bra through the wet, smudged cotton, remembered the thought she'd had earlier – that when the time came – when she was back in her cell and had a hand free—

Still there, still intact. Moving that arm slightly, she could feel it. Given the chance, she'd have done it now, this moment. She'd been right in that guess, you didn't have to *think* about it.

Prinz's voice: 'They tell me you tried to drown yourself.'

Focusing on him. He'd looked taller behind the desk. Short legs, fat hips, Himmler-type pale face. Prime specimen of the Master Race.

'Obviously more drastic persuasion is necessary. I won't allow you to kill yourself – you'll either endure quite incredible levels of pain, or you'll see reason. Again, I *advise* the latter.'

If only in that forest she'd been quicker off the mark. Dashed out after Romeo, for instance, so they'd have *had* to shoot her. Or had a gun, as he'd had – that would have done it. She remembered Marilyn offering her one, in the cabin of that old paddle-steamer.

An *age* ago ...

Prinz had turned away, opened a desk drawer.

'This may do the trick.' He held the object in front of her face: a pair of pliers, handles encased in red rubber, the business-end shiny steel, new-looking. She thought – cringing, an immediate reflex, it was one of the things she'd feared – *Fingernails. Oh, Jesus Christ ...*

Help me, Jesus?

'Strip her.' Pointing, with the pliers. 'To the waist.'

Not fingernails.

The bra, the cyanide ... Slam of the door – *no* way out? Beyond that – much closer – a mounting awareness of overwhelming horror – understanding – she couldn't *not*, couldn't hold it off, couldn't continue to keep out of mind the recollection of a whisper heard a year or so ago and deliberately – imperatively – shut out. She begged frantically, *No, not possible, not even* these *people – Christ, don't* let *them!*

'No!' Her own voice, high and querulous: repeating on an even higher, longer note, '*N-o-o!*'

The big one clumsily pulled her blouse open, jerked it back over here shoulders. A wet rag – the cord held it there. She'd shut her eyes: not to see either Prinz or the other, and by shutting them out coming as near as she could to not letting them see *her*.

Prinz's voice: 'Yes – of course, that too.'

Her bra.

A hand on her shoulder held her forward against the cord: thick fingers between her shoulder blades fumbled at the catch.

'Here.' Prinz used a knife: she heard it click open, then felt a tug and the bra came loose, was pulled away: opening her eyes, she saw him just let it drop. He was staring at her breasts. Fingers gripped her chin then, tilting her face up . . . 'Look at me!'

'No. No – please—'

'Guessed what I'm going to do, have you?'

Jesus had prayed, *Take this cup from me*—

'Guessed, have you?'

The other one had murmured something in German. Prinz said in his atrocious French, 'She knows how to stop this. Open her eyes, pull the lids up.'

More German. An appeal, by the sound of it.

'Do it!'

Hazy, unfocused, and pulsing actually in her eyeballs: as if her brain was swelling, about to burst out. Heart thudding, shaking her whole body.

'So pretty. *Very* pretty.' Fingers stroked her breasts, touched the nipples. She struggled to twist away against the chair, the cord, the big one's hands: the thumb and middle finger of one hand pulling her eyelids up, the other now brought into use, clamped over her mouth. Prinz was asking her, 'Are you choosing to cooperate?'

She might have nodded. Agreed to *anything*. There'd never been any concept in her mind of such horror: the threat in itself, her certainty that he'd go through with it, terror of something even beyond the ultimate in pain – and with it, a part of it, the disfigurement – and virtual certainty that her screams would fuse into outpourings of treachery, self-destruction in the course of destroying everything of the greatest, truest value.

'Look. *See* this.'

The pliers: through a fog of terror as well as utter loathing. She was fighting, trying to get her teeth into that hand, screaming like an animal, writhing, Prinz murmuring calmly, 'Now then . . .' Cold steel touched that nipple, moved against it as the pliers opened: 'If you want to change your mind—'

'She's gone.'

'What d'you mean, *gone*? Fainted, is all—'

'Not so sure, looked more like a heart—'

'Revive her. Get a bucket – cold water—'

Surfacing, she heard a door open. Something like a wire was biting into her chest. Gagging, mouth open, slime welling, hanging – the feel of it made her retch again. Somewhere close, Germans were shouting at each other. Heels stamped across a board floor and a door banged shut. A hand on her shoulder pulled her upright in the chair, and the wire cutting into her – it was a cord, she remembered – went loose. Whoever it was – oh, the big one, Prinz's subordinate – jerked the sodden blouse together over her breasts, muttered in heavily accented French, 'Seems you're in luck.'

18

She'd been dragged back to her own cell, left there in semi-delirium for – she'd little idea – one hour, six hours – then hauled out again – thinking *This time, they'll finish it, please God* – and pushed into another one – bigger – in which a blanket-covered human form crouching against the back wall had turned out to be a man.

'Pascal Erdos. Who are you?'

'Jeanne-Marie Lefèvre.' Her knees still felt as if they were on fire, and her legs were throbbing agony from ankle to hip. She'd more or less collapsed into the corner behind the door. Telling him – Erdos – after some interval – 'If you don't mind, I want to sleep.'

The bucket routine was going to be an additional discomfort now. It was part of the reason she resented having to share a cell with him. Would have preferred to have been alone in any case, psychologically to lick her wounds, work up new strength: if she could find any ... Also, though, she suspected the motive behind this – theirs, and *this* person's.

Sunburnt face, balding head – a lot of forehead anyway – and the whites of his eyes unnaturally bright in the tanned skin. Staring at her, and beginning to chatter – somewhat chimp-like ... 'Why they'd have put you in with me, is what bothers me. No offence – but usually it's either solitary or all-women or all-men. Not that I've been locked up before – going by what one's heard, I admit ... Might you be S.O.E. – by any chance?'

'I suppose they've set this up so you can question me.'

Aesop's fable about the sun and the wind competing to persuade some character to strip off. Kindness succeeding where violence had failed. It was an old dodge, anyway, one had often been warned about it. Erdos told her, 'I was wondering the same of you.'

'Well – I'd be content not to exchange another word ... Except – you said your name's – Erdos? Are you French?'

'Born Hungarian, French by adoption. My guess is you *are* S.O.E. – or you *were* – but I don't mind telling you – these bastards know it already – I'm RF Section, or was. Tell you another thing—'

'Don't tell me *anything*.'

RF Section was a kind of parallel to F Section – hers – set up as a separate operational unit and employing only French agents. The object had been to propitiate de Gaulle, take the steam out of his anti-S.O.E. attitudes and manoeuvrings. They liaised with his people and had a base of their own in Dorset Square.

'Tell you, anyway. Not that I'd want you to count on it – my guess, that's all – that they've put us together because we're both on our way to Paris. What I *can't* tell you is whether it'll be Avenue Foch or Rue de Saussaies. This lot here *were* all S.D., you see, Gestapo have now displaced them. What the English call a bit of a bugger's muddle, at the moment.'

'What makes you think we're being moved?'

'I know *I* am, and they've stuck you in here with me, so' – he shrugged – 'if there's any method in their foulness ... Have they been giving you a bad time?'

She shut her eyes, leant the intact side of her head back against the wall.

'Sooner not talk about it.'

'OK. For what it's worth, though, I'm sorry.'

If he was right about being moved to Paris – well, it was pretty well par for the course, and whether one would be in Gestapo or S.D. hands at that stage didn't make much difference. After they'd finished with you, you might be shunted on to Fresnes prison for a while, en route to Ravensbruck or one of the other death-camps. Or, miss out Fresnes.

Prinz's assistant hadn't let her have her bra back. He'd allowed her to recover her wooden shoes, but when she'd wanted the bra he'd growled something negative in German – perhaps that with the strap cut it wouldn't be any use to her – and he'd physically stopped her when she'd reached to pick it up. So – effectively, one was a lump of meat. Or an animal waiting to *become* a lump of meat. No hope, no exit. Shut the mind.

Pascal Erdos had his head back too, and his eyes shut. Monk-like more than monkey-like, in that blanket. He'd watched her closely while they'd been talking, must have seen that she had on only the thin, damp blouse and that she was shaking like a jelly, but he'd done nothing, offered nothing.

Perhaps the blanket was all he had. If he was naked under it he'd hardly have offered it to her.

The sickening fact that was beginning to sink in now was that her carefully contrived Jacqui Clermont setup had gone for six. She'd been so sure that she'd got it up and running and that it would continue to run either with or without her own participation, but it had hinged on Romeo getting to London and telling S.I.S. about the 'Rosalie' password. Jacqui wouldn't deal with anyone who introduced herself in any other way, so – full stop. She – Rosie – had *not* been so bloody clever.

The field reports would come in, of course – to César, or whoever came in to replace him. Plumier's death would have left a gap in that chain, unfortunately – but the others would all know of it, make their own alternative arrangements. And a lot would go straight to London – touch wood – some of it no doubt by the secret mail route to the Brittany coast and across-Channel by hand of Ben Quarry, *et al.*

Interception of Baker Street's signals *had* to be the

Achilles heel. It couldn't have been César because if it had been it would mean he personally had instigated the ambush at Hêtre de Poilu, and to have done that he'd have had to be in touch with the local Army Command: so this lot upstairs would have been in the know, would hardly have gone to such lengths to extract information which they'd already have possessed – the drops, locations, recipients, all the stuff she'd given César in writing.

And they *knew* about him, for Christ's sake! Prinz's complacent tones swam up out of memory: *I'll have Rossier on that chair, before much longer.*

She'd caught her breath, gasped '*Oh, Christ*—'

'Huh?' The Hungarian . . . 'You all right?'

'Yes. Only' – she shut her eyes again – 'talking to myself.'

'Best not to think about any of this more than you have to. Think about pleasant things, if you can . . . Married are you? No – too young . . . How about a lover?'

How about minding your own bloody business, she thought. But her first impression might have been wrong, perhaps he wasn't all that bad. He nodded – thinking back on the advice he'd just given her – 'Easier said than done, I know.'

She managed a smile, in response to his. 'Have they hurt *you*?'

'Well.' A shrug, inside the blanket. '*Hurt* I think is rather a funny little word, in that context . . . But – yes, they know what they're about, don't they . . . D'you know – oh, I don't want to be a bore, come over all introspective—'

'Go on.'

'Well – I think it's the first time I ever found myself actively *hating* someone. Consciously, actually *full* of it. Of course, hate and fear are first cousins, I realize that, but—' He paused . . . 'Do *you* hate them?'

'I have done for a long time. Not just for *this*. In fact I think I'd say *hate* is a funny little word.'

'Oh, I couldn't agree. To me it's like a knife – either the

sound or the look of it on paper. It has an edge to it, it *cuts*!'

'Something to do with language, are you?'

'Was.' He raised his hands in surrender. 'I was a lecturer at the Sorbonne – for two years—'

The bolt scraped back on the outside of the door. Erdos finished – 'In modern languages ... Whatever this is, good luck.'

'Same to you.'

'The two of you—' It was the big man, Prinz's assistant. In uniform, with a pistol on his belt. He was a sergeant. 'On your feet ... Out!'

'Out –' struggling up, using both the walls in her corner – 'like *this*?'

Meaning the way she was dressed: the thought of being moved to Paris in such a state ... The German grabbed her by an arm, jerked her into the doorway, saw the pain she was in, and let go: she leant there, two uniformed guards in the passage staring at her out of quite startlingly brutish faces. Behind her Erdos murmured, 'I'd give you this blanket, except—'

'Thanks, but—'

'No talking to each other!'

The passage – not towards the lavatory, the other way – to narrow stairs leading up into the vestibule. Stone pillars, printed notices on some of them – posters in red and black announcing executions carried out. Two black-uniformed Germans and a Frenchman in plain clothes paused in their jokey conversation, staring at her and the Hungarian as they passed. Outside, she saw that it was early evening: she'd thought of it as being later, wouldn't have been surprised by pitch darkness. Hobbling down the steps to the pavement, wooden shoes clacking on the stone although she was putting them down as gently as she could so as to jar her knees as little as possible – and the guard beside her in his jackboots and helmet staying level but showing impatience at her slow progress. Erdos behind her with his own guard clomping down: he was bare-footed, she remembered.

There was a camouflage-painted staff-car waiting, with a soldier-driver behind its wheel. Prinz's man got to it ahead of them, jerked the rear passenger door open and gestured brusquely at her to get in.

Her knees didn't like being bent . . .

'Isn't this a treat.' Erdos, shoved from behind, dumped himself beside her, the door slammed and the big man was going round to the other side, to the front passenger seat. Erdos nudged her: 'Notice we're not handcuffed?'

Until that moment, she hadn't thought of it. Prinz's man was forcing his bulk in, in front of her, and having some difficulty getting that door to shut. The other guards were going back up into the building. Erdos muttered, 'Door's not locked either, this side.'

'Talking is not permitted!'

He'd shouted it with his head slightly sideways – as if trying to see out of his left ear. Too bulky to swivel round, and on that colossal neck his head probably couldn't turn much either. The driver pushed the car into gear, revving the engine as he pulled out from the kerb: Erdos whispered, 'Any chance we get – out *this* side – join me?'

It took a moment to sink in . . .

Then: *Why not?*

Even at the cost of a broken neck. Cost – or prize . . . And – the odds would be against one getting far or being free for long, but *possibly* long enough to get to the Belle Femme, warn César to burn those notes.

And the message for S.I.S. about contacting Jacqui?

Probably not. Because the odds were that César would be bagged too, soon enough. Therefore (a) no point, (b) extreme danger for Jacqui. But – think about it . . .

Erdos muttered, 'Heading for Gare Rive Gauche, I'd guess.'

'No talking!'

Via the Pont Pierre Corneille, presumably. It was right on top of the station, which was just across the river there. They could have driven straight down and over the Jeanne d'Arc bridge but the driver was obviously making for the Corneille. Swinging left into Rue aux Ours: he'd turn right near the cathedral, get down to the river there and left along the Quai Corneille.

The big one was wearing a Luger, she remembered.

Better than Rue de Saussaies or Avenue Foch, though. Pliers, for instance . . .

Thank God for Pascal Erdos, she thought – for even the fleeting *ghost* of a chance . . . She was watching him out of the corner of her eye as the driver braked – slowing for *this* corner . . . There was a troop-transport thing parked right on it, and he was having to swing out . . . She glanced directly *at* Erdos, then – seeing the chance or the hope of one at the same moment as his hand closed on her arm. His other hand creeping to the door-handle. For a moment her brain flared, telling her *You're mad, in the state you're in already*—

She part threw herself out after him, was also part dragged out *by* him. He'd misjudged it – sheer bad luck, hit a lamp-post as he dived – in so doing softening *her* landing – slightly, she cannoned into him and then fell, spinning, hitting the paving and rolling, arms wrapped round her damaged head to protect it but nothing she could do to protect her knees: in the next second she'd fetched up with literally stunning violence against an abutment of the cathedral's wall. Erdos was on his knees out near the kerb, stooped forward like a Muslim at prayer. She yelled – in surprise at being alive – 'You all right?' Brakes squealing, there'd been shouts, a car's horn blowing repeatedly and now solidly, continuous – but other traffic still passing – until *now* there *had* been. Erdos bawled at her 'Go on! *Go!*' Two priests were staring open-mouthed at her, and some children too, jumping up and down and shrieking, pointing – but he had more than that round *him*, a small crowd gathering. She was half-running, half-hobbling – a wave to the children, a goodbye wave that said *Please, don't follow*: instinct telling her that if they thought she was all right they'd lose interest, transfer it to the naked monk – then she was round the southeast corner of the cathedral, slowing to a limping walk so as to be less conspicuous.

Still was, though. Two young girls with bicycles – on the pavement, pushing them, talking and laughing – one glanced at her, did a double-take, muttered to her friend and they both stared – open-mouthed, speechless. She must look like something really special, she realized. Horns were still blaring at each other back there – beyond, around the two corners she'd somehow managed to put between herself and them: she could imagine the staff-car having to back out of that short-cut alleyway into the mainstream of traffic, and Prinz's outsize assistant going berserk – he'd have got Erdos back in the car by this time, she guessed. Poor man – his incapacity and easy recapture would have delayed any pursuit of *her*, she guessed.

'Hey, hell*o* there!'

Female voice: a straggle of women had been passing, several of them giving her hard looks, but—

She saw her, then, recognized her – the tart who'd told her at Ursule's that the hot water had run out. In a tight, short, hip-hugging, low-cut pink dress, skirt with a flouncy hem swirling around her skinny knees. Artificially auburn hair, and all that make-up . . . Rosie stopped, with a vague thought of *Any port in a storm* – of highly dubious benefit, admittedly, but – someone one knew – after a fashion . . .

'Hey – *you've* been in the wars!'

'Yes – I have, I—'

'Baby, are you *showing*!'

Her blouse lacked some buttons and seemed to have shrunk on her; and with no bra, her nipples would be visible through the thin material.

'Jeanne-Marie – right? I asked Ursule about you. You sell perfume, don't you . . . Some bastard roughed you up, that it?'

'Yes.' Glancing back, towards the corner. Back at this *poule* . . . 'Look – I suppose you wouldn't – do me a favour and—'

'Why wouldn't I? Where d'you want to get?' She took her arm. 'Long way back, mind . . . I could call my friend – if he's there he *might*—'

'Walk with me to Place de la Pucelle?'

'Oh, *that*'s no distance. Sure, why not . . . Hey, looky here—'

A bright green scarf, chiffon, she'd had it over her arm, for some reason. She looped it over Rosie's head – round her neck, with the ends hanging loose in front. It made for a great improvement . . . 'My God – side of your head here, what's—'

'I'll get it seen to, don't worry. Thanks for this, you're immensely kind, I'm sorry, I don't know your name?'

Arm in arm: like sisters . . . Thinking it out: around the top corner there and across the cathedral square, into Gros Horloge. The girl was telling her that she could call her 'Misty'. She reeked of some scent which by Pierre Cazalet's standards might have been classified as disinfectant . . .

'—short for Mistinguette, see. Like it? Sort of sexy but it's got class too, know what I mean? Hey, you *are* hurting bad, aren't you!'

'My knees mostly. It's not as bad as it was, anyway. You're *very* kind, Misty.'

'Think you're one of us, won't they?' She flashed a smile at a policeman on duty in the *Place*. 'Nice boy, that. Just got married, though, the silly fucker . . . Tell me what happened?'

'I'd sooner forget it, Misty.'

'German?'

'Oh – yes . . .'

'Yeah. They can be sods – without trying, even. Can be nice too, mind . . . But you're not on the game, are you? Shit *that* feller'll know you next time he sees you. Hold up, dear—'

'Sorry. Damn knees . . .' They felt they might seize-up solid at any moment: and the cobbles in Gros Horloge didn't help much. She was trying to keep to the middle, the narrow smooth strip of the rainwater channel, but there were a lot of

other pedestrians and cyclists, you couldn't *all* the time . . .
'This is taking you miles out of your way, Misty.'

'Never mind. Known the bugger long, have you?'

'What?' Catching on, then . . . 'No. Not long at all.'

'I'd steer clear, if I was you.'

'Yes.' Rosie laughed, glancing at her. 'I will. If I *can*.'

Left into Rue la Vicomte. Reasonably smooth pavement,
on this side. Misty asked her, 'Is it the Belle Femme we're
making for?'

'Yes.' From the corner, getting over to the other side –
cobbles again. Misty informing her that this was Margot's
territory . . . 'The blonde one, you must've seen us together?'
Rosie agreed, yes, of course she had . . . Thinking of Pascal
Erdos – what they'd do to him now, and what he'd done for
her: then facing the huge, immediately vital question:
whether César would still be here.

Might well not be. Might be on his way to the Pyrenees
– or out in the sticks somewhere, gone to ground . . .

Gaston, the younger son, saw them coming. He was
among the pavement tables with a napkin over his arm,
waiting for custom. Only two tables were occupied at the
moment, Rosie saw.

'Gaston . . .'

'Madame.' He'd taken in her roughed-up state: was
looking now at Misty, seemed to know her too. 'Mam'selle,
I regret—'

'I know, dear. Maman doesn't like us, does she? Reckons
I might eat you up – you *and* your brother . . .' Facing Rosie,
holding her arms: 'You going to be all right now?'

She nodded. 'Misty, thank you *very* much . . . Oh, your
scarf—'

'Give it back at Ursule's, no hurry. Someone here who'll
look after you, though, is there?'

She'd met Gaston's eye, and he'd nodded, with a slight
movement of his head towards the café's upper regions.
Relief was enormous: she kissed Misty's cheek. 'Yes, there
is. And thanks a million.'

'I'll be off, then . . .'

Gaston asked her – leading her inside, to the stairs – 'Were you involved in an accident, madame?'

'Yes. But I'll be all right . . . Monsieur Rossier's in, is he?'

'Oh, yes. Madame, if I might assist—'

'No – thank you. You go on, tell him I'm here.' She was hauling herself up one stair at a time, using the banisters. Gaston ran up ahead of her. Rosie telling herself, *No rush now. Thank God he hung on . . .*

'What is it Gaston?'

'Believe it or not, monsieur – Madame Lefèvre!'

'*What?* You *mean* it?'

She was at the top, then: he came bounding to the door: arms outstretched . . . 'Angel!' Gaston, smiling, pulled it shut behind her. She told him, 'I *must* sit down . . .'

'Are you hurt? Oh, my God, you *are*!'

'Yes. But don't panic. Not all *that* bad. Looks worse than it really is, I'm sure.' He was helping her: she subsided into the deepest of the chairs. 'Michel, I've a lot to tell you, and not much time. Did you hear what happened at the landing-field?'

'That there was an ambush and you'd got away. That was four days ago – I've been going crazy. Where've you been, what – Angel, you look *terrible*!'

He was more human, she thought, than she'd realized. He'd seemed a cold fish, until now . . . 'Is today Tuesday?'

'Wednesday. Hell, don't you even—'

'I just wasn't sure. Lost a day, somewhere. But listen – tell you this quickly, then – well, just listen. It's worse than you imagine, much worse. No, not talking about my injuries – of our situation generally – yours as much as mine. Michel – I didn't get away – whoever told you that was misinformed or lying. I've been in the Palais de Justice here – Gestapo, I was tortured—'

'My *God*—'

'I didn't tell them anything. Except one thing, I admitted

the radio transmissions were for arms drops. I didn't tell them where, or any names – so those notes I gave you, please burn them, that's the *most* important thing. They know about you, you see—'

'*What* about me?'

'Not from anything I said, I promise you. This Gestapo man – Prinz, I don't know his rank – told me they knew enough that if I lied he'd catch me out, and for instance they knew you were my Organizer, code-name César and nom-de-plume Michel Rossier. He said 'I'll have Rossier in here, before much longer'. So maybe he doesn't know where you are or what you look like – they've just taken over from the S.D., incidentally, there seems to be some element of confusion—'

'So – go on?'

'What he wanted from me most was about the drops. To whom, where and when. So the lists I made on your insistence, Michel—'

'I'll destroy them. As you say, burn them. Right away. What else?'

'Well, I'm a dead duck, obviously. I'd imagine you are too – or would be if you stayed. But they've got my radio – and even if I still had it I doubt it'd be safe to use it. They *must* be reading our signals – *must* be!'

'If they were, wouldn't they have the names and locations, as on your lists?'

'Yes. Yes – of course ...' He was right – she *thought*. Struggling to keep herself thinking straight ... 'They would, wouldn't they ... So it must be Baker Street's stuff they're reading. The Lysander R/V, for instance – and the interceptions during the previous *réseau*'s time – all blamed on poor old Romeo—'

'My own thinking's been – well, rather similar, in a way – that we might have a traitor in Baker Street. There was a Frenchwoman they sent over – you may have heard of her?'

'La Chatte. Behind bars now.'

'Exactly. But having tried once – eh?'

'Possible, I suppose. Anyway – as far as you and I are concerned, here and now – no radio communication, no question of calling for another Lysander pickup – which'd be out anyway, in the circumstances—'

'So?'

She nodded. 'The way I came in, this time – by sea. Train to Paris, then the Brest express – tomorrow morning. I must get to Ursule's first, mind – to get some clothes. Crazy, really – talking about Paris and Brittany, mightn't even get as far as Rive Gauche. But I'll need money, please. I've no papers of any sort, of course ...' Staring at him, shrugging. 'Hopeless, isn't it?'

'I wouldn't say so, Angel. A lot of us have travelled right across France and back without being asked to show papers ... Where, though, and how will you make contact?'

'I know how. Don't worry.' She nodded. 'From Paris I can make a phone call to say I'm coming—'

'Perhaps say *we* are coming. I could travel with you?'

'Yes. Except – well, as I just said – I might not get half a mile from here. Might you not have a better chance using your own contacts – ones you used when you took the airmen from Lyon?'

'I don't see why it should be better.'

Gazing at him: getting it together: at least, trying to ...

'Because – well, they know *exactly* what I look like, and that I'll be on the run. You don't want to be seen even *looking* at me. I may not get far anyway – as I say. I only came here to tell you what's happened and – to burn those notes. But – *maybe* I'll get lucky ... Well, look – if this is what you *want* – suppose I get the first Paris train in the morning – the milk train. You come on a later one, we'll both get on the mid-morning express to Brest. Goes through – oh, Le Mans – and Rennes. And St Brieuc. And – if you were just to keep me in sight, get off where I do—'

'Where'll that be?'

'You don't need to know – do you? What's more, there'd be no point – you couldn't make it on your own, those boys wouldn't take you on trust – I mean if I'd fallen by the wayside . . .'

'Which boys are you talking about?'

'*Men*. This escape *réseau* on the Breton coast. But – Michel, the Gestapo and all the others too will be looking for me, and they know you by name . . . Right? Well – at least one of us doesn't *have* to know – isn't that good sense?'

'You think if I was caught and they put the screws on me—'

'It's *possible*. Believe me. I've *had* the screws on me, they had me screaming. I had the suicide pill but I couldn't get at it; if I could have I'd have taken it without a moment's hesitation. I wouldn't be here now. I'm not going to talk about what they did to me – and threatened – but I learnt one thing – no matter *what*, I couldn't give names – simply *couldn't* – I hate to *know* them even—'

'All right – but steady on, you're—'

'Shouting. Sorry . . . It's been – very, *very* bad, Michel.'

'Your head – over that ear—'

On his feet, stooping over her, peering at it . . . 'What did *this*?'

'—at the ambush – I was hit with a pistol-barrel. They'd shot Romeo – I saw that happen—'

'Shot all except you, I heard, and you'd made a bolt for it, got away. So I've been waiting, *hoping*—'

'From whom did you hear that I'd got away?'

'Mattan. I tried the Plumier house but a German answered . . . Angel, we must bathe this wound. I have some iodine, too.'

'All right.' She let her eyes close. 'Thank you.'

'How on earth did you escape from the Palais de Justice?'

'They were sending me to Paris. To Avenue Foch or – I don't know. They put me in a cell with an RF Section agent, and – cutting it short, it was all his doing. This car was taking us to the station, they didn't bother putting handcuffs on us, and when it slowed at an awkward corner he jumped out and pulled me with him. I got away without much trouble but I think he'd hurt himself, they'd have recaptured him.'

'Must hand it to you, Angel—'

'Those papers – all the stuff I gave you—'

A nod. 'I'll burn it all. Other notes too. Will you stay here tonight?'

'No. At Ursule's. I said, I must get some clothes – but I'll be close to the station too, for an early start, take the first train that's going – and I'll telephone, say we're coming—'

'We'll meet at the Gare Montparnasse at what time?'

'Not *meet* – just both of us *be* there ... The Brest train leaves at eleven-twenty or eleven-thirty. Say be there about eleven. But don't come near, or speak – they *might* be watching me, you know? You could sit behind me – in one of the open carriages, if I'm near the front of it—'

'And I'm not allowed to know where we'll be getting out – eh?'

'I thought I'd *explained*—'

'Well, you did, but—'

'Buy a ticket to Brest, and get out when I do. Get a return ticket, d'you think – for camouflage? Just going for a day or two, to see some relative?'

'What about you?'

'As it happens I do have a story that would fit. Of course I've no papers to back it up now, but—'

'What if you were arrested?'

'Change trains, go your own way. The more distance you put between yourself and me, the better chance you'd have!'

'I suppose' – he got up, stretching – 'you have a point. But—'

'Also – as I said – on your own, these other people wouldn't take a chance on you. A stranger just turning up – well, you told me that when you took those escapers from Lyon you had a job getting them to accept you – wherever *that* was?'

'Yes. Yes, all right.' Glancing at her as he limped to the nearer window ... 'You're a tougher nut than you look, Angel. In fact you're – astonishing.' He was stooping, looking out. 'Light's going. We'd better see to that head-wound – if you want to get over to Rive Gauche before curfew.' Turning back: 'How'll you get there? Your bike's not here – no, obviously—'

'I left it at the Plumier's place, inside our van. Which the owner will say was stolen, incidentally, when they trace it to him. Wise precaution of Romeo's, wasn't it ... Listen, might Gaston know of a taxi-driver we could trust?'

They'd given her a meal – soup, bread and cheese, and coffee with a fair amount of brandy in it. Then César had come with her to Ursule's, in a diminutive *gazo*-converted Renault van which Gaston's brother Emil had provided – probably borrowed, but some black-market involvement, she guessed. The brandy might have been a product of it, too. César had produced the bottle from the cupboard in which he also stored his briefcase: and it had been just what she'd needed – for its medicinal effect in general but even more so after the shock of seeing herself in the bathroom mirror – the bruises on her face and worse ones on her neck, eyes like holes in sodden blotting-paper, and the open wound – now clean and iodine-tinted but still not exactly decorative ...

At Ursule's she'd hobbled straight up to her room, anxious to avoid any more explanations – and sympathy, curiosity, etcetera. And she'd be leaving long before any of them were out of bed.

Leave Ursule's rent money in the kitchen. And Misty's green scarf.

Her room didn't seem to have been disturbed, or searched. She wouldn't have been totally surprised to have found it ransacked. She started by putting out the clothes she'd wear in the morning. A rather well-worn woollen dress, a café-au-lait scarf to cover her hair and most of her face, a skirt that was far from fashionable but would reach well down over her knees. And her old falling-apart cardboard shoes. Clean underwear including the spare bra with its *empty* pocket. She'd have to take the smart holdall – incongruous with this *ensemble* – but she could carry the old tweed coat draped over it.

She'd look different, all right. Sad little country bumpkin, dowdier even than she'd been when she'd arrived in Paris and called on Louis.

That was a thought: call on him again, give this case back in exchange for her old one. Or if he'd thrown that one out – probably would have – use a cardboard box with a bit of string round it.

Who'd ask for identity papers from a down-and-out?

Well – *they* would. If they were looking for a female on the run . . .

César would be back in his room at the Belle Femme by this time: she hoped, on his knees at the grate, burning her notes. He'd sworn it would be the first thing he'd do. Anything that had a name, an address or a telephone number on it. And the copies of her transmissions, obviously.

The notion of calling on Pierre Cazalet and swapping luggage wasn't a bad one. Until now she'd only thought of telephoning to ask him to alert the *réseau* leader at Lannilis to the fact she was on her way – or they were on *their* way – but he might also be able to get a message sent to Baker Street about recent events. He didn't have a radio in his own control, she remembered, but relied for communication on his contacts with neighbouring *réseaux*.

Probably very wise . . .

A new thought, then: through *him*, to get word to S.I.S. about the arrangements she'd made with Jacqui. Conceivably by radio, but even better – if he had any way of doing this – by word of mouth, someone en route to London who might stand a better chance of getting through than she did.

That would *really* be an achievement. Also, though, it told her how slowly her mind was working – that she hadn't thought of it before. Even an issue as vital as *that* was.

In the bath – the water was still warmish – she paid special attention to her breasts. Soaping them very gently: thinking how they *might* have been, poor darlings ...

Another thought, though, suddenly. Inspired by the prospect of bed and deep sleep, and then contrarily of the possibility of that sleep being shattered by German shouts, boots heavy on the stairs, her door bursting open and the Gestapo crashing in ... It *was* a possibility. She'd half expected to find the room ransacked anyway: now they'd be hunting her, and if they had a clue or acquired one that this was where she'd been living ...

Out of the bath, wrapped in the thin towel, thinking *Jacqui? Jacqui's flat?*

No. Leave Jacqui alone, in this sense uncontaminated.

In any case, there was the curfew. Crazy even to think of getting across town ... It limited the prospects, rather. Have to stay here, but not in the room. And better not bring Ursule into it, if that could be avoided ... The little room behind the kitchen, maybe? Ursule had her desk there, the back door and a W.C. led off it, and there was an old horsehair-stuffed sofa. Sleep fully dressed – in tomorrow's clothes?

Dried and dressed and carrying her bag and coat, she went carefully and painfully downstairs, saw her rent money still on the kitchen table – with Misty's scarf ... No sound from Ursule's apartment: none from anywhere. Might have brought a pillow down, she thought, shutting the small room's door quietly behind her. Wasn't worth climbing the stairs again, though – neither the effort nor the risk. Roll the coat for a pillow ... The back door was locked; if Ursule came in the front way she mightn't even look in here, wouldn't know one had been here at all. Further thought, then: get the rent money and the scarf, put them on this desk, to be found in the morning rather than tonight. She did that: crept back in, shut the door again ... Getting her legs up on the sofa hurt her knees almost as badly as kneeling on that bloody shovel had.

She managed several short periods of sleep, and having

washed in the kitchen sink was out of the house by four-thirty. It was light by that time, with a milky-bright sky, the hazy early warmth of a very hot day to come. She'd thought she wasn't going to be able to walk at all, when she'd started easing herself off the sofa, but she'd massaged her knees and exercised them gradually before putting her weight on them, and now she was walking almost normally.

Almost. A scruffy little woman, shuffling up Rue Malouet ... With three blocks – if you could call them that, two crossings anyway – before the Gare Rive Gauche, also known as Gare Saint-Sever. Where, for sure – there'd be a heavy police presence, Boches too most likely, all of them up early – or all night even – watching out for any single female traveller or would-be traveller.

The only hope came from the fact that she didn't look anything like Jeanne-Marie Lefèvre. No-one who looked as she did now could possibly be employed as a parfumeuse. More likely to be seen following a handful of cows down some country lane, wielding a bit of stick ...

There was no noticeable police presence. No grey or green uniforms either – or burly louts in plain clothes. Station staff, and a couple of ordinary policemen: the clerk in the ticket kiosk didn't even look at her. The Paris train left just after five, and at seven-ten she was in a call-booth outside the Gare Saint-Lazare, dialling Pierre Cazalet's private number.

It rang for some time, and she was thinking he might be out of town. Then: 'Yes?'

'May I speak to Pierre Cazalet, please?'

'May I ask who's calling?'

'His cousin, Jeanne-Marie Lefèvre.'

'One small moment, madame.'

Toutou, she guessed. The giant ...

'Jeanne-Marie, my *dear* girl, where are you?'

'Sorry to disturb you at such an hour—'

'Perfectly all right. Are you in Rouen?'

'No – I'm at the Gare Saint-Lazare, just arrived.'

'Don't tell me you're throwing up the job?'

'Well – you must be psychic, Pierre, but unfortunately, I have to. If I could see you – *please*—'

'Of course. Come right along, my dear ... You can't really mean it, though – are you really deserting us?'

She hesitated ... Then told him quietly, 'It's – no joke, Pierre.'

'I see.' He'd got the message. 'Well – breakfast will be waiting for you.'

It took her less than half an hour. Two Metro stops south to Champs-Elysées Clémenceau, then via Rue la Boétie. Nobody had done more than glance at her. She'd felt dowdy on her previous visit, but now 'Louis' was really going to get an eyeful.

Toutou was waiting in the shop, opened the door for her and relocked it immediately behind her ... 'Madame was not followed?'

'Definitely not.'

'If you please ...' He ushered her upstairs – into the same room, the one graced by Goering's portrait. Pierre Cazalet hurried forward to embrace her ... 'Angel!'

'Louis ...'

'Come, sit down. You can put the coffee on now, Toutou ... Oh, my God.' Peering at her: 'My first thought was that you'd been at a jumble sale, but I see now – an accident?'

'If you call the Gestapo an accident.'

'Oh, my *dear*—'

'Pierre, I have to get out.' She sat down – gratefully – on a Louis Quinze *fauteuil*. 'Could you contact the *réseau* leader at Lannilis for me?'

'Vidor. Yes. Not directly, but – yes, I can ...' He perched himself on a stool in front of her ... 'So – tell me?'

'I'm on the run. I escaped yesterday – from a moving car, it caused *some* of this ... Well – I may not get much further, but I'm going to try. There'll be two of us – my chief from Rouen is with me – *will* be, he's going to follow me, get off where I get off – Vidor's people wouldn't know him, you see, wouldn't—'

'What if you *don't* get that far?'

'What about him, you mean. Well, he'd go elsewhere. Change trains at Rennes, perhaps. He has contacts in the south, as an alternative. But as we've agreed it, we'll both be on this morning's train to Brest – disembarking at Landerneau, of course. I don't know about the moon-state, when a gunboat's due ... Oh, you could tell them – in case they're talking to London – this man is Michel Rossier, code-name César.'

'You said—'

He was goggling at her ...

'Something the matter?'

'Something.' Pressing the fingertips of both hands to his face: she could smell his aftershave powder ... He'd shut his eyes. '*Something* – my God, yes ... Angel, there's *something*, all right ...'

'What—'

'Code-name César, nom-de-plume Michel Rossier. In Lyon, about three weeks ago – he died under torture. I heard only yesterday, I have to get it passed to London. Oh, my *Angel* ...'

19

Westward out of Montparnasse: four hours later, time to draw breath – the train picking up its rhythm as it left the Seine behind. She had a bench to herself, near the front of one of the open carriages: wooden-slatted benches, their waist-high backs forming the only partitions. A thin, elderly man and his huge wife faced her: behind her, about five booths away, César had an old priest on his left and a woman opposite with two small children. Across the aisle from him was a man with one arm: sparse grey hair and lean, aristocratic features. His name was Jean-Paul, and she'd gathered he was a full-time pimp – from a remark Toutou had made. Pierre Cazalet frowning at him warningly – *Spare our Angel's sensibilities . . .*

Pierre had been marvellous, though. She put one hand down, touched the wooden seat: aware that marvels didn't always last, that things could still blow up in one's face. A police inspection now, for instance: *Your papers, madame*?

Could happen. But if it did it would be only a chance thing: she no longer believed they'd be looking for her. If they had been, she'd never have got out of Rouen. Now, she thought, she had about as much chance as you ever had: you got stopped, or you didn't. If you did and your papers weren't in order – well, bad luck . . . The best thing was – as always – not to think about it, simply to be oneself, concentrate on *that* . . . Jeanne-Marie Lefèvre, going home to ma-in-law and *l'enfant*. Having failed to get a job, and on top of that having fallen in the Metro, hurting herself badly *and* having her travelling-bag run off with, with all her papers in it. Ration card, everything: God alone knew what she'd do for money now, what she and the child would live on. Beg – or at best, scrub floors. Meanwhile, in telling the story, shed tears . . .

Tears had helped last time, she remembered.

She'd fielded a very dangerous ball, at the Montparnasse station. She'd spotted that César didn't have his briefcase with him – only a holdall that couldn't possibly have contained it. Whereas both she and Pierre had expected him to have brought it with him. Actually it had been Pierre's logical expectation, and she'd agreed with it – having forgotten the extent of César's carelessness, the possibility he *might* have left such an object just lying around for anyone to find.

Pierre had told Toutou, 'Have Jean-Paul take care of the briefcase. Make that his special care. He's to bring back whatever luggage or other appurtenances our man may have, but the briefcase is of paramount importance, tell him.'

Jean-Paul's other job was to identify César to those who'd be boarding the train to deal with him. Rosie was to identify him to Jean-Paul initially and would from there on be in the clear, wouldn't need to speak to anyone or even look at them, or have any idea that anything at all was happening. Little country mouse running home with her tail between her legs: disembarking then at Landerneau – César would have been taken care of by then – and the rest would be up to Vidor.

Who'd said he couldn't help, with César. Pierre had shrugged as he put the phone down: 'Better to come straight out with it, than try against the odds . . . Especially as I have another string to my bow.'

To start with – before breakfast – he'd listened intently to all she'd had to tell him, which had included the fact that she'd told César about *him* . . .

'Exactly what, about me?'

'That you were providing my cover – your name and code-name – the fact you're a friend of Goering's—'

'His reaction to *that*?'

'Surprise, and keen interest. As you'd expect. It came up because he'd asked me what my cover was – which as my boss he was entitled to know, obviously. But I'm dreadfully sorry—'

'It's not necessarily fatal. In fact – Angel, I'd put money on it that he won't have made any report, as yet. At any rate, not on the subject of yours truly. First, I haven't been – approached, questioned, investigated – and second, I'd have been told well in advance if any such thing were contemplated. I have *very* well-placed and highly reliable contacts, Angel. Including – well, doesn't matter – but if there'd been talk about me even in the most secret and – oh, the most *elevated* circles—'

'You'd know.'

'Yes. I would. For a long time now it's been essential to my survival.'

He'd become quite calm, by this time. Having realized that he *could* retain command of the situation.

Rosie nodding: 'And if he hasn't passed *that* on, you're saying—'

'Yes, the same would I think apply to all the rest of it. Piling it all up – for a grand slam, you might say. A fat dossier to drop on his general's desk. For his own advantage – one might guess – but also he wouldn't want them arresting people prematurely, scaring the rest away.'

'Must have arranged the ambush, though?'

'He'd have had no option – except to let Romeo fly away. And on that score – listen, here's how it looks to *me*. I may be jumping to false conclusions but – listen, and tell me what you think ... He told you he'd heard you got away, he was waiting for you to show up. I think that's nonsense – his information would come from his own people, not from some – rumour, out of the countryside ... On the other hand, from what you've told me I'd strongly suspect they *arranged* your escape. Too easy for you, otherwise, too grossly inefficient for them – in those departments especially they aren't stupid. Try these questions: why put you with Erdos, why bother moving you from one cell to another? Why fail to put you in handcuffs? Why only one escort to two prisoners? Why unlocked car doors and a route with tight corners so they had to slow down to that extent? Why no shots and no pursuit?'

'All right.'

'Erdos would have been acting under their orders – a bargain for his life, maybe. Bet *your* life, Angel, they wanted you out. And why? Well, he's making use of you now, isn't he? Why else, this day-trip to Brest? To get into the escape route and whoever's handling it – all it *can* be. Uh?'

'Shades of La Chatte ...'

'Who's she?'

'They faked *her* escape. But it was her idea.'

'Never heard of her. But listen – what if you weren't supposed to have been taken prisoner in the first place? This is on the same track, you see. If he'd arranged that you'd be allowed to get away, he'd have assumed you *had*. And there again, in his shoes I'd have wanted Romeo caught, not shot dead – and I'd have wanted that Lysander on the ground – complete with this Romeo-replacement – huh? I think they cocked it up, Angel – if you'll allow the expression. I think he *assumed* you were on the run – you'd have run back to your Organizer, wouldn't you? Then he must have discovered – Angel, are we getting somewhere?'

'So the interruption – when they were on the point of doing this dreadful thing to me—'

'*How* would he have discovered you were there, I wonder?'

'From his own people – as you say. Whoever they may be ... If he'd called in – here, Paris, the operation would have been run from here, wouldn't it – transferred from Lyon to head office – he might have begged them *God's sake order them to let her out* – especially if he's S.D. – or S.S. even,

recruited to S.D., and the Rouen operation's now in Gestapo
hands.'

She'd paused, remembering. Only *yesterday*, for Christ's
sake ... 'It was good timing, Pierre.'

'My poor Angel ... There are times one can *hope* there's
such a thing as hell-fire.'

'Too good for them. I'm not sure there's *anything*—'

'Well, I think perhaps there is. But we haven't time now
for – philosophical discussion ... We've – let's see – about
one and a half hours ...'

He'd made two telephone calls by that time, and while
they were talking Vidor had responded from Lannilis.
Cazalet telling him, 'I'm almost a stranger to you, monsieur,
but you'll remember my young cousin whom you helped not
long ago – a very pretty girl, known to her close friends as
"Angel"? You do ... Well, she'll be on the train from Paris
– reaching you late afternoon – and I wondered if you could
arrange to have someone meet her. Exactly – but – one
moment, monsieur – there's a complication. Another passenger on the same train – *not* deserving of your hospitality...'

'Ah. Ah ...'

Listening, frowning ...

'Well, I understand. Yes.' A long intake of breath ...
'Don't concern yourself – except for the young lady – all
right? But listen – I shall make other arrangements, and may
I ask you to call me again – so you'll know what's arranged
– in say one hour?'

Hanging up, he'd buzzed for Toutou and asked him to put
a call through to Jacques Delage in Rennes. Or, get his wife,
locate him through her. Tell her please drop everything else,
just *get* him ...

Delage, he explained to Rosie, was a road-haulier whose
wife had a boutique and dealt in Maison Cazalet products.
They were both – to coin a phrase – kindred spirits. He went
on then, 'You understand the basis of my thinking, Rosie –
first, assuming all the information our German friend has

gathered is either in his head or in his briefcase, and second the hope he'll have the case with him. This is the only weak spot, I think. The remedy for the head is obvious, and if the case is with him, no problem *there*. I think he *will* have it – don't you? It's a *little* speculative, but – look, he's working solo, knows he may have to call for support from either his own crowd or the *milice* – at Landerneau, perhaps – and he'd need documentation . . . It *is* speculative, but—'

'I think you're right.'

Toutou had buzzed through then to say the haulier was on the line. After some banter about whether he or his wife wore the perfume, and chat about how the road-haulage business was doing, Pierre had asked him whether he could spare a small team for say half a day. Today, yes. If they could board the Paris–Brest express . . . Well, at Rennes, presumably. Two men at least. They could return by some other train – late evening, perhaps. He, Cazalet, would defray all expenses. 'Those specialists of yours, Jacques . . .'

Still over breakfast – rolls with cherry jam, and – incredibly – *real* coffee – he'd told her with his mouth full, 'I'll ask Toutou to be at Montparnasse, Angel. He'll collect Jean-Paul and take him along, I imagine.'

She'd spread her hands: 'Words fail me, Pierre . . .'

The train clattered westward, snaking around a wooded hill. The front end was just disappearing into a tunnel: she pulled the window up, met the fat woman's stare, explained, 'A tunnel . . .' It always stank, in tunnels. The big woman nodded, shrugged her massive shoulders; she'd already consumed an apple and a large piece of sausage.

At the station – Montparnasse – Rosie had boarded the train and bagged this seat, hadn't been at the window long before she'd seen César coming along the platform. Loosely cut grey linen jacket hanging open, checked shirt, narrow khaki trousers, and a soft leather holdall swinging at his side. He'd seen her too then – checked abruptly and limped to a door at the rear end of this same carriage, and a closer sight of him as he'd appeared inside had confirmed her first impression – that he had no briefcase, and there wouldn't have been room for it in the bag. She'd thought about it for a moment: meanwhile seeing Toutou and his friend Jean-Paul a little way down towards the barrier, watching her: she guessed they'd have seen *her* watching César, and nodded to them, gestured in that direction: the one-armed man moved off towards that door, and Toutou smiled, raised a hand discreetly. She'd made her mind up, meanwhile – what to do about the briefcase. She left her coat and canvas grip – supplied by Toutou – on the seat, and disembarked, carefully not looking either César's way or Toutou's: guessing César would be watching her, might even follow. But he didn't – might have checked and seen she'd left her things on the seat. She'd checked a second time that he wasn't with her – saw Toutou looking after her, and the other one leaving the train to rejoin him – and continued out through the central concourse to the ornate stone portico where there were telephone booths that might almost have dated from the Franco-Prussian War.

Sure enough, the first two she tried didn't work. But the third did. She joggled for the operator, and gave him Marc Pigot's number in Rouen.

Ringing, ringing. Taking awful risks with telephones, she was well aware of it. Of Pierre having done so earlier his morning, too ...

'Auto Normande.'

'Marc – it's Angel.'

'*Angel...*'

Coughing ... She could *see* him: pale, hunched over ...

'I have to be quick ... Marc – a great and very urgent favour?'

'Tell me.'

'The Café Belle Femme, Place de la Pucelle. Top floor, a room's let to a man calling himself Michel Rossier. He's not there – he's in Paris, so the coast's clear. You could say he sent you, if you needed to. Anyway – from the doorway, in the far right-hand corner there's a floor-level cupboard with blankets in it, and under them there *should* be a briefcase. It has information in it which would be fatal to some of our friends. D'you follow?'

'I'll go now.'

'Take it, and burn everything?'

'As good as done. You all right?'

'So far. But Romeo—'

'I know. Good luck, Angel.'

Toutou and the one-armed man had very conveniently placed themselves at the newspaper kiosk near the barrier. She stopped beside them, bought a copy of *L'Illustration* and spoke as if she was reading it to herself: 'Tell Louis I've arranged for the removal and destruction of the briefcase from the Café Belle Femme in Rouen. He can count on it, tell him not to worry. I take it you saw him, Jean-Paul – grey jacket, checked shirt?'

'Like a sore thumb.'

Toutou muttered as she turned away, 'Good luck, madame.' A stickler for the formalities, old Toutou. The Cazalet training, no doubt. . . . She went on through the barrier, showing her ticket for the second time. Grateful to Romeo for the gift of a man such as Marc Pigot, in whom one could have such faith. Romeo, Pigot, Vidor: men of the same stamp, she thought.

And by contrast – *that* thing . . .

César – his head out of the window, searching as she came trudging back along the length of the train – shabby, breathless, with a cream-coloured scarf – a gift from Pierre, not *too* new – over her head to hide that wound and at least the worst of the facial bruising . . . César backed in, leaving the door clear, and the train looked and sounded as if it was about to leave, so she used that door herself – hauling herself awkwardly up the two steps, then not glancing at him any more than at his neighbours as she pushed past them. Jean-Paul boarded behind her: he'd left possessions of his own, she saw – a case, and a straw hat – on the seat diagonally across from César's.

So far, so good. Except for feeling she'd just run five miles and had had no sleep for about a week ... Back in her own place, she nodded to the elderly couple who'd got in during her absence, murmured politely 'Monsieur-madame ...'

'Ah, so those are yours ... Going far, my dear?'

There was a shine of sweat on the fat face. The husband's was skeletal, grey as putty. Rosie smiled at them both, as she sat down. '*Too* far. And what a *price* ...'

At Chartres, the train was held up while they inspected tickets and, at random, papers. In Rosie's case a glance at her return ticket satisfied them. There were armed police on the platform, but no arrests or trouble. The fat woman's husband had had to open his eyes during the ticket inspection, and as the train pulled out he actually spoke – a mutter of 'Who'd believe this was France?'

'Hush, André.' His wife glanced at him, frowning: he stared at Rosie until she looked away, not wanting to involve herself.

After Vidor had called back – when Pierre had told him it was all fixed, his cousin would have no escort by the time the train reached Landerneau – putting the phone down, he'd told her, 'He's highly relieved. *Must* have problems. But he's a good man, he won't let you down.'

'I know. We had breakfast in his house – me, and the one who was arrested when we got here.'

'Guillaume.'

'Did you hear any more?'

'No. Nothing. Angel, do you understand why we're going about this as we are? Delage's men boarding at Rennes, so forth?'

'I assume they'll kill him – but where or how—'

'Leave that to them. No need for you to know it's happening. Make sure you *don't*, in fact. What I mean is – the strategy, you might call it. The German's got to be eliminated – obviously. It can't be done here in Paris –

equally obvious. It can't safely be done in the earlier stages
of the transit from here to Landerneau, because with such a
lengthy period of exposure, allowing for instance for the
discovery of the body – not necessarily in the train but on the
track even – well, the train could be stopped, everyone
searched – including you, lacking papers ... On the other
hand it has to be done before Landerneau. Another point, by
the way, is that by and large the train starts full and empties
as it goes along. Rennes, Saint-Brieuc, Morlaix – not exactly
empties, but—'

'These men get on at Rennes, Jean-Paul points him out to
them—'

'—and all you have to do is make sure you wake up for
Landerneau.'

She blamed herself for not having guessed, about César.
Or at least suspected ... But she *had* – and dismissed the
suspicion – despite finding him fairly unpalatable, at
times ...

You know, Angel, you rather grow on a man?

Bloody cheek ...

'What?'

She'd jumped: had been semi-dozing. The fat woman
apologizing: 'I'm very sorry – hadn't realized—'

'It's all right – I was awake, more or less—'

'No, I think you'd dropped off, I spoke before I'd realized
... But tell me – am I right in thinking you've hurt your
knees? You rub them so frequently. A fall, perhaps?'

'Yes. In the Metro. Quite a bad one.'

'Oh, poor doll!'

She'd slept through Le Mans, was woken by the clatter and
sudden flurry when Fatso dropped a knife with which she'd
been slicing a tomato into a half-open stick of bread which
she'd already lined with sausage. Rosie picked the knife up
for her: it had been under her feet, more or less, and the
woman couldn't have bent down that far – not without
rupturing something.

'Thank you so much. And once again, *so* sorry—'

'No reason—'

'You're obviously exhausted. Could have cut you, what's more!'

It certainly could have. It was a carving-knife with a horn handle and six-inch blade, and from the way it sliced that tomato, razor sharp.

Pierre was going to get the message about Jacqui and the password 'Rosalie' out to London – preferably, he'd agreed, by word of mouth. So even if she herself didn't get through, that operation would go ahead. She thought that if she had the job of organizing it from Baker Street she'd think about using transient agents, routing some to or from their various *réseaux* via Rouen. Or even one-off visits for no purpose other than to empty the postbox, so to speak; parachute in, exit by Lysander a day or two later.

But of course it would be S.I.S.'s business, not S.O.E.'s.

Might settle for a quieter life, though, after this?

The top brass might decide it for her, anyway. Might decide she'd done her bit, in the field. Especially after Rouen: might wonder about her making it, another time.

She thought, *Might well* ... Leaning forward again to massage her knees. The next stop would be Rennes, where the Delage team were to join the train. At least two men, Pierre had thought, perhaps three or four. Resistance, presumably. But what if he evaded them somehow – if they couldn't do it and he stayed on her heels, got off with her at Landerneau?

'Care for a tomato, dear?'

'Why yes, thank you ...'

It would quench her thirst, as much as anything. And since the old bag had found she'd got more there than she could cram in ...

At Rennes, disembarking passengers were required to show their papers. She watched it happening, from her window, noticed that quite a lot got out and very few got in.

A trio of nuns. Road-hauliers in disguise?

It wasn't funny, though. Nobody embarked who could possibly fit that bill.

Two German officers got in up front. Then further back, a schoolmistress with a flock of children.

Doors slamming, a whistle blowing. Rolling ... The fat woman told her, 'We disembark at Morlaix. *Such* a long way, still.'

'Morlaix ...' Getting her mind to it – from extreme anxiety to total disinterest. With the Delage men still uppermost, for the moment: whether they could have boarded without her having seen them ... She didn't think so. 'I've heard Morlaix's a charming town. But – excuse me, madame ...' She got up, needing to visit the *toilette*, which was at the rear end of this compartment. César's slitted eyes followed her towards him, picked her up again on her way back. Jean-Paul gazed at her too: grey head tilted back, dark eyes questioning. As if *she* could know the answer, for Christ's sake ...

She felt ill. Facing the fact that Delage or his people had let old Pierre down. Missed the train, or Delage hadn't been able to get hold of them, or – whatever ... He might have phoned back to Pierre to tell him, even. Not a damn thing Pierre could have done. He'd be sweating *his* guts out.

So – alternative to hopeless panic – what to do?

Stay on board right through to Brest, then go through the motions of looking for some non-existent individual, pretending to be shocked, horrified, etcetera? You'd end up arrested and back in the hands of someone like Prinz, but at least you wouldn't have led them to Vidor. Disembarkation at Landerneau, in fact, was out of the question.

Morlaix? Try to use this odd couple as cover: get out with them, then run for it? One would have a chance, at least: if one got away with that much, then live rough in the countryside for a day or two and make it *eventually* to Lannilis?

Saint-Brieuc came and went. Nobody joined there who could have been any use.

But nobody would. They'd have joined at Rennes, or nowhere.

Face it – you're on your own ...

Next stop, Guingamp. Then Plouaret ...

'Your ticket, mam'selle?'

She showed it – tired, defeated, hopeless ... Might just as well act the part; it was what she looked like anyway. He'd called her Miss instead of Mrs, perhaps because it wouldn't have occurred to him that anyone would have married such a plain, dull-looking creature.

It would be Morlaix, next.

'My dear ...'

Glancing up at her. Like a great barrage balloon ...

'Like to try this cheese?'

It didn't look bad, and she was being offered it with half a loaf of bread and that knife for a tool. She *was* quite hungry: the sandwiches from Pierre's kitchen had been flimsy little things, and there mightn't be much of a meal on offer tonight.

Wherever the hell one might find oneself, tonight. It wasn't by any means a cut-and-dried situation, now.

'Very kind of you ...'

'My pleasure, dear ...' She added, 'Not far to Morlaix now.'

'Where you live ...'

'Not *at* Morlaix, exactly – a short distance ... Go on, dear, tuck in!'

After Morlaix there'd be Landivisiau: then Landerneau.

'It's excellent cheese.'

'I'm glad you like it. My husband only needs a sniff of it to make an absolute pig of himself ...' She nudged him: 'André – we'll be there, in just a minute!'

'Thank God.'

He'd shut his eyes again. His wife meanwhile packing things back into the picnic basket ... 'No, my dear, finish it.

Please. We do very well down here, you know – and you've still a long way to go, eh? Going where, did you say? André – our bags are under the seat – if you could disturb yourself for just one small moment—'

'When the train stops, I'll disturb myself.'

The cheese had been wrapped in some kind of grease-proof paper. The bread had also been wrapped. Rosie had sliced most of the bread, was about to pass the knife back when she saw the woman repacking her basket: having forgotten the knife?

Apparently ...

The heap of crumpled paper hid it. If she didn't catch sight of it, wasn't reminded ... The train was slowing, letting off steam, southern outskirts of Morlaix drawing in on both sides. Rosie's hands clutching each other tightly on the wrappings ... 'You've been extremely generous, mad-ame.'

'Oh, not in the least ... André, will you *please*—'

Jean-Paul passed slowly up the aisle, up to the front end, his one hand transferring itself from seat-back to seat-back as he progressed; he glanced down and back at her as he passed. At the end he opened the connecting door and peered for a moment into the next carriage. There was no lavatory at this end, though – if that was what he was looking for. He shut the door and turned around, leaning back against it. There were very few passengers in this part of the train now: those for Brest, she thought, were all up front.

He was looking straight at her. She shrugged: a gesture of helplessness. Then he'd started back.

'Monsieur—' She'd stopped him ... 'Am I right that the next stop will be Landivisiau?'

'Indeed.' He didn't look like a pimp, she thought. More like an ex-officer, a man of some distinction. A cold look, though: thin lips and eyes like brown flints ... He'd nodded. 'Landivisiau, then Landerneau. One other small halt shortly before Brest ... Oh, Le Relecq-Kerhoun, is it?'

The knife was like a splinter in her mind. It had been there with a question mark beside it since the moment she'd realized it was hers. To start with, thoughts as vague as not looking a gift horse in its mouth: but fooling herself, surely, as much as clutching at a straw: there was at least the *possibility* – frightening as it was – of actually making use of it.

To put the lid on it now, Jean-Paul's cold stare: asking her wordlessly *What for Christ's sake are* you *going to do about it?*

The obvious thing was to work it into the sleeve of her dress – the left one. One *had* done things with knives – as well as pistols – at Arisaig, the first stage of the S.O.E. agents' training course. Glancing up at Jean-Paul again: 'I think we're approaching Landivisiau, monsieur. Shouldn't you return to your seat?'

Because he had only one arm, and the train sometimes stopped in a series of powerful jerks. He was still staring down at her as she spoke, and she let him see the knife. Then when he'd moved on – with a surprisingly decisive nod – she craned round for a look at César, found him watching her over the seat-backs, looking anxious. She half-smiled, nodded reassurance to him before settling down again.

Bastard . . .

There were *miliciens* on the Landivisiau platform, one civilian policeman, a woman with several crates of hens. Nobody either boarded or disembarked. The guard's whistle shrilled, the train jolted and began to roll.

Diddle-de-dum, diddle-de-dum, diddle-de-dum . . . Beautiful countryside, clear sky, enough breeze to move the upper branches of the trees. Sun well past its zenith, shadows growing from trees and telegraph-posts, cattle grazing in low-lying pasture where a river curled. The train pounded over a bridge.

Better not cut it *too* fine. Or wait so long that one's faltering reserves of courage ebbed away.

Twenty minutes to go, say. Even twenty-five. Wait another ten?

Think of the pliers ...

He watched her coming. She nodded to him as she approached, gestured to him to get up and come with her. The pliers could as well have been in his hand as Prinz's: it was effectively the same hand. But in any case – no option, this whole thing now devolved on her. César still rooted – in surprise, uncertainty: she stopped, leant down to mutter '*Must* have a word.'

Assuming he'd follow ... The other passengers either gazing out of windows or slumbering. Even with all the windows open it was very warm, but that wasn't the reason she was wringing wet. He *was* following – thank God ... She got the end door open, and held it for him to take – her right arm out behind her, the left one doubled against her with the knife in that sleeve.

Jean-Paul was coming behind César. She'd have been twice as scared if he hadn't. And the sign on the door of the *toilette* mercifully read *Libre*. She'd let César catch the compartment door as she let go of it, and pushed the *toilette*'s open, side-stepped into it. Gesturing to him to follow ...

'So, what's—'

He was stooping in the small doorway, confined by it. Rosie, inside, with more room to manoeuvre, and Jean-Paul *out*side, behind him: 'Shut up and don't move!' César jerked near-upright, banged his head, was attempting to twist around, Rosie stopping that movement with an answer to his question – '*This* is what ...' The knife at his throat – letting him feel it: Jean-Paul's hand clamped over his mouth. The slits of his eyes above the Frenchman's dark, crooked hand were wider open than she'd ever seen them. She brought the knife down swiftly, slashing a hand as it grabbed at her – Jean-Paul's hand shifting too, his forearm locking across César's throat, wrenching his head back and crushing the windpipe, jerking the shocked eyes from Rosie's in precisely the moment that she drove the knife in – two handed, under his lowest rib on the left side and upwards into his heart. One of the moves they'd taught at Arisaig. Jean-Paul had the dead man's full weight on his one arm then: Rosie leaning back as far as she could, away from the flow of blood. He told her, 'You'd better clear out. Come round this side. No, wait – the knife – leave it in the basin.'

'Can you manage on your own?'

'Of *course* I can—'

'What about his luggage – could be papers in it, incidentally – yours too, though—'

'Leave it. I know what I'm doing.'

Something more than a pimp, she thought.

And what about *me*, Christ's sake?

She had blood down the front of her dress and on her cardboard shoes. Back in her seat – hands shaking, body cold with sweat, pulse-rate about two hundred to the minute – for the moment, limp, played out ... Forcing herself back into motion then, she pulled an unlaundered blouse out of her grip and used it to *try* and clean up with. Without much success: it turned red itself but a lot had soaked into the wool. Brownish stains anyway, on the neutral-coloured material: she didn't think anyone would know at a glance that it was blood. Might wear the old coat, though. Look like some village idiot, on a day like this, but – not exactly the Queen of Sheba anyway ... Resting again – head back, eyes closed, trying to control her breathing, slow the pulse-rate ... Wondering how Jean-Paul would be coping. Extraordinarily confident, purposeful – *professional*, in contrast to the frightened, fumbling amateur that she was.

César's face – a brain-imprint of it, nightmarish – above that larynx-crushing forearm, the bulge of blue eyes forcing the slits open ... Would he have understood – guessed *why*?

Pulse down to maybe one-twenty now. A mere two beats to the second.

The train too – *that* rhythm slowing ...

Opening her eyes: *Landerneau, already*?

She'd only got as far as spreading the coat like a rug over

her knees, was still clutching the bloodstained blouse in one hand. Looking at it now, wondering what to do with it: you couldn't hide anything under these slatted seats ... Then: *Shove it back in the bag, stupid* ... Slower-witted than usual, even in a state of shock, perhaps. Blind panic only just round the corner: it had happened so fast, she'd been so unprepared ...

So who'd *done* it? Other than little Rosie Ewing – aided by an assassin masquerading as a pimp ...

Coat ... Checking where the worst of the staining was on her dress, and how she might cover it by keeping her left hand in that pocket and holding it across her, letting the right side flap open. She pulled it on, then groped under the seat for her one piece of luggage. Thinking, *Call these oil-stains* ...

From where she'd fallen in the Metro – and any that actually looked like blood, same thing, from the cut on her head ... Be vague, no need to be sure whether its blood or oil, you can be *wrong*, won't matter ...

No-one else in this carriage seemed to be disembarking here. Maybe they *could* get out at Brest, from this end of the train ... She was on her feet at the window, seeing the front part of it curving round. Beyond the signal-box, was where the platform would start. On the straight, now, thumping along very slowly. Signal-box coming up – now ...

There were German soldiers on the platform – at this end of it – facing this way, about a dozen of them, watching the train puff in ... They were waiting to board it, she saw then. Kitbags, etcetera ... Beyond them, a group of railway staff and – yes, *milice*. Unfortunately ... So she'd be asked for her papers. Bound to be: with very few disembarking here. She might even be the only one.

She sat down for a moment – irresolute, conscious again of her racing heart, not sure she had the strength ... With no papers, and spattered with fresh blood – probably reeking of it—

It looked like a funeral party, beyond that group of

uniformed officials. Men and women in dark clothes –
twenty or more, most of them elderly – women in hats and
veils, and—

Vidor?

Tall and well made, in a dark suit. It *was* him. Beside him,
a girl, reddish hair visible under a floppy dark hat. And on
her other side – that was Vidor's wife, the rather chubby,
jolly person who'd cooked breakfast. In black, like all the
others. Either a funeral or – she guessed it – a mock-funeral,
for her own reception? Vidor had spotted her, now – he'd
pointed, calling back to the others, was moving along this
way as the train began jolting to a halt: she reached down,
got the door open as he came trotting up, reaching to take the
bag from her, all the rest of them crowding up too. The
redheaded girl called to her 'Lucinde! *Magnificent* that you
could come!'

Vidor's wife was calling out that name too. Vidor helping
her down, meanwhile – into the middle of the crush.
'Remember me – Vidor?'

'Of course, but—'

'Your name's Lucinde. This kid here is your sister
Solange Brodard. Your father – Josef Brodard – died two
weeks ago, you couldn't make the funeral, it's a Memorial
service you've come for. Nobody's going to question who
you are, see—'

The redhead kissed her – screeching, 'Lucinde dearest,
wonderful of you to have come!'

'My dear – this is for you.' Vidor's wife presented her
with an awful hat with a veil on it . . . Vidor explaining while
other women embraced her, 'There was a family row, you
and your father weren't on speaking-terms, that's why we're
all so happy you've turned up. Angel – I'd put the hat on if
I were you – is the other business taken care of?'

'Yes. It has been.' Glancing back, murmuring 'I can't
believe this . . .' Thinking again of Jean-Paul – wondering
how he'd been handling it . . . There were passengers at just
about all the train's windows by this time . . . She'd heard

Vidor say 'There's something else you truly *won't* believe!'

'*Ma chère Lucinde.*' A priest – ruddy complexion, curly greying hair, kind eyes – cut in on him: 'Bless you, my dear – ' his voice was resonant, would certainly be audible to the *milice*, twenty or thirty feet away – 'that your father's soul may now truly rest in peace. We are all thankful that you should have found it in your heart—'

'Father – excuse me—'

'What? Yes, of course – we should move on ...'

'Angel.' Vidor had taken one of her arms, the redhead was clinging to the other, the crowd still surrounding her as they left the platform. 'The thing you *won't* believe—'

'Ben sends his love.' The redhead, interrupting him. Very young, and pretty – *lovely* eyes ...

'You said – Ben—'

She nodded, and told Vidor, 'Her name's Rosie, anyway, not Angel.'

'Rosie, then. But it's true, he's here. He was stuck here three weeks ago – the visit after they landed you. He wanted to come with us, to meet you, but that would have been insane. Same at the church, this service – we have to go through with it, you see, but afterwards—'

'Not sure *I*'m not insane.' She'd stopped, grasping his arm with both hands as if it was all that was holding her up. 'Vidor – if it's possible – please – I need a drink. *Now*, not afterwards ...'

20

Subject to the usual confirmation – broadcasts from London later in the day – a motor gunboat would be collecting them from Guenioc island tonight. Friday. She remembered as she woke up – in a strange bed which turned out to be Solange's – that Vidor had told her this. In some *gazo* ... She got it, then: it had been on the way from Landerneau station to his and Marie-Claude's house. Yesterday afternoon – Thursday. It still called for a conscious effort to get the days right – having lost that one during her time in the Palais de Justice. Clock gone haywire through nervous strain, she thought: on top of which one had packed in a fair amount of action, in the past two days. Drifting back to sleep – half in, half out, thoughts and dreams intermingling. There was a touch of hangover in it too, but that would be only a by-blow, the basic cause was – whatever she'd thought just now ... Nervous exhaustion. By holding out, of course, one actually racked up the strain oneself: plus the strain of worrying oneself half to death with the absolute dread of *not being able* to hold out. The Hungarian, as an example – Erdos – in retrospect he seemed to her to have been a lot more relaxed than she'd been, and this might tally with Pierre Cazalet's guess that he'd sold out. To that bastard Prinz – about whom quite a separate question in her half-sleep was whether out of office hours so to speak he might be a kind, devoted family man – or might *become* one, or adopt that guise, if in the long run justice failed ... *What did you do in the war, Daddy? Oh, I pulled girls' nipples off with pliers* ... The mind jumped, rather: Erdos to Prinz, Prinz then to Jean-Paul – what he might have done after she'd left him – left *them* ... Locked or jammed the door from the outside, somehow – got out at the other station he'd mentioned? The train would be in Brest perhaps for some while before railway staff forced the door: Jean-Paul would have taken off with his own and César's luggage – and surely a lot more blood on him than *she* had? He'd have made sure the corpse wouldn't have had anything in its pockets to make it easily or quickly identifiable as German.

Something like that ...

Something still wrong, though. Something *she*, at any rate, didn't understand ...

Waking again, she'd found Solange sitting on the bed, smiling at her. They'd shared this bed, apparently. Solange had been out attending to some of the animals, had also got porridge on the stove for breakfast, and she'd come up to see if Rosie might be ready for some.

'I'll get up.'

'My, but you had some dreams!'

'Oh, I spoilt your sleep ...'

'No. Really. But I think one was about the man on the train – the one you killed—'

'Christ, you know about that?'

'You *told* us, Rosie!'

Lying back, remembering – last night, telling Ben about it – which she wouldn't have done if she hadn't been plastered – and Ben staring at her unbelievingly – as if he'd thought she was mad, or fantasizing, or still drunk ... The drink element had arisen because they'd stopped – she, Vidor and his wife and Solange – at Vidor's house, en route to the church at Broennou, and Marie-Claude had given her half a tumbler of brandy which she'd downed in one and then asked for another, and she'd passed out during the Memorial service. They'd got her out between the two of them – Vidor and Marie-Claude – supporting her as they'd have supported any other mourner overcome by grief – and put her in the priest's charcoal-burning motorcar, in which he'd then driven them out here to the Brodard farm. She'd still been dopey, but remembered Ben loping out across the yard, the lower half of his face chalk-white where he'd just shaved off his beard, dressed as for a Flannagan and Allen show and howling 'Rosie, Rosie, oh *Rosie*, this can't be bloody *true*!'

Then in a bear-hug he'd caught a whiff of the brandy fumes, muttered 'My God, you've been at the grog *again . . .*'

They'd forced a bowl of soup into her, apparently. That would have been when she'd told them her no-doubt garbled story. Then she'd flaked out again, and they'd carried her up here. Or Ben had.

Solange left them at the kitchen table after a while, went out to milk goats. Rosie said, 'She's a darling, isn't she?'

A nod. 'Been through it, too. She really has.'

'How long have you been here with her?'

'Oh – ten days, thereabouts. Why?'

'Just curious.' She glanced at him: then at the window, a distant back view of the girl. 'But don't worry – I'm asking no questions, Benjamin.'

For a second she thought he was going to take her up on it, burst into song – *their* song. Instead, a double-take, catching on late to the innuendo . . . 'I'd damn well *hope* not!' He added, 'When I got here, she was in shock. It was a hell of a thing she went through!'

'Yes. I didn't mean—'

'I'd say you did, but it doesn't matter. Long as you don't insult her with any *more* so-called non-questions.' His hand covered hers, on the scarred old table. 'You've been through more than any person ever should but it's over now, Rosie. You can relax, be yourself again. You're safe – almost. Also you're with me, and I'm not letting go of you. By this time tomorrow – well, best not to speak too soon—'

There'd been some doubt whether they'd be using this
pinpoint at all, apparently. The deadline yesterday had been
for Vidor to make up his mind whether to give London the
all-clear or warn them off. Vidor had been due to come out
to the farm some time yesterday afternoon, to talk it over
with Ben, but he'd arrived on his bicycle at about midday
and asked 'Remember there was a girl you landed here that
last visit – I told you, she went on the train with the man they
arrested? Well, she's on her way. Paris train, this afternoon.
God knows how I'm going to get her off it, the way things
are ...'

It had been Ben's brilliant idea – Vidor had told her this,
she remembered, on the way to his house – Ben who'd
thought of pretending it was Solange's sister coming and
having a crowd there to welcome her. Vidor had then set it
up – briefed the station-master and persuaded both Solange
and the *curé* to take part: the *curé*'s condition for doing so
had been that they should do it properly – a genuine
Memorial for old Brodard.

The news that she was coming had also clinched the
decision about the M.G.B. Vidor would have voted for it
anyway: he had eleven people here to get away – alternatively either to house and feed for another month, or to try
to shift to one of the other three established pinpoints. There
were four flyers left over from last time – from Ben's fiasco
with the dinghy – three more who'd arrived a few days ago,
plus Ben and his two seamen, and now Rosie.

After breakfast – it had been getting on for mid-morning by
then – Ben had shown her the view from a small window at
the back of the attic, a view along the coast and over the
southern part of the expanse of sand that was uncovered at
low water. The tide had been about halfway down: a
shimmery, hazy summer seascape under a flecking of high
white cloud. In the foreground there was an island called
Garo, and beyond that the inshore end of the rock-strewn
channel the M.G.B. would be coming down. Familiar

territory, to Ben – though less so in daylight. She'd asked him what kind of danger there might be, if local suspicions of a leak about arms shipments proved to have been justified: would you expect military activity on the coastline, or interception of the M.G.B. at sea, on its way in or out?

'Perhaps both. If I was the Kraut in charge I'd have an R-boat or two standing by. Destroyer, if available. Round the corner there, say – other side of the peninsula. It's a long inlet, decent anchorage, small warships do use it.'

'Any there now, do we know?'

'*Weren't* – up to last evening. But the buggers could slip in after dark. They'd want to catch us bending, wouldn't advertise their presence. Come from the other direction too – round from Brest, for instance. But – worst came to the worst – which it won't, don't worry – if the bastards handled it right, we'd be sitting ducks.' He'd pointed to the left, southwestward: 'Down there – three-quarters of a mile, no more – that's the nearest of the coastal batteries. Just that end of the village. The other two are closer to where we'll be crossing the sand bar.'

'What a place to pick!'

'Wouldn't expect us to, though, would they?'

'I remember – you said that.'

'The other pinpoints aren't all that much better ... You know, Rosie, we're both sort of taking this situation for granted, but – well, Jesus—'

'What else should we do?'

'I know – but still—'

'I've thought of you, from time to time.'

'Thought of *you*, practically non-stop!'

He'd kissed her – gently, carefully, as if conscious that she was an invalid. 'You're lovely, Rosie.'

'I'm a wreck.'

'Hell, you are.' He did it again, for longer and less carefully, and this time she felt herself responding. 'Rosie—'

'No.' Pushing free. 'Ben, I *am* slightly wrecked. Let's go down?

*

They'd been setting out after a midday lunch of bread and cheese. The gunboat's visit wouldn't be confirmed until this evening, but the sand bar could only be crossed an hour or so either side of low water – which would be around two p.m. – and they had to be on Tariec in time to be rowed over to Guenioc as soon as it was dark enough. Vidor and Léon would be bringing their boat up to Tariec from the Aberbenoit inlet. They'd have heard the BBC broadcast by then, too.

If the gunboat was *not* coming—

Well, you'd be stuck there. So forget it, assume it *was* bloody well coming.

The seaweed-gathering cart would be here quite soon, and the doctor from Lannilis would be bringing Bright and Farr and the two R.A.F. sergeant-pilots. A cousin of Léon's would be driving the cart, and Rosie was to ride in it – with some children, apparently. The other party – five escapers, one R.A.F. and four U.S.A.F., with a friend of Vidor's guiding them, would already have started, Ben told her. They'd ostensibly be shell gatherers, armed with buckets. Seaweed and shell gatherers had been out there regularly all summer, weather and tide permitting, so to the Germans in the coastal batteries there'd be nothing out of the ordinary going on.

Again – touch wood . . .

Solange bathed and disinfected the cut in Rosie's head for her. It seemed to be clean, also less tender than it had been. Her knees were better too: strong enough for a limp around the farm, with Solange as guide. The dog – Marco – seemed to have accepted her as a friend although he was still warily hostile to Ben. Old Brodard hadn't been very kind to him, she gathered.

Léon's cousin – Albert, who was older, bald, and had a huge moustache – brought the cart, and came into the house while Ben took the horse out of the shafts and tethered it near the water trough. Then he rejoined them, and they'd hardly given up on the bread and cheese when the doctor's *gazo* pulled up in the yard. Ben shot out again, and from the doorway she saw him greeting his long-lost shipmates and two airmen. The doctor shook hands quickly with them all, then turned his car and drove away. Léon's cousin went to put the nag back in its harness; the rest of them trooped into the house, where Solange introduced them to Rosie. Bright and Farr remembered her – or said they did.

Solange would be staying behind now, but she'd be going down to the beach in the early hours of tomorrow morning to meet three agents who'd be landing from the gunboat, and bring them up here. Ben put an arm round her shoulders: 'So you'll have company again. That's good.'

'Not for long, though.'

Rosie thought, *Not the company you'd choose, either* . . .

Ben was telling them all, 'She's some girl, this. I mean it, she damn well *is* . . . Solange, how can we ever thank you?'

'It's for me to thank *you*, Ben.'

'We'll come and look you up some time. Won't we, Rosie?'

'Definitely.' She kissed her. The others were drifting out, ready to go. 'Solange, if you *should* come to England, ever—'

'I know. I know.'

She – Rosie – knew that Ben had suggested it, at some stage: Solange had mentioned it, during their tour of the farm. He was hugging her now, and she was trying to hold back tears: Rosie agreeing in her heart that he was right, she *was* rather special . . . She heard Ben saying, 'If you decide to come – or need to – ask Vidor if he can't fix it. Rosie might even get you a job in her outfit . . . Meanwhile, though – when Pierre gets back, tell him from me he's an exceptionally lucky guy, will you?'

Rosie asked him, crossing the yard, 'Pierre?'

'Her boyfriend. In some labour camp in bloody Germany. Very good *hombré*, Vidor says.'

*

The cart was far from comfortable to ride in. Constant jolting, and a tarpaulin over the top making it greenhouse-hot, and a stink of seaweed. Flies were abundant, too. Then on the track from the road to the beach they stopped to pick up three boys and a girl – twelve- to fourteen-year-olds – who climbed in with her, by no means improving matters. They were needed, Albert had explained, to make up numbers on the return journey across the sand, for the benefit of Germans watching from their lookout posts. It wouldn't be the same number coming back as had gone out, but it would be enough to fool them, he'd said. Rosie found it best to sit upright against the back-end of the cart with her legs out straight, having warned the kids to keep off them. It was better once they were on the sand, the cart then meandering from one area of seaweed to another, the men using hayforks to toss the stuff up without much of it actually landing on the tarpaulin. She put her head out from under it only once, to catch a sight of the others – the shell gatherers with buckets, in two widely separated groups – distant, mirage-like figures across the sultry haze of sand.

On Tariec, where they all met up, Ben found the dinghy where they'd hidden it, under a mound of rotting seaweed weighted down with stones. There'd evidently been no storms on this coast in the past three weeks. No Germans, either – unless they'd left the boat here deliberately, to watch and see who came for it. Ben worked with the two seamen, getting the muck off it and checking for any damage: Bright asking him, 'You'll be taking us out in her, will you, sir?'

'No, I bloody won't!'

'Ah.' A wink at Rosie. 'Shame, *that* is.'

The cart was on its way back by this time, zigzagging across the sand with the young girl handling the reins while Léon's cousin and the three boys forked up seaweed – loading the cart properly, now. Here, with a long wait ahead of them, they settled down on the island's blind side, sprawling in the coarse sea-grass.

Wondering about Jean-Paul again ...

Primarily, what he'd been *for*. Partly because the allegation that he was a pimp didn't wash: therefore that old Pierre had indulged in at least *some* deception. Second, if those men had boarded at Rennes, *she* could have identified César to them, surely – as long as she'd had some way of recognizing *them*, which surely wouldn't have been too difficult. Third, the feeling she got when she thought back to the way he'd looked when he'd been standing over her – before she'd shown him the knife.

The feeling she'd been in danger herself, at that moment. A suspicion that if she hadn't made her move when she had – and hadn't by sheer luck had the knife in the first place . . .

Jean-Paul could have broken César's neck. In retrospect she was sure of it. But he'd only held him, allowing her to do the killing. Despite the considerable disadvantage of all that blood. Letting her prove something?

Pierre's long-stop, she thought. If César had somehow looked like getting away with it – have *her* killed. She'd said to him herself, 'Shades of La Chatte', and he'd brushed that off with 'Never heard of her' – but Pierre was a clever, very devious man: it must surely have occurred to him at least as a possibility?

Hence the provision of a long-stop?

Except – countering that devil's advocacy now – one, she'd already told him that César knew about *him*. César would therefore have been a prime target even if Vidor's *réseau* had been saved by Jean-Paul killing *her*: and two, she needn't have come to Pierre at all, could have stuck to her original intention of only telephoning to ask him to let Vidor know she was on her way.

That was the clincher, surely. She wouldn't have gone near him. And he'd have seen that, it wouldn't have taken him *this* long to work it out.

So Jean-Paul was – more or less – what Pierre had said he was? But in a more generally supervisory capacity, perhaps? If he hadn't wanted to tell her that in effect he'd been lending her a one-armed bodyguard?

Drop it in their laps at Baker Street, she thought. Let *them* lose sleep over it.

'Will they send you back, d'you think?'

'I don't know, Ben.'

She'd been asleep. Easier in her mind for having decided that old Pierre had probably *not* had thoughts of having her killed. Awake now, yawning, she had the feeling that she was more or less back in her right mind: at least, capable of logical thought to *some* degree. Plucking a blade of the thick, sharp-edged grass, tasting the salt on it.

'Well.' Ben was on his back, gazing up at streamers of white cloud in a mellowing sky; the sun was well down, by this time. Turning his head, he had to shield his eyes against it. 'I hope you won't, Rosie.'

'Won't what?'

'What we were saying. Be sent into France again.'

'Oh. Sorry . . . Well – I expect I'll do just what I'm told.'

'*I'd* say you've done enough.'

'My lords and master may think so too. May not. We'll see.'

Hansen, the American major, joined in. 'Once would be enough for me, I'll tell you that. Our safari down to Bordeaux – hell, *I* wouldn't volunteer for *that* again . . . And that'd be nothing, to you, I guess . . . Ben, one question I meant to ask you – your motor gunboats only operating when there's no moon – must leave a lot of time you're inactive – huh?'

'Not really. Maintenance is one thing, training's another. Training never stops. Landing practice on our own beaches, for instance. This kind of job – like tonight's pickup – it's not *all* they use us for. For instance, we work quite a bit with what are called Small Raiding Units. Commando teams – snatching prisoners from a certain area for interrogation, say.'

'Like from one of these coastal batteries, you mean?'

'Exactly.'

'But that'd be moonless period stuff too, wouldn't it?'

He nodded. 'Point is, it's another type of operation, different field of training. And operating with other gunboats or M.T.B.s, for instance. You have to work out new techniques and practise them. More humdrum jobs too, on occasion – we've even been known to escort convoys around the coast, for God's sake.'

Rosie said, 'I've wondered the same thing. Thought perhaps you all went up to London and chased girls.'

'We do that too, of course.'

Looking at her. Willing her to look at *him*. She did, finally. Asking him, deadpan, 'You do, do you?'

'Haven't for quite a while, as it happens. Might again soon, though. Matter of fact—'

'Are you going to be in trouble, Ben –' Hansen cut in, over their murmurs – 'on account of that piece of bad luck you had?'

'It's on the cards. Might lose my job, even.'

'Well, that'd be too bad!'

'Kind of you to say so. If they sent me back to a desk job – yeah, it would. I did have one, before this, and – to put it mildly, I'd sooner not.'

'It was because he'd had his eardrums flattened, getting shot up in some action in the Channel. German destroyers, Ben, wasn't it?'

'Only one eardrum, actually.'

'Your hearing seems pretty normal again now, anyway. Could it have become *un*-flattened?'

'Let's try it out. Come here, whisper a few sweet nothings. This ear first?'

'Stupid bloody colonial!'

Soft laughter in the fading light ... Hansen asked him, 'Knew each other before, did you?'

'Well, yeah.' He reached out, found her hand. 'Sort of.'

'Rosie?'

'Hello. Oh – it's quite dark ...'

'*Is* dark. They'll be here pretty soon – or should be ... You had a good long zizz, Rosie. Caught up, yet?'

'Should've, shouldn't I . . . Unless it's sleeping sickness . . . I suppose your time here's been fairly restful?'

'Oh – mostly.'

'Apart from comforting Solange?'

'Only breaks in the monotony – well, I got chased across some fields, by Krauts – and before that I helped shift a weapons cache – to a tomb in a churchyard, would you believe it?'

'Believe *anything*.'

'You can, really, can't you? Even more so in *your* world, I'd imagine.'

'Absolutely *anything*.'

'Tell me more about what you've been doing?'

'Some time, Ben. One day.'

'Official Secrets Act, or you don't trust me yet?'

'I *do* trust you.'

'You didn't, though. Thought I was a shyster taking advantage. If we hadn't run into each other again – by purest chance—'

'You know how it was, Ben, how—'

'It was glorious, that's how it was. You know what I'm talking about too. But you ran away – *stayed* away—'

'Going to hold it against me for ever, are you?'

'Not holding it *against* you for one *second* – merely bloody commenting—'

'How about changing the subject, then?'

'All right. Good idea, let's do that. Water under the bridge. Quits. New start. OK?'

'OK.'

'Where's home, Rosie?'

'Place called Passenham. Near Stony Stratford – Buckinghamshire. You take a train to Bletchley, and I meet you there. I'll give you the address and phone number, and when you have leave – and when *I'm* home—'

'I'm finding it difficult to believe my semi-functioning ears.'

'My mother tends to be a bitch, I warn you.'

'That's incredible too. Anyway, never mind, I'll de-bitch her with my famous Aussie charm. You know, this *is* incredible?'

'I've got an uncle you'll get on with very well. My mother's name is de Bosque, by the way – I think I told you my father was French? And the family name – Uncle Bertie's – is Mathieson. My name's Ewing.'

'Rosie Ewing. Rosie Ewing. I like it . . .'

'I don't, much. Ben keep your voice down. Beaches are all ears, you know?'

'Yeah, but stuff 'em. Listen – don't like Rosie Ewing, how's Rosie Quarry sound to you?'

High broken cloud, a few early stars, a light wind from the west. The noisy lop of sea along Tariec's craggy western edge came from a swell heaving in lazily from the Atlantic. Farr heard the rowing boat coming, the sound of creaking oars: then one of the sergeant-pilots spotted it. McDonnell, the Irishman. Ben, Bright and Farr waded in to meet the Frenchmen, hauling their boat in high enough for embarkation, Vidor calling 'Ben – it's OK, gunboat *is* coming!'

'You're a genius, Vidor!' Then to Rosie, 'Hear that, did you?' It was Hansen who answered: 'Sure did. Sure did, Ben . . .'

Rosie telling herself, *It's real, we* are *on our way . . .*

And the job done, by and large. Counting on Marc Pigot – which she was certain she could do. An echo of Romeo's words reinforced her own instincts, in that: *Trust him to Kingdom Come, you know?* And subject to Jacqui sticking to *her* guns, seeing it through. She would have, for sure, if her friend Jeanne-Marie had been able to stay with her, and the only reason for less than total certainty now was that she'd have some interval of time with only contrary influences working on her.

Persuade the people in St James' not to leave her

unattended any longer than they had to. Wasn't anything else
one could do . . .

Ben and the two sailors were getting the dinghy down into
the surf. They'd decided – Rosie heard snatches of this as
she was getting down there herself – that the three of them
would make the crossing to Guenioc in it, under tow from
the larger boat. It would save Vidor having to make a second
trip, and the dinghy had to be brought out with them anyway.
Léon queried, 'Why should we tow you? You have oars
there?' Then it turned out they didn't have a line suitable or
long enough for towing anyway. Léon suggested, 'Stay close
under our stern, Ben.' Face to face in the dark, the swirl and
heave of white water thigh-deep around them, and the others
wading out to embark. 'We'll watch for you, too.'

'All right. Fine. Do without a tow-rope. *Work* for your
living, for a change.'

Farr muttered, 'Oh, my sainted aunt.'

Ben helped Rosie into the Frenchmen's boat. 'See you on
Guenioc.'

'I *hope* you will.'

It was an easy trip across, seemed to take no time at all. They
hauled the dinghy up beside the larger boat and joined the
rest of them in the cover of the rocks. Vidor and Léon would
be waiting for them, to meet the agents who'd be landing
from the gunboat and row them to Tariec; Léon would then
take the boat back into L'Abernoit, and Vidor would have
about two hours to wait for low water, until he could take the
newcomers across the sands and hand them over to Solange,
going on home himself by bicycle. If there was a weapons
container being landed – he thought there would be, but it
hadn't been confirmed – they'd leave it cached here on
Guenioc.

'Until things become easier with us, you know.'

Ben said, 'We'll be saying prayers for you, Vidor.'

'Thank you. But you have three other pinpoints, after all.'

'Right. And navigationally this is the least easy. Still

would't want you to close down.'

'From my point of view – ours – we'd be very sad. In theory we could leave – join the Maquis perhaps – but it's our home, we make our living here, have our families and friends. If the pinpoint goes – that's it, I'm a vet, he's a fisherman, Luc's a barman.'

'A few jobs on the side like the one at St Renan?'

'Oh – when they come up . . .'

The rendezvous on the beach was set for 0045 G.M.T., meaning 2300 C.E.T. The gunboat would be in the anchorage by about midnight, that meant. Bright asked Ben, 'Reckon it'll be 600 coming, sir?'

'Could well be. Skipper'll be wanting to pick his own men up, I'd imagine.'

'Yeah, I suppose.'

'Wanting my guts for garters, is what *I* suppose.'

'Will Baker Street give you some leave now, Rosie?'

'Not right away. There'll be a lot of debriefing to get through first.'

'What – a few days?'

'Could take a week or two. Depends.'

'Well. If I get leave, I'll give you a buzz. Take you out for a meal or something.'

'I may be out of circulation for a while, though. The debriefing might not even be in London. But you could leave a message – or write a note – and I'll get in touch once the dust's settled.'

'Mind you, I'll be putting in some sea-time – touch wood – so if you don't hear from me right away—'

'I'm sure you *will* be back at sea. Of course you will. It wasn't *your* fault.'

'Whose was it, then?' He didn't expect an answer. He told her, 'Listen – we'll start at the Gay Nineties – maybe dine and dance at Hachette's—'

'Steer clear of railway hotels, that's the main thing.'

'Hear it, sir?'

Tommo Farr – first *again* ... This was the northwest corner or the island, as close as they could get to the gunboat's approach route. There was a fresh breeze now, west-northwest, over the mass of hissing white water at their feet. Farr called again, 'Hear it now, sir?'

'Not yet ...'

Rosie squawked, '*I* do! Engines! *Listen*—'

'Crikey, you're right ...'

The last time he'd heard that part-smothered, deeply resonant thrum he'd been in the dinghy with his seasick passengers and the sound had been receding, leaving him utterly appalled. The moment had been so awful that it had seemed unreal.

This one was real, all right. Getting more so every second. He called back, 'Well done, Farr. Buy you a pint, first chance we get. Buy you both *several* pints, in fact.' Dropping his voice, then, adding, 'I owe you, God knows ... Come on, Rosie.' He pulled her up, 'Mind your step now ...'

Half an hour later, Ball came wading out of the surf and wrung Ben's hand. 'Ben. Oh, terrific!'

It was how *he* felt, too. Telling him, 'This is Rosie. Only she's not allowed to give her name. You landed her, remember, trip before last?'

'Of course.' He shook her hand. 'Ben, I shouldn't have lost you, as I did. Did you realize I'd gone off-course?'

'Can't say I did. I was using a shore light to steer by, and the bloody thing went out.'

'*I* saw that light – on one of the Gerry observation posts, I reckon. Yeah, well ... You hung on to the dinghy all right, I see ...'

The boat he'd come ashore in was a sixteen-foot surfboat, which they'd brought from Falmouth in tow. Making sure of it, in case the passenger-list had grown any longer at the last minute, after the long moonlit interval.

A weaponry container was being landed. There was also a parcel of sweets for the local children and Scotch whisky for the *réseau* leaders. Bright and Farr lent a hand with the container, assisting their shipmates who were making jokes about lead-swingers taking French leave. Vidor had told Ball that he and Léon would see to the burial of the container, having plenty of time in hand; he was explaining to the three agents, one of whom was a woman, that they were going to have to wait on Tariec for the tide to fall.

Rosie patted the girl-agent's arm. '*Bonne chance.*'

'*Merci.*'

She stalked away, up towards the rocks. Tall, angular, anonymous, keeping herself to herself. Well, one did – always *had*. Rosie could guess how she'd be feeling, and felt in herself an enormous depth of empathy. It surprised her, made her think *Ben's right, I probably have had enough ...* The four sailors were coming back to the surf-line, having parked the container up there in a cleft between rocks; one of them – Robertson, a leading hand – took Léon to show him where it was. Ball had been dishing out Mae Wests: he asked Hansen, 'If you're ready, sir? And – er – Rosie?'

They had a tow-line on, this time. A much shorter trip, but a much smaller point of destination, and again pitch-dark, with no compass. Easy passage anyway, not a drop of water shipped. All the way out, the final farewells with Vidor and Léon were echoing in Ben's ears. He doubted he'd see them again, particularly as it was most unlikely he'd set foot in another dinghy.

Terrific guys, he thought. Incredible. Rosie had told him that most Frenchmen only wanted to sit tight and keep their heads down, tended to believe in the double-think doctrines propounded by Marshall Pétain, and in an eventual Nazi victory. A man like Vidor, she'd agreed – and for that matter all the others he'd met in the past three weeks – made up for a hell of a lot of *that* species.

Come back and see them when the war's over, he thought. Honeymoon trip with Rosie.

Well – not honeymoon. The honeymoon wasn't going to

wait *that* long. Second honeymoon, maybe.

The gunboat's sheer side loomed over them. The other boat was at the ladder, passengers climbing up, sailors reaching down to help. From this dinghy there were oars to be passed up and lines to be received and hooked on, ready for her to be hoisted in a minute, when Ball's surfboat had been led aft, clear of the ladder.

As it had now. Bright hauled the boat up to it, Ben grasped the ladder's chain sides, and went up. M.G.B. 600 was moving quite a bit, pitching at her anchor with the long swells from the northwest rolling under her.

'Quarry?'

Surprisingly, Mike Hughes was there in the waist to meet him. Rosie was the slight figure behind his shoulder. There were busy men all round them: seeing to the boats, ushering the passengers into the bridge and thence down below, and up for'ard he guessed they'd be shortening in, not hanging around in here any longer than they had to. The six-pounder was manned, he saw as he came off the ladder; the Oerlikons too, gunners up there on the bandstand in black silhouette against star-dotted sky. He faced Hughes: 'Can't salute, sir, haven't a cap. Actually I'm dressed like Charlie's aunt.'

'Suit you to a 'T', no doubt.' Hughes reached to shake his hand. 'Glad to have you back, Ben.'

They had a substitute navigating officer on board, a friend of Ben's whose own boat was in Portsmouth being re-engined. With Hughes' concurrence, Ben left him to it. He'd worked out his own courses in relation to the tides and so forth, which Ben would have had to have got down to from scratch and to no particular advantage. Having said goodnight to Rosie and hello to most of the ship's company's personalities, therefore, he slung his own binoculars on and joined the skipper, Don Shepherd and Petty Officer Ambrose in the forefront of the bridge. The gunboat was under way by this time, at slow speed, only the outer pair of engines rumbling through their silencers and drowned exhausts.

The coxswain, Ambrose, eased rudder off her as she nosed out around the west side of Guenioc.

'Wheel's amidships, sir.'

'Steer north ten west.'

'North ten west, sir . . .'

Rolling a bit, with the swell sliding under her from not so far off the beam. She was at action stations, all weapons manned and eyes skinned. Here in the bridge, two lookouts at its after end and the signalman, Crow, as well as the three of them up front, all had glasses at their eyes.

'Course north ten west, sir.'

'Very good.'

The ritual response ... Don Sutherland asked, without lowering his binoculars, 'What's the panic about, Ben?'

'Panic?'

Hughes took over: 'Right up to about five minutes before we shoved off there was some doubt whether this pinpoint would be usable.'

'Oh, yes. Boches swarming all over – not that you'd notice especially, if you didn't live there, but a lot more than usual, anyway – looking for arms dumps. Theory is, if they've got that far – and it's a persistent effort, still going on – they may also have ideas how the stuff's been getting in. In which case – who knows?'

Shepherd commented, 'Seems they *don't* have any such idea.'

'We aren't out yet.' Hughes, his glasses sweeping slowly across the bow. 'Let's not jump to conclusions.'

Rolling, rumbling, and the swish of sea, white water splitting ahead and spreading astern, melting into the surrounding blackness. Ben lowered his binoculars, wiped sea-dew off their front lenses, put them up again ... 'Brisante coming up abeam to starboard, sir.'

'Can't think what we did without you, pilot.'

'Must admit *I* wondered, sir.'

The coxswain, Ambrose, cackled briefly.

'Bridge?'

Hughes answered the voicepipe from the pilot. 'Bridge.'

'Be better on north thirteen west, sir.'

'Very good. Cox'n – steer three degrees to port.'

'Three degrees to port, sir . . .'

Otherwise, Ben appreciated, you might be shaving the Grande Fourche rocks a trifle close. Navigating by echo-sounder, as Tony would be doing now, you sometimes got readings or sequences of readings that told you *exactly* where you were. He had his glasses trained out that way, out across the two channels which both led into the L'Abervrac'h inlet and anchorage – where this morning he'd told Rosie that enemy small ships might conceivably lie in wait. Recalling also that the last time he'd left this place they'd darned near run into some armed trawlers, but had stopped engines and lain doggo while the bastards passed ahead.

Rosie'd be fast asleep, he hoped. Having sweet dreams, not the kind Solange had told him she'd had last night. Visualizing her, in the skipper's little cabin. They'd all had ham sandwiches and coffee when they'd boarded; he'd forced a couple of sandwiches down himself, before he'd rather formally wished her a good night's sleep and left her to it.

'Petite Fourche in sight fine to starboard, sir.'

'Very good . . .'

After that, the Libenter. Easy conditions, tonight, a lot easier than when you were being flung around. Grande Fourche was abeam, at this moment. Searching to starboard, looking for the loom of the searchlight on Ile Vierge; no such thing though, yet. Although the line of sight should have been clear, just about. Or maybe they weren't using it tonight. Sweeping back very slowly: over La Pendante, then the littered water over the inshore end of the Libenter bank.

Shepherd said, 'Got the place to ourselves, sir, by the look of it.'

How it *should* be. Fifteenth Flotilla gunboats had to be just about the only seagoing units of the Royal Navy that did *not* seek action of a violent kind. Action for these small ships meant only stealth: silent approach, invisible inshore presence, withdrawal still undetected. Perhaps surprisingly, there was enormous satisfaction in it – *triumph* even – as much as there ever was in the crash and flame of gunfire.

Especially when you had a cargo that was – to put it mildly – somewhat precious.

'Pilot.' That would have been for him, but the skipper was addressing Tony Swanton. Telling him, 'Petite Fourche will be abeam in about thirty seconds.'

'When it is, sir, alter to north fourteen east.'

It was *now*.

'Starboard wheel, Cox'n, steer north fourteen east.'

'Starboard wheel, sir. North fourteen east . . .'

Ben saw the searchlight, at last. 'Loom of the light on Ile Vierge about green seven-oh, sir.'

Nosing smoothly towards the new course: Ambrose already easing rudder off her.

'Ben – the girl we have on board now – isn't she the one we landed here, trip before last?'

'The very same, sir.'

'And didn't you know her, before that?'

'Course north fourteen east, sir.'

'Very good. Ben, didn't—'

'Had met before, yes. About the end of my time with N.I.D.'

'Ah – of course . . .'

Telling no lies.

Telling no nothing.

Ignoring some stupid dig from Shepherd, too. He was all right; just – well, stupid . . . Ben thought, lowering his glasses, I'll paint this. Paint this *moment*. The black sea peeling white, gunners crouching over it like leashed hounds – paint it as I'm seeing it now and call it *Rosie Sleeping*.

POSTSCRIPT...

In researching the naval side of this story, the role of the
15th Motor Gunboat Flotilla and detail of the gunboats,
I was fortunate in having the most expert of advice from
Commander Christopher Dreyer DSO DSC* RN (Rtd.), and
through him (as President of the Coastal Forces Veterans'
Association) further help from John Townend VRD, Charles
Milner DSM and W.R. Cartwright DSM, respectively Navigating Officer, Leading Telegraphist and P.O. Motor
Mechanic of M.G.B. 718. I was also privileged to see some
autobiographical notes left by the late David Birkin, another
of the flotilla's navigating officers; for this I have to thank
his widow, the actress Judy Campbell.

In June 1944 718's first lieutenant, Guy Hamilton, who
had landed on 'Bonaparte' beach (near Plouha) with two
ratings, was unable to rejoin the gunboat – she'd dragged her
anchor. They had to be left ashore, and were suspected by
the Resistance of being Nazi decoys. He writes – in January
1995 – 'we were several days and nights on the run ...
Suspicions were mutual. When at last we cast our lot, I
remember a long walk through the night led by a young and
equally suspicious lady. Was she just walking us into a trap?
We entered a darkened cottage, and I heard a sigh of relief.
The blackout curtain was of rubberised canvas. The material
used by S.O.E. to pack agents' stores and equipment. I knew
we were in good hands.'

In later years, Guy Hamilton was to become famous as a

film director, one of his major successes being *Goldfinger*.

Into the Fire is a novel, and all the characters in it – except for Maurice Buckmaster and François Mitterrand (who did travel with the 15th Flotilla, on occasion) are fictitious. The real-life leaders of the L'Abervrac'h *réseau* were Paul Hentic, code-name 'Mao', Pierre Jeanson – 'Sarol' – and their radio operator 'Jeannot'. David Birkin recorded in his notes that soon after Christmas of 1943 all three were arrested, tortured at Gestapo headquarters in Paris and sent to their deaths in concentration camps; but happily it has more recently emerged that this is not so at any rate in the case of Paul Hentic, who in the summer of 1993 was alive and well and living in the south of France.

NOT THINKING OF DEATH

Alexander Fullerton

'It is regretted that hope of saving lives ... must be abandoned'
Admiralty signal to C-in-C Plymouth at 1610 hrs on 3.6.39.

As the shadow of Nazism descends in Europe, and Britain at last begins
to prepare her defences, trials for the first of a new class of submarine
are taking place in the mouth of the Clyde.

Royal Navy submariner Rufus Chalk, on board as an observer of the
trials, has one or two misgivings. There are certain technical problems,
small enough in themselves but in aggregate possibly dangerous; and on
this first dive in the open sea, with twice the boat's normal complement
on board – shipbuilders' representatives and technicians as well as naval
observers like Chalk – if there *were* an accident the precious air supply
would last only half as long as normal ...

Based loosely in historical fact – the tragic loss of H.M. Submarine
Thetis in Liverpool Bay in 1939 – NOT THINKING OF DEATH is a
vivid evocation of the lives and loves of characters intimately involved
in a tragedy that shakes the nation.

'What le Carré is to the spy genre Fullerton is to novels of naval warfare'
South Wales Echo

LOVE FOR AN ENEMY
Alexander Fullerton

1941: the louche and exotic city of Alexandria is virtually under siege by the Afrika Korps.

A vortex of ancient loves and murderous intrigues, it is the Royal Navy's major Eastern Mediterranean base, and a particularly lethal threat to warships is being posed by Italian frogmen and their so-called 'human torpedoes'.

Hardly the time or place for a British submarine commander to fall in love; especially as the girl in question is half-italian, and Alexandria's large italian population is only too eager to welcome Rommel and his troops into town.

Interspersed with scenes of naval action described in gripping and authentic detail – and seen through Italian as much as through British eyes – the human drama unfolds, its actors ever aware of the mounting threat of a German breakthrough.

'The most meticulously researched war novels that I have ever read'
Len Deighton

Other best selling Warner titles available by mail:

☐ Not Thinking of Death   Alexander Fullerton   £5.99
☐ Love For An Enemy   Alexander Fullerton   £4.99

The prices shown above are correct at time of going to press, however the publishers reserve the right to increase prices on covers from those previously advertised, without further notice.

WARNER BOOKS

WARNER BOOKS
Cash Sales Department, P.O. Box 11, Falmouth, Cornwall, TR10 9EN
Tel: +44 (0) 1326 372400, Fax: +44 (0) 1326 374888
Email: books@barni.avel.co.uk.

POST AND PACKING:
Payments can be made as follows: cheque, postal order (payable to Warner Books) or by credit cards. Do not send cash or currency.
All U.K. Orders   **FREE OF CHARGE**
E.E.C. & Overseas   25% of order value

Name (Block Letters) _____

Address _____

_____

Post/zip code: _____

☐ Please keep me in touch with future Warner publications

☐ I enclose my remittance £ _____

☐ I wish to pay by Visa/Access/Mastercard/Eurocard

                                                    Card Expiry Date

_____